TWELVE YEARS GONE

A DETECTIVE EMILY TIZZANO VIGILANTE JUSTICE THRILLER

KJ KALIS

This is a work of fiction. Names, characters, places and incidents either are the products of the author's imagination or are used fictitiously. Any resemblance to actual persons, living or dead, or locales is entirely coincidental.

Copyright © 2021 K.J. Kalis
eISBN 978-1-7352192-3-3
ISBN 978-1-7352192-4-0
All rights reserved

Without limiting the rights under copyright reserved, no part of the publication may be reproduced, stored in or introduced into a retrieval system, or transmitted, in any form, or by any means (electronic, mechanical, photocopying, recording, or otherwise including technology to be yet released), without the written permission of both the copyright owner and the above publisher of the book.

The scanning, uploading and distribution of this book via the Internet or via any other means without the permission of the publisher is illegal and punishable by law. Please purchase only authorized electronic editions, and do not participate in or encourage electronic piracy of copyrighted materials. Your support of author's rights is appreciated.

ALSO BY K.J. KALIS:

The Kat Beckman Thriller Series:
The Cure
Fourteen Days
Burned
The Blackout
The Bloody Canvas
Sauk Valley Killer

Christian Non-Fiction (Karen Kalis)
Miserable Christians: Eliminate Discontent, Rediscover Your Joy and Live an Abundant Life

1

Five years had passed, and she could still feel the cold metal of handcuffs being clicked around her wrists. Former Chicago PD detective, Emily Tizzano, stepped out the front door of her small house just outside of Chicago. The morning air was cool. Somewhere in the distance, she heard a single bird chirp. It was far more cheerful than she was. She looked up and down the street, half expecting someone to be staring at her, but they weren't. It was a feeling she hadn't been able to shake, even after all these years.

She reached over to the black mailbox that was just outside of the front door, flipping the lid open. Inside, there were two letters and a magazine with coupons in it. There was also a fat envelope with nothing written on the outside. Emily pursed her lips and shook her head. It was the first of the month. The envelopes kept coming.

Emily clicked the door closed behind her, twisting the deadbolt and hearing it click into the frame. Her neighborhood was safe — she knew that — but for some reason it didn't feel that way. It felt like all the safety and security she knew in her life had been stripped away and sat just out of reach.

She padded down the hallway, avoiding stepping on her dog, Miner, named for all the holes he dug in her backyard. "We'll go for a walk soon," she said, taking the mail to the kitchen. It landed on the counter with a slap. The only thing she bothered to open was the fat envelope. It was filled with hundred-dollar bills, just like every other envelope had been for the last five years. The first of the month, it appeared out of nowhere, filled with five thousand in cash from someone. Who, she couldn't be sure, though she thought she had a pretty good idea.

She picked up the money and stuffed it in a drawer in the kitchen. It would go to the bank later. She had long ago given up the idea of trying to talk to the person who was giving it to her. Even if she confronted the person that she thought was giving her money every month, she knew they would deny it. As a former detective, she knew she had no other evidence besides the fact that it replaced the salary she had lost when she'd been terminated from the Chicago Police Department. The money should have made her feel better, but it only left a bitter taste in her mouth.

Pushing the thought aside, Emily scooped out dark black coffee grounds from the container on the kitchen counter and put them in the coffee maker, hearing the bubbling of the water starting to boil. While she was waiting, she refilled Miner's water dish with fresh water. He wouldn't drink anything that had sat for more than a few hours. She didn't know why. She glanced at him. He was standing right behind her, staring at her. "I know you want to go for your walk. Just let me drink a little coffee first, okay?"

The silver and black Australian Cattle Dog grunted and laid down on the floor. She'd gotten him two years before, after visiting a local dog shelter. He had looked up at her with such sweet brown eyes that she couldn't resist. He was only six months old at the time. "Now, you know that blue heelers require a lot of exercise, don't you?" the girl who was helping her with her adoption paperwork said, "The young couple that brought him to us left him here because he was taking up too much of their time."

Emily nodded. She knew what the girl was really asking her, which was if she was prepared to take care of this dog or if she'd be like so many other people that got a dog and then decided it was inconvenient and left them at a shelter, hoping for a better home. "I've got nothing else to do," Emily said.

The girl tilted her head and squinted a tad, as if she was wondering how it was that someone so young had nothing to do. Emily decided to finish her thought for her. "You could say I'm retired." The girl nodded.

Emily and Miner had been inseparable ever since. No matter where Emily went, Miner was there, too. After tripping over him in the kitchen, she looked at him and mumbled, "Maybe I should rename you Shadow?"

She took a moment and refilled his food dish and then set it down, hearing a few mouthfuls of crunching behind her. Emily checked her phone. There was nothing new on it. She'd check her email later. Before the pot finished perking, she poured herself a cup of coffee and took a sip. The bitter liquid scalded the roof of her mouth. She put the cup down quickly. It was too hot to drink. Emily walked down the hall, grabbing a leash and a bottle of water. Miner ran to the door and sat in front of it as if saying to her, "If you're going somewhere, you'll have to take me!" Emily clipped the leash to Miner's collar, pulled on a light jacket and slipped into her tennis shoes, stuffing her cell phone in her pocket.

Emily had repeated this same process nearly every morning for the last two years, except if it was pouring down rain or too cold, as Chicago winters were prone to be once in a while, the winds howling off of Lake Michigan at a sub-Artic level. Miner would go for a walk no matter what, but there was a point at which it made little sense to suffer through the weather.

As Emily ran down the steps, she glanced around the neighborhood. It was filled with small bungalows that had mostly been built in the 1960s. Some of them had been fixed up — even fully remodeled with new landscaping. There were others that looked like they were stuck in a time warp, as if nothing had changed since the day the first family that owned them had moved in.

Miner stopped for a second, sniffing the grass and poking at a bug with the tip of his black nose. Emily waited patiently, knowing that she didn't have anywhere to go or anything to do that was pressing. That had been the hardest part of adjusting to life after the Chicago Police Department. The adrenaline, the shift work, the calls in the middle of the night — it was something that kept her going and gave her life structure. Now, all of it had been taken away from her.

After about an hour of walking, Emily knew that Miner had had enough for the moment. As they stepped inside the door, Emily unclipped Miner from his leash. The dog trotted to the kitchen where she could hear water being lapped up. She slipped off her shoes and walked into the front sitting room that she had converted into the office after Luca left. It wasn't much, just an old desk with a creaky chair and a file cabinet in the corner. If her mother had seen it, she would have scolded Emily for her lack of decor. Unlike her mother, decorating and cooking wasn't her thing. Emily plopped down in the chair, pulling her long black hair up into a bun on top of her head. She flipped open the lid to her laptop, hearing the whirr of the fan inside start to hum. The screen lit up and Emily typed in her password, walking back to the kitchen to get a fresh cup of coffee while the machine woke up and loaded. Back in the office, Emily sat down again and stared at the screen. She had more than one hundred emails, most of them junk. Scanning the names that popped up, she saw that some of them were retailers and some of them were places she had ordered from trying to sell her more things she didn't need. She quickly deleted those, getting down to a list of seven emails. They were all the same. People had found out that Emily was a former detective who sometimes helped solve problems, problems that no one else could. How they found out about her, she wasn't sure, but the number of requests for her help seemed to grow every single day. She sent each email to the printer which started to clatter in the corner, feeding the paper through and spitting it out. She closed the lid on her laptop and got up, pulling the sheets off the tray.

Emily sat down at her desk chair, the old wooden back creaking again. The monthly mystery cash would have allowed her to buy new furniture, but she liked the old chair. Taking the sheets from the printer, she spread them out across her desk, looking at each one individually. She started with people's names — Leo, Jane, Sal. Reaching for the sheet on her left, she picked it up and looked at it, scanning it quickly, setting it down again. As she picked up the second one, Miner came into her office, curling up by her feet, resting his head near her toes. "The second one is a no," she said to him. Jane's husband had left her. She wanted Emily to kill his new wife. Not exactly a cold case. Emily knew Miner didn't understand, but it didn't matter. It made her feel better to have someone to talk to since most of the people she used to hang around with were either connected to the police department or her ex-husband. Loneliness had become her new partner. Whether that was by design or because she learned the hard way that people couldn't be trusted, she didn't know. It didn't matter.

Emily scanned the other emails and picked them up in one pile, all except a single sheet she set off to the side. So many requests, most of them for cases that weren't really cases at all. Someone got offended by something—a marriage that went bad, a brother that supposedly stole money from a sister—those weren't the cases Emily was interested in. She was only looking for cases where a wrong needed to be righted, one that was something deeper than just some hurt feelings or broken dreams.

Emily stood up from her desk and took two steps toward the corner where there were two cardboard boxes stacked. She opened the lid and slid the rejected emails in, adding them to a pile that had to be five hundred sheets thick, years of requests for her help.

Emily sat back down at the desk, picking up the single sheet of paper she'd set aside, twisting back and forth in her chair as she read it again. It was a sad story, one she hadn't heard before. The boxes were filled with the history of people's lives, their anger at people who had done them wrong, the injustice that they felt with no way to rectify the situation. She understood their pain, every single one of them. But just because they were hurt didn't mean that she could do anything about it or that she'd even want to.

"Miner, this is one to think about." Emily stood up from the desk, taking the email with her into the kitchen. She popped her cup of coffee into the microwave to heat it up, noticing there was another cup — the one she had poured before she went on her morning walk — still sitting by the coffee maker. She would work her way through both of them by lunchtime.

While she was waiting for her coffee to heat, she reread the email a couple of times. It was from a woman named Vicki Schmidt, who lived somewhere in Ohio. Her daughter, Sarah, had disappeared twelve years before. No matter what Vicki had done, she wasn't able to get closure. Sarah's body was never found. "I ran across your name in an online forum about unsolved crimes. Someone mentioned that you were one of the best cold case detectives that Chicago PD had ever seen. I'm sorry to bother you with my daughter's story, but I can't sleep. I haven't slept in the twelve years since Sarah went missing. My doctor thinks my newly diagnosed heart condition is a coincidence. I don't believe that for a minute. I'm sure the real problem is a broken heart..."

In her mind, Emily tried to imagine what Vicki Schmidt might look like. She wondered about her house and the town that she lived in. But one thing Emily knew was that she couldn't commit to a case too fast. She had done that once, and that was the single case she'd not been able to close.

She put the email down on the kitchen counter. She had errands to run. Vicki's email would be waiting for her when she got home. The woman had waited twelve years, she could wait a few days more while Emily made up her mind.

2

Sleep didn't come easily to Emily that night. She tossed and turned so much that at some point, she felt Miner jump off of the bed and curl up on his blanket in the corner. He only did that when she had nightmares. Unfortunately, it was more nights than she would have liked. The image of her own arrest, the handcuffs, the video cameras, her partner whispering in her ear, "I'm sorry, Emily," as he led her out of the front door of her house were mixed in with the images of the crimes she had seen, the dismembered bodies, the old photographs and the vacant faces of family members that had long ago given up hope.

Startled, Emily sat straight up in bed. The room was still dark. She glanced over at her cell phone sitting next to the semi-automatic pistol by her bed. It was four o'clock in the morning. She sat for a moment, waiting for the memories to slide back into the box they emerged from nearly every night. She heard rustling from the corner. Miner jumped back up on the bed, coming close. She could feel his hot breath near her face, then the damp lick of his tongue as he kissed her on the cheek. He turned around twice and curled up near her feet. She didn't move. She sat stock still, waiting for reality to soak back into her skin. Although she desperately wanted to go back to sleep, the longer she sat there, the more she realized that it wasn't going to happen. Not tonight.

Swinging her legs over the side of the bed, she padded towards the bathroom, brushing her teeth. There'd been many times as a detective she had been woken up in the middle of the night, but much of that stopped once she had been moved to the cold case division. That's where she really found her calling. Somehow the pain of the families who didn't have answers and the victory that criminals felt at getting away with things so evil they could barely be spoken about for years, if not decades, fueled her.

SHE WAS on her fourth year of working in the cold case division, closing more open folders than anyone else ever had, when she noticed people started to whisper around her. At first, she thought it was just office gossip. Police officers were worse than anyone else when it came to gossip, worse than anyone else she had ever met. Over the next week or two, the whispers became stares. Finally, she asked her partner, Lou Gonzales, what was going on.

"Why do I get the feeling everybody's staring at me?" she said to him one afternoon while she was pouring over one of the newest cases she was working on, the rape of an elderly woman from ten years before.

Lou looked startled, something that Emily picked up on right away. "I don't know. Why would you say that?"

Emily caught him glancing toward the captain's office that was stationed at the end of the hallway. Something was going on, she knew it. She just didn't know what.

Two days later, her doorbell rang at eight o'clock at night, hours after her shift was over. She opened the door, her hair up in a ponytail, her face scrubbed free of makeup, wearing leggings and a T-shirt, barefoot. Lou was at the front door, his badge dangling around his neck between the lapels of his brown suit coat. He wasn't the only one. There were two detective cars and two cruisers. Lights from news channel video cameras blinded her momentarily. "What's going on?"

She glanced to her right, down on the sidewalk in front of her house. The captain of the cold case division, Deion Lewis, was standing in full uniform, his arms crossed in front of his chest. He didn't approach the house, didn't call to Emily. She stared back at Lou, who had put his hand on her right arm. She felt her body go limp, Lou's voice in her ear, "Emily Tizzano, you are under arrest for bribery, dereliction of duty and improper conduct. Please put your hands behind your back." As the bracelets from the handcuffs jingled behind her, she felt the cool steel clamp around her wrists. Lou leaned forward, "I'm sorry, Emily. I didn't have a choice…"

She didn't say anything. All she could do was stare forward. She put her head down and started down the steps as more officers pushed their way past her into her house. She didn't need to ask what they were doing — she knew they were executing a search warrant. But, for what, she had no idea. Her brain raced ahead. What did they think she had done? Her husband at the time, Luca Tizzano, came down from upstairs. He stared at the crowd out the front door, wearing only a pair of shorts. "Emily, what's all this? What's going on?" She didn't answer him.

The officers who brought her in at least had the decency to take her through the back entrance of the precinct. That was where their mercy ended. The next few hours were filled with visits from her union rep and the lawyer the union had hired for her. Captain Lewis came in and stood in the doorway, staring at her like a common criminal, glancing at the shackles on her wrists. He said he couldn't have contact with her anymore, no one from the cold case division could. IAB—the Internal Affairs Bureau — would take over.

A slight, scrawny man with thinning gray hair smeared over the top of his head came into the interview room about an hour later. She still wasn't sure why she was there, why she was handcuffed like so many of the criminals that she had put away throughout her career. "Detective, I'm Richard Henry. I'm with IAB."

Emily didn't say anything. She knew better. The criminals she had managed to convict were the ones that decided to talk. It took everything she had in her not to scream at them and tell them to get her out of the handcuffs.

"I imagine you're wondering why you're here." He opened a manila folder in front of him, tipping it towards him on his lap so she couldn't see. Emily knew the tactic well. It was meant to create tension in the room. He had information she didn't. It was supposed to keep her off balance. It didn't. Every moment that went by she became angrier. He pulled some pictures out of the file and slid them across the table to her. She glanced down, realizing it was a picture of the inside of one of her desk drawers. There was an envelope filled with money inside of it. The second picture was much the same, except that it looked like the money had been stuffed in an old suitcase she kept in the garage.

She blinked but kept silent. Her mind was on full alert, searching for answers. She'd never seen those envelopes of money. She knew that, but they didn't. Was it planted? Maybe.

Richard's voice cut through her thoughts. "Would you like to tell me about these envelopes of money?" He leaned back in his chair, a satisfied smirk on his face. "I'm sure there's a logical explanation. If you can give me something here, I'm sure we can take those handcuffs off and send you home."

Emily knew better. Richard's tactics were basic and boring. No wonder he ended up in IAB, she thought. She looked at him, staring directly at him. He looked away first, his eyes dipping back to the file. At least she had that. "Lawyer. I'd like to speak to my lawyer."

The next morning, they released her pending a full investigation and her court date. The lawyer the union had sent had been replaced by one that her father-in-law had hired. Anthony Tizzano was a powerful man. Powerful in a way that her husband hadn't bothered to explain to her before they got married. Emily thought he was in real estate. It turned out that he was involved in quite a bit more than just that.

Once Anthony's lawyer got working on Emily's case, two things happened: he quickly filed a lawsuit for wrongful termination and unlawful imprisonment, and Luca left. Emily wasn't surprised by either. Emily came in from grocery shopping a few days after her arrest and found a note on the table from Luca. "I love you, babe, but this isn't good for business." Emily dropped the bag of groceries on the ground, slid to the floor and sobbed, the first time since her arrest. It wasn't that it surprised her Luca left, just the callous way that he did it. Just like that, it was over.

Not that their marriage was that good to start with. An architect, Luca had issues with other women during late nights spent at his office working on drawings for major buildings in the Chicago area. His father had helped him to get a job in a premier architecture firm. The longer they were married, the longer Emily was sure that Luca was doing work for Anthony on the side, work that she couldn't know about as a detective.

EMILY STOOD up and glanced out the window, leaving the warmth of her bed behind. A puddle of light from the streetlamp left a bright circle that cut through the early morning darkness. She padded downstairs, Miner on her heels, the jingle of his collar following right behind her. Flipping on the bulbs underneath the cabinets, she realized she didn't want to turn on all the kitchen lights. Sleep might not come back to her that night, but it seemed way too early to deal with the full glare of brightness in the kitchen. She started a pot of coffee and grabbed a bottle of water, before opening the back door and letting Miner out.

Once he was back in and the coffee was ready, she poured herself a cup, taking the water bottle with her into her office. Vicki Schmidt's email was still sitting on top of her computer. Emily looked at it and read through the details again, flipping open her laptop. She took a sip of coffee. It was strong and bitter, a brand that Luca had discovered right after they got back from their honeymoon. It was one of the few habits left from their marriage.

"What's the name of Vicki's daughter?" Emily said out loud. Miner only groaned, curling up in a corner and going back to sleep. "Sarah, that's right." Emily typed in her name and quickly did a search to see what information was available on the Internet. Within a fraction of a second, a whole slew of articles popped up about Sarah's disappearance. Emily leaned forward and clicked, the article leading with a picture of Sarah, probably her senior picture, her hair carefully done, and her makeup carefully applied, sitting outside on a bench. She scanned the article. From the details, Sarah was eighteen when she disappeared from a small town in southern Ohio near the Wayne National Forest. She was out hiking one afternoon before work, about a month before she was due to leave for college on a cross-country scholarship. She never came back.

Emily folded her legs up underneath her, clicking on links for more articles. Most of the reporting had been done right after Sarah's disappearance. After about ninety days, there had been no more reporting. Apparently, the Sheriff, a man named Jerome Mollohan, had gone on television about two months into the investigation pleading for leads, but none ever came. Emily scrolled down the page and then went back to the top, clicking on a link for recent news. A different batch of articles came up, "Victim's Family Refuses to Give Up After Her Disappearance," one article was titled, dated two years previously. Emily clicked on that one. The image the reporter used was of Vicki Schmidt and one of Sarah's cousins, a girl named Liz. From the pictures Emily had seen of Sarah, she looked a lot like her mom, the same mid length straight brown hair, the same round face with gently sloping eyebrows. Years of worry and unresolved grief had etched lines into her mom's face. The cousin, who looked to be about the same age that Sarah would have been, was blonde with a square jaw and a small nose. The two of them were seated next to each other, holding a picture of Sarah between the two of them. "We need answers," the article read, quoting Liz, "It's been ten years and we still don't know what happened to Sarah."

Emily spent the next few hours scanning articles and looking at maps. Stockton, Ohio, was located just a couple miles from the main entrance to the Wayne National Forest, a vast wooded preserve, where Sarah had been hiking when she disappeared. The information in the article she read was repetitive — Sarah had gone hiking, only one shoe had been recovered, her family was still looking for her to this day. One article, though, mentioned another detail. Emily sent that one to the printer. She pulled it off the tray and took a sip of her coffee, which was now lukewarm. She stood up, carrying the article with her as she went to heat her coffee. It read, "Eight months after the disappearance of Stockton, Ohio teenager, Sarah Schmidt, good Samaritans called the police after they found a picture of a young woman dropped in a gas station parking lot approximately five hundred miles from Stockton. Authorities, to this day, don't know if it was actually Sarah Schmidt, or someone else, although her family believes it was her." Emily stared at the image of a young girl, her hands and ankles bound, her mouth covered with duct tape.

As Emily poured more coffee into her mug, she realized the sun had come up. She left the article on the kitchen counter, knowing that it would be there when she got back from walking Miner.

3

Slow and steady wins the race, Emily thought as she followed Miner down the sidewalk, passing a few other people on early morning walks with their dogs. She tended to pull Miner off onto the grass or into a driveway, so he didn't bark too much when others passed. He was a handful, that was for sure.

About halfway through their walk, Emily passed Monroe High School. It was early enough that the teenagers were still filtering into the building, their bodies slumped from being dragged out of bed at an ungodly morning hour, facing a long day of what she expected was boring, tedious instruction. At least it had been for her.

Like Sarah, Emily had run cross country in high school, that was until she tore her ACL during her junior year. She'd had surgery and was fully recovered by the time she graduated. She went away to school, got a degree in criminal justice and then went to the police academy, courted by Chicago PD, even though she had to scrap her way through. "We need more strong women to join the force," the recruiter had said to her. The job fit her perfectly until it didn't.

Emily stopped for a second, staring at the teenagers wandering into the high school. Sarah Schmidt hadn't gone to school in Chicago. She hadn't ever been to Chicago as far as Emily could tell, but Emily could imagine a girl like her walking into that school building, excited to have been offered a scholarship to run cross country in college. Was she alive somewhere? There had been a case in Cleveland of three women that had been abducted and kept in a house just two miles from where they lived. They had been locked inside, bearing children for their abductor for ten years before one of them finally escaped. Was Sarah like that? Or maybe her body had been long nibbled at by wild animals somewhere in the forest near her house? Or maybe she had been dragged overseas and sold? The questions rattled through Emily's mind.

One particular girl caught Emily's attention as she stood at the fence line. She had brown hair like Sarah's, was probably about her size based on what Emily could guess from the pictures, and was walking slowly into the building, next to someone Emily guessed was her friend. The girl turned to look towards Emily, a big smile on her face, before disappearing into the building. Emily kept walking.

Back at the house, Emily let Miner off his leash and went right back into her office, lifting the lid on her laptop. As she sat down, an image of Sarah popped up on the screen. Emily furrowed her brow, realizing how much Sarah looked like her own younger sister, Angelica. The image of her own mom passed through her mind. Her mom had died about a year after she got married to Luca. In a way, Emily was glad that her mom hadn't been witness to the destruction of her marriage and her career. It would have broken her mom in a way that Emily wasn't sure she would've been able to recover from. It had been hard enough for her mom when Angelica had finished medical school, worked for a few years at a local hospital and then decided to go to Europe. Angelica had only been back one time since she left, and that was for her mom's funeral. Emily had seen her sister a couple times, flying one time to Madrid and another time to Rome where her sister was living at the time. Angelica lived a nomadic life, going here and there, making money, helping people.

Emily leaned back in her chair and looked up at the ceiling. She could either agree to help Vicki or not. She knew it was time to decide. The settlement she had gotten from the Chicago PD for wrongful termination had set her up. She didn't need to work if she didn't want to, but solving cases was in her blood. The money that came to her mailbox each month just gave her that much more freedom to do what she wanted. The question was, did she want to use some of that freedom to help Vicki find justice?

Emily got up from her desk and walked out through the back door, the jingle of Miner's collar following her. He could be dead asleep and if she got up, he would too. He was very dedicated to her, and she felt the same way about him. He was one of the few good things that had come out of her life in the last few years. She grabbed a frisbee from on top of a storage box just outside the door and tossed it to him a couple times, sitting down on a plastic chair facing out into the little backyard. It was surrounded by an eight-foot-high privacy fence. She couldn't see her neighbors and they couldn't see her. When they moved in, Luca had insisted that they make some improvements around the house—a new kitchen, a new bathroom, paint and carpet and new landscaping and a deck in the backyard. He designed them himself, using a drafting table he set up in the extra bedroom. All of it had been a gift from her father-in-law, Anthony. At the time, Emily told him it was too much. She remembered the moment when he was standing in the backyard, looking at the landscaping that had just been installed. "Anthony, I can't thank you enough for all the help," Emily said.

"It's nothing, honey," he said, a smile tugging at the corners of his lips. "We are family. We help each other."

When Luca and Emily got divorced, it was done quickly and quietly. Emily got everything. Anthony could help Luca put the pieces back together again. Anthony knew his son had run around on her, Emily was sure of that.

Miner ran off, catching her eye, growling at something in the corner of the yard. It was probably a squirrel or a chipmunk. Emily got up off of the chair and wandered over to the vegetable garden that was in the back corner of the lot. It was on its last legs, the plants withering under the cool night temperatures. It would be time for Emily to turn the soil under for the winter soon, but not yet. Not yet.

Vicki Schmidt's face flashed in front of her mind's eye. How could a young girl, especially one that was as fast and in shape as Sarah, disappear without a trace, Emily wondered? Not that she hadn't seen cases like this throughout her work as a detective, but something about it didn't make sense. It was as if the truth was right under the surface, but Emily couldn't get to it. If she felt frustrated after only knowing about the case for one day, she couldn't imagine how Vicki Schmidt felt after twelve years...

4

"Can you watch Miner for a couple of days?" Emily said to Mike Wilson on the phone the next morning.

"Yeah, sure," he stuttered. "When are you leaving?"

"As soon as you get over here."

Emily met Mike Wilson at a dog park just before one of her earlier cases, a cold case where a family had lost a young child. The body was recovered, but no one had ever figured out how the child died or who did it. Mike was a whiz with everything technical. He had a way of finding information and resources that Emily couldn't. When she went on a case, he was her lifeline. He was also a good dog sitter.

About an hour later, Emily heard the key in the lock of the door. Miner bolted to see who it was, barking and growling, his alert quickly turning into tail wagging and panting when he saw Mike. Mike shifted the backpack off of his shoulder and sat down cross legged on the floor, his scraggly hair hanging over his eyes.

"Still haven't gotten a haircut, huh?"

"It doesn't bother me," he said.

Emily looked at him as he stood up. He had on baggy jeans and a loose T-shirt with a pair of worn tennis shoes. Everything about Mike was unkempt. They'd met at a dog park, Mike hanging on the fence watching people as frisbees and balls sailed between the pups. Emily had noticed he was standing alone, so she wandered over. Mike didn't have a dog of his own, but he liked them. At first, he was hard to understand. He'd grown up in an abusive family and had developed a stutter from his father smacking him around. Over the next few months, Emily would talk to Mike whenever she saw him at the dog park. They finally exchanged cell phone numbers and Mike came over one night, sharing pizza, Mike playing ball with Miner until the dog was so tired he grunted and found a spot on his bed. They were just friends. Mike was at least fifteen years younger than Emily, she guessed. She still didn't know exactly how old he was.

Mike had been staying at her house dog-sitting Miner when Emily discovered his technical skills accidentally. She had called to check on how they were doing and started complaining that she couldn't get the financial records of the father in the cold case she was trying to solve. She suspected he was the one that had killed his child, but she didn't know why. "I can get those for you," Mike said.

"How?" Emily said.

"Don't worry about that. Give me a half hour."

Sure enough, twenty-eight minutes later, Emily's phone chirped. It was a text from Mike with some documents attached. "This what you're looking for?" the text read. Emily still didn't know how Mike managed to dig up the information she needed. The part she was sure of is that his methods were likely on the shady side of being legal, but in her line of work — solving the unsolved crimes that people were left to wrestle with — it didn't matter. After years of trying to do things the right way, Emily had gotten to the point when she cared more that things got done, not how they got done.

Mike picked up his backpack and set it on one of the kitchen chairs. He took his duffel bag and set it in the corner. "So, where are you off to this time?"

"Ohio," Emily said, pushing her laptop into the sleeve in her backpack. She turned and walked across the kitchen, opening a drawer. From it, she pulled a full-sized Sig Sauer pistol. She bought it after she'd been dismissed from the Chicago PD, once her name had been cleared. There was something about carrying a gun on your hip for that many years that made it a hard habit to break. That, and many times, it had come in handy. Sometimes her cases required radical action. She wasn't above pulling her gun and using it if she needed to protect herself or to protect the people whose cases she was trying to solve.

A familiar lump formed in her throat. There was always a moment before she left on a case, where she wondered if she was making the right decision and what she would be faced with on the journey ahead. It never stopped her, but it had threatened to a few times. She slipped the gun into the holster, feeling the familiar click as it settled into place. She pulled her shirt over it so the imprint of the rear grip wouldn't be so obvious.

"Are you going to tell me a little about the case before you go?" Mike had his head in the refrigerator already. Emily paid him for watching Miner, but part of his pay was being able to raid the refrigerator. He was nice about it, though. There were many times Emily got back from a case to find food Mike had cooked for her.

"Are you offering to work as tech support again?" Emily said, a smile spreading on her face.

"Of course. I can't let Miner take up all my time!"

As soon as Mike stepped away, Emily reached into the

refrigerator and pulled out two water bottles. The drive to Stockton, Ohio, would take about seven hours. It wasn't long enough to warrant a hotel stay in the middle of the drive, but it would be easier if she had at least a couple of bottles of water with her. "Twelve years ago, an eighteen-year-old girl named Sarah Schmidt, disappeared after going for a hike in the Wayne National Forest."

The scrape of the kitchen chair on the tile floor caught Emily's attention. Mike had already pulled out his laptop and was typing furiously as she talked. "What city did you say this was in?"

"Stockton. It's near the Wayne National Forest. From the map I pulled up looks like it's pretty far south in Ohio, almost to the West Virginia border."

"Why this one?"

Emily wasn't surprised by the question. Mike had taken up asking her the same thing on pretty much every case she took. She had shown him the boxes of requests that she got one night, late. "All these people want your help?" he had said at the time.

Emily had nodded.

"How do you decide?"

THE QUESTION WAS the same today. It was a good one. Why this case? Why did the story of Sarah Schmidt resonate with her more than any of the other emails she had gotten in the last few weeks? "I don't know… Her mom is the one that sent me the email. Her name's Vicki Schmidt if you want to look her up," Emily heard typing in the background as she checked her bag.

"Yeah, I've got her."

Even though Emily had worked with Mike for the last couple years, it still surprised her how quickly he could acquire information. On more than one occasion, that information had saved her life or helped her close a case. It wasn't that she didn't think she could do her job without him, it just made it a whole bunch easier to have him available to fill in the blanks. Emily zipped her duffel bag closed and pulled her cell phone charger out of the plug on the wall.

"Looks like the Schmidt family has lived in Stockton for generations. From what I can gather, looks like Sarah's dad died a couple years ago." Mike glanced up from his laptop, catching Emily's eye.

"Anything else I should know about before I go?" Emily's car keys jingled as she pulled them off of the counter.

Mike frowned, leaning further over his computer, "I don't know. I'll do a deep dive while you're in transit. I can have a full brief to you by the time you arrive."

Emily tried not to chuckle. Whenever she headed out on a case, Mike's demeanor completely changed from the goofy awkward twenty something-year-old to a very focused black hat techno wizard. "That would be great. Any extra info you can give me would be helpful."

"Roger that," Mike said, his hair flopping over his face.

Emily reached down and stroked Miner's thick fur. "I'll be back, boy. You be good for Mike, okay?" The dog had already curled up at Mike's feet. She knew he was in good hands. "All right, I'm gonna head out. Long drive ahead of me."

Mike was silent as Emily locked the door behind her, only the sound of his fingers on his keyboard following her as she left. She walked into the backyard and opened the garage door, tapping the key fob in her hand. The alarm system for the blue pickup truck she drove chirped. It was the one luxury she allowed herself, that, and lots of treats and toys for her dog.

The engine roared to life as Emily put the big truck into gear, carefully backing out the driveway. When she had first bought it after her settlement with the Chicago Police Department, she brought it home and immediately wasn't sure it was going to fit in the garage. She must've gotten in and out of the truck five times, trying to decide whether it would fit or not. Luckily, it did. She shook her head, the view of her little house disappearing in the rear-view mirror. There was nothing worse than scraping a half inch of ice off the windshield of your truck in the middle of a Chicago winter.

5

The countryside didn't change much once Emily passed outside of the metropolitan Chicago boundaries. Within the city, it was all small homes, expensive lakefront properties and high-rises. Outside the city, it started to look more like the pastoral scenes of the Midwest that were captured on travel postcards. Rolling hills, fields filled with corn that had yet to be harvested and clear blue skies. A couple hours into the drive, Emily stopped to fill up the truck with gas.

The time in the car gave her a chance to think about the case in front of her. All the cases she took put her at risk. Personal risk. She was no longer a commissioned police officer, so anything she did—whether good or bad—was on her. She could be prosecuted just like anyone else, probably more so with her history. Now that she was no longer married to Luca, she didn't think that his dad, or anyone else for that matter, would come to her rescue. She was on her own. Other than Mike, no one knew where she was heading, not even Vicki Schmidt.

Just over the border into Ohio, the clouds opened up,

pounding the truck with pelting rain. The wipers whipped back and forth, clearing the glass just enough that Emily could see without having to slow to a crawl. The question Mike asked her before she left about why she chose this case rattled in her brain. It was hard to explain — that's why she never really gave him an answer. Word had gotten out about Emily's ability, and more accurately, her willingness, to go after unpunished criminals in cold case forums all over the Internet. At first, the requests came in like a trickle, one or two a month. From the beginning, Emily didn't respond to any of them. She didn't want to commit herself to something before she was sure she was willing to go the last mile. Over time she figured out which cases were for her. She knew they were meant for her in a way she couldn't explain. Something inside of her clicked when she read the story. That wasn't to say that many other requests she got weren't compelling—missing children, murders, suicides that didn't actually look like suicides—there was no lack of injustice in the world, that was for sure. But this case, the case of Sarah Schmidt, it pulled a string inside of her she hadn't felt for a long time.

She shifted in her seat, feeling the tightness in her back after driving for half the day. To top it all off, Sarah had an uncanny resemblance to Emily's younger sister, Angelica. Just thinking about her softened Emily's heart. It had been several years since they had spent any time together. "Maybe when this is over, I'll head over to Europe and go see her," she whispered.

Her phone rang. It was Mike. "What's going on? You miss me already?"

"Very funny. Not exactly, though I think Miner does. You ready for some news?"

"I thought you were losing your touch. I'm nearly halfway there."

"I had things I had to take care of here. You know, the whole dog sitting thing kinda gets in the way. Miner insisted on going for a walk before I was allowed to sit down to work on my computer."

Emily smiled. She knew exactly what Mike meant. Miner was perfectly happy to shadow her all day long as long as he got out first thing in the morning. If he didn't, he would stand at the door and whine and bark until she took the time to get him some exercise. "Well, better you than me. What did you find out?"

"Okay, well, I'm not sure I'm going to be able to tell you anything that you don't already know."

"Tell me anyway," Emily said, staring straight ahead, letting a semi pass her in the high-speed lane.

"So, Sarah Schmidt was a division one cross-country prospect. She had gotten full ride scholarship offers from the University of Michigan, Ohio State University and Northwestern."

"She was a Big Ten girl, huh?"

"Yeah. She committed to Northwestern after winning the state cross country meet in her age bracket. On top of that, she was an excellent student and wanted to go into medicine."

Another tie to Angelica, Emily thought. "What else?"

"Well, it looks like she disappeared about four weeks before she was scheduled go to school. Early August, about twelve years ago. She'd be thirty if she was still alive today. There's not a lot of information about what happened to her. The story goes that she went for a hike on one of the trails in the Wayne National Forest, which looks like it's only a couple miles away from Stockton. I'm thinking it was a familiar place to her. Maybe she just wanted to get away from the family for a few hours, maybe clear her head? You know that whole going to college thing can be stressful…"

Emily raised her eyebrows. She knew that college hadn't been an easy time for Mike. He was probably projecting his own life onto the case, but it didn't matter. "Okay, so you think she goes into the forest to clear her head, get a little nature therapy, and then what?"

"The obvious. She doesn't come home. Her mom, Vicki and her dad, Dan Schmidt, call the police and file a missing person's report. Based on the information I could find in news reports, it seems that the local sheriff made them wait twenty-four hours since she was eighteen years old."

Emily shook her head, the heat of anger bubbling up in her chest. An eighteen-year-old girl was hardly an adult in Emily's mind. The only thing someone Sarah's age could be responsible for was figuring out what kind of breakfast cereal they wanted in the morning. If Emily had a dollar for all the teenagers that had made bad decisions, she'd be a billionaire. "So, she's gone, then what happens?"

"By the next morning, the whole city was aflame. I don't know if I'd exactly call Stockton a city, though. Technically, it's incorporated as a Township."

"Stay on the topic, not on government," Emily groaned.

"Right. Anyway, by the next morning the Sheriff's Department had been convinced that it was time to start looking for her, whether it had been twenty-four hours or not. From the news reports, it looks like search parties were brought in from the community, people that knew Sarah and other people that just wanted to help. A couple hours later is when they found her shoe."

"One shoe?"

"Hold on. Let me confirm."

Emily could hear tapping in the background, as if Mike was working on his search parameters.

"Yes, it was one shoe. It doesn't say if the police saw it or if it was one of the search parties, but they found it off to the side of the trail under some brush. It was her left shoe."

Emily pursed her lips together. If that was the only information they had about her disappearance, it wasn't much. This was the reason that she never emailed anyone back when they sent a request. More than once, she'd driven to the area where a case had emerged, walked around for a few hours and then turned back and went home. The victim's family never knew she was even there. Emily was beginning to wonder if Sarah Schmidt's case would be one of those. Before Emily could get too far off track, Mike's voice interrupted her thoughts.

"Then there is the whole picture thing…"

"Yeah, I read about that. Give me your take."

"An image was found in a gas station parking lot about five hundred miles away from Stockton, somewhere in West Virginia. The thing is, it turned up eight months later, which implies she was alive at the time the picture was taken. There's one sticking point though. No one could ever verify if it was actually her."

"How is that possible?" Emily said. "This happened twelve years ago, not fifty. Why couldn't facial recognition have been used to verify it was actually Sarah? Why was the picture five hundred miles away?"

"That would be your department, boss. What I can tell you is that facial recognition software is still in its infancy. I wish it was better than it was, but it doesn't surprise me that a degraded picture left in a gas station parking lot wouldn't give anyone definitive evidence."

Given the fact that Mike didn't have any police experience, she was always surprised that he was able to come to the conclusions he did. "Anything else?" There was a pause on the other end of the line. Emily could hear Mike moving around, but she wasn't sure what he was doing. "You still there?"

"Yeah, sorry. Was just checking something else. So, it seems that after the picture was found, there was a brief flurry of information on the investigation, but no traction. Then, two years ago, Vicki Schmidt and one of Sarah's cousins, Liz Schmidt, took matters into their own hands. There's been a fairly consistent push of information from the family over the last couple of years. I'm not sure if they made any headway, but it's not for lack of trying."

Emily had seen a picture of Vicki, Sarah's mom, and Liz, Sarah's cousin, sitting together on a couch in one of the articles she had read. From the picture, Liz didn't look anything at all like Sarah, who was brown haired with soft features like her mom. Liz was as blonde as blonde could be with a strong, square jaw. "Any idea why all of a sudden the mom and the cousin are so involved?"

"None."

That Vicki and Liz had gotten so involved in the case could be a good thing or a very bad thing, Emily reasoned. It would be good if they were available to give Emily the information she needed to figure out what happened to Sarah. It could be bad if they wanted to interfere. Emily was a one-man band, aside from Mike who was back in the city. She worked alone. She didn't trust anyone enough to work with them. Not after what happened to her. The interference factor alone had sent her home from several cases. Families wanted to be in the middle of the investigation, and more critically, they wanted to be in the middle of the revenge. It didn't work that way, at least not for Emily.

6

Emily's blue truck passed the small "Welcome to Stockton" sign on the side of the road with no fanfare at all. The tiny sign was mounted on a couple of wooden posts on the outskirts of the township, flanked by a field of overgrown corn on the left-hand side and a field where the hay had been cut on the right.

The smell of crops filtered through the cab of Emily's truck as she cracked the window open. After living in the city for so long, her sense of smell quickly picked up the difference between city and country. For a brief second, she wondered what it would be like to live in a small town, out in the middle of nowhere. She shook her head, refocusing on the road. It was hard to stay anonymous in a small town. It was much easier to blend in amid the rows of bungalows and lines of traffic in Chicago.

It didn't take her long to find what would be considered the center of town. The road where the sign had been posted was about a mile from it. She passed an old church with peeling paint and a sign that announced Sunday services at ten AM, a shop that sold tires across the street, and a feed store right next door. The road was peppered with small buildings with one big box grocery store push off the back of the road.

There was no one really walking through the town. She saw trucks and cars parked on the side of the road, a cluster of them stopped in front of a small restaurant perched on the corner of the main street and a narrow side street. Emily couldn't read the name on the street sign as she passed. She kept going to the end of the main drag, the buildings spreading farther and farther apart. Her phone pinged just outside of town on the other side. Picking it up, she read the text, trying to keep her eyes on the road, "You passed the hotel," the text read. It was from Mike. She smiled. "Turn around and go back a quarter-mile. It'll be on your right-hand side. I made you a reservation." How he knew exactly where she was, she wasn't sure. He had probably installed some sort of GPS tracking software on her cell phone or attached something to the truck. She made a note to ask him later. Not that she minded. He had gotten her out of enough jams in the past she appreciated him watching her back. "Thanks for the reservation. I'll check in later." It was the nicest thing she could think of to say to get Mike to leave her alone while she looked around.

She pulled the truck into a parking lot attached to a pediatrician's office, backed it up, and turned it around, heading back through town. On the next corner, there was a gas station. The overhang looked like it was original, but the pumps and displays were new, probably mandated by their supplier to avoid an EPA fine. She popped the door to the truck open and slid down, landing on two feet. As she put her credit card into the reader, a man came out from inside the store, wiping his hands on a greasy blue rag. "Well, hello," he said, stuffing the rag into his work pants. "You need anything else besides gas?"

"Nope, but thanks for asking."

The man, with thinning dark hair, turned away. He walked

like he had a bad back. Emily called out to him. "Actually, there is one thing."

"What's that?"

"Any good restaurants here?"

The man narrowed his eyes a little, "Sure, you probably passed it on the way in. Just go back up about a quarter mile on your right-hand side. You'll see it on the corner. Sandy's. She's got just about everything you could want. Staying for a while in Stockton?"

"Naw, just passing through. Headed to visit family in West Virginia." Emily had gotten good at lying. It wasn't something she was proud of. The words just seem to slide out of her mouth before she had a chance to filter them. Not that it mattered. It really wasn't any of the man's business who she was or why she was in Stockton.

The man nodded. "Have a good meal and a good trip. Thanks for stopping to fill up."

Even after just a brief drive through the town, Emily knew she would stick out like a sore thumb. The only saving grace was that she was dressed casually enough — jeans, a shirt and light jacket — that she'd match nearly everyone else in town. The story that she was just passing through to go visit her family would buy her a little time while she decided whether it was worth it to solve the case. She felt a little ball of nervous energy form in her gut and tugged at her dark ponytail. It was the same feeling she used to get when she was on duty and about to go into action. It was the same feeling she had the day she'd been arrested.

Emily got back into the truck, the fuel gauge now reading full. She pulled out of the station and turned right, her back tires sliding on loose gravel near the edge of the road. The man inside the station looked up, right at her. Emily gave him what she hoped would be considered a friendly wave, though she wasn't feeling friendly at all.

Finding the restaurant was as easy as the man said. She saw it when she was driving through the town on the first pass. Pulling down the side street, she turned left into the parking lot behind the restaurant. She loved her truck but maneuvering it into small parking spots could be a chore. There were two other trucks already lined up in spots, a motorcycle leaning on its kickstand nearby. It didn't look too busy for late in the day. Not that there was much of a dinner rush in this small of a town.

A woman with a long braid dangling over her shoulder approached her, "How many?"

"One."

The woman gave a brief nod and motioned for Emily to follow her. She set a laminated menu down on the table, one of the ones closest to the window at the front of the restaurant. Emily chose the seat where she could watch the front door. It was an old habit, one that she had found hard to break, though she thought it was a smart one. Always good to see who was coming in before they saw you, she thought.

"Coffee? Water?" the waitress asked.

"Both, please," Emily said, fingering the menu. It had been used for so long that the lamination was starting to curl at the corners. Emily wasn't sure how long they had used the same menus, but she guessed it was a while, probably years. Totally different than in Chicago, where if you weren't changing your menu regularly, you couldn't survive, except for the historic restaurants, of course.

While she glanced at the menu, Emily looked around. The chair seats were red vinyl, cracked in a couple places, covered with silver duct tape to hold them together. The tables were pale yellow Formica, with metal edging. Pushed to the edge of each table was a metal caddy with condiments, salt and pepper, and an old-fashioned sugar dispenser and a napkin holder. The way the restaurant was outfitted screamed old-fashioned diner, but not quite. It was like the restaurant was trying to be something it wasn't. People were like that, too, Emily thought, looking up from her menu and sizing up the people sitting nearby. There were a couple middle-aged guys wearing jeans, cowboy boots and button-down shirts at a booth on the other side of the restaurant. There was one guy wearing a leather jacket sitting alone at another table. Emily guessed he was the one who had the motorcycle parked out back. Time stood still for a moment. Emily wondered if she came into the restaurant ten years ago or ten years in the future if it would look the same. She guessed it would.

The waitress returning to her table caught Emily's attention, the cup of coffee and glass of water suspended upright on the palm of a single hand. She set them down in front of Emily pulling a straw out from her apron. "You ready to order?"

"Sure. I'll have the BLT and some french fries."

"Anything else?"

"Not right now. Thanks."

Emily heard her phone chime again. She pulled it out of her pocket and looked. It was Mike. "I got Vicki Schmidt's address for you and some other information you might find interesting. Sending it now. Check your inbox."

Emily tapped on her email and saw three different messages from Mike. They didn't come directly from him. They came from an encrypted service that he used. He cloaked his identity whenever he emailed her. Emily wasn't sure exactly why — probably some techno geek protective cover, she guessed. She tapped on the first one. It was her hotel information. She closed it and looked at the second one. It was a list of additional articles about Sarah Schmidt's disappearance. She'd take a look at those later on in the evening.

The third email had something she hadn't thought to find. It was the location of the empty grave where Sarah would be buried if they ever found her. How Mike thought to dig for that information, she wasn't sure. There was also a list of people that were involved in the case when it happened. Emily shook her head. She guessed that most of those people had long retired from the police department.

Within minutes, the waitress was back with her food, the smell of bacon and freshly cooked french fries curling up off the plate. Emily hadn't realized how hungry she was until she smelled it. As a waitress dropped off the food, Emily glanced up at the woman. If she had to guess, she probably wasn't much older than Sarah Schmidt would have been if she'd still been living in Stockton. "Can I ask you something?" Emily said, pushing a french fry into her mouth.

The woman put a hand on her hip, "Sure."

"This is my first trip to Stockton. Have you lived here your whole life?"

The woman nodded. "Yep. My family's been here forever. We live on the outskirts of town. My dad's the local pediatrician."

In Emily's mind, the odds that the waitress knew about Sarah Schmidt, or even possibly knew her, had grown by leaps and bounds. If her father was the local pediatrician — and Emily suspected there wasn't much competition in the area — then this girl, or at least her family would know about it. "Oh, that's so interesting. He's worked here his whole life?"

The girl seemed to relax. She pushed a blond hair off of her face, "Yeah. He came here right out of medical school, met my mom and they got married. Most people you see walking around the town had my dad as their doctor at some point or another. If they haven't, then probably somebody they know has."

"That's so cool!" Emily sighed, faking some enthusiasm. "So, anything interesting ever happened here in Stockton?" she said, dipping a second french fry in ketchup.

"In Stockton? I don't know where you're from, but not much happens here in Stockton."

"I'm from Chicago."

"Oh, I always wanted to go. You live there?"

Emily nodded. "Yep, just passing through." She kept to the lie. Emily leaned back against the chair and looked at the waitress a little more carefully. Her name badge said Kathy. "I did a little research about Stockton before I came here. Wanted to figure out if I could get a hotel here on my way. I read something about a girl named Sarah Schmidt that had gone missing? You know anything about that? Sounded so strange to me."

It was as if every door that had opened between them immediately slammed shut. Kathy's body stiffened, "I don't know anything about that." Emily watched Kathy for a second. "I'll go get you some more coffee," she said, except she didn't look at Emily. Her eyes were fixated on the kitchen. Emily looked at her and then looked back at the kitchen. There was no one there, at least no one that Emily could see. "Okay, thanks."

Kathy walked away, her personality shifting back into professional waitress mode. Emily took a bite of her BLT and looked up. She saw one of the men at the table looking at her. Watching, would be more correct. Why, she wasn't sure. They were far enough away that Emily wasn't sure the man could have heard their conversation.

Kathy came back to her table a minute later with a pot of coffee. She topped off Emily's cup without saying anything and then walked over to the two men at the table. Emily watched as she filled their cups as well. Neither of the men said anything to her. They just watched her. Emily's eyes traced Kathy's path as she made her way back to the man in the leather coat. She filled his coffee to and then looped back to the kitchen. She could see Kathy's mouth moving, like she was talking, but she wasn't holding her phone and Emily couldn't see who the other person was based on the angle where she sat. Emily moved slowly, not wanting to attract any other attention, picking up her sandwich and taking a bite and then setting it back on the plate.

Kathy made one more loop back to Emily's table, dropping off an old-fashioned order ticket with the total. Emily looked at it closely, hoping there was some sort of message, something she could work off of, but there wasn't. Just her order listed in scrawling handwriting, the total and the tax. Emily pulled cash out of her pocket and left it on the table, including a hefty tip. She wasn't sure it would make up for any discomfort Kathy felt, but it was the least she could do.

Emily walked out of the restaurant without checking behind her. She didn't want anyone to think she knew she was being watched, even though she was pretty sure she was. She got into her truck and drove straight to the hotel, checking in and taking her backpack and her bag up to her room.

The hotel was a three-story building, part of a chain of hotels scattered throughout the country. Emily had stayed in buildings like these before, she thought, recognizing the pale gray painted walls as she walked down the hallway on the third floor. They were nondescript, every single room identical. As she slipped the key card into the lock, it clicked open and gave a beep. She dropped her bags just inside the door letting it click behind her and checked the bathroom, behind the shower curtain and then scanned the rest of the room. Old habits die hard, she thought. She didn't want any surprises.

Once the room was clear, she locked the door and went into the bathroom to wash her face, changing into a T-shirt and a pair of leggings. She pulled her long hair into a ponytail and sat down at her laptop, calling Mike on speakerphone. "How are things at home?" she said.

"Nothing to report here. You?"

"I had an encounter of the strange kind at a local restaurant."

"Do tell."

"I asked the waitress, a gal named Kathy who had to be close to Sarah Schmidt's age, if she knew anything about the case. I did it real casual, but she got freaked out. You should've seen her body language."

"What d'you think happened?"

Emily could hear typing in the background. "Not sure. She said her dad's been the local pediatrician for decades. As soon as I mentioned Sarah's name, her body stiffened, and she went from friendly to busy real quick even though the restaurant was pretty much empty. I had some guys across the restaurant eyeballing me. Not sure if they were just curious or not. I don't think they could hear what we said, though."

"You said her dad's been the local pediatrician? What was her name again?"

"Kathy. I don't know her last name. The pediatrician's office is down the street from where I'm staying. I pulled in and turned around there when I first got into town."

"Barnes. Dr. Barnes."

A new email from a different encrypted account popped up in Emily's inbox. Emily clicked on it. Inside, there was an article with a picture of someone identified as Dr. Barnes hugging a couple of kids. The title read, "Local Pediatrician Celebrates Thirty Years in Business." Emily scanned the article. It was nothing more than a fluff piece, describing the fact that Dr. Barnes had decided to spend his career working in Stockton instead of taking an offer he had to work in Nashville.

"Based on what this article says, doesn't look like there's much of a chance that your waitress didn't know about Sarah Schmidt."

Emily tapped her fingers on the edge of her laptop, staring at the picture. Dr. Barnes looked like a kind man, someone that you'd want to send your kids to, with a shock of thick gray hair, square rimmed glasses and a broad smile. He was the kind of man Emily imagined would have a bowl of candy and stickers ready for each of the kids. "I guess that's right," she said. "I mean, if he's the local pediatrician for the whole area, what are the chances that Sarah wasn't one of his patients? If he's the guy they describe in this article, then he would've gotten pulled in on the case or at least knew about it."

There was more typing in the background. "Based on what I can see here, it looks like Kathy Barnes, if she's the same person that you met at the restaurant, is two years older than Sarah Schmidt. She's thirty-two right now. Not married."

Emily stood up and started to pace, not drifting too far, otherwise Mike wouldn't be able to hear her on the speakerphone. She walked to the window and pushed the sheer curtains aside. The parking lot was pretty much empty except for her blue truck. As she looked to her right, she saw another couple of vehicles parked, but there weren't many. She guessed the hotel was maybe ten percent full, if that. "Here's what I don't understand, Mike," she started, "Why the strange reaction from Kathy? I mean, she practically bristled when I asked her about Sarah."

"Did you come at her like a detective?"

"Now, that's not nice. And no, I didn't." Emily knew she had a tendency to be all business, but she had been more than casual with Kathy. She chewed her lip. "Her reaction just didn't fit. And then, after she refilled my coffee, I saw her start talking to somebody in the kitchen, but I couldn't see who it was. She didn't look happy."

"Hmmm... that's a little strange."

"My gut tells me that the mere mention of Sarah's name raises eyebrows in Stockton. Why, I have no idea."

"Well, I guess that's what you are there to find out."

7

Emily slept surprisingly well, given that it was a lumpy hotel bed in a strange city without Miner curling up next to her for half the night. She got up, took a shower and went downstairs. Mike had wisely chosen a hotel that offered a free morning breakfast. Not that it was much to talk about. There was cold cereal, stale bagels and lukewarm powdered eggs. Emily grabbed a couple pieces of sausage and a granola bar to go with her coffee and sat down in the corner where she could watch the guests walk by. There weren't many.

What Emily knew about Stockton, which wasn't much, was that it seemed like a stop off place for people on their travels. When she had told the story to the guy at the gas station about her passing through to visit family the day before, he bought it hook, line and sinker. As she thumbed through her phone, looking at some information Mike had sent overnight, she realized the very nature that Stockton was a pass through was how the town stayed anonymous. Only the people that lived there knew the secrets. To anyone else driving through or even staying for a night or two, it just looked like a slightly rundown Midwestern town.

The day spanned ahead of her. Emily didn't have a real plan, but she knew that by dark she needed to decide on whether she was staying to work the case and get justice for the Schmidt family or she was getting back in her truck and driving home. A knot of nervousness formed in her stomach. At the beginning of the case, she often felt like she was circling the drain. She'd go around and around and around, looking at the case from all angles before either drifting away, leaving no clue she'd investigated or taking the plunge and getting justice. But one thing she knew was that once she decided, her decision was final. After what she'd been through with the department, there was no negotiating. If she took the case, she would finish it. She would get justice for the family in whatever case she was working on, no matter how long it took or what danger it put her in. On the other hand, if she decided that it wasn't a good case for her, she walked away. That's why she never told the families she was coming.

She stared at her phone for a minute, trying to decide where to start. Mike had sent her an interesting link in the middle of the night. It was the location of a cemetery plot that had been purchased for Sarah. It had never been used. The empty grave didn't help the knot in her stomach at all. She took a sip of lukewarm coffee. Emily put herself in Vicki Schmidt's shoes. Her daughter had been missing for years, with few leads and even less hope. More than anything, Emily imagined Vicki would just want to put her daughter to rest. Emily cocked her head to the side, wondering if filling the grave or getting justice was higher on Vicki's list.

Emily abandoned her dishes and lukewarm coffee on the table and walked out of the sliding glass doors of the hotel, starting up the truck. She plugged the directions to the cemetery into her phone and pulled out of the lot.

There was very little traffic. Emily glanced around, passing the same restaurant she had eaten in the day before. She wondered if Kathy was there, starting her shift. She passed the pediatrician's office where Dr. Barnes had seen generations of children come and go, grow up and leave, some of them staying to spend their days in Stockton. Making a right turn just before the gas station she had stopped off at the day before, she headed down a side street. There were houses lined up on each side of the road, each with matching white clapboard, the lots probably at least twice the size of the ones that were common in Chicago. From driving into town, Emily knew that this would be as much of a neighborhood as there would be in Stockton. The remainder of the township residents lived on farms just outside of the city center.

The road hit a dead end, Emily facing a small white church with a single stained-glass window at the base of the steeple. She hadn't seen a country church like that in years. The GPS reminded her to turn right and she did, the engine of the truck humming as she gave it a little gas. She followed the road down another five hundred feet until the GPS told her to turn left. Slightly offset from the back of the church was the cemetery. Emily pulled the truck onto the side of the road, not pulling into the cemetery itself. She shut it off, sliding out the door and slamming it, arming the security system. Walking up the driveway into the cemetery, glancing left and right., she stopped for a second, shading the screen on her cell phone, pulling up the exact coordinates for the plot. She shook her head slightly. Mike was thorough, if nothing else.

Emily stopped for a second to look around, getting her bearings. The church was slightly behind her to her left. Ahead of her the road curved first to the left and then to the right, accommodating graves that had been in the ground for generations. There was a metal fence that cordoned off the cemetery from the rest of the neighborhood and a stand of thick pine trees on the right-hand side that shielded the homes from the ghosts that roamed there.

It didn't look like anyone else was at the cemetery early in the morning, except for one car, a white sedan parked up ahead. Emily looked at her phone and saw that she needed to walk down the road. The plot would be on the right-hand side. Looking up, she realized that the plot was probably just ahead of the white car. A knot formed in her throat. She wondered who might be there. Maybe a new widow? Maybe a groundskeeper? The lawn looked freshly mowed, so she wasn't sure that would be the case.

Dappled morning shade covered part of the road as Emily passed the car. She followed her GPS, the sound off. Somehow having the automated voice giving her directions seemed disrespectful to the people that were buried there. When she was close, she turned off her phone and stuck it in her pocket, glancing to her right. There was a small park-like setting, a circle carved into the grass that had been paved with slim concrete sidewalks. A white stone bench had been installed on the back side of the sidewalk, facing out into the cemetery. A woman sat there, alone. Emily walked on the path glancing down every few feet to read the names. Jackson, Hildebrandt, Barnes… Emily wondered if the Barnes that she saw on the ground was related to Kathy Barnes and her dad, the pediatrician. As she rounded the back of the walkway, opposite of where the woman was sitting, she saw the name Schmidt. There were six plots. She walked over the grass and stared at them, feeling a little funny that she was standing literally on top of someone's remains. The names weren't familiar to her, so she took a picture and was quickly sending it over to Mike when a voice broke through the silence. "Why are you taking pictures?"

It was the woman who was sitting on the bench. Emily hadn't given her a close look, not wanting to be rude if someone was trying to grieve or remember a loved one, but glancing up she realized that the woman in front of her looked very much like the pictures she had seen of Vicki Schmidt. Emily decided to answer Vicki's question with her own. "Are you Vicki?"

The woman looked instantly surprised, her eyes wide. She stood up, as if she was ready to run from the cemetery and the stranger. Leaning a hand on the side of the bench, she said, "I am. Who are you?"

Emily didn't say anything. She walked over and sat down next to Vicki, letting the silence speak. After a minute or two, Emily pulled her phone out of her pocket and pulled up the email that Vicki had sent to her. "Recognize this?"

Vicki glanced down at the email and then glanced at Emily. "You're Emily?"

Emily nodded, but still stayed quiet.

"You got the email about my daughter?"

"I did." Emily looked down at the ground, sliding her boots on the grass, watching it flatten and then pop up. She didn't look at Vicki, but she heard some soft sobbing next to her. "I don't want you to get your hopes up," Emily said, "I haven't decided yet if I'm going to take your case."

The sobbing stopped. Emily was glad for that. She couldn't imagine the amount of pain that Vicki had been under for all these years, or maybe she could. It wasn't unlike any of the other cases she worked on, she realized. "I wasn't planning on running into you this morning. Generally, I don't let anyone know that I've come or gone until I decide what I'm doing."

"I understand." Vicki dabbed at her eyes, "Well, at least you're here."

Emily stood up and walked over to the cemetery plots across from the bench where Vicki sat. "Why don't you tell me about the plots?" Emily paced around the edges of where she thought bodies may have been laid to rest, careful not to step on top of them.

"My parents are buried over there," Vicki pointed. "After a few years, when Sarah didn't come home and we didn't have any more leads, I decided the only thing I had left to do was to buy her a plot. At least if she's found someday, there's some place for her to go to be with her family."

Emily stood in front of the headstone that had already been partially engraved. It read, "Sarah Marie Schmidt, loving daughter, born May 17, 1990." There was a blank for her death date.

"The thing that's hardest," Vicki said, "is that I can't end this. The pain is with me every day. There is no date I can have engraved on the stone. There is no way to know where she is or what happened to her. I'm at the end of my rope, Ms. Tizzano. Reaching out to you was my last best hope."

Emily nodded. It was a familiar story. All the cold cases she had worked—either while she was still with the Chicago PD or on her own—had left the victims with exactly the same set of feelings. There was something unresolved, something undone in all the cases. It was as if the families of the victim were frozen in time. They couldn't move forward with their own lives, no matter how hard they tried, no matter how good they made it look, because of their loved one that had been lost. The questions that haunted them kept them leashed to a past that they couldn't explain.

"Do you come here a lot?" Emily asked, still standing by Sarah's headstone.

"Yes," Vicki whispered.

Emily looked up from the headstone toward Vicki. She had unkempt blonde hair cut just above her shoulders, gray roots showing. Deep lines of worry were etched into her face and into the corners of her mouth. She sat balled up on the bench, her purse on her lap, her feet pressed together next to each other. It was as if she was trying to stay as still as possible, worried that if she moved, she might fray the edges of what life she had left.

Neither of them said anything for a moment, but Emily

knew that the question of what would happen next was hanging in the air. The cool breeze picked up, cutting its way through the trees and manicured grass of the cemetery. "I'm guessing you're wondering what I'm going to do now?" Emily said.

Vicki looked up from the spot she was staring at on her lap, staring straight at Emily. Her face hardened, "Actually, I was going to see if you'd like to come back to the house so I could make you a cup of coffee."

Emily raised her eyebrows. It wasn't the response she expected. She knew that Vicki wanted to know whether she would take the case or not, but she had to come to that in her own time and in her own way. Not that she wanted to leave anyone in their pain or that she was unwilling to help, it was just that she only took cold cases she thought she could solve. Handling things outside of the law meant considerable risk to her. Every case had to be worth the personal consequences. "Yes, I'd like that very much."

Emily followed Vicki as they walked back out of the cemetery. The only noise around them was the breeze rustling in the trees. Vicki pulled the sweater around her a bit tighter as they got close to her white sedan. "I only live a couple miles from here. Follow me?"

"Sure. I'll be in the blue pickup truck."

As Emily got into the truck and started the engine, she felt a small sense of relief. Vicki was neither hysterical nor needy. Hysterical people made Emily nervous. There had been more than one case, on more than one occasion, Emily refused to take because after meeting the family they were so emotional, she couldn't make any progress in solving it. Her decision making had two layers—a case that couldn't be solved any other way and people that had been steeled by their devastating memories. That was the whole purpose of what she did. Solving the case. Getting vengeance.

Emily put the truck in gear and followed the white sedan back past the small church and out onto the main road. They passed the gas station Emily stopped at the day before, then zig zagged their way out of town on the opposite side from the direction Emily came in. It was new territory. She chewed her lip, grateful for a few minutes to regroup before going to Vicky's house.

The little stores and offices that were clustered together in the center of Stockton quickly dissipated into longer and longer stretches of farmland. As they drove, they passed a sign for Wayne National Forest, the white paint and script lettering reminding Emily of signs she had seen fifty years in the past. "That must be where she went hiking," Emily said to herself. Slowly, she could feel the pieces of the case start to fall into place within her, like the tumblers in a lock. She still wasn't sure she was going to take the case, but she was getting closer to making that decision.

Vicki Schmidt's house was a square, pale yellow bungalow near the side of the road. The tires on Emily's truck crunched on the gravel driveway as they pulled in. The garage door opened. Vicki pulled her white sedan inside. There was a small blue Buick parked in the other spot. It was covered with dust and had a flat rear tire. Emily wondered if that had been Sarah's car.

Emily hopped out, slamming the door and locking it. It probably wasn't necessary to close it up that tightly in Stockton, but it was an old habit, one that was hard to break. No one left their cars open in Chicago, that was, unless you wanted it stolen. Emily walked into the garage, the smell of damp filling her nostrils. "You can come this way," Vicki said, holding the door open.

Inside, Emily followed Vicki up three steps and immediately ended up in the kitchen, yellow linoleum on the floor, and white countertops around the edge of the room. The house was a bit cluttered on first glance, Emily realized, but it was a controlled clutter. Things were stacked up, piles of magazines, letters, jars of flour and sugar pushed against the back of the kitchen countertops, a teapot sitting on the stove.

"Make yourself at home," Vicki said. "I'll start a pot of coffee."

Emily nodded and continued through the kitchen into the family room. It was carpeted and covered with a rug, a couch and a couple of chairs arranged in the space, facing a television. There were bookshelves along the back wall. Emily wandered over to the bookshelves.

Pictures were arranged on each shelf, carefully maintained. Emily could imagine Vicki taking time each week to wipe off each shelf and each picture. Many of her clients had exactly the same display. It was a memorial to whoever they had lost. Pictures of two young girls and then the girls singly littered the shelves. Family pictures and pictures from generations before were there as well. "You probably think it's strange that I keep so many pictures of Sarah," Vicki said from behind her.

Emily looked over her shoulder at Vicki, who seemed to be frozen, her face simply staring ahead. "I don't. Many of my clients do exactly the same thing. You aren't any different from any of them in that respect."

Vicki nodded at the picture Emily was holding. "That's from when Sarah was fourteen. That's my ex-husband and Sarah's sister Carrie. Ed and I got divorced a few years after Sarah disappeared. Our marriage fell apart. The stress of never knowing where Sarah was destroyed our relationship."

Emily nodded. "That happens. And Sarah's sister?"

Vicki looked down for a second and then back at Emily, "Carrie left Stockton as soon as she could. She was sixteen when Emily disappeared. She went off to college and I've hardly heard from her since."

"Where did she go to college?"

"Purdue."

Emily walked over to the second bookshelf. It didn't look much different than the first one. Pictures of the girls were clustered together amid a few trophies and other mementos. Vicki had walked away. Emily guessed she was attending to the coffee. The smell of the fresh pot brewing made its way into the family room. Emily looked out the back window into the yard. There was still a swing set in the back. Behind it there was a field, filled with corn that looked like it could be harvested any day. "Is that all your land, too?" Emily asked, nodding toward the backyard.

"Yes," Vicki said. She was pouring coffee into a couple of mugs and arranging something on a plate that Emily couldn't see. "My husband used to keep up with the corn, but after we divorced, I rented the land out to a neighbor. They take care of getting it planted and harvested for me."

Emily had heard of rental houses before, but not rental fields. Although living in a little town like Stockton seemed like a simple way of life on the face of it, Emily was beginning to feel like there was more going on than appeared at the surface. "Is renting out a field a normal thing to do?"

Vicki waved her back into the kitchen. "Coffee is ready." Vicki lowered herself down into one of the chairs before she answered Emily's question. She moved like her back hurt. "To answer your question, yes. Land is a pretty valuable commodity around here. Ohio is one of the largest agricultural states in the nation. Empty land doesn't last for long before somebody either offers to buy it off of you or rents it for the season."

On the table were two mugs filled with coffee, the tendrils of steam curling up above them. Vicki had set a plate on top of two of the placemats, each hosting a folded paper napkin and a fork. Vicki cut a piece of Danish pastry and set it on Emily's plate as if she had been expecting her to stop by for a visit.

"Thank you," Emily said. "You always have food to feed to

complete strangers?" As the words came out, Emily hoped that they didn't land wrong. She didn't mean it in any way to be insulting, just to probe a little.

"I have a couple of people that like to stop by unexpectedly. I always like to have something I can offer them." Silence hung in the air for a second as Emily took a sip of the hot coffee. It nearly scalded her mouth.

"So," Vicki said, slurping at the edge of her own coffee and then setting the mug down. "You're from Chicago?"

Emily knew this part of the dance well. People always wanted to know about what happened to her but were never sure how to start the conversation. It's like they needed to know more of her story before they felt like they could trust Emily with their missing child. Emily wasn't ever sure why that mattered. In her mind, it was just the results they were after. Find the perpetrator. Punish the perpetrator. Her past shouldn't matter, or maybe it should… "Yes, I was born and raised in Chicago. Was married for a time and then got divorced."

Vicki nodded. "I know how that feels." She shook her head slightly. "I don't know about you, but mine came as a total surprise."

Emily took another sip of the coffee, which had cooled enough that it didn't burn her mouth. She set the cup back down, "Mine came as a surprise. My ex-husband had some issues and after a while he decided he needed to go work on them on his own."

Vicki stabbed at her pastry, the white frosting chipping off the top and landing on her plate with quiet clink, "I'm sorry to hear that. I read in the forums you'd had some trouble in Chicago and now you help people like me."

Emily glanced at Vicki. She was staring down at the table as if ashamed to be questioning Emily about her past. As she looked up again, Emily realized she looked like a woman who'd had much of the life drained out of her. It was common among

Emily's clients. Her heart tightened for a second, thinking about all the nights Vicki was probably awake, pacing, waiting for Sarah to come home, or some news of her that didn't come. Some of her other clients had described it as a hole that could never be filled. The reality was that even if Emily could somehow get justice for Sarah, it was unlikely that the emptiness in Vicki would ever go away. Those types of wounds didn't heal, they just scarred over.

Before Emily could answer, there was a knock on the door. Emily looked up at Vicki, "Are you expecting someone?"

Vicki shook her head, "No. But that doesn't mean someone might not stop by. It's pretty common in this area. If we didn't do that, we'd never see each other with the houses so far apart."

Vicki pushed up off of the table to get herself into a standing position, walking over to the door. She disappeared out of sight, although Emily could hear voices in the background. She was on high alert. The feeling of being cornered covered her. Emily glanced to her left, noticing there was a door that led out into the backyard. She got up quietly and unlocked it, just in case she needed to leave quickly. Emily sat back down again, making no noise, before Vicki came back. Knowing she wouldn't have to fumble with a lock gave her some comfort.

Behind her was a younger woman with blonde hair. Emily recognized her immediately. She was the same woman that Emily had seen during her research, Sarah's cousin, Liz. "Ms. Tizzano, let me introduce you to Sarah's cousin, Liz."

Emily gave her a quick nod, "Please, call me Emily."

"Liz stops by to check on me sometimes. I guess this was just one of those times." Vicki lowered herself back down to her chair and motioned to Liz. "Go get yourself a mug and a plate. Sit with us for a little. We were just starting to talk."

As Liz turned toward the cabinets, Emily was able to get a better look at her. She was of average height and a moderate to thin build, with long blonde hair. Emily guessed Liz had the same hairstyle her whole life. A second later, Liz came back and sat down at the table, bringing the pot of coffee with her. "Anyone need more?" Vicky nodded yes. Emily shook her head no.

Emily scratched her forehead. This was the stage of the case where things got uncomfortable. They weren't sure whether she was going to take the case or not and they didn't know her at all. Emily still wasn't sure if she was going to take the case. It was time to break the ice and see what was there. "I don't like to waste a lot of time when I look at cases to take," Emily said. The two women stared at her strangely, as if she had passed over all the pleasantries. She had. "I wasn't planning on running into you at the cemetery this morning, Vicki," Emily said, leaning back in the chair, cradling the mug between her fingers. "In fact, most of the time I'm interested in a case, I'll be in town for about twenty-four hours before the family has any idea I'm there. You found me a little early. That said, I won't make any promises. I haven't decided yet if I'm taking Sarah's case or not."

Vicki straightened in her chair as if she just realized this was a job interview. "That's fair, I suppose. What do you need to know from us?"

Emily took a sip of her coffee and set the mug back down on the table, "How about if you start at the beginning?"

Liz stood up from the table, staring at Emily. "Wait, you want us to go through the whole thing, everything that's gone on with Sarah since the day she disappeared, but you're not sure you're going to take the case? What is this? Some sort of scam?"

Emily sat still, waiting. She saw Vicki reach out and grab Liz's wrist, "Liz, Emily drove the whole way here from Chicago. If she decides to take the case, that's at her own personal risk. I think you can understand why she wants information, can't you?"

Liz stood there for a second, "I guess. I think you should tell us if you're going to take the case or not first."

Emily raised her eyebrows. She hadn't expected Liz would be so hot tempered. "As your aunt said, I'm no longer attached to any law enforcement agency. If I decide to take the case and something goes wrong or I get caught, I go to jail."

Liz slid back down into her chair, crossing her arms in front of her chest, "So you're nothing more than a glorified criminal, that's what you're saying."

Vicki's face froze, her eyes wide, her mouth open, "Elizabeth! What are you doing? Do not treat our guest like this. I asked for her help."

"And I told you not to go this route," Liz said. "If we want to get to the people that got to Sarah, we've got to do this the legal way."

Vicki lowered her voice, "We've been through this, over and over again. We've given law enforcement twelve years to figure it out and they haven't. I need closure and so do you."

Liz stared at Emily for another minute and then got up from the table, pulling a glass out of one of the cabinets and filling it with water, drinking half of it while she was still standing at the sink, as if trying to cool the anger that was burning inside of her. She came back to the table, her eyes watery, "I'm sorry, I don't know why I just acted like that. It's just the stress…"

Vicki tapped Liz's arm and looked at Emily, "Liz has two little kids at home. Her husband works long hours and she and Sarah were best friends. Losing her was very difficult on the whole family."

Emily narrowed her eyes. Unlike Vicki, Liz was over the top. "Where're your kids now?" Emily said.

Liz wiped her eyes, "With the neighbor. She's got a couple of kids, too. We switch off so we don't go crazy with them home all the time." She took another sip of water, "I thought I'd just run over here and see Aunt Vicki, and I found you."

Emily smiled, "I guess it wasn't the surprise you were hoping for, huh?"

"It's the surprise I was hoping for," Vicki said.

Emily looked at Vicki again for a moment. The more time she spent with her the more she noticed there was a strong core underneath the dark circles and etched lines of grief on her face. Vicki might look fragile on the outside—there was no doubt that the disappearance of her daughter and a fractured relationship with her other daughter had taken a toll on her—but inside of her, Vicki was holding tight, holding onto any last shred of hope that they could resolve Sarah's disappearance. "Let's try this again. Can you tell me a little about what's gone on with the case?"

Liz shot Vicki a look that seemed to say that Emily should already have all the information. Vicki took a sip of her coffee and looked at Emily. "I'm sure you've read about the case, otherwise you wouldn't be here."

Emily nodded. "Yeah. But I like to hear the story from the family. Written reports never do the case justice."

Vicki pursed her lips together. "Sarah was born just a couple years after Liz. Liz's mom and I are sisters. The girls played together a lot while they were little. It's not like there are tons and tons of people here in Stockton. Growing up, Sarah was good at school, she was friendly, and she liked to run. She discovered running in middle school and quickly joined the cross-country team. Sarah always said she liked to feel the wind in her hair and the way her body moved through space. Didn't matter what the weather was, she'd go for a run nearly every single day. By the time she was a sophomore in high school, she was on the radar of some big cross-country programs. We had scouts from Michigan, Ohio State and Northwestern come out to watch her run. When she won the State Championship in her Junior year, the scholarships started rolling in." Vicki looked down at her coffee. Without a word, Liz got up and retrieved the pot, refilling Vicki's cup. Emily wondered how many times the two of them had sat together telling the story. Families who lost someone were forced into reliving it over and over again, every time a new investigator came on the scene. It was a strange sort of torture never allowing the family to move on.

"We took a road trip to some schools between Sarah's Junior and Senior year. The scouts came back out at the beginning of her Senior year. They all seem so excited about Sarah."

"What did she want to study in college?" Emily asked.

"Medicine," Vicki said, "at least something in that field. She wasn't sure. That fall, she committed to Northwestern. She said they had really good academic programs and she liked their cross-country coach. We had visited the campus. She even liked the school colors." Vicki picked up her napkin and dabbed at her eye.

Although Emily didn't move, watching the families go through reliving the disappearance of their family member was a kind of quiet torture for Emily, too. When she was with the police department, she had to do these types of interviews, but she had access to all the case files, so they were usually quick, cursory meetings. Many times, there was so much information in the case file that the only time she met the family was after they had made an arrest. It wasn't that way now. "I read that Sarah disappeared right before she went to college."

Vicki looked down at her lap. Emily saw Liz glance at her and then draw in a breath, "That's right. My cousin disappeared four weeks before she was due to leave for school, August 4, 2008." Liz stood up and leaned against the kitchen counter as if she was trying to get some distance from the pain of the story. "She went out hiking that morning. She told my aunt she wanted to save her legs. Sarah knew there would be a lot of running and training coming up as soon as she arrived on campus. The Wayne National Forest is just down the road."

Emily nodded, "I passed the entrance. Looks like they need to update those signs."

Liz cracked a weak smile, "You could say that. You learn pretty quickly that here in Stockton not much moves fast at all. Probably nothing like it is in Chicago."

"That's true. You are saying Emily went hiking that day in the forest?" Emily glanced at Vicki, who was still staring at her lap. She couldn't imagine how many times Vicki had told the story. Clearly, it was enough times that she felt comfortable having Liz relay the details of that day.

"Yeah. She left before lunch. She had a cell phone with her for safety reasons in case she got hurt. By midafternoon, she still hadn't come back, and Aunt Vicki was getting worried. They drove down to the parking lot and found Sarah's car in the lot."

"Is that the blue car that's parked in the garage?"

Vicki looked up, "Yes. Honestly, I can't get rid of it. You know, just in case..."

Emily nodded. It was common for family members to hold on to items from their loved ones just in case. She even knew one family that constantly kept their missing son's favorite foods in the house in case he suddenly came home and got the itch for a peanut butter and marshmallow sandwich. "That's okay. I see that a lot."

Liz seemed to have calmed the more they talked. "As I said, Sarah didn't come home. By dinnertime, Aunt Vicki and Uncle Ed were freaking out. They tried calling Sarah's phone, had gone down to the parking lot and found her car, but there was no sign of her. They called the sheriff's office but the officer they spoke to said that because Sarah was eighteen, they had to wait for twenty-four hours before they could file a missing person's report."

Emily shook her head. In most states the law read that if someone was considered an adult — meaning they were eighteen or older — the family had to wait twenty-four hours before they could get any help at all from law enforcement. It was a ridiculous statute. In her career, Emily had seen people who had disappeared and never come back because of the delay. It was designed to prevent law enforcement from going on a wild goose chase if somebody went on a bender in a local bar and didn't end up coming home that night. She understood that part, but in the heat of the moment it was often difficult to tell if it was some sort of lack of communication between family members or if someone was in a dangerous position.

Vicki cleared her throat as if she was fighting back tears and looked at Emily. "I finally called a friend of ours who's a park ranger over at Wayne and asked him if he could help."

Emily knew that Vicki met Wayne National Forest. "How quickly did they look for Sarah?"

Vicki glanced at Liz and then looked back at Emily, "Well, probably by the time I called him it was after dinner, getting close to dark. I don't know if they have different rules in the park, but they were definitely more helpful than the local sheriff."

Emily frowned. While there were many good police officers out there, she'd run into her fair share of law enforcement officials that simply didn't want to get involved if they didn't have to. She heard one guy who joked that he'd drive slowly to any calls that involved a heart attack. He didn't want to have to give mouth-to-mouth and would rather get there after the squad. That was the kind of law enforcement attitude that turned her stomach. It was the attitude that caused her to lose her job. "Who was the local sheriff at that time?"

Vicki scowled. "It's the same guy we have now. His name is Jerome Mollohan. I think he's more of a career politician than anything else."

Emily found herself getting lost in the story. "So, at some point after dinner, the park rangers get involved. Then what happened?"

Vicki pressed her lips together. "Not much overnight. There wasn't a lot they could do in the pitch black."

Liz interrupted, "Things started to move quick the next morning. I don't want to make it sound like nobody tried to help Sarah. They did."

Emily shifted her gaze to Liz. When she wasn't angry, Liz was a beautiful girl, with almond-shaped brown eyes, a square jaw and blonde hair. "What happened the next morning?"

"I didn't sleep much that night. Neither did Ed," Vicki licked her lips. "As soon as the sun came up, which was right about five thirty in the morning, we got a call that the town was assembling a search party and we were asked to come down to the park and bring some of Sarah's unwashed clothes."

Emily nodded. It was typical to bring articles of clothing that had been worn to a scene if they were bringing in scent dogs. That was at least a good move.

"By the time we got to the parking lot, there had to be at least a hundred people standing around, ready to help. The Sheriff was barking orders at people like he had been on the case from minute one, which wasn't true. There were three guys there with their hunting dogs and five people on horseback."

Emily looked at Vicki, "I'd imagine the terrain up in the forest is pretty rugged, right?"

"It can be. The trail that Sarah used was well marked and cleared. The Rangers up there don't want to have people get lost. It's a hassle for them. They brought in the horses and the dogs in case Sarah had gotten off trail somehow."

There was a pause in the conversation. Emily said nothing, giving Vicki and Liz a moment to collect themselves. She knew that telling the story, no matter how long it had been, could be very emotional for the families. She glanced at Vicki, not wanting to stare. The color in her face had drained, as if someone had opened a tap somewhere on her body and the life had simply oozed out. Emily bit the inside of her lip. She'd seen this way too many times. The thing she knew was that the family's pain would fuel her. The question was whether Sarah had just gotten lost and her body was somewhere out in the forest and had never been found or whether something else had happened to her. It was a painful question, but one that needed to be asked. "Let me ask you this… Is there any chance Sarah just got lost in the woods and was just never found?"

A flash of anger passed over Liz's face. "I don't know why everybody asks that question. It's so ridiculous!"

Vicki reached out and put her hand on Liz's wrist, "You know why they ask, Liz." She looked back at Emily. "I can't imagine that's the case, Emily. Sarah practically grew up in those woods. We spent a lot of time there as a family. The other thing is the picture…"

Emily's mind flashed back to part of the information that Mike had sent to her. "Yes, I read about that in your email and in our background research. Can you tell me a bit about that?"

"About eight months after, it was May, I think, we got a call from the Sheriff's office. It wasn't Jerome that called. It was somebody else. They asked us to come down to the station. When we got there, I thought for sure they had found Sarah's body. I had hardly been able to breathe the entire way. But when we got there, they brought us into a conference room and showed us a picture that was sealed up in a bag. Said it was found at a gas station about five hundred miles away. They said it resembled Sarah and wondered what we thought."

What Vicki described was typical police work. Ask the family to come in without any information and then judge their reaction when you show them a piece of evidence. The family was always the first suspect. But looking at Vicki and Liz, Emily knew they hadn't done anything to Sarah. "What did you think of the picture?"

Vicki raised her eyebrows, "At the time, I was shocked. I didn't know whether to be hopeful or sad. It wasn't a great picture. The officers said it looked like it had gotten caught in the rain. Sarah was sitting on a bench, duct tape around her wrists, ankles and over her mouth." Vicki's voice began to shake, "I kept looking at the picture, wondering if it was her. The hair color, the shape of her face, all of it looked like her."

"The officers had questions about whether it was her?"

Vicki nodded. "They said because it had been so long and it was so far away, they just weren't sure it was her, but then I noticed something."

Emily found herself leaning just forward in her chair, waiting. This was the information that could never be represented in a report or in any background that Mike could provide.

"Her hair was pushed off to the side. I saw a scar, a scar on her forehead." Vicki pointed over towards the fireplace. It had a brick hearth around it. "When Sarah was three, she tripped over a cord that my husband had laid across the floor to plug in a video camera. She went headfirst into the fireplace. There was blood everywhere. We rushed her to the hospital. It was a little tiny cut, but it still had to be stitched. Sarah had a small white scar on her forehead exactly in the same spot where the girl in the picture did."

"And the police officers didn't take that into consideration?" Emily knit her brows together. It seemed like a pretty conclusive piece of evidence to her.

"They said they would look into it..."

Liz walked into the kitchen and mumbled over her shoulder, "That's what they always say. They say they'll look into it, but then you never hear from them. That's why Aunt Vicki and I decided to start doing some research on our own."

Vicki nodded, "That's how we ended up posting in the

forum. And that's how you ended up here, sitting in my kitchen."

"Was there any evidence found at the scene? Emily asked. "Did anyone ever nail down the spot where they think she was taken?" Emily thought she knew the answer, but she wanted to hear it from them, from their perspective.

"They found one shoe." Vicki said. "That's how I know someone took her. Why would she wander off into the woods with only one shoe? It just doesn't make any sense."

Emily looked down at her lap for a second. If what they were saying was true, then it did make more sense that it was an abduction and not the tragic case of someone just getting lost in the woods. "The next morning, did anyone find anything? You said there were scent dogs on the scene?

Liz walked around the table and picked up the plates, stacking them, the china making a little clanking noise as the dishes touched each other. "The scent dogs were how they found Sarah's shoe. We were all waiting in the parking lot. The Rangers had erected a little tent they were using as a command post, when someone radioed in, they'd found something. We were excited and scared at the same time. We hoped it was Sarah, but the Rangers had explained to us that if Sarah had gotten lost in the woods, it would be nearly impossible to find her unless she could get to a clearing or back onto a main road. The tree cover was simply too thick for a helicopter to spot her, even though they had one doing passes overhead. A couple minutes later, we heard the engine of an ATV come down the trail. The officer hopped off — we saw him talking to a couple other guys and then he looked at us. He had a bag in his hand. It was Sarah's shoe." Liz sat back down at the table, her shoulders slumped. "That was all they found of her until they found the picture later on."

Emily found herself staring out the window, thinking. It certainly was possible that Sarah had gotten lost in the woods, except for one thing… the shoe. "Is there anything else besides the picture and your gut instinct that tells you that Sarah didn't just get lost?"

Vicki shook her head, "I've gone over this in my mind a million times. There was no real stress at home, no reason for her to run away. She had everything — her whole life — ahead of her. We had been buying everything in sight so she could get ready to go to Northwestern. Her relationship with her sister Carrie was good. She knew the trails. The weather was good that day." Vicki's eyes narrowed, "Are you thinking she ran away or got lost?"

Emily stood up and walked back into the family room, not answering the question. She stopped in front of the photos in front of the bookshelf, staring at the pictures of Sarah and her family, each one showing her to be a bit more mature. Nothing Vicki or Liz had told her made her think that Sarah had just gotten lost, but there was always the possibility. Emily wasn't sure she wanted to put herself out there if that was the case. From behind her, she heard Liz clear her voice. Emily turned.

"There is one other thing Aunt Vicki hasn't told you."

Vicki shook her head, "Liz, I really don't think you should…"

"We've heard rumblings the people in this town know who did it."

The words hit Emily like a ton of bricks. If any family had ever buried the headline, this was it. "What do you mean?"

Liz bit her lip and looked at Emily, "It's hard to say, really. We've all heard some rumblings from people in the community, people who heard something from someone else, that it was a person from Stockton that did it. The first time I heard it was about three months after Sarah disappeared. I was with some friends. It was a cold night. We'd built a bonfire in the backyard. We weren't supposed to be drinking, but we were. One of the boys there whispered in my ear that he had heard what had happened to Sarah. I've heard it a couple other times over the last twelve years and Aunt Vicki has too. She just doesn't like to talk about it because she says it's speculation."

"It is," Vicki said, pushing herself up out of the chair and walking into the kitchen. "The idea that someone who lives here could do something to my Sarah is just sickening," she said, fumbling through her purse. She pulled a business card from a pocket somewhere inside. "Here," she said, extending it to Emily, "This is the police officer we've had the most recent contact with. His name is Cameron Nolan. He seems like a nice young man."

Liz shook her head, "I think he's afraid of Sheriff Mollohan, though."

Emily took the card. She pulled out her phone and took a picture of it and handed it back to Vicki. "Thanks. You guys have been very helpful. Thank you for sharing Sarah's story with me."

Vicki tilted her head to the side, "Are you going to help us?"

That question always got Emily into trouble. She swallowed and looked back at the two women. "I don't know."

8

Emily said a brief goodbye to Vicki and Liz and walked back out to her truck, passing Sarah's dusty sedan in the garage. As Emily pushed the key fob to unlock the door, she heard a motorcycle coming down the road. She watched for a second and realized it was the same guy from the restaurant the day before. He was wearing the same red and black leather jacket. He was hard to miss. Strangely, he turned and looked at her as he passed. He didn't slow down, but Emily found it to be odd, odd enough that shivers ran up her spine.

Getting into the truck, she pulled out onto the main road and headed into Stockton. It was time for lunch, a good opportunity to see if she could track Kathy Barnes down again.

There wasn't a ton of traffic in the small city. After Emily got through the fields filled with hay and soybeans and corn, she found herself back on the main drag. Stockton wasn't exactly a complicated city with a single main road running north and south. She parked the truck behind Sandy's Restaurant again and looked around. No motorcycle. It gave her a funny feeling, one she couldn't explain. What she did know was that she needed to listen to her gut. She checked her cell phone as she locked up the truck. It was noon. She would give herself one hour and then decide. By one o'clock she would either be back on the road headed to Chicago or she would be visiting the local police station.

Inside the restaurant, there were a few more people than the day before. Two women, each toting a young child with them, had settled into a booth near the door, filling their kids mouths with french fries so they could have something of a proper adult conversation. A table filled with older men was in the corner. Emily guessed the same guys came and ate at the same time every week. They looked like regulars, their body language slumped and relaxed, their chuckling and laughter making Emily think they were telling old stories they had probably shared with each other dozens of times.

Two waitresses were working. One of them she didn't recognize, but the other one was Kathy Barnes. The other waitress, an older woman wearing a name tag that said Scarlett, approached her. "You eating by yourself, honey?"

Emily nodded. "Yep. It's just me today."

The woman waved her to a booth in the corner. As she was sitting down, Kathy Barnes turned from the table she was serving and saw Emily. She stiffened, staring. Her head dipped down, and she scurried back into the kitchen. Why she was so uncomfortable, Emily didn't know. It might be something worth finding out.

Scarlett set down a glass of water in a menu in front of her. "Do you need a few minutes? Can I get you something other than water?"

"Thanks. Yes, a glass of iced tea, please."

"Sounds good. Our lunch special is creamed chicken. I'll be back in a minute to take your order."

As Scarlett shuffled off, her round frame and curly black

hair carrying her away from the table, Emily glanced around the restaurant. No one was looking at her funny, unlike the day before. Everyone seemed to be absorbed in their own little world. Emily guessed it was pretty normal for people to stop in the middle of town to get something to eat or fill up their vehicle with gas before they continued on. She knew the longer she stayed in Stockton, the more questions would be asked about her.

Her phone chirped. She looked down. It was Mike. "Any news?"

"It's decision day."

Her phone chirped again, "I love decision day! What time?"

"One o'clock. How are things at home?"

"Fine, except for the fact that Miner dug a new hole in the backyard."

After the heaviness of the morning, Emily was glad to smile. Miner had gotten his name because of how much he loved to dig. The girl at the adoption center had told them they spent a lot of time filling in holes. Emily texted back, "Par for the course. Anything else?"

"No."

Scarlett brought back Emily's iced tea and set it on the table, leaning her hip on the side of the booth, her head tilted toward Emily. "Did you decide what you want for lunch?" she asked.

"I'll take the special. It sounds good."

"It is. You'll love it," Scarlett said, wandering off again.

Emily sat for a second, trying to catch her breath. Not that she was physically winded, she just felt emotionally drained. The only question she had rattling in her mind was whether Sarah got lost or whether Sarah was abducted. She picked up her phone and texted Mike. "Any chance Sarah got lost in the woods? Are we sure this was an abduction?"

It took a couple minutes before her phone beeped again. She imagined Mike typing on his computer, looking for any evidence that Sarah had gotten lost. Emily took a sip of the iced tea. It was sweet. Her phone chirped. "Don't think so."

That wasn't good enough, not if Emily was going to risk her neck to try to solve the case. "Why?"

"Remember that picture they found eight months later?"

"Sure. What about it?"

"I just ran a facial recognition program I've been testing out. It's her…"

The idea that technology had evolved to the spot where Mike could get better results in her kitchen at home than any law enforcement agency more than a decade later wasn't a surprise. That surprise was that Mike had written his own program. Emily grinned.

Emily set her phone down on the table just as Scarlett came back and set a plastic plate down in front of her, covered in chicken and vegetables with two biscuits on the side. "You have to let me know how you like this. I had some this morning. I thought it was good."

"I'll let you know in a minute, but while I have you, can I ask you a question?"

Scarlett nodded. "Sure. Shoot."

"How long have you lived here?"

"My whole life. My family's been here forever. We have a big farm on the outskirts of town." Scarlett didn't look up.

"You were here when Sarah Schmidt was abducted?" Emily watched and waited to see if Scarlett's reaction was any different than Kathy's had been the day before.

Scarlett lifted her eyes toward Emily. They narrowed a bit and she set down the pot of coffee she was carrying on the table. "Now, why would you ask about that? Are you family?"

"You could say I'm a distant cousin." In a small town like

Stockton, Emily knew saying you were family was one of the only ways to get people to talk, even it if was a lie.

Scarlett leaned over the table, pulled a cup to the center and filled it with coffee even though Emily hadn't asked for it, her long hair dangling dangerously close to Emily's lunch. "That's not a question that will get you many favorable answers in this town," she whispered. "It's not something I'd recommend talking about." She stood up, "The coffee's on the house. Enjoy your lunch."

Emily gave Scarlett a brief nod as she walked away. There was something about the amount of silence hovering over Stockton when it came to Sarah's disappearance that wasn't right. Her mind flashed back to sitting in Vicki's kitchen and hearing Vicki and Liz talk about the fact that everyone in the town knew who did it. Emily imagined the night Liz was out drinking with her friends, trying to bury the memories of the past only to have them rear up their ugly head in the most painful way possible.

Emily took another sip of her iced tea before she dug into lunch. She had learned long ago that the edgier people got, the closer she was to the truth. The truth mattered. She stuck her fork into the pile of chicken and vegetables on her plate and took a bite. Scarlett was right. It was good. After a few bites, she set her fork down and took a sip of the coffee that Scarlett had poured for her, glancing around the restaurant. The two women sitting with their kids were packing up, scooting the kids out of the booth, wiping hands and faces, and gathering up crayons and coloring books, the women never missing a beat in their conversation. Scarlett was tending to the table of men in the corner. Their low voices and chuckles could be heard clear over where Emily was sitting. The little bell on the door into the restaurant rang and attracted Emily's attention. She looked up, taking another bite of her lunch. It was someone from the Sheriff's Department. She studied him for a moment. He had on the tan uniform shirt of a County Sheriff, black pants, his gun belt slung low on his hips. He had a scruffy beard and a faded cowboy hat on his head. Emily looked back down, trying to determine if that was the sheriff that Vicki and Liz had told her about or if it was someone else. She didn't want to appear to be staring at him. If she had to guess based on his age, she would think it was Jerome Mollohan.

The man passed her, going straight for the table of older men in the corner. As he walked by, Emily stared down at her lunch, pretending to look at her phone. There was no point in attracting any additional attention at this point. Her stomach tightened, seeing the handcuffs resting at the small of his back. There were times she could still feel the cool metal of the ones used the day of her arrest. It was a visceral memory, one that had been etched into her bones. It was one she wished she could forget.

She could hear chuckling from the men as they talked to the sheriff. Emily took a couple more bites of her lunch and realized she'd had enough. From her wallet, she pulled a twenty-dollar bill, more than enough to pay for her lunch, the coffee and a nice tip for Scarlett.

Emily slid out of the booth and walked out the door, the little bell signaling her departure. She walked around the side of the building and over to her truck. As she did, movement from the back corner of the building caught her attention. Kathy Barnes was outside, leaning against the brick of the building, smoking a cigarette. Emily paused for a second, looking down, pretending to fumble with her keys, weighing her options. In a burst of movement, she made the decision, striding over to where Kathy was standing. Kathy looked startled at the speed of her approach, her eyes widening, "What do you want?" she said, folding her arms across her chest and taking a drag on the cigarette.

"Just to tell you I'm sorry. I didn't mean to make you uncomfortable yesterday." Apologizing wasn't exactly part of Emily's repertoire, however she had learned that a well-placed "I'm sorry," could open doors that no amount of force ever could. "It's just that the story of Sarah Schmidt is so interesting."

"Interesting?" Kathy dropped the cigarette butt on the ground and used the toe of her worn black tennis you to crush it out. "I'm not sure I'd call it interesting. It was a horrible time. This town has never recovered."

"What do you mean?"

Kathy looked back over her left shoulder, as if she expected someone to come bursting out of the back door of the kitchen onto the parking lot at any moment, "Listen, I can't really talk about it. No one does. It upsets people if you know what I mean. But I'll tell you, Sarah was one of my best friends in high school."

Emily sized up Kathy for just a second. Clearly, someone had put the fear of God into the people of the town. There was a reason they didn't talk about Sarah. What that was, she didn't know. "Okay, I get it," Emily said holding her hands up. "Can I ask you just one question, though?"

"I guess, but then I've got to get back to work."

"Do you think there's any chance she just got lost in the woods?"

Kathy looked away for a second and then looked back at Emily, practically glaring at her. "Sarah? You've got to be kidding me. We lived in those woods as kids. She knew them better than anybody else. She didn't get lost. That's a fact."

"Could she have run away?" Emily felt reasonably confident that Sarah hadn't, but talking to someone who knew her during those years could sometimes shed a light on circumstances that would be pertinent to the case.

"I gotta get back to work. My break is over. The answer? No. She had everything going for her. Unlike the rest of us…"

Kathy walked away without saying goodbye. Emily wasn't

surprised by it. She turned and walked back to her truck, opening the door and sliding inside. The engine roared to life as soon as she put the key in the ignition. Before she put the truck in gear, she sent two texts, one to Mike and one to Vicki. "Decision made. I'm in. Let's find Sarah."

9

The next steps in the case started to form in Emily's mind as she pulled out of the restaurant parking lot. She turned the truck down the main drag through Stockton and then passed the gas station. Two blocks past she saw a sign on the corner that pointed to the Sheriff's office. That would be her next stop. If it was the Sheriff that was at the restaurant at the same time as her, then he wasn't in the office at the moment. There could be good news for Emily. Maybe she could get some help with the case.

The Stockton County Sheriff's office was nothing more than a small brick building with a standard pitch roof on it and one basic front door, painted gray, facing the parking lot. Emily parked near the door, picked a spot that was marked for visitors, hopped out of the truck and went in. Inside, the walls were painted white with two plastic chairs in the corner, a steel door separating the lobby from the work area where the officers were. She went to the glass window and rapped on it, getting the attention of an officer. "Can I help you?" the young man said.

"Hi, my name is Emily, and I'm a third cousin to Sarah

Schmidt. I was wondering if I could talk to someone about her case," she lied. No one needed to know her identity.

For a moment, the officer looked a little confused. She heard the door buzz and stepped over to pull it open. At least she had made it inside. The young man had stepped over to meet her at the door. The interior of the Sheriff's office was tiny. There was a small conference room off to the right, half a dozen desks scattered around an open floor plan and a steel door at the back that read jail in bold letters. It was nothing like the precinct where she worked in Chicago, that was for sure, and nothing like Chicago Police Headquarters. Not that she'd ever want to step foot in any of those buildings again.

Emily sized up the young officer in front of her. By his look and the way he carried himself, she guessed he'd only been out of the Academy for a couple years. His dark hair was cut high and tight on this head, his uniform was wrinkle free. He looked like he could finish any fitness test that was set out by the Sheriff's Department at any time, not that they would be that aggressive with their officers. Usually only the feds had high fitness standards.

"Who did you say you are?" the officer said, his eyebrows furrowed.

"Emily. I'm a third cousin to Sarah Schmidt. I was doing some genealogy for a graduate project and thought I would travel down here to meet family and see if I could get more information. Is that possible? Vicki thought you might be able to help." Hoping that dropping Vicki's name would buy her some favor, Emily had swapped out her normally direct personality for one that was pretty and flirty.

"Okay, the sheriff isn't here right now, but let me see if I can get you some help."

Emily read the name badge on the officer's uniform. Nolan. He was the one Vicki had told her about. "Thank you, Officer Nolan."

He didn't reply but started rapidly typing on a computer terminal that was near where they were standing. She tried not to be obvious about watching over his shoulder, even though that's exactly what she was doing. It looked like they used the same basic system she had used when she was with the Chicago PD. Officers could reference case numbers or victim names in order to get to the files. She glanced away as a result popped up, pretending to pick at the cuticle on her fingernail. "Well, I have good news and bad news. The good news is we have a case file here for Sarah, but it hasn't been converted to the digital system. If you'll give me a minute, I'll see what I can find." He pointed, "Why don't you go have a seat in the conference room? I'll be just a minute."

Emily nodded and walked into the conference room, surprised he hadn't asked for her ID. Maybe it was a small town thing, Emily wondered. The conference room was outfitted with a wobbly table and two chairs with torn vinyl seats. You'd think that for the Sheriff's office of an entire county they could afford better furniture, she thought to herself, waiting for Officer Nolan to come back.

Emily positioned herself toward the back of the room where she could watch what was going on while she was waiting. There were two other officers hanging out in the office. One of them was working at a desk, typing things into the computer and staring at paperwork alternately. The other officer, a woman, was standing at the coffee maker stationed against the wall. She kept fussing with her gun belt, as if trying to make it more comfortable. Emily looked down and tried not to smile. She remembered the first few months of working for the department. All the gear had been designed and engineered for men. Trying to get used to wearing a heavy gun belt had taken her a couple months to figure out. She knew exactly how the woman was feeling.

Another minute or two went by, Emily sending a quick text

to Mike to let her know where she was. "Having my first encounter with the Sheriff's office," she wrote.

"Have fun with that."

Anyone else would have been startled by Mike's sarcasm, but Emily liked it. Before Mike could reply again, Officer Nolan came back in the room, a manila folder in his hand. "I found the file, but there doesn't seem to be much in it." He set it down on the table, his hand keeping it closed. "Now, before I let you take a look at this, you need to understand the rules of the road."

"The rules of the road?" Emily tried to say sweetly, "I just so appreciate your help. You have no idea. I am just trying to graduate, and it has been so awful." The lies rolled off Emily's tongue without much thought. When she was on a case, she did what she needed to do.

"Listen, the Sheriff is out of the office and if he was here, I couldn't let you take a look at this. So, I can give you about five minutes, but you can't tell anyone, and you can't take any pictures of anything that's in here, okay?"

Emily nodded, pasting a smile on her face. The officer still hadn't asked her for an ID. It just showed how few visitors they got. "Of course. I so appreciate your help."

"And I'm going to stay right here with you. I gotta keep an eye out for the boss, if you know what I mean."

"Of course. I'll just be a minute."

"If you have any questions about anything, just let me know. I can help you get through the law enforcement terminology."

Emily nodded and gave him another one of her big smiles. Inside, she was fighting the urge to put him in a choke hold and walk out the door with the file under her arm, leaving his unconscious body under the conference room table on the dirty floor. But even in this small town, she had noticed there was video surveillance. And it was a little too early in the day for her to take revenge on anyone.

She quickly flipped open the manila folder, taking Officer Nolan at his word that she only had a couple minutes. There were maybe five pages of content in the file. On the left side, there was a picture of Sarah and her pertinent details—her date of birth, height, weight, license number and Social Security number. On the right, there was a single picture of the shoe. Emily flipped the pages over and quickly scanned the information. They were handwritten, scattered notes, clearly written by more than one person, based on the looping scrawl on the page.

She ran her finger over the paper trying to find any details that Mike had already uncovered or that Vicki or Liz hadn't shared. The notes were badly written. The only information she could see was about Sarah's shoe and that they hadn't found the other one. There was a brief mention at the end of the third page about the photo, but there was no copy of it in the file. Emily looked up and caught Officer Nolan's eye, "Is this all the information that you have about my poor, sweet cousin?" Emily said. "I would just think with such a complex case there would be more documentation than this?"

Officer Nolan leaned out in the hallway for a second, eyeing the front door. "I'm sorry, that's all there is in the file. I wish there was more I could tell you, but there isn't." He leaned over and pulled it away from Emily, quickly closing it. "My boss will be back here at any minute. I need to get this back to the file room. You can show yourself out."

Without saying another word, she did just that. The last thing she needed was to be on the radar of the county sheriff before she ever got started.

Pulling out into the intersection, Emily felt her stomach tighten. How was it possible that there were only five pages of notes on the case? It just didn't make sense. Was it possible that the Rangers that worked for Wayne National Park had more information? Emily chewed her lip while she drove, heading over to the hotel. It was, but it wasn't likely. The Sheriff's office would have jurisdiction. That meant they would maintain all the records and evidence. Someone had kept enough paperwork to make it look legitimate, but not enough that anyone would have any leads to go on. The idea that there was a cover-up in town seemed to be a real possibility. The question was who was behind it and why?

Halfway to the hotel, Emily swung the wheel hard on the truck and made a U-turn, heading back out of town. Stockton was laid out on the north, south, east, west grid. It had only taken her a few hours to figure out where things were, at least in a basic sense. She passed the restaurant and the gas station again, heading back towards Vicki's house. If the Sheriff's office didn't have information, or more likely, was hiding the information, maybe Vicki had the records Emily needed.

Ten minutes later, Emily heard the truck tires crunch on the gravel in Vicki's driveway. Vicki's white sedan was still in the garage, resting next to the blue sedan that had been Sarah's. Emily stopped for a second, looking at it. It was if the car had been lost in time, a memorial to an owner that no longer loved it. Emily walked inside the garage and went to the back door, rapping on it. Emily heard Vicki's voice from inside, "Come in."

As Emily went up the steps, she called out to Vicki, "Vicki, it's Emily."

"I know."

Vicki was still sitting in the same spot at the kitchen table where Emily had left her a couple hours before. The kitchen smelled like coffee. Emily glanced back in the corner and heard the pot burbling. She wondered for a moment if that's how Vicki spent her day, sitting at the table and waiting, waiting for any news of Sarah. The thought was painful. Emily clenched her teeth. She could feel the anger rising inside of her. She liked the feeling. It was anger that drove her forward. It was the kind of anger that had allowed her to solve cases and get the justice she needed for her clients, the justice she had not been given.

"Can I look through Sarah's room?" Emily didn't bother with any pleasantries. It didn't matter. Without access to Sarah's things, the case would be nearly impossible.

Vicki looked at her and blinked, not saying anything for a moment. "What happened?"

"I went to the Sheriff's Office."

Vicki looked down at the table, her head swinging from side to side slowly. "I'm guessing they didn't have much for you, did they?"

"That's correct." Emily's mind drifted back to Officer Nolan and the few minutes she had spent in the Stockton County Sheriff's Office. She wondered if they handled all their cases — the few they got each year — with the same cavalier attitude. God forbid something serious would happen in the county. It was like they couldn't be bothered to deal with the issues in front of them. She suspected the Sheriff was too busy glad-handing his constituents to do his job. "I need to get into Sarah's room."

"Down the hall. Second door on the left." Vicki pointed to a short hallway where Emily could see at least one door was closed. "Before you ask, the only thing I've done in there since the day she disappeared is dust and vacuum. Everything else is exactly as it was."

Emily walked down the hall without saying another word to Vicki. She paused at the door for a moment, a plain slab door with an old brass knob. She knew it wasn't really brass, but she felt the warmth of the metal under her skin as she turned it. With a creak, the door opened, the hinges complaining that they hadn't been used enough.

Light streamed into the room from a window that was directly opposite the hallway. White sheer curtains had been pushed to the side, covered by a mauve-covered drapery. Emily stood in the doorway for a second, getting her bearings. To her right was Sarah's bed, neatly made, the bedspread pattern in the same rose and green color as the curtains. The floor was wood, covered by a rug. Directly ahead of her and to the left of the windows was a small desk, awards hung above it, probably from her cross-country days, Emily realized. To her left, there was a closet, the doors closed. The room had a musty smell, the hint of body lotion or perfume still hanging in the air. Emily couldn't tell which. It was a sweet smell that when combined with the musty odor of her unused room, caused Emily to swallow hard.

Emily scanned the room for a moment and then took a few steps across it to look at Sarah's desk. She sat down in the chair, the cushion tied with bows on the backrest. Emily looked at the pictures stuck to the wall. She recognized Sarah's sister, Carrie, but no one else. There was one girl that looked a like Kathy Barnes, slightly off-kilter, and another one that looked a little like Sarah's cousin, Liz, but it was hard to tell. "People change a lot in twelve years," she mumbled. The awards hanging on the wall, suspended from blue and red ribbons, told Emily that Sarah never got anything less than either a first or second place in the division that she ran in. It was no wonder that she had been offered at a Division I scholarship in cross country. Emily shook her head, the weight of the lost life landing squarely on her. The friendships, her family, and her future had been left behind. Sadness rose through Emily. She shook it off, knowing that those kinds of feelings wouldn't be helpful in solving the case and getting what the family needed, answers. Hopefully, by the time things were over, Emily could get them justice, too, but there was no guarantee of that.

The desk had a few small drawers. Emily pulled the top drawer open, hearing the rattle of pens and pencils. There was a sheet of unused stickers, a calendar from 2008 and some gum. Emily went through the rest of the drawers on the right side of the desk, pulling them open one by one. Emily found Sarah's acceptance letters to Northwestern, Ohio State and the University of Michigan. Underneath them was more information from Northwestern and a note from the cross-country coach, "Sarah, we are so excited to have you join the Northwestern family!" it read. Emily instantly wondered how many of those notes the cross-country coach had written, or even if she wrote them herself. It sounded like a good job for a graduate assistant.

The bottom drawer in the desk had some old folders filled with homework from the subjects Emily had to take in high school — English, Math, History, Government. There was nothing of note in the drawer, nothing that would tell Emily much more about Sarah, other than she was a great runner and a good student.

Frustrated, Emily got up and looked under Sarah's bed, quickly lifting the mattress up off of the box spring. Teenagers were known for hiding things in all sorts of places. There was nothing there. She turned to the closet. As soon as she opened the door, the smell of dusty clothes filled her nose. Emily expected Vicki to look in on what she was doing any minute, but when she glanced at the doorway, it was empty. A brief moment of relief passed through Emily. It was easier for her to do her job without the family hovering, that was for sure.

The closet held the remnants of what anyone might expect to see in a high school girl's closet — a couple of dresses, a few skirts, pairs of jeans and shirts. On the floor there were piles and piles of shoes. More shoes than Emily would have expected. She frowned and knelt down. There were a couple pairs of boots, ones that Emily would guess Sarah wore in the winter time, a couple of pairs of heels that might go with the dresses and skirts she had in her closet, but more than anything else there were lots of pairs of tennis shoes. Nike's, to be exact. The prominent swoosh on the side of the shoe was enough to let Emily know that Sarah had been a fan. Emily, herself, had used the same brand for running over the years.

Emily started pulling the shoes out of the closet, pair by pair, lining them up on the floor. There was carpet at the bottom of the closet, old burgundy carpet that Emily guessed had been there before the floors had been stripped and restored back to wood. The carpet smelled funny, like sweat and dust and mold. As the last pair came out, there was one shoe left. A pink shoe without a match.

As Emily knelt down, pushing the clothes aside, she wished she had worn leggings instead of jeans. She wasn't dressed to be digging through closets, but her jeans and shirt would have to do. She pushed the shoes off to the side and leaned over, kneeling back into the closet. Something about it didn't seem right. Emily pulled her phone out of her back pocket and used the flashlight to check the corners. There was a small ledge in the carpet in the back right-hand side of the closet. Walking her fingers through the dirty burgundy pile, she felt for the edges and realized that whatever it was, it laid flat and was flush against the corner of the closet where it would be hard to find. Emily sat down, realizing that no matter how clean she tried to stay, whatever dirt or grime that was in the closet was now on her. She pushed through, the clothes still on hangers making a curtain that blocked her from the rest of the room. Using the flashlight by holding it in her mouth, she tried to pry up the carpet that covered the lump. It came up easily, the flap of red carpet launching dust particles into the beam of light. Underneath, she felt around, realizing there was a notebook hidden under the carpet. She pulled it out and flipped it open, her heart skipping a beat. Why had Sarah hidden it in the closet? Had Vicki not ever found it in the twelve years that Sarah was missing? Emily flipped open to the first page and realized there was handwriting in the book and dates, dates that started in 2007. She heard rustling from the hallway, the floorboards squeaking. Slipping the notebook into the back of her waistband, she sat with her back to the closet, staring at all the shoes.

Vicki came around the corner, poking her head into the room, "Finding everything okay?" she said before she saw the pile of shoes on the floor. Her face paled as her eyes landed on the pink shoe. "Oh, you found it."

Emily stood up, keeping her back away from Vicki. She didn't want her to see the lump under her jacket. "Yeah, you didn't mention that you had this."

Vicki stammered, "I guess, I guess I had put it out of my mind."

For a moment, Emily wondered if that was actually the case. She had seen other situations where families had conveniently forgotten about clues and other things that had to do with a case. Whether it was an honest mistake or an intentional move to prevent Emily from finding the truth, she didn't know. "Really? How did you end up with this? Why doesn't the Sheriff's Office have this with the evidence?"

Vicki stepped more fully into the room. "A couple years ago, one of the officers came by and dropped it off. It was still in the evidence bag. He said something about them cleaning out old evidence they didn't need anymore. Wanted to know if I'd like it. What was I going to say?"

If that was the truth, it left a sour taste in Emily's mouth. Once a piece of evidence was removed from the chain of custody, it couldn't ever be used in court. No matter what the officer said, there was a finality to the act. It was as if the department had made a decision that no one would ever be able to solve the case. "The other one has never been found, is that right?"

Vicki nodded. "Once they found the shoe you have right there," Vicki nodded, her eyes barely looking at it, as if it was a reminder of the reality of her life, she said, "They scoured the area, looking for the other one. They even brought the dogs in. None of them picked up Sarah's scent or found the other shoe." She looked down for a moment. "It's all I really have left of her, I guess."

Emily saw her glance down at the pile of shoes. "I'll put these back." She pulled her phone out of her back pocket and took a picture of the one that remained, sending it quickly to Mike for the file. Her phone chirped back instantly with a thumbs up. Emily knelt down and put the shoes back in the closet, trying to replace them as she had found them. She felt Vicki's eyes on her. For some families, there was something superstitious about a missing family member's room. They might live for years, if not decades, with it exactly the same way. In a few cases, when a family member had been found after a long period of time — in one case, she remembered a boy that had come home seven years after being abducted and having his name changed — the room didn't even feel like it was their own anymore. It felt foreign, as if someone else had lived in it. In many cases, that was correct. Time passed and so had their life.

Emily dusted off her jeans as she stood up. By the way that Vicki was eyeing up the shoes, she was sure that Vicki would be back in the closet putting each one back in place as soon as she left. "Did you find anything? Anything that would help you solve the case?" Vicki asked, leaning forward and looking at the closet floor.

Stepping away from the closet, Emily shook her head no. "Not really. Did the department happen to give you anything else when they dropped off the shoe?" Though Emily wanted to believe that Vicki wouldn't hide anything from her — at least not consciously — she wasn't so sure that was the case.

A moment passed. Vicki didn't answer right away. "They gave me some papers, too." She looked away as if the memory was uncomfortable. "I've never looked at them. Liz said we should, but I've always said I wanted to remember Sarah the way she was."

"Where are they?" Emily felt half excited and half angry. Why Vicki and Liz hadn't mentioned that before, she didn't know. A part of her knew that people who wanted justice and didn't get it became suspicious over time. That's how she felt about her own betrayal. When she was in Chicago, she didn't even drive past the station anymore. It felt like too bitter of a pill to swallow.

"In the basement. I'll get them."

Emily followed Vicky out to the kitchen where she opened a door that led down a narrow flight of stairs. The smell of moisture and laundry filtered up through the air as they descended, Emily trailing Vicki as she held onto the rail. For someone who was relatively young, Vicki wasn't in good shape, even physically.

At the bottom of the steps, Vicki reached up and pulled on a string that illuminated a single bulb. To the right, Emily could see a washer and dryer at the back of the basement. To the left, there was an abandoned workbench with a few boxes stacked on top of it. "Never have gotten around to cleaning out the basement since Ed left. Just don't have the energy."

That was one thing that Emily could understand. It had taken her a while to get Luca's stuff out of the house after he left her. Not years, though. She was so angry that two weeks after he left, she texted Sam, one of the guys that worked for his father. "I've got the rest of Luca's stuff. I'm putting it out on the lawn. Have someone come and get it before trash gets collected in the morning."

She never heard back from Sam, but a few hours later, after dark had covered the street, she saw headlights wash over her front windows. Three minutes later, they were gone and so was Luca's stuff. "It took me a while after my husband left, too." Though she was irritated that Vicki had been slow to give her the information she needed, she was all in on the case. She would get justice for Sarah, even if she had to pull the information out of Vicki with pliers.

Vicki rustled through a box and pulled out a sheaf of papers that were in a brown paper bag with the words, "Evidence" printed on them and lines where notes and signatures could land. It was a generic bag, not even one that had the Stockton County Sheriff's Office logo on it, if they even had a logo. "Here. This is what they gave me." Vicki handed it over like it was a nuclear bomb. The only thing she didn't do was pinch it between two fingers like it was a hot potato.

Emily opened the bag and stared inside. In the murky light of the basement, it was impossible to see the contents. "I'll take this back to the hotel and then get it back to you."

Vicki shook her head. "That's okay. I don't want it back. If you can't help us, I'm done."

From the sound of her voice, Emily knew she was serious. This was her final shot at justice. The question was, could Emily get it for her?

10

Now that Emily knew Stockton a bit better, getting back to the hotel from Vicki's house took just a few minutes. As she drove, she glanced over at the brown paper bag sitting on the passenger seat. The fact that the Sheriff's Department had casually dropped off the files at Vicky's house told Emily pretty much everything she needed to know — whatever was in it was of no value. It was worth taking a look anyway, though.

Emily furrowed her brow as she pulled into the parking lot. Why would one of the officers have given Vicki any papers about the case at all? And the shoe? When she worked for the Chicago Police Department, they kept evidence and case files forever. There was never a date or a time in which they simply gave up and turned over whatever they had to the family. Not to say Emily didn't have case files at her house. While she was still active with the department, she had made copies and taken a few things home that she probably shouldn't have, but only because she wanted to work on them. Just thinking about it made her stomach turn, the feeling of cold steel handcuffs reminding her of the past. Pushing the thought away, she refocused on where she was and what she was doing. She turned off the truck, grabbed her cell phone and the bag from the front seat and fished the key card for her room out of her pocket. Taking the steps this time, she emerged at the end of the hall, finding her way to the hotel room door, slipping the key card in until she heard a quiet beep.

Inside, the room had been left pretty much as is, except that the bed had been made and fresh towels were in the bathroom. She decided to wash her hands before opening the bag, giving herself a moment to collect her thoughts. The towels smelled like a combination of commercial detergent and bleach.

Emily glanced around the room, wondering where to spread all the materials out. The bed was the logical choice. She plopped down, the bed springs giving us squeak, and opened the bag. Before she pulled the contents out, she grabbed her cell phone and called Mike, putting it on speaker, setting the phone on the bed near her leg.

"Hello?" Mike sounded like he was chewing.

"I've got something. How are things at home?"

"Things are fine. Miner and I just got back from the store. We were running out of dog treats."

"Already? I just bought some before I left."

"I'm teaching him a new trick. What did you find?"

Emily adjusted herself on the bed. "It's not so much what I found is what was given to me."

"What does that mean?" Mike mumbled, still sounding like he had food in his mouth.

"Well, I tried going to the police station. The file they showed me on Sarah was maybe five pages."

"Five pages? For a missing person in a case that's twelve years old? That doesn't sound like much investigative prowess. My grandma could do better."

Emily smiled. She'd met Mike's grandma one time. She was one of the few people that Mike kept in contact with in his family. Based on what she had seen, the spry, sharp tongued woman could indeed do better than the Stockton Sheriff's Department. "For sure. I went over to Vicki's house after that so I could dig through Sarah's room. Interestingly, they released the single shoe back to her. I found it buried in the back of Sarah's closet. I also found a journal that was wedged underneath the carpet. My guess is that no one had found it since Sarah disappeared."

"You're kidding? Man, if I was Sarah's mom or dad, I would have torn that room apart. Or are they the museum types?"

Emily nodded, though she knew Mike couldn't see her. "Museum for sure. Vicki even said that nothing was touched since Sarah disappeared." Emily pulled the journal out of the back of her pants and set it on the bed. "Turns out, Vicki had some paperwork that the Sheriff's office had given her in her basement."

"And she didn't bother to tell you about that when you were there before?"

Emily could hear the concern in Mike's voice. He'd been through enough cases with her to know that if a client didn't cooperate and wasn't forthcoming with information, it wasn't likely that Emily would stay on the case. "Nope. But I have this funny feeling that she isn't intentionally hiding things from me. I think she's just piecing it together the best she can. It's like only half her brain is working because the other half has shut down from the pain."

"That's a terrible way of looking at it, I suppose..."

The sarcasm in Mike's voice told Emily that he was feeling a little protective over her. It was nice, in a way, though she was fully capable of taking care of herself. After what happened to her, the first decision she made is that she would never put herself in a position of being vulnerable again. Helping the vulnerable, yes. Being vulnerable, no.

"So, what's in the bag?"

Emily picked up her phone and tapped the video call feature. "I'll put this on video so you can see the same stuff I'm seeing." She positioned the phone so he could see the bag and then opened it, looking inside. At the bottom looked to be a jumble of papers. She flipped the bag over and dumped it out onto the bed. There looked to be about twenty or thirty sheets of paper of different sizes, which struck her as strange.

"Geez, that looks like receipts or something?" Mike said, his face pressed up against his phone.

Emily frowned and started going through the papers. The first two were nothing but logistical information about where Sarah had disappeared from, dates and times and contact names and phone numbers. After more than a decade, Emily was relatively sure that most of the contact information was no good, although in Stockton, time seemed to stand still for some reason. The next couple pages were a few handwritten notes that were difficult to read. "I can't make this out," Emily said, leaning closer to the paper, "It looks like maybe the log sheet from when Sarah first disappeared?"

"That handwriting is pretty bad. If you want to take a picture of it and send it to me, I can try to decipher it for you," Mike said.

Emily laid out the next few sheets of paper on the bed. There was a copy of Sarah's class schedule, a copy of her driver's license and birth certificate. The last page in the pile was a photocopy of her fingerprints. "No wonder they handed over this information to Vicki. It's basically useless. Vicki probably provided most of this information to them at the start of the investigation," Emily said.

"Strange," Mike said. "Maybe they were just trying to give her something, so she'd get off their backs?"

Emily wondered if he was right. Families with an open cold case varied greatly. There were families detectives never heard from, having given up and moved on with their lives, to the ones that called every single week, no matter what was going on in their life or yours, to see if there was progress. They could go on for years. She wasn't sure Vicki was that way.

Emily lined up all the pages on the bed, "I'm gonna take you off speaker now and start taking pictures of the stuff and get it to you."

"Hold on. There something missing here?"

Emily chuckled. "Pretty much the whole case file is missing, Mike. I'd say that's an understatement."

"No, I mean there's that other photo, the one that showed up eight months after Sarah disappeared. Where's that? Did you see it in the file they showed you at the police department?"

Emily froze. Mike was right. The photo that Mike found online had been nowhere in the file that Officer Nolan showed her at the police department. There was also no copy of it in the bag of paperwork that the department had turned over to Vicki. Where was it? "That's strange," she whispered. "That seems like one of the most important parts of the case, and yet there's no record of it, not here and not in the case file I saw at the department."

Emily had learned to trust her gut when she worked cold cases. Her gut was clenched into a small ball, telling her that there was a significant problem with the case, and it had something to do with that picture, or the lack of it.

Emily started taking pictures of the paperwork, Mike mumbling in the background as he got them. She started stacking up the sheets of paper, squaring them off and setting them back inside the bag. As she stood up, something on the floor caught her eye. Apparently, a small slip of paper had escaped the stack and had landed near her feet. "Wait, there's one more," she said, bending over to retrieve it. It was a small sheet of paper, the size of a receipt. She sat back down on the bed and looked at it. The front was faded. The numbers and letters pressed into it by a cash register were obscured after years of being trapped in a dark, damp basement. On the back a name and a phone number were scrawled. "We might have something here," Emily said, cocking her head to the side. She tried to make out the writing. "Looks like it's a name and a phone number, Mike. Nate Gillibrand?" Emily pressed her lips together. "I wonder who he is and why his name and phone number is on the back of this receipt?"

Mike grunted in the background. "Based on the way this case is going, it's probably a receipt from the local drugstore that somebody scrawled a name and phone number on it just tossed in the bag as a filler."

Based on the way the case was going, Emily wasn't sure she could disagree with him. Frustration started to work its way up Emily's arms, tightening all the muscles on the way to her neck. "You're probably right, but can you give it a look anyway?"

"Sure, boss. Send it along."

Emily knew that any time Mike called her "boss," he wasn't happy about what he was being asked to do. Not that tracking down a name and a phone number was that big of a deal. "All right, I've sent you all the papers I've got here."

"What about the journal?"

Emily looked at it, sitting on the edge of the bed. "Yep, that's going to be this afternoon's reading. I'll let you know if I find anything."

"Okay."

As soon as they ended the call, Emily picked up the bag and set it on the little desk that was in the corner of her hotel room. She slipped off her shoes and took off her jacket, propping herself up in bed. Flipping on the television, she turned the volume to low. She found a national news station and let it run in the background. The drone of the announcers giving their opinion on everything the president did or didn't do was entertaining at best, irritating at most, but the noise of other human voices was good. Silence was not her friend.

She took a close look at the journal. It had maybe one hundred pages to it and was hardback, the binding like any book you could find at a store, not spiral-bound like the notebooks that high school kids, like Sarah, had used for their classes. On the front the manufacturer had inscribed the words "My Journal," in white lettering. The background was red, almost the same color as the burgundy carpet under where Emily had found it. At the house, Emily had noticed that the dates were from 2007 and 2008, right up until the time when Sarah disappeared. Two questions floated in her mind: Was there anything in the journal that would help Emily solve the case? And why had Sarah taken the time to hide the journal so thoroughly? By its location, Emily would bet her house that Vicki didn't know it was there. If that was the case, that journal had been sitting there since the day Sarah disappeared. Chills ran up Emily's spine. If that was true, then the last hands to touch this journal had been Sarah's. Emily was the first person to find it.

Emily opened the cover and saw that the date on the first page of writing was dated April 2007. The first several pages were nothing more than Sarah's musings about the day and her worries about going to college the following year. "I have no idea where I want to go," she wrote in flowery handwriting. Emily wondered if she had practiced that when she was bored in class at some point along her high school journey. "All I know is that mom expects me to go to college and do well. It's not that I don't want to do well, it's just that I want to have some fun, too. High school hasn't been that fun. I'm ready to leave Stockton."

Emily flipped the page and then thumbed to the back of the journal. There were about ten pages that hadn't been filled, the white of the paper still bright even though it had been buried in the corner of a closet. The last entry in the journal was dated the last week in July, just a few days before Sarah had been abducted.

Over the next few hours, Emily spent time going through each one of the entries. Much of it was nothing more than teenage angst, Sarah's worries about high school, her friends and what to wear. As the entries drew farther into 2007, there were comments about which college to choose and an ongoing worry Sarah had about who she would room with and if they would be nice. She seemed to be a girl that desperately wanted to make friends when she went to college. Emily wondered if she felt alone at Stockton High School.

Emily set down the journal for just a second and grabbed her phone, googling the enrollment of Stockton High School. Currently, there were not more than about six hundred kids in the entire high school. It wasn't very much for a district that spanned an entire county. Emily stood up off the bed and stretched. She rolled her neck from side to side and then sat back down on the bed, wanting to finish what she had been reading. She made it all the way through the first year of entries.

As Sarah got closer to graduation and moving out, her handwriting became less flowery and the entries were shorter. It seemed strange to Emily. Why the change? The emotion on the page was raw. Sarah seemed to worry about everything — her mom, her dad, her sister, leaving Stockton, not leaving Stockton. There didn't seem to be a direction that Sarah could turn that she wasn't worried. Emily started to wonder if that's why Sarah ran. Maybe she ran because she was running away from something. Maybe her talent was more about emotion than it was the physical nature of her feet pounding the pavement.

Emily settled back into the chair for a moment, closing her eyes before refocusing them on the page in front of her, the letters small and dark. Emily's breath caught in her throat as she read Sarah's words, "I feel like I'm stuck in-between. I'm not in high school anymore. I'm not in college. I'm nothing."

EMILY KNEW about feeling that way. After her issues in Chicago had been cleared up, she realized she had a lot of time on her hands. One morning, before she had gotten Miner, she found herself driving around the neighborhood and passed a boxing club. With nothing else to do, she went in and stood in the shadows until an elderly black man approached her. "You here to box?"

"Me?" Emily wasn't sure how she appeared to the man. It wasn't as though she was petite, but she was female and everyone she had seen in the gym definitely wasn't.

"No reason for you not to. Come back tomorrow. Same time. Be dressed to sweat. My name's Clarence. I'll be here waiting for you."

Emily remembered the confusion she felt for the rest of the day. She had managed to isolate herself pretty well from everyone, including from her family after her arrest and separation from Luca.

The next morning, she got up and got dressed to box. She got in the truck and drove back to the boxing club and sat in the parking lot for twenty minutes before she actually got out. Clarence was waiting by the door when she walked in. "You just did the hardest part," he said, not bothering to say hello or good morning.

"And what's that?"

"You got out of your truck. Next time it'll be faster. It won't take you twenty minutes."

A surge of embarrassment ran through Emily, but she tried not to show it.

Sitting on the bed in the hotel room, Emily wondered if

that's how running was for Sarah. She read the next few entries that spanned from April 2008 to the end of June. Picturing Sarah with a pen in hand, probably curled up in her bed after a long day, pouring herself out on the page to no one in particular, not realizing these would be potentially some of her last entries sent a wave of sadness through Emily.

After sitting for a few more hours, reading and rereading Sarah's entries, Emily got up and stretched again. Spending hours sitting in a strange hotel room reading a stranger's journal was odd. Emily felt her skin crawl a bit. Had Vicki truly not known about the journal? Or maybe, she just left it where it was, afraid to read what it said.

After a couple minutes of trying to work the kinks out of her body, Emily wandered back over to the desk. There was a room service menu in the corner. She had no desire to go out after spending the afternoon digging through Sarah's journal. Glancing at the menu, she called downstairs, ordering herself a burger, some fries and a salad. She knew she'd probably only pick at it, but she was at least a little hungry.

While she was waiting for the person to come and bring her dinner, she went and took a quick shower, wanting to get the dust and smell off of her from Sarah's closet. The hot water felt good on her shoulders. Coming out of the shower, she dried off and slipped on leggings and a T-shirt.

A knock came at the door just as she was pulling a comb through her wet hair. "Just a minute," she said, peering through the peephole in the door. Oftentimes, the worst part about going on these jobs was staying in the hotel. There was nothing she liked about it. A couple of times, she had actually slept in her truck. At least in her truck, things were familiar.

When she opened the door, a young man stood there, carrying a tray. "You ordered room service?" he said, blinking.

"I did." Emily took the plate from him. "Have anything for me to sign?"

The young man shook his head no. Emily pressed a couple of dollars into his hand. "Thank you," she mumbled, quickly closing the door behind her.

The TV was still droning on in the background as Emily perched on the bed, uncovering the food she had ordered. She flipped open Sarah's journal again. The entries in July in the weeks leading up to Sarah's disappearance started to shift before Emily's eyes. "I haven't written a lot in my journal about my love life," Emily read. The comment got Emily's attention. "There's a guy. His name is Nate. He seems interested in me. We've gone out on a couple of dates, but I told him I'm going to college and leaving Stockton. He keeps calling, though. Sometimes it makes me uncomfortable."

Emily stopped chewing and wiped her hands on a napkin, picking up the journal and rereading the entry. There had been no mention of Nate anywhere earlier in the journal — Sarah had admitted that. Most girls would write about their love life, Emily thought. That was natural. The fact that Sarah hadn't struck Emily as strange. She looked up from the page for a second, glancing out the window, only seeing the brush of branches from a tree against the building and blue sky in front of her, sky that was turning slightly dusky. Emily reread the section again. Why was Nate making Sarah uncomfortable? She took a picture of the entry and texted it to Mike. "Here's a connection to that name I found on the receipt earlier."

Emily thumbed through the remaining entries. There was no other mention of Nate. She flipped the pages, counting. There were twelve more entries after the one about Nate. Twelve more until the journal ended. She was picking up her phone to text Mike again, when it rang. "Great minds think alike. I was just about to call you."

"So, you figured out who this Nate is, huh?"

Emily tilted her head to the side. "Well, there could be more than one Nate, but the fact that this is such a small town makes me think it's probably the same guy."

"You would be right."

Emily shook her head. Most of the time, she loved Mike, but he could be frustrating, especially when he wanted to make sure that she knew he had all the information and she only had part of it. "Why don't you tell me what you found out?"

"Was it that obvious?"

"Yes."

"I'm gonna have to work on my covert techniques."

"You can save that for another time. What's the story on Nate?" Emily could hear some tapping behind her. Her phone beeped. A document loaded.

"Turns out Nate Gillibrand was in the same graduating class as Sarah Schmidt. The phone number on the receipt looks to be a phone number that is still live. Probably a cell phone."

"He still lives here in Stockton?"

"From what I can tell," Nate said, "Looks like Nate went to the University of Cincinnati for a couple of years, flunked out and then came back to Stockton. When I accessed his tax records, it looks like he works for a roofer in the area."

"So, he never graduated?" Emily heard more tapping.

"Nope. Doesn't appear that he is married or has any kids that I can find."

"Where's he living?"

"Already sent that to you. Looks like he lives a few miles outside of town, approximately seven point three miles from your current location."

Emily shook her head. Mike had slipped over into acting creepy. Gotta love tech people, she thought. "Did you find any information on his relationship with Sarah? In her journal," she tapped on the page, "it says that he seemed pretty interested in her, but she told him she was going to school and so there was no point in pursuing the relationship."

"No. Whatever they had going didn't leave a footprint."

"Any social media?" Emily didn't personally have her own social media profiles. She thought they were a waste of time. That was, however, until she needed to find someone and make them pay for what they did. She was always surprised what people put up on their walls or feeds or whatever they were called. They'd often posted details that if they knew who was looking at them, they would take them down immediately.

"Are you talking about from twelve years ago? There wasn't much social going on then, so nothing for Sarah that I could find. Nate, on the other hand, there's a picture of him with a motorcycle. Give me a sec and I'll send it to you."

Emily's phone chirped. She looked at the picture, a warning coming up on her phone before she could see it that her battery was running low. "Hold on. I gotta plug my phone in." A surge of frustration ran through her as she dug through her bag to find the cord. She plugged in, the warning disappearing. The image of Nate popped up on her screen. He looked to be about six feet tall, with an average build and brown hair, about the same color of Sarah's that Emily had seen in the pictures in Vicki's house. He was standing in front of a motorcycle, his arms folded, not much of a smile on his face, wearing a red and black leather jacket. "Wait. I've seen this guy. Twice, in fact." Tension crawled up Emily's back.

"Where?"

"He was at the restaurant when I got into town yesterday and then he buzzed by Vicki's house a couple hours later. I swear, he looked at me as he passed."

"Could you tell for sure it was Nate?" Mike asked.

Emily shook her head, "Not by his face. He had a helmet on. But it was the same make and model of motorcycle. An Indian, right?"

Indian motorcycles had been launched in the early 1900s. They were an American brand, sort of like a Harley, but most of them had saddlebags in the back with fringe on them and rode quite low to the ground. They were cult classics.

Mike snorted on the other end of the line. "How do you know about motorcycles? You just drive a big old truck."

"Luca. He always wanted one. He said that if we moved farther out of the city someday, he'd get one. Obviously, that never happened."

Mike pivoted the conversation. "Do you think this guy was trailing you?"

"I have no idea…"

11

Kathy Barnes ended her shift at Sandy's restaurant and got into her car to drive home. It had been a long day. Not that there had been a ton of people in the restaurant but having to talk to that Emily woman had stirred up a lot of feelings from the past, feelings that she didn't really want any part of anymore. She sat in the parking lot of the restaurant for a few minutes and then started her car, a sedan that had more rattles than anything else. It barely got her back and forth to work every day, but it was all she could afford. She hadn't been one of the lucky ones like Sarah's sister, Carrie. Carrie had gotten out. She'd gone to college. Kathy couldn't remember exactly where, but she had heard recently that Carrie was living in Nashville and was engaged. That was a far cry from Stockton and Kathy's own dreary daily life.

Kathy turned her car out of the restaurant parking lot and headed down the side street that was next to it. She had wanted to move out and get her own place, but she still lived at home with her parents. Luckily, their house had a basement. She moved into it a couple years before, wanting her own space, promising herself that she would save money so she could either get out of Stockton or at least get away from her parents. It never happened. She'd tried to leave after high school, her parent's offering to pay all of her expenses. She'd gotten accepted to a little school called Hiram College just a couple hours away, but became so panicked at the idea of leaving home she never went. It wasn't the first time she'd made a plan to leave, and yet she was still in Stockton…

Kathy's car bumped up the curb onto the driveway in front of her parent's house. She got out, the jingle of her keys the only noise other than the slam of the car door and walked around the side of the house, using the back entrance to go straight to the basement. She didn't feel like talking. Not today.

After washing her face and changing her clothes, trying to get the grease smell off of her, she grabbed her lighter and a cigarette and walked back up the steps and into the yard. Her parents didn't like her smoking so they wouldn't let her do it in the house. It didn't matter how cold or windy or rainy it was, there was no smoking. She walked toward the back of the lot, out of earshot from anyone that was in the house and tapped the screen. It was a number she hadn't called in almost a year.

"Kathy? That you?"

Kathy and Nate Gillibrand had dated briefly a couple of years after Sarah disappeared, after Nate got kicked out of the University of Cincinnati. One night, Nate told Kathy the story he told his parents was that he wasn't sure what to do with his life. The real story was that he had found out he liked drinking and partying a lot more than going to school. They had broken up when Kathy found out that Nate was running around on her with another girl from a nearby town. For a while, she thought Nate and the other girl might get married, but six months after she and Nate broke up, he broke up with the other girl.

"Listen, I've got somebody who's asking a lot of questions about Sarah." Kathy got right to the point.

"Really? And how's that?"

"Not sure. She showed up in town yesterday. Started asking questions about my dad and then quickly jumped to realizing that my dad probably treated Sarah. She found me again today on my break at the restaurant."

"What did she want?"

Kathy could hear the steel in Nate's voice. "Not sure. Just asking a lot of questions. Told me she's on her way through town on her way to West Virginia."

"You believe her?"

"I have no idea. That's probably something you should be more concerned with than me."

There was a pause for a second. Kathy waited, wondering if Nate had hung up on her. He did that sometimes. After school didn't work out for him, he had become angry. He'd been such a nice guy in high school. Kathy remembered him even though he was a couple years younger than her. Somehow being stuck in Stockton brought out an aggressive side that wasn't necessarily pretty. She had heard that a couple years before, one of the guys on the crew he worked with shingling roofs fell off and broke his leg. The guy blamed Nate. Said Nate threw him off the roof because he got mad. No charges were ever filed, but it made Kathy wary.

"You know what kind of vehicle she's driving?" Nate asked.

"Blue pickup truck. Illinois plates. She said she's from Chicago."

"Oh yeah, I saw her yesterday at the restaurant. I think that same truck was parked out in front of Schmidt's house, too. What is she, a reporter or something?"

"No idea. Just giving you a heads up."

It was Kathy's turn to hang up. She didn't want to hear anything more that Nate might want to say to her. All she wanted to do was give him the information and be left alone. But Nate was one of those guys that kept circling around in her life. Kathy dropped the cigarette on the ground, crushing the butt with the toe of her shoe. A crawling sensation hit her skin. Hearing his voice was enough to make her want to pack a bag and get out of Stockton, that night.

12

Emily woke up the next morning to a cramp in her calf and the steady pelting of rain against the windows. Dark clouds pressed against the sky. As she looked out the window, she saw a break in the line of storms to the west. Emily hoped it wasn't an all-day rain. She changed into a pair of jeans and a shirt, slipping her boots back on. She checked her phone. Mike had texted overnight. How she had slept through it, she wasn't sure. Not that she had slept well. Between the lumpy mattress and the words from Sarah's journals whirling through her head, she felt like she had hardly slept at all.

The text from Mike said he was unable to find anything interesting in the paperwork that the police department had dropped off with Vicki. That wasn't a big revelation. Emily could've told him that. She texted him back, knowing that he was not likely to be awake unless Miner got him up for his walk. "Someone has to have those files. The real files. Someone has to know what is going on here."

Sending the text to Mike, she knew her next step. It was time to shake some trees. Enough with the gentle research. If she ever wanted to get out of Stockton and get back to Chicago, and more importantly, figure out what happened to Sarah, it was time to try something new. She trotted downstairs, leaving Sarah's journal and the papers in her hotel room along with her backpack. Where she was going, she wouldn't need it.

Emily didn't even pause at the doorway to the hotel, charging right out into the pouring rain and making a beeline for her truck. She hopped in, shaking the water off of her jacket and starting the engine. She headed out the driveway towards Vicki's house.

The drive only took a few minutes. Emily felt like she was on autopilot even after only a couple days in Stockton, the anger at the idea that it was possible Vicki was hiding information from her building inside. Was it really true that Vicki didn't know anything about Sarah's journal? If it had been Emily's daughter, the first thing she would have done was tear her room apart, down to the studs if necessary. Even if it wasn't intention, Emily couldn't shake the feeling that there was something going on, though. As she pulled into Vicki's driveway, she saw the white sedan still in the garage. She couldn't imagine that Vicki would go to the cemetery with the weather. She slammed the truck door closed and walked in the house without even knocking. "Vicki?"

As she had been the day before, Vicki was sitting at the kitchen table, reading the paper. Emily furrowed her brows together. In Chicago, all the newspapers were pretty much digital. It was strange to see someone sitting and staring at words on newsprint.

"Emily? I wasn't expecting you this morning."

"Where's Liz? We need to talk." Emily stood in the doorway, not moving. Depending on the words that came out of Vicki's mouth next, she would either wait or she would drive back to the hotel, get her stuff and head back to Chicago. These women knew more than they were telling her. The hidden journal, the scant police file... there was something going on. Vicki and Liz wanted her help, but did they really? Anger burned inside of Emily. She had driven the entire way to Stockton, seven hours of long road, leaving her life behind. She didn't need this. They needed her. They needed to remember that if they wanted her help.

"Is there something wrong?"

"Just get Liz here."

Vicki nodded and picked up her phone, which was right next to her on the table. While most people kept their cell phone handy, families who had lost someone without explanation kept them even closer, always having them nearby in case news, good or bad, became available. "Liz? Hey listen, Emily's here. She needs to talk to both of us. Can you come over?"

Emily could hear murmuring on the other end of the line. Vicki was nodding. "She'll be here in a minute."

Vicki pressed her palms into the arms of the chair and stood up. "Can I get you something while we wait? A cup of coffee? I just made a fresh pot."

Emily shook her head no. Thoughts raced through her head — the feel of the paper from the evidence file, the look on Kathy Barnes' face. The last thing that she wanted to do was get involved in emotions or social graces. She needed answers and she needed them now. She had given up doing things other people's way a long time ago. This wasn't the time for her to go back to pleasing people.

Not more than about three minutes passed before Liz came up the back steps, the door slamming behind her. "Morning," she said, setting her purse down on the counter. "Lucky for you guys my husband wasn't going to work early this morning so he could watch the kids. What's going on?"

Emily struggled to control her temper. She didn't want to be angry but the pace at which Vicki and Liz gave her information made solving the case nearly impossible. There were too many gaps. "When I talked to you guys yesterday, you said that everyone in the town knows what happened to Sarah and who did it, but you conveniently left out any information tied to that. Now, I've been patient. I need all the information, not just part of it. All."

Vicki threw up her hands, "I've given you everything we have! I don't know what you want!"

Emily didn't say anything, she just pivoted her gaze to Liz, who stood, leaning against the countertop. Neither of the women said anything for a moment. Emily knew by the look on Liz's face that she was calculating. What she was thinking about, Emily wasn't sure. A moment later, Liz said quietly, "Are you talking about what I heard at that party?"

"You know darn well that's exactly what I'm talking about," Emily said, a little louder than she normally would have. "I can't work with people that hold information back on me." She looked at Vicki, "That bag of information that you gave me has absolutely nothing in it. The only thing we found was the name of Nate Gillibrand. Neither of you mentioned that Sarah had a boyfriend at the time."

Vicki stood up, her head hanging. She carried her coffee mug into the kitchen, not saying anything. Emily watched her carefully, wondering if she would remain under control or become emotional. Emily didn't want to upset her, but something had to be done. She had to push these people otherwise she would never solve the case and get back to Chicago.

"I didn't mention Nate to you because I didn't really think it was pertinent to the case. Liz and I have talked about it. We don't think he did it. Or we don't think he knows anything, maybe."

Vicki sounded decidedly uncertain to Emily. She folded her arms across her chest, "It's not up to you to decide who may or may not be the suspect and responsible for Sarah's disappearance. That's why you reach out to me. That's my job. It's my life on the line if things go badly. So, I need all the information and I need it now."

Liz's shoulders slumped. She blinked a couple times. "I guess we've just been at this for so long that we know what we think happened, or least we have some of the pieces," she said.

"And they are?"

Liz sat down in the chair next to where Vicki had been sitting. "The spring before Sarah graduated from high school, Nate was interested in her. That much is true. I think I remember her telling me they went out on a couple dates. Nothing serious, just a couple trips to go get some ice cream. Not that there's a lot you can do here in Stockton. I don't remember if Sarah told me or she told you, Vicki," she looked at Vicki, who was still standing in the kitchen, "Sarah just didn't want to get involved with anyone before college. She wanted a fresh start and she wanted to concentrate on her studies."

"Why did she need a fresh start?" Emily unfolded her arms and listened carefully. The women were finally starting to talk. This might the break Emily needed.

"Have you seen this place?" Liz said, raising her eyebrows. "Stockton is not exactly a booming metropolis. There's not a lot of opportunity here, but there is a lot of talk between a lot of families who have been here for generations. Not all those relationships are good. A lot of people have history that has brought a lot of bad blood."

"Did any of that bad blood have to do with the Gillibrand family?" Emily asked.

"Not really," Liz said. "I think it was just that Sarah didn't want to get involved with anybody from Stockton. She had friends growing up, don't get me wrong, but she never seemed to connect with anyone, if you know what I mean."

Emily did. Especially in the years since she'd been fired from the Chicago Police Department, she kept to herself, except for Mike and the people she talked to at boxing. Her stomach clenched, wondering if the idea of connecting with other people was something that maybe she should work on. She shook her head, pressing the thought away from her. Emily didn't need that kind of distraction right now, not while Liz was finally opening up. It didn't seem that Vicki had information about Sarah, or maybe she didn't want to have information about Sarah, but Liz seemed to know way more than she had said the day before.

"What about that party you went to?" Emily said.

"You mean the one where somebody said they knew what happened?"

Emily nodded, "Yes."

"Like I told you yesterday, that was a couple months after Sarah disappeared. There were few of us left here in Stockton. We had a bonfire out of the old Morris farm. The people that owned the place didn't care. We all showed up there one night after a football game. One of the guys brought a cooler of beer he had stolen from his dad and we sat out drinking pretty late."

"Who was there?"

Liz looked up, like she was trying to access the memory. Emily had read a study one time in a psychology journal that said the placement of people's eyes determined what side of their brain they were using. When they looked to the right, they were using the left side of their brain, when they looked left, they were using the right side of their brain.

"I don't know, that was a long time ago. There were a bunch of us there. Some people who had already graduated high school, like me, and some people who were seniors that year. It was all people that had been in high school together, you know what I mean? Like the people who had been underclassmen when I was a senior." She shook her head, "There aren't that many people in Stockton to hang out with, so it probably seems strange, but even after I graduated, for the first couple years I still hung out with people who were in high school."

"Who was the person that told you they knew what happened to Sarah?"

"Daniel Nichols."

"And who's he?"

"Other than a guy who wanted more than I was willing to give? He was a year behind me in school, which meant he was a year ahead of Sarah." Liz wrinkled her nose, "I can still smell his beer breath. I was sitting and chatting with a couple of the girls. I had a pretty good buzz on, so the details are a little fuzzy. All I remember is he somehow appeared behind me, sitting off to my right. As I turned to see who it was, he leaned in. I thought he was going to try to kiss me, so I jerked back." She shook her head, "He wasn't someone I was interested in at all. Instead, he leaned towards me and said, 'I'll bet you'd like to know what happened to Sarah, wouldn't you?' The only thing I remember from that moment is being so surprised he'd say something like that. I must've looked at him funny and nodded, because he continued talking. He said something like, 'everyone knows what happened to her. Everyone knows who did it, too. I'm surprised you haven't figured it out yet.' As soon as he said it, he got up and walked away. He probably figured I'd follow after him and he'd get what he wanted, but honestly, he was so creepy there was no way I'd follow him anywhere."

Now Daniel Nichols was a suspect, Emily thought. "Did you tell anyone about what he said to you?"

Liz shook her head. "A week or two went by and I finally mentioned something to my mom. I think she called Aunt Vicki and told her, but I just chalked it up to Daniel being drunk and stupid. It's never really crossed my mind that somebody in Stockton could do anything to Sarah. Everybody seemed to like her."

"So, your assumption is that someone outside of Stockton did something to Sarah? It wasn't someone who knew her?"

Liz's eyes grew wide. "Of course! Stockton may be backward, but the idea that someone from the town would kill Sarah? I don't know, that just seems impossible to me."

"Then tell me this. Why are the police files such a mess?"

Vicki furrowed her brows and shook her head, "What do you mean?"

"After I left you guys yesterday, I went to the police station. I guess the sheriff was out so Nolan — that same officer you told me about — let me look at the file for like three seconds. Not that there was much to see in there, there were only five pages in the entire file. That's not typical for a case like Sarah's."

"I don't know what to say about that," Vicki said, wrapping her hands around her mug of coffee. "I remember Cameron Nolan from when he was a kid at church. Family has lived on the outskirts of the city for generations. Not super smart, but he wouldn't intentionally turn you the wrong way."

"I'm not saying he did," Emily said, correcting her. "What I'm saying is that whoever was in charge of the investigation had some reason for not doing the file correctly. Any idea why that would be?"

Liz snorted. "Other than the fact that the most lethal crime in Stockton up to that point was a couple missing cows from one of the farms? Listen, Stockton is small. When I say small, I mean small. I don't think that those officers know how to do much more than write tickets for underage drinking and an occasional speeder down Center Street. They weren't equipped to deal with Sarah's disappearance."

Emily sat down in one of the other chairs at the table. "You said that the Rangers from Wayne National Forest were involved. There weren't any notes in the file from them either. Stockton had control of the scene, right?"

Vicki nodded, "I think so. I mean, that's pretty much who we talked to all the time. Me and Ed, we never really had any contact with anyone from the Park service. They seemed to help out during the search but then kinda disappeared. We worked with Sheriff Mollohan, but other than a lot of nice words, he didn't really have anything for us."

Emily's mind began to race. If the Sheriff's office had been in control of the scene, someone had been responsible for keeping notes and logs on the case, or at least someone should have been. She stood up from the chair and started to pace. She felt Vicki and Liz's eyes on her, but she was too busy thinking to speak. There had to be more than five simple pages in the case file. It looked like something that someone had put together just to keep in a drawer in case anyone ever asked. She needed the real file. "Okay. I gotta go."

As Emily started for the door, Liz and Vicki followed her. Liz called out, "Wait! What are you going to do next?" Emily walked down the steps and out into the garage without saying anything. She never answered that question. Her clients asked all the time, but sometimes it was better if they didn't know.

As Emily walked out of the garage, the two women trailing her, she noticed there was a police cruiser parked behind her truck. A large man with a mustache and a cowboy hat leaned on the hood, his ankles crossed, and his arms crossed across his chest. He had half a grin on his face. When he saw the women, he stood up, "Well, Vicki, I heard you had a visitor."

Vicki and Liz stopped in their tracks. Emily stopped too, but stared at the man. He extended his hand to Emily, "I'm Sheriff Jerome Mollohan. Welcome to Stockton." Emily didn't take his hand.

Vicki spoke first, "Sheriff? What are you doing here?"

"Now, that's not the way you should greet someone who has worked so hard on your daughter's case for all these years."

Emily tried not to laugh. The lack of case file alone told her that the Stockton Sheriff's Department was inept at best and responsible for creating a cover-up at worst.

Vicki raised her eyebrows. "Really? Have you come to give me information about my Sarah?"

The Sheriff's face became a blank canvas. His tongue reached out between his lips and touched the upper one before answering, "As much as I'd like to be coming here with news, I don't have any. I was just coming to welcome your visitor." He looked at Emily. "I'm sorry, I didn't get your name."

"I didn't offer it," she said. Emily had developed an instant dislike for the Sheriff. He was everything about law enforcement that made her stomach turn. He was about the politics, not about the people. Emily walked to her truck, opened the door and got in. As she started it up, the Sheriff walked to her window. She rolled it down. "You still didn't tell me your name?"

"Sarah Schmidt," she said, rolling up the window, throwing the truck into gear, making a noisy U-turn on the gravel driveway.

In her rearview mirror, Emily saw Vicki and Liz standing in the driveway with Sheriff Mollohan. The rage was building inside of her. She felt angry not only for Sarah, whose entire future had been cut short but also for the people of Stockton. They didn't have many options and even if they did, they didn't have many people they could count on to protect them. That was plain.

Emily drove back through the town and headed to the cemetery. She needed time to think. She parked the truck out on the street and walked up the long driveway, her mind reeling. The conversation she had with Liz ran back through her mind. Daniel's beer breath, his comment that everyone knew what happened to Sarah and who did it, the fact that Liz was too ashamed of her drinking to tell her mom. As she got to Sarah's empty cemetery plot, she stared down at it, realizing there were two options. Either someone in the town had killed Sarah and they had managed to keep it covered up for twelve years or it was just a bad rumor that had been started by some teenagers. The real perp could be in the town or long gone by now. Based on the thin facts she had, and the location of the town, it made a lot more sense that some drifter had come through, gone for a hike on the trail and decided to do something to Sarah. Finding that person would be nearly impossible with the slim information available.

Emily squatted down and started picking at the grass around Sarah's headstone. The people that maintained the cemetery trimmed the grass, but they hadn't bothered to edge right around it. Emily took her frustration out on the plot. At this point, she didn't have enough information to go on. Emily didn't have any records, and she didn't have any real information that gave her any real leads other than the name of Nate Gillibrand.

Emily stood up and walked over to the bench where she and Vicki had sat when Emily first got into town. She pulled out her phone and called Mike. He answered after two rings, sounding out of breath. "What's up?"

"What are you doing? You sound like you're out of breath?"

"I guess I am. We just got back from the pet store. Miner needed a new bag of dog food. He convinced me he needed a toy while we were at it. I just dragged like fifty pounds of kibble into the house."

"When I get home, remind me to take you to boxing class. Clarence would have a field day with you."

"Very funny."

"You think I'm joking? I'm not. But that's not why I'm calling."

"What's going on? Did you find anything out?"

"I just had an encounter with the local sheriff. He is a creepy guy, for sure. Pulled right up in Vicki Schmidt's driveway and was waiting for me when I came out of the house."

"No way!" Mike said, "What's up with that?"

"Well, apparently my presence in Stockton has raised a few eyebrows. But here's the thing, I can't make any headway on this case if I don't have the case files. There's no way that there are only five pages of information on this case. There's no way."

"You went to the police station yesterday, right?"

Emily nodded, hearing tapping from Mike's end of the conversation. It sounded like he was on his computer. "I did. The officer there gave me like five seconds a take a look at the pages. Not that there was anything there that would've helped us anyway."

"You think there are records somewhere else? Is that what you are saying?" Mike asked.

Emily heard Miner bark in the background. "That's exactly what I'm saying. Even if the police in Stockton don't know what they're doing, they had the help of the National Park Rangers. Those guys go through some pretty extensive training from what I've heard. They have to be ready to deal with rugged terrain, lost people and some significant injuries. They aren't just out there counting squirrels, if you know what I mean."

She waited for a moment. Mike didn't say anything, but she could hear the persistent tapping of his computer keys in the background. She felt her chest tighten, impatience flooding through her. This case just shouldn't be that hard, she thought. "Anything?"

Mike didn't answer for a minute, making Emily even more impatient. "I'm gonna have to get back to you," he said. "I'm not sure you're right, but we'll see. Gotta go."

Mike had practically hung up on her, but Emily didn't mind. He sounded focused. That's where she needed him to be. The breeze had picked up. It was blowing hard enough that Emily felt the need to zip up her jacket. She took a deep breath and looked out over the cemetery. In some ways, she could understand why Vicki came here on a regular basis. There was no noise, no ringing of phones or chirping of texts, no whirring of laptop fans or the drone of televisions in the background. There was just an occasional chirp of a bird and some wind rustling through the trees. It was peaceful, or at least as close to peaceful as Emily had found in a while.

Soaking in the quiet made Emily wonder why she still lived in Chicago. She'd grown up there, that was one thing, but there was something about the city that didn't seem to want to let her go. It was as if the handcuffs that had been put on her wrists that night had been taken off, but not removed. She was still chained to the city.

Emily stood up, smoothing her jeans down over her thighs, finding a stray dog hair from Miner's coat on the denim. Emily blew it away, but instantly missed being at home and sleeping in the same bed with Miner and going for walks in the neighborhood. She missed going boxing. Emily sighed. She knew she could go home at any time. Emily wasn't under any obligation to finish the case. She wasn't getting paid. Emily's mind drifted toward the pictures of Sarah displayed in her mom's house, the bookshelves filled with memories, the images printed on paper the only thing that the Schmidt family really had left of their daughter. She knew she couldn't go home, at least not yet.

Emily walked back to the truck, wondering if there was something in the papers back in the hotel she could have missed. As she got into the truck and started it up, she thought back to meeting Sheriff Mollohan an hour before. Him tracking her down at Vicki's house hadn't been a coincidence, she knew that. He must've gotten wind of her arrival from someone in Stockton. Who, she wasn't sure. It could have been someone at the restaurant, maybe Scarlett, maybe Kathy Barnes. Maybe he had been the one Kathy had been talking to in the kitchen the day before, but either way, someone had decided that Emily's questions were enough to roll out the welcome wagon. It wasn't much of a welcome, Emily thought, turning the wheel of the truck into the hotel parking lot. She shut off the engine, leaving it in the back corner of the lot, backing it in. She slid out, staying close to the driver side looking around. There was no one in sight. Backing the truck in meant she had a little cover from peering eyes in the hotel. Leaning near the door, she grasped a small gold key and leaned over under the driver's side.

When she got the truck, one of the first things that Emily did was purchase a lockbox. The installation was pretty easy. Remove the bolts that hold the seat to the frame, slide the lockbox in underneath the flanges and re-bolt the whole mess down. If anyone wanted to break into her truck, they could take anything that was out and visible, but the chance that they'd have the time or the energy to break into the lockbox was small. She jiggled the key in the lock. When she slid the small drawer open, seeing the blue fabric that lined the box, she also saw the butt of the pistol she always carried with her. It was a Sig Sauer. Not the same brand that she had carried when she was with the Chicago Police Department. Definitely an upgrade. She pulled the pistol out and pressed the slide just enough to see the brass of a round sitting in the chamber ready to fire. If the Sheriff was going to come and make idle threats, she needed to be ready just in case.

As she put the pistol back in the drawer, she saw two other magazines filled and ready to go in the drawer. She closed it and locked it. Before leaving the truck, she opened the back door, lifting the bench seat. She had made changes there, too. Inside, there was a rifle, extra ammo for both the rifle and her pistol, and extra rifle magazines. Technically, she knew she shouldn't be transporting guns over state lines. Not that she'd bothered to take a look at the laws between Illinois Indiana and Ohio before she left, but if anyone knew she had the guns with her, it could be a problem. It was a chance she was willing to take.

Emily closed up the truck, looking around, making sure that no one had been watching. As she slammed the back door, a man came walking out of the hotel, a backpack slung over his shoulder. He was staring at his phone. Emily shook her head, wondering how many people had missed the threat right in front of them because they were busy with a random text or checking their email.

Leaving the guns in the truck, Emily decided to go upstairs to her room to have another look at the papers she had left behind. Other than Nate Gilbrand's phone number and name, there had to be something in those papers that was valuable information. She needed a lead. She knew she had one in Nate, but she wanted to take another look at the papers before she tracked him down. It wasn't her style to go into a confrontation unprepared. She didn't know enough about Nate, she didn't know enough about Stockton, and she certainly didn't know enough about Sheriff Jerome Mollohan in order to make a move. She just hoped that Mike could come up with something. In the meantime, it made sense to go back through the information she did have.

The key card slid quietly into the slot and the door gave a beep as the light turned green. Emily walked into the room looking down for a second, shoving the key card in the back pocket of her jeans. As soon as she looked up, she knew something was wrong. She looked to her right, toward the bathroom. She instantly wished she had grabbed her pistol before she came up. Her room had been ransacked, the papers all over the bed and the floor, her backpack and bag pulled apart and tossed.

She listened just for a moment, keeping the door to her back so she could run out if needed. For a second, her heart pounding in her chest, she considered going back down to the truck and getting her gun and coming back up, but she didn't hear any noise. It was likely that whoever had been in her room was already gone. She sidestepped to the bathroom and reached around the doorframe flipping on the light, the blood rushing in her ears, carefully checking to see if anyone was in there. It was empty. Her bathroom was intact, the toothbrush and toothpaste still sitting where she had left them on the sink counter. She turned her attention to the main area of the hotel room. From her vantage point, she could see the corner of the bed and things strewn about. What she couldn't see was around the corner. She inched forward, her heart still pounding, anticipating someone coming around the corner with a knife or a gun. If they had either of those, her odds weren't good. The search for Sarah could be over before it ever got started. She pushed towards the corner and decided to stick her hand out, knowing that anyone who saw it would likely move forward exposing themselves. There was no reaction. Emily couldn't hear anything, except for the continued rush of blood in her ears, her heart pounding, the adrenaline surging through her body. It felt like she was tingling all over. She decided to make the only move she had. In one motion, Emily charged around the corner. There was no one there. Emily let out a breath, now being able to get a view of the entire room. She quickly checked under each of the beds, but they were blocked off so that guests didn't leave things behind.

Now that she knew there was no one in the hotel room, she could better figure out what happened. A wave of relief flooded over her. The television was still off, so they hadn't used noise as a cover. By the looks of it, she realized they had probably come in using a master key card, looked for whatever it was they were trying to find, and then quickly left the room. Was it a message or threat? Emily wasn't sure. It might be both. The reality was the wrong people knew she was in town and that she was looking into Sarah's death.

She pulled out her phone and took a couple pictures of the mess, sending them to Mike. "Another visit from the welcome wagon," she wrote.

"Yikes," the reply read. "You okay?"

"I'm fine." Truth be told, Emily was anything but fine. She was ticked. Whatever hornets nest she had managed to stir up by coming to Stockton, she'd had about enough of it.

Emily gathered up her personal items that had been dumped all over the floor. She made piles of her clothes, refolded them, and stuffed them back into the bag. There was no reason to leave anything in the hotel room from now on. She went into the bathroom and retrieved her toiletries, stuffing them into her backpack. Would she tell the front desk? No. The fewer people involved, the better.

That left the paperwork that Vicki had given to her. Emily had gone through it once already and then stuck it back in the bag. Though she had taken pictures of it, without a lot of time and painstaking work, there'd be no way to know if the person that came in the room took something out of the bag, unless it was obvious. Emily's pulse started to slow down after the surprise of having her room ransacked. She sat on the corner of the bed, gathering up the papers, making a new stack, deciding to lay them out one by one on the bed to give them a last look. As she did, she noticed that the slip of paper that had Nate Gillibrand's name and telephone number on it seemed to be gone. Curious, she thought. She lifted up the corner of the white hotel comforter and knelt down, checking the floor. Out of the corner of her eye, Emily saw something. She scooted towards the headboard on her hands and knees. It looked like a piece of paper had blown halfway under the blocking the hotel had put under the bed. She used her fingernail to drag it forward. It wasn't the receipt with Nate's name and telephone number on it. It was something else. Something Emily hadn't seen before. Emily frowned for a second, twisting around and sitting with her back against the bed. A couple of dust bunnies blew past her on their way to the corners of the room. Clearly, the cleaning staff at the hotel needed to be brought up to speed on proper methods, she thought. Emily glanced down at the piece of paper again. There were some notations on it, numbers in a series. There were a few breaks between the numbers. She could barely make them out.

   Emily took a picture of the numbers and sent it to Mike without a note. If nothing else, they'd have it for reference later. She frowned and squinted at it. The numbers were written on an angle as though someone had been sitting in a car or on the move when they jotted them down. They almost looked like coordinates to her, but it seemed like some of the numbers were missing. There should have been about twelve digits if it was coordinates, if she remembered correctly from the last time she used GPS coordinate, but she couldn't be sure. There only seem to be about eight digits in the list. As she stared at it, there were two more lines of numbers. The second two were so faded out that if someone wasn't staring directly at the paper, they would've been hard to see. It almost looked like they had been erased and just enough of the graphite had been left on the paper in order for someone to see them if they looked carefully. Emily stood up and walked over to her computer. A flutter of nerves ran through her. She realized she hadn't checked it when she got back into the room. Luckily, it appeared that nothing had been damaged or taken. Her machine was password-protected with some fancy encryption that Mike insisted on. The odds of someone other than her being able to get in were small, or at least that's what Mike had told her. She typed the numbers into the search bar, wondering what would come up. Nothing. The search engine sent back some nonsense results about blood pressure and electrical currents, nothing that made sense to Emily. Nothing that related to Sarah or her case. Emily stood up and started to pace. She walked past the lineup of papers that were on the bed and checked again. There was no sign of the slip of paper that Nate Gillibrand's name and phone number had been written on. The question was, who would take his number? Was the slip of paper she found with the numbers on it new and left behind or something that had simply fallen out of the bag when she first did her investigation?

Emily slumped down in a chair in the corner of the room. She moved the sheer curtains away so she could look out in the parking lot, checking on her truck. There was no one near it. A minute later, she saw a black sedan with rental plates pull in and park. The same guy she'd seen earlier that day, the one with the backpack who had been staring at his phone got out, his car chirping as it was locked. He walked back in the hotel still staring at his phone. Emily chewed her lip. She didn't know who he was, but he didn't fit the profile enough to be a suspect in her mind. From underneath where she was sitting, Emily heard an engine start. It wasn't a car engine. It was a motorcycle engine. She stood up, pulling the curtains back, staring straight down. Out from under the overhang of the hotel, she saw the front wheel and handlebars of the motorcycle emerge, the rider wearing a black helmet and a red and black jacket. "Nate," she said. A surge of energy ran through her. Had he been the one in her room? It would make sense that he would want his name removed from the case. Maybe somebody had tipped him off. But who? Emily stared out the window. There was no point in running down to try to get in the truck and follow him.

Gathering up her clothes, the bag she brought them in, her backpack and computer, and the papers that Vicki had given her, Emily shoved them into the front of her backpack. She grabbed the key card for the room and the keys to the truck and headed out, making sure she hadn't left anything behind. She could still bed down at the hotel, but she wasn't leaving anything there.

Emily took the steps down to the parking lot at a run, giving the front desk clerk a nod as she moved towards the front door. She opened up the truck, putting her bag and backpack inside. Inserting the key into the lock box, she pulled out the pistol ready in its holster. She clipped it to the back of her pants and covered it with her jacket. There was no reason to take any chances, no reason to expose herself, not after the state her hotel room had been left in.

Emily started up the truck, clicking the doors locked as she sat in the parking lot. She thumbed through the texts and information that Mike had sent her, looking for an address on Nate Gillibrand. It was time to talk to him. She'd find out quickly whether he was responsible for Sarah's death or not.

13

On his way out of the hotel parking lot, Nate noticed his motorcycle was running low on gas. He decided to stop at old man Adams' gas station on the way out of town. It didn't take long to tank up the motorcycle. That was the good thing about two wheels instead of four. It didn't take a lot of cash to get a whole lot of miles underneath you.

In the winter, Nate drove an old truck that had about three hundred thousand miles on it his dad had given him, but spring, summer and fall, he drove the Indian as much as he possibly could. He liked the feel of the motor underneath him, the vibration running through his body. As the miles passed, he didn't pay much attention to where he was driving. There wasn't much in Stockton to pay attention to these days. He took a turn off onto a dirt road that had only a few pieces of gravel left on it from when someone had cared. That had been decades ago. A clearing in the woods opened up in front of Nate, the trailer he called home poking out from behind a stand of trees. Just beyond the trees was a creek that ran and bubbled all year long. The trailer was on the back acreage of land his family owned. Working as a roofer helped him pay the bills, but there wasn't much left after the end of the month, depending how much drinking he did.

As he got off the motorcycle, he heard the crunch of tires coming. He pulled his helmet off and set it on the handlebars, waiting. He saw a blue pickup truck with Illinois plates approach.

The truck stopped and a slender brown-haired woman got out, her ponytail hanging down her back. She had on a pair of sunglasses, a jacket and jeans, work boots on her feet. She took her sunglasses off and looked at him, "We need to talk."

"Who are you?" Nate balled his fists. He had seen the truck around town for the last day or so. That some woman he didn't know from out of town decided to come charging up to him on his property without an explanation made him furious. He tried to push the anger back down, remembering what the judge had said the last time he was in court for getting into a fight. "This time I'm going to give you a chance to make a change. Next time I'll send you right to jail, no questions asked," he had said.

Answering his question, the woman shoved her hands in her pockets, "I'm someone who's very interested in your ex-girlfriend, Sarah Schmidt."

Nate didn't answer for a minute, sizing up the woman in front of him. After a second, he placed her. It was the woman from the restaurant. He'd been surprised enough that someone was on his property that he didn't put the truck and the woman together right away. Squinting at her, he realized she was attractive. Nate guessed she was a little older than him, maybe by ten years or so. He could tell she was tough by the way she stood and the way she spoke to him. If he'd met her at a bar, his reaction might be different. "Sarah was never my girlfriend. I don't know who you are or what gave you that idea." He looked down, pulling the key out of the ignition of the motorcycle.

"Now, if you'll excuse me, I'd like to go inside. It's been a long day."

"You had a long day doing what?" the woman said. "Trashing my hotel room?"

"Your hotel room?" he said. "I don't even know who you are! Why would I be interested in your hotel room?"

"Maybe because your name is on a piece of evidence in the Sarah Schmidt disappearance?"

For a second, Nate's stomach clenched. This woman knew an awful lot about him and Sarah. She was clearly an out-of-towner. Maybe she was some PI that the Schmidt family had hired. "It's no secret I was interested in Sarah before she disappeared, but I didn't have anything to do with her disappearance."

The woman shifted her weight onto one leg. It looked to Nate like she was trying to decide whether he was telling the truth or not. "Funny thing. I went back to my hotel room a little while ago. Papers strewn everywhere. The evidence with your name on it was gone, but I have a copy, so nothing to worry about there. Even stranger, I saw you leave the hotel right after I got back. Can you explain that?"

Nate pressed his lips together. It was everything he could do not to charge the woman and punch her right in the face. "Listen, lady. First of all, you're trespassing. Second of all, I don't even know who you are so I couldn't care less about your hotel room. Third of all, Sarah's been gone for a long time and she and I never really dated. Fourth, for your information I was at the hotel because I was applying for a job."

A smirk crawled across the woman's face, "I hope it wasn't for housekeeping."

Nate turned to walk into the trailer. "Listen, this has been an interesting conversation, but as I said, I'm tired." He glanced back. The woman hadn't moved. "I'm going to get a beer and sit out by the creek. You want one?"

The woman nodded. "All right."

"I'll meet you out back." As the woman turned to walk around the trailer, he saw a bulge at her back. Whoever she was, she was carrying a pistol. Nate swallowed. His day had just become a lot more interesting.

14

Emily wasn't sure what to make of Nate Gillibrand. He was handsome in a rugged way, his hair cropped short but tousled, like he didn't care about his appearance. She wondered if he had been one of the guys that all the girls had chased after when they were in high school. As she walked around the side of the trailer, questions formed in her head. Nate wasn't exactly what she expected. Did he look to be hot tempered? Yes. Did he react in a way that made her think he knew anything about what happened to Sarah? She wasn't sure.

Emily had learned long ago that what people didn't realize is they all have a series of tells, little habits or mannerisms that show in their bodies when they lie. Everything from blinking to chewing a lip to rubbing two fingers together could be indications a person isn't telling the truth. Emily had gotten good at figuring out who was lying and who wasn't. It was really the only way for her to solve cases that have been unsolved for decades. Somebody always knew something. That was a fact. Did Nate know what happened? It wasn't clear at this point.

Around the back of the trailer was a homemade fire pit, the

remains of a couple of charred logs and burned beer cans in the middle of it. Emily could imagine Nate sitting around with a couple of his buddies from work hanging out late at night and getting drunk. There were a couple of plastic chairs nearby. She glanced down toward the creek, just as the back door of the trailer banged closed. Nate came out, carrying a couple of bottles of beer. "This way," he said. "It's not much, but it's better than living with the folks."

"This is your parent's property?" Emily asked.

He squinted at her for a minute, settling into a plastic chair with a view of the creek. He motioned for her to sit down and offered her a bottle. "I'm not gonna answer any more questions until you at least tell me what your name is."

"Emily."

"Are you a PI or something? Did the Schmidt's hire you?"

"You could say something like that."

Emily waited for a moment, silence settling over the two of them. The only noise was the burbling of the creek as the water ran over and around rocks. "You sit out here often?"

Nate nodded. "Helps me stay calm. Last time I was in court, the judge told me I needed to stay under control. Not too many people I can punch when I'm sitting out here relaxing."

"Tell me about Sarah," Emily said, taking a sip of the beer.

"Sarah?" Nate looked down for a second and then took a sip of beer, settling the bottle between his knees, leaning back in the chair. "Sarah was a nice girl. Pretty. Great runner. Great runner's legs, if you know what I mean," he glanced at Emily. "Her disappearance, it's hurt this town."

"What do you mean?" Emily said, setting the beer down on the ground next to her. The last thing she needed was to have too much alcohol in her system in a strange town while she was carrying a gun after someone had ransacked her hotel room. That sounded like a recipe for disaster. She picked up her phone, waiting for Nate to answer her question, sending Mike a ping of her location, just in case. It wasn't much, but at least if she disappeared, Mike would have a place to start looking for her. In this town, you never knew what could happen.

"Well, before Sarah disappeared, people just seemed to be friendlier. Ever since Sarah's disappearance, everybody's suspicious."

"What about you? What do you know about the case?"

Nate took another swig of his beer. "Other than the fact that Sarah went on a hike and never came back? Not much. I mean, I went out to help just like everybody here, but there was nothing we could do."

The fact that Nate had gone out on the search surprised Emily. "You went out on the search?"

"Yeah. I got a call from one of my buddies that she had gone missing late that night. I woke my parents up and told them I was going to go help. We met at the local church. Everybody brought a flashlight, and we started looking. That was before the formal searches started in the morning. From what I've heard, it sounds like the Sheriff's office didn't move very fast on this one."

Emily had gotten the same sense from Vicki, but it was curious to her that Nate brought it up. "What do you mean?"

Nate shrugged and set his empty beer bottle on the ground, "I don't know. It just seems like everybody here knows everybody else, you know what I mean?" Emily didn't, but she nodded anyway. Chicago was a big town. There was no way you could ever know everybody there. Nate continued, "I didn't know Sarah well, but I did know that she was kinda outdoorsy, so it makes sense that she'd know the trails. When she didn't come home, you'd think that the police would do something about it right away, but the Sheriff, he didn't." Nate stood up and walked towards the creek for a second, then turned back. "That's why I went out with my buddies to try to help that night. We didn't find anything." He kicked a rock with the toe of his boot, "For all I know, we were on the wrong trail. There are lots of trails over there in the park. One of Sarah's friends told me later that she was up there all the time. Knew those trails like the back of her hand. I don't know," he shrugged. "Maybe it was just a story."

"I need to ask you about something and then I'm gonna take off," Emily said.

"What's that?"

"Emily's cousin, Liz, said there is a rumor going around in town that everybody knows what happened to Sarah and who did it. Is that true?" Emily watched him carefully, looking for any signs of him trying to mask the truth or lie to her. She waited for a second, her attention focused on him completely. What he said could be the difference between whether she continued to consider him a suspect or not.

"Liz? She said that?"

Emily nodded and waited. He still hadn't answered her question, but he apparently knew her.

Nate turned and looked at her dead on. "Yeah, I've heard some of the same rumors. Nobody ever gave me any names. Just heard some stuff in passing that it was somebody local, not some out-of-towner. I have no idea what his beef could've been with Sarah. From what I could see, she was a nice girl."

Emily sat for a second watching him. There was no indication that he was lying about anything. He had turned and looked at her straight on. "So, you're saying you have no idea who they were talking about or why?"

"That's right. If it's true, though, that's a problem. There are people in this town that would go after whoever it is and take care of whoever did it."

Emily stood up. "One more thing. Why do you think I found your name and cell phone number in some evidence the Schmidt's gave me?"

Nate started to smile. "Well, it's probably because I made no secret that I was interested in Sarah. The morning after she disappeared, some police officer from the park asked me why I was helping, and I told him about it. That's probably how it ended up in whatever paperwork you found." He looked down for a minute and then back at Emily, "Listen, I've had my share of troubles. I've made some bad decisions, there's no doubt about that. But I'd never hurt a girl. That's not how I roll." He tilted his head to the side slightly, "You're going to try to figure out who did this?"

Emily stood up, "I'm going to try." She headed back to her truck.

"Let me know if you need anything," Nate called behind her.

As she pulled away, Emily considered what Nate said. Although it would've been easy to say that Nate had something to do with the break-in at her hotel room or Sarah's disappearance, she just didn't think it was the case. The fact that he'd heard the same rumors that Liz did around town that somebody local had hurt Sarah gave Liz's story more credence.

It was nearly time for dinner, but Emily didn't feel like eating at the restaurant or ordering room service. She didn't even really particularly feel like going back to the hotel. There was one fast food place in town, next to the old gas station where she had filled up when she first got there. As she pulled through, the woman handing her a bag of food and a drink, her phone pinged. It was Mike. "I've got something you're going to want to see."

Since she was driving, Emily tapped her phone and called him back instead of texting. "What's up?"

"You know those files you wanted?"

"Yes. The real case files?"

"I've got them."

A surge of excitement ran through Emily. Having the actual case files could be the difference between running around town chasing dead leads and actually getting somewhere. For a second, her mind went back to Vicki. She could practically see her sitting in her kitchen, making yet another pot of coffee, dusting the pictures of the daughter she'd lost. In reality, she had lost both daughters with the fractured relationship she had with Carrie.

"How did you get them?" Emily asked, pulling out into traffic.

"Probably better if you don't know. The only thing you need to know is there's about a twelve-hour window before somebody figures out that a digital copy has gone missing. You better hustle up and get the information you need from them."

"Thanks. I will. You'll email them?"

"Already did. There's a link for you to follow. Remember, the clock is ticking."

Emily pressed the accelerator in the truck, anxious to get back to the hotel and do a deep dive on those files. Why they were on the clock, she didn't know. She didn't always understand how Mike got access to things. But if he said they only had twelve hours, then they only had twelve hours. She needed to get to work.

15

After Sheriff Jerome Mollohan left the Schmidt house, he drove back to the station, trying to get into his office without any of his officers pestering him. That's how he preferred his days. He wanted to go about his business and not deal with requests and suggestions from people that should know better. It was his town. Stockton had been his for a very long time and it was going to stay that way.

As Jerome closed the door to his office, he glanced at the walls, filled with pictures of him with dignitaries that had rolled through Stockton at one time or another — a Presidential candidate, a woman that was running for Congress, and an NFL player. There were some pictures of him with community leaders and his family. The office hadn't been updated in a long time. For a second, Jerome tried to remember when, then the thought escaped him. He had a phone call to make.

His meeting with the woman from out of town hadn't gone exactly as he expected. He was hoping she would have been more friendly. A quick check of her license plates gave him her name, Emily Tizzano. The records came back that she was a resident of Chicago. He didn't know much about the city, although it was big and probably not some place he'd ever want to visit. What she was doing here hanging out with the Schmidt's, he could only imagine.

Jerome sat down at his desk, the chair complaining under his weight. He took off his hat and set it on the corner of the desk, thinking. After a moment, he leaned forward and started typing on his computer, doing a little research on the visitor that had arrived in his town. Researching visitors wasn't something he did on a regular basis. Most of the time people came through town, got gas, ate a meal at Sandy's restaurant, maybe stayed a night or two at the local hotel, and then headed out. For some reason, this one seemed different.

A quick search on the Internet gave Jerome a gold mine of information. News articles popped up about Emily. They weren't flattering. "So, you were a police officer," he mumbled, talking to himself.

He flipped through a few of the articles. It was usually harder to find information on people, but not on this Emily woman, he realized. There were literally dozens of articles about her arrest and then a few dozen more about how the charges had been dropped. One of the articles linked her to the Tizzano crime family. The journalist speculated that somehow the mob had gotten involved in her case and got her off of whatever charges had been filed because she was married to the boss's son, Luca.

Uneasiness started to gnaw at Jerome's stomach. He reached into his desk drawer and popped a couple of antacids. Before her arrest, she was a top cop in Chicago, rising to the level of detective awfully fast for that big of a department. He clicked on a couple more articles. She had closed a record number of cold cases. The uneasiness inside of him grew. If she was in Stockton to look into Sarah's case, there could be trouble. Big trouble.

He picked up his phone and then set it down again. Caution

was the name of the game. He needed to think carefully about Emily and what he did next. Maybe it was just worth watching her for the time being, he thought.

Leaning to the side, Jerome reached down and unlocked the bottom file cabinet drawer in his desk, his gun belt pinching into his side. He pulled the drawer open and thumbed through the files there were in there. There were three of them, three files that could cause him trouble. Sarah Schmidt's was one of them. He closed the door without pulling it out or looking at it. He'd done that too many times already. He locked the drawer again, knowing he was the only one with the key, the only one who had access to those files.

Jerome felt more settled knowing that the information about Sarah was still under lock and key, especially his. Not that anyone in the department would care. All the officers that worked for him knew they owed him their careers. They were loyal. If they weren't, they had to find themselves another job in a different department. He'd been the sheriff for too long to give up what he had built.

He got up from his desk and went to the file room where all the original documents for the cases they worked were stored. Closing the door behind him, he wondered if he was being paranoid, but there was no reason to take any chances. He found the drawer that was labeled "cold cases" and pulled it open, thumbing through the worn edges of the manila files. He pulled out the one for Sarah. The thin file was exactly where it should be, just like he had left it after he removed the real file. Things were still in place, at least for now.

16

As soon as Emily got back into her hotel room, she tossed the bag of fast food on the bed, slipping off her boots and lifting the lid on her laptop as soon as she dug it out of her bag. As it warmed up, she fished a power cord out of her backpack and plugged it in. The lights on the screen popped up right away. After she put in her password, Emily pulled off her jacket and opened the bag of food, pinching a few French fries from the bottom of the bag. She pulled the rest of the food out, crushing the bag down on the side of the desk near her laptop. She'd eat and work at the same time.

As soon as she opened her email, she saw a message from Mike, marked with an exclamation point to let her know it was an important message. There wasn't any actual content in it, just a link. She clicked on it and immediately two hundred and thirteen pages of information popped up on her screen. "This looks more like it," she muttered, unwrapping the chicken sandwich and taking a bite before wiping her fingers on a napkin and scrolling down.

Based on a quick scan of the information, Emily felt more

confident she was looking at the actual case file, not the watered-down version that Cameron Nolan had shown her at the station. For a second, she wondered if Nolan knew that he was giving her a staged file. She pushed the thought away, knowing that twelve hours wasn't a lot of time to go through more than two hundred pages of data. A message popped up on the screen from Mike. "I see you in the file. Don't try to print it off. There's a line in the coding that will wipe it off of your machine if you do."

"Thanks, I think," Emily wrote back. Mike sent her back a smiley face.

From inside her bag, Emily pulled out a notebook. She'd have to go old school when reviewing these notes. For a moment, she felt like she was back at her cold case job in Chicago, the wash of memories passing over her — the smell of stored files and stale coffee in her nostrils, the feel of the thin paper in the files. That wasn't her reality. She was far away in a tiny town in Ohio, alone. She looked at the first page of the report. It was a typical report cover sheet, giving the basic details of the case, the name of the victim, a basic description and identifying information, including her address. Emily looked at her cell phone. It was just after seven o'clock at night. With the number of pages in the file, she'd likely be up all night.

By the time she looked at her phone again, it was dark outside, the parking lot lights at the hotel having popped on. Emily glanced at her cell phone. It was after ten o'clock and she was only through the first thirty pages. She got up and stretched, taking a moment to look outside in the parking lot from the window of her hotel room. For a minute, she wondered what Vicki and Liz were doing. She wondered if Nate was drunk and passed out in his trailer, waiting to hear from the hotel on his job application. She shook the thought from her head. The people who were part of the case were not her concern, except if they were suspects. Her one and only focus was Sarah. She went to the bathroom and refilled her water bottle, sitting back down at the desk. "Keep going," she mumbled to herself.

The next page of the report had the first crime scene photo. There were detailed pictures of where Sarah's shoe had been found and some images of footprints on the trail. After each page, there were comments from the investigative team. Based on the fact that it had been twelve years prior, Emily doubted that any of the people still worked for the same department. "Single shoe found near trail. Alternate footprints belonging to a male, size ten shoe, found as well. Trail is well used, so impossible to determine conclusively whether men's shoe prints belong to perpetrator." On the following page, there were some wide-angle shots of the trail as well as interior pictures of Sarah's room and her car. "The presence of a single shoe creates suspicion of abduction," the author wrote. "However, with no ransom note or call from the abductor it is impossible to rule out the fact that the victim simply got disoriented and lost in the forest."

Emily felt her system start to settle, whether it was because she was tired or because it looked like someone had actually taken the time to do their job, she wasn't sure. The more that she read the file, the angrier she got at the Stockton County Sheriff's office. Why they were hiding this information, she didn't know. The possibilities swirled in her head. Were they protecting someone? If that was the case, then it was possible what Liz had heard at the party was true.

Emily clicked on the next set of pages, the image of a water-damaged photo popping up on the screen, cockeyed to the left. It was the picture that was found at a gas station five hundred miles from where Emily had been taken. "Object was found at the Loudonville Gas Mart and reported to the Stockton County Sheriff's office forty-eight hours after it was found. Upon seeing the picture, the family is relatively sure that is Sarah Schmidt, however there is some question by the local law enforcement agencies whether that is her, given the time since the initial disappearance and changes to her look."

Emily scowled. She understood why the person writing the file notes couldn't be sure it was Sarah, but Mike's new facial recognition software had proven that it was. In Emily's mind, if Mike said it was Sarah, then it was Sarah.

Emily stopped and stared at the picture for a moment. If she had been shown a picture of Sarah from her mom's bookcase in this picture, there would be no doubt in her mind that it was the same person. Why was there even a question? She leaned back in her chair. She stared at the picture for a few moments, taking in all the detail. It wasn't just Sarah she was interested in, it was her surroundings.

It looked like Sarah was seated on a bench in the back of some sort of vehicle. The walls were dark around her. Underneath her, there appeared to be a blanket. Her wrists and ankles were duct taped together, another piece covering her mouth. Her eyes were at the same time both wide and sad, as if any hope she had of being found had evaporated. There were no shoes on her feet, just a pair of socks. Emily flipped to the next page of notes, scanning them quickly looking for details on the image. "Family reports that the outfit Sarah is wearing in this image is the same one she had on the day she disappeared."

Emily frowned. That made figuring out when the picture was taken difficult, if not impossible. If Sarah had been wearing a different outfit, it could be argued that time had passed between her abduction and when the picture was taken with the need to change her clothes. Since she was wearing the same outfit, any investigator would quickly realize that the picture could have been taken an hour after she was abducted, or weeks or months later. It was impossible to tell. Emily clicked back to the picture itself. The blanket underneath Sarah had a pattern to it in yellows and greens. There didn't appear to be anything special about it. Emily squinted at the picture and then used two fingers on her screen to enlarge it. There was something between Sarah's knees. Emily leaned forward, trying to get a better look at the grainy picture. There was a hint of pink, but it was hard to tell what it was. Emily flipped back a page earlier in the file, pages that had pictures of the evidence from the scene in the park. She flipped back and forth between the picture of Sarah and the picture of the shoe. The pink was almost the same. Emily wondered if whoever had taken the picture had taken off Sarah's other shoe, probably so they could bind her ankles together more tightly. Sarah was an athlete, probably stronger than she looked. Whoever grabbed her would have had to have been considerably stronger, probably a man of at least her age if not a little bit older.

Emily could feel her mind starting to work, digesting the details of the case. She had solved other cold cases with less information, but those cases had more to go on at the start. The Schmidt's had so little information, it was difficult to make any headway without the file. She whispered a quiet thank you to Mike and his technical skills. Without access to this file, figuring out who did it would've been a slow, if not impossible, process.

Emily got up and started to pace. Questions were popping up in her head. She walked back and forth, her fingers interlaced behind her back. She realized she had a few pieces of information that were helpful. First, Sarah didn't get lost. If someone had a picture of her bound and gagged, that was obvious. That theory was out the window. No one needed to go searching for her scavenged bones somewhere in the Wayne National Forest. Second, the picture that was found at the gas station could have been taken the day she disappeared or shortly thereafter, or it could have been taken months later.

That part she didn't know. Third, Emily knew that whoever had taken her had to be strong and probably took her by surprise.

As the pieces started to fall into place in Emily's mind, realized the odds of a stranger running across Sarah while she was out hiking in the woods was pretty small. Maybe there was something to the rumor that people in Stockton knew what happened to Sarah and who had done it? Emily shook her head. Small towns often held the most secrets. Stockton appeared to be one of them.

AT EXACTLY SEVEN the next morning, Emily was staring at page one hundred ninety-five of the document when it disappeared from her screen. Luckily, she had taken the time to glance at the last twenty pages or so as she saw the time drawing near. Just like that, it was gone. She leaned back in her chair, barely able to keep her eyes open, when a message popped up from Mike. "Did you get the information you needed?"

"Maybe."

17

By the time lunchtime rolled around, Emily had grabbed a few hours of sleep, showered and put on a fresh set of clothes. She repacked her bag and took everything she owned down to the truck, shoving the key card in her back pocket. She wasn't taking any chances that someone would come into her room and find the pages of notes she had taken last night. If it was someone in Stockton, that would give them far too much information.

Emily started up the truck and headed out of town, towards the main entrance for the Wayne National Forest that she passed on the first day in town. It was time for her to take a look at the scene. Based on the files Mike had gotten her access to, there were actual coordinates that she could use to pinpoint the spot where the investigators thought Sarah had been taken.

She pulled into the main entrance and then off to the side of the road. On her phone, she pulled up a map of the area and compared it to the notes she had from the file from the night before. She found the parking lot where Sarah had left her blue sedan. For a moment, Emily wondered who had driven Sarah's car home when they realized Sarah wasn't coming to get it. Had it been Vicki or maybe a family friend? That had to have been an awful moment for the family, Emily realized, and then pulled herself back. She wouldn't be useful if she got too emotionally invested in the case. She was in Stockton for justice. That was it.

She parked the truck and locked it, deciding to leave her pistol in the car. From what she could tell by the GPS coordinates, it wasn't a far walk. The last thing she needed was some overeager park ranger to notice the bulge on her back and haul her in for questioning when she should be making progress on the case.

The day was bright and sunny, the type of early weather many places in the Midwest enjoyed. Cooler temperatures, low humidity and bright, blinding sunshine. According to the calendar, it had been just over twelve years since Sarah had disappeared. The foliage was still thick, although the leaves had started to turn a dark mottled green, the first whisper of fall colors already beginning. She could hear the cicadas and the peepers, what people in the Midwest called toads, already making noise in the woods, even though it was just after lunchtime. The changes in humidity and noises from the wildlife let people know that colder temperatures were coming whether they liked it or not.

Emily approached the trailhead, watching the GPS on her phone and tracking the trail ahead of her. It looked to be about a half-mile walk to the spot that had been noted in the police report. As she looked back towards the parking lot, there was only one other car parked there, the owner of it nowhere to be found. Emily figured they were out on the trail somewhere probably hiking or taking in the scenery.

From the Wayne National Forest's website, it looked like most of the people that visited the area were locals or people from the Midwest who are searching for a quick jaunt away from their hometowns to a place where they could be outdoors and enjoy nature. As the cool air rubbed against her face, Emily understood why people liked getting outside. It made her wish that she lived farther out of Chicago. That would be something worth thinking about when this case was over, she thought. She imagined for a moment that Miner would like a bigger yard to play in.

There was no time to think about that now. Emily hiked up a steep rise, the cinder covered trail grinding under her boots. She still wore the same rugged boots on her cases she used to wear when she was on duty. They were made for any kind of terrain you could possibly run into, although they were hot and could be a bit clunky. Her right foot slipped on a chunky stone and she nearly lost her balance, but recovered at the last second, noticing that she was almost on top of the area where Sarah had been taken. Emily stopped for a second and looked around. The trees seemed to be bigger than the photo she had seen the night before, but there was something familiar about it. She walked slowly forward glancing left and right past where the GPS said she should go and then turned around and walked back the other direction. Had Sarah been on her way out for her hike or on her way back when she had disappeared? Emily wasn't sure anyone would have that piece of information except for Sarah. Whether it was important to the case or not, she didn't know.

Walking back towards the trailhead, she saw the slope of the trail go downhill. The image of Sarah's shoe being lodged in some brush off to the side filled her mind. She stopped for a second and took a few photos with her phone and then looked up, trying to think through what could have happened to Sarah on that day.

Emily remembered the crime scene photos and the comment that the author had made that there was a set of footprints in a men's size ten at the same area where Sarah's shoe had been found. Was it possible that the person that took her moved her with an ATV? Maybe, but there would have been tracks. There weren't any.

Stopping for a moment, Emily looked around. The only noise around her was the brushing of leaves together in the trees as the wind passed by and a few birds high up giving an occasional chirp. She could barely hear their calls. Pulling out her phone, she took a few more pictures, squatting down in the area where she believed Sarah's shoe had been. Not that she was trying to find new evidence — twelve years had passed. The odds of finding anything new in the brush were slim to none. She stood up again, turning, trying to position herself where Sarah might have been, running the scene through her head. The possibilities flooded through her mind in a rush. In her mind's eye, she could see Sarah moving along, thinking about school, running, and the new friends she might make. Just the circumstances of her life would make her distracted and probably not as focused on what was going on around her as usual. The one piece of information that Emily didn't have was what direction Sarah was going. Emily furrowed her brow and licked her lips. Did it really matter? She pulled up her phone and found the picture of the pink shoe. It had been kicked off on the side of the trail, down a slight slope, the toe of the shoe facing up, the heel going downhill. The undergrowth had partially hidden it from the people searching for her. Emily tried to figure out what direction Sarah had been standing when her shoe had come off. She sucked in a deep breath and then sighed. Without more information, she wasn't sure she'd be able to figure it out.

Emily took one more look around and started walking back to the truck. Seeing how the crime scene was laid out helped a little, but not enough to help Emily figure out who might be behind it. She put her head down and started walking the trail back to the truck. Lost in thought, the notes from the file she had digested the night before ran through her head. The images of Sarah from Vicki's bookcase in the file flashed in front of her mind's eye like a movie.

Emily hiked down a small slope in the trail and then up the other side. As she was getting ready to go down the last hill to the parking lot, a deer ran across her trail and startled her. For a second, she stopped in her tracks, wondering what the deer was running from. Maybe it was just the fact that there was a person on the trail. Emily had no way of knowing how well used the trails were this time of year. As she continued her descent down the hill, the prickles on the back of her neck stood up. Something about the deer running across the trail didn't seem right to her.

She picked up her pace a bit, her stomach clenching in a little knot. Emily could see the trailhead in front of her. Why a simple deer crossing her path seemed to make her so uneasy, she wasn't sure. Maybe it was the lack of sleep, she thought as she crossed into the parking lot. As she walked to the truck, she scanned the area. It seemed to be clear. The only car left was the black sedan that had been there when she arrived. Emily went directly to her truck. When she opened the driver's side door, she noticed that the chassis was sitting at a funny angle. The front tire was flat. She knelt down, looking for the source of the leak. There was a slice in the side wall. This wasn't some random nail she'd picked up in the road. Someone had intentionally knifed her tire. As she stood up to check around her a man charged her, the glint of a blade catching in the sun. She felt a searing pain in her thigh and immediately dropped to the ground. Before she could fight back, the sound of a car passing caused the man to turn. He ran off before he could get a second shot at Emily.

A wave of nausea hit Emily, the pain from the wound in her leg coursing through her body, a surge of adrenaline catching up with what had already happened. She knew she needed to move. She couldn't risk waiting for the man to come back.

Whether he had meant to kill her or not, she didn't know. It wasn't time to find out. Emily pulled herself up using the side of the truck for support, trying not to pass out. She opened the door and retrieved her gun, her hands shaking. As she slid down to the ground again, pressing on the wound in her leg, she took a few deep breaths. The sound of her heartbeat rushed in her ears, pain pouring into her system. Only a few seconds had passed, but it felt like hours. She knew she needed to stay calm and get herself patched up. She looked down at her leg, her hands red with blood. The good news was that it wasn't spurting. Whoever had attacked her hadn't managed to hit the femoral artery. That was good news. If they had, she would be dead already.

Emily glanced to her right and to her left, knowing she had to get out of the parking lot, but she wasn't sure whether she could drive the truck. Limping to the back of the truck, she found a spare tire kit. She grabbed a jack, looking over her shoulder and managed to lower herself to the ground, keeping her wounded leg out in front of her. It took some time, but she was able to lift the truck up and start changing the tire.

From behind her she heard a voice, "You need some help with that?"

She nearly drew her gun from her holster, but as she turned, she realized it was an older man, wearing a camouflage jacket and a matching hat. He had a white beard and a walking stick. "Sure," she breathed.

As she turned around, the man must have seen the blood on her hands on her pants. "What happened to you? Maybe I should call the park rangers?"

"Oh no," she lied. "I just had surgery on my leg a couple of days ago and I think I popped a couple of stitches trying to change the tire. I was pressing on it with my hands. I've got a first aid kit in the back, but I just didn't get it. I figured I'd head over to the clinic here as soon as I got the tire changed."

Emily wasn't sure if the man would buy her story. She didn't have time to explain the circumstances to him or the park rangers.

The man nodded. "My wife popped a couple stitches a few years ago after some surgery. Nasty business. Let me give you help with the tire and we'll get you on your way to the clinic."

Without saying anything more, the man went to the back of the truck and pulled the spare out, quickly tightening the lug nuts and putting the damaged tire in the back of the bed. The tailgate closed with a slam that caused Emily to jump. "You sure you're okay to drive? I can follow you to the gas station in town if you'd like."

"No, no, that's okay. I'm probably gonna have to wait till I get paid to get the tire fixed anyway. I appreciate your help. I'll just head on over to the clinic now."

The man gave a nod and picked up his walking stick, moving towards the black sedan that was parked in the corner of the lot. Feeling relieved, Emily opened the cab of the truck and crawled inside, pressing the wound in her leg. She could tell it was deep by the pain she was in. Slow, deep breaths, she told herself, as she started the truck. She needed to get out of the park as quickly as possible.

As Emily drove, the pain got stronger and more persistent. A couple miles outside of town, Emily started to see spots in front of her eyes, a sure sign she was about to pass out. She pulled the truck off the side of the road. The last thing she needed to do was to crash headlong into a tree because she passed out. She opened the door to the truck, grabbed a water bottle, her phone, and the first aid kit from the backseat. She limped around the other side of the truck and sat down on the ground. To anyone passing by, it looked like the truck had been abandoned on the side of the road. As she maneuvered around the front of the truck, using the hood for support, she noticed there were no houses around on either side of the road, just fields filled with corn, their tassels sticking straight up, dancing in the sunshine.

On the far side of the truck, out of sight, Emily slid to the ground, her boots making a grinding noise against the gravel on the side of the road. She leaned her back against the passenger side door, resting her head for a moment. She cracked open a bottle of water, knowing that any type of severe stress or blood loss could quickly lead to dehydration. No one in Stockton could be counted on to help her. She sent a quick ping to Mike with her location, but no notes. If she told him she'd been stabbed, he'd call her and probably try to send the cavalry to help her. She didn't need that kind of attention, not now. Still holding her cell phone, she scrolled through her contacts and tapped a number near the bottom of the list. Immediately, the phone started the strange double ring of a phone connecting in Europe.

"Emily? Is that you?" the voice on the other end answered.

Emily nodded, "Angelica. Yeah, it's me. Where are you?"

"Barcelona. Just finished a job here. What's going on?"

Emily closed her eyes for a second. Angelica Rossi was Emily's younger sister. She'd gone to Europe after finishing her residency in the United States. After an expensive medical education, Angelica had told their father she didn't want to work for some stuffy hospital administrator.

Angelica had always been a wild child, her mane of long, red curly hair following her wherever she created headaches for their parents. Angelica had been the kind of teenager who'd broken out of their house, disappeared for entire weekends and then would come back and get straight A's in school without ever cracking a book open. Emily remembered all the times when her mother would sit up late in the kitchen, sipping a cup of tea, waiting for Angelica to come home. If anyone ever asked, all her mother would say was, "She's a force of nature. She's like the wind. You can't stop it."

Emily hadn't seen Angelica in about three years. The last time they'd been together, Emily had hopped on a plane and flown to Rome. They hung out for a week, darting in and out of cafés and bars, Angelica always flirting with the men, but never leaving with any of them. Emily had rented a motorcycle for her stay. It was the only way she could travel with Angelica. Angelica had never had a car, but went from place-to-place on a Ducati. It fit her personality perfectly.

Angelica supported herself by putting people back together who had gotten into scrapes throughout Europe that preferred to stay anonymous. She'd get a call on her phone, hop on her motorcycle with her backpack filled with medical equipment and patch people together. Emily had asked her once about the people she treated and Angelica shot her a look, "It doesn't matter to me how they got hurt, it only matters to me that I can try to help." By the way Angelica was treated in the towns they visited, Emily could tell that she had helped everyone from a poor family to the local police officers to criminals. It didn't matter to Angelica who they were.

While Emily was visiting her in Rome, Angelica had gotten called off to a case, returning a couple hours later to the small apartment she kept on the outskirts of town. Emily had walked in on her while she was unpacking her medical bag, opening cabinet doors and restocking the supplies. From the bottom of the bag she pulled out an envelope. "Is that cash?"

Angelica nodded, her wild red hair caught in a tumble that traveled around her neck and over her shoulder. "Of course. How else would I get paid?" Emily watched as Angelica lifted a painting off the wall, exposing a safe. As the door clicked open, Emily saw stacks of cash inside, tilted up against the inside wall.

"Don't you worry that someone will break in and steal all that cash?"

"Oh, sweetie, the locals would never allow that." Angelica didn't say any more.

The memory of the last time they had spent together flashed before Emily's eyes as she tried to take another swig of water. The nausea was getting worse. "Listen, I'm on the side of the road. Somebody stabbed me."

There was a pause for just a second. "All right, walk me through what happened." Angelica turned her medical doctor's voice on.

"I'm on a case in southern Ohio. Was coming out of a hiking trail. Somebody slit my tire. As I started to change it, they came up behind me and stabbed me."

"Where?"

"Right thigh. It's not spurting."

"I guessed that. You wouldn't be calling me if that was the case. You'd already be dead."

"Thanks for the comforting words, sis. What do I do?"

"Do you have any medical supplies?"

"Yes, I ordered the medical kit you told me to get a couple years ago. I've got it right next to me." Over a glass of wine, the last time that they had been together, Emily had told Angelica about her life. She had told her sister more than anyone else knew. Angelica didn't say much, the sunset mimicking the color of her hair. She looked far away for a second, took a sip of wine and then looked back at Emily. "Once you get back to the States, I'm going to send you a link for a medical kit. Wherever you go, I want you to take it with you. You never know. Someday you might need it."

That day was today. Emily set the phone down, putting it on speaker so she could hear her sister while she opened the medical kit. "Can you take a picture of the wound for me? You'll have to cut your pants away a little so I can get a good look at it."

Emily reached into the medical bag and pulled out a set of

medical scissors, carefully peeling the blood-soaked denim away from her leg. As she looked at the wound, a new wave of nausea covered her. She picked up her phone and snapped a picture, trying not to throw up. "Okay, I got it."

Emily leaned her head back against the truck, trying to keep her composure. She opened her eyes, looked left and right making sure that no one was approaching her. There wasn't even any noise on the road. "Okay, what do I do?"

"Well, since I'm guessing you don't want to go to the hospital, you're going to have to clean it and stitch it. Think you can do that?"

"I have no idea. Do I have to stitch it? Can't I use those butterfly bandages from the kit?"

"Depends on if you're willing to see a doctor at some point today or tomorrow to have it properly dealt with. I'd do it, but I'm a little too far away."

Emily groaned, moving her leg a little. "No, I don't want to go to the doctor." Small towns like Stockton were known for their gossip. The last thing she needed was to draw any attention to herself, especially if she had any hope of finding out what happened to Sarah.

"Then you're going to learn how to do sutures today."

Although getting the wound cleaned and closed didn't take too long, it took longer than Emily thought it should, most likely because she had to keep taking breaks so she wouldn't pass out. The good news was that the first thing Angelica had her do was spray some topical anesthesia onto the wound and then numb it up using small injections of lidocaine around it. Within a couple of minutes, Emily couldn't feel that section of her leg at all. It was a distinct disadvantage if anyone should approach her, but it was the only way that she was going to manage to do the rest of the work Angelica needed her to do. "Once the wound is clean, you're going to stitch it up, just like mom taught us to sew. The only difference is you're going to make single stitches with knots rather than ones that run along. Does that make sense?"

"Yes." After cleaning the wound as best as she could with some iodine pads, Emily threaded the suture needle with the filament. It took thirteen stitches to get the gash in her leg closed. "Okay, that's done. What do I do now?" Emily took a picture of her work and sent it to Angelica.

"Those look good. You could have had a career as a surgeon, Emily!" Angelica laughed. "Grab some four-by-four gauze and two gauze rolls out of the bag. Put the gauze pads over the wound and then wrap the rolled gauze around your leg. Tie it off so the wound stays clean."

Emily suddenly felt exhausted. The inclination to go back to the hotel and curl up in bed was strong. She tore open the gauze pads and carefully laid them across the wound. Even though it was numb, she didn't want to feel any more pain. Not today. As soon as she laid the gauze pads on her leg, she realized that the bandages would be obvious to anyone who looked at her. She didn't need that. "Hold on for a sec," she said into the speaker.

"What are you doing?"

"Taking off my pants." Emily scooted up against the truck, using it to help her balance. She unzipped her jeans and pushed them down to her knees, bending over and picking up the gauze pads and the rolled gauze. She pressed the gauze pads onto her thigh and then began rolling the gauze around her leg, securing it with some tape. It just took a second, but a wave of fear covered her. She looked left and right and listened, hoping that no one would choose this moment to pull up and check on her. No one did.

As soon as the wound was covered, Emily pulled her jeans back up and sat back down on the ground. "Okay, that's done. Now what?"

"Did you get those antibiotics I told you to get?"

"Yeah, I think so." Emily rooted through the medical bag, finding a pharmacy sized bottle of Amoxicillin in the bottom of her bag. "I've got them."

"All right, I want you to take two of them now. Take another two before you go to bed. You probably want to take them with some food, so they don't upset your stomach. Keep at it until you can get some medical attention, okay? No longer than ten days on the antibiotics, okay?"

Emily opened the bottle and used her thumb to punch through the paper seal at the top, pulling out the cotton wad that protected the pills during shipping. She pulled two out, the white capsules shiny in the sun, downing them with what was left of her water, "Yeah, I'll try to get in to see a doctor at some point."

Angelica's voice changed, "Emily Marie, you will need to see a doctor. I don't even care if it's a veterinarian. Just find somebody who can take a look at that wound in the next twenty-four hours, okay? The last thing I need is you calling me and telling me it's all infected and then you have to have your leg amputated."

Emily smiled as she stuffed the medical supplies back in the bag. There were times that Angelica sounded just like her mother. Emily knew Angelica would be furious if she said that to her. Angelica had never wanted anything to do with their parents, but Emily knew they were good people, or at least they tried to be. "All right, boss," she said. "How long is my leg going to be numb?" The idea of trying to drive with the numb leg presented a new set of challenges.

"A couple of hours. There should be some pain medication in the bottom of your bag. In about an hour, take one of those. No more than one every four hours. The ones I told you to get are pretty strong."

By strong Emily knew that Angelica meant they would

make her woozy. She didn't need that. "I'll just take some over-the-counter stuff. I have a bottle in my truck."

"If you can do that, that would be better. Remember, go find a doctor."

"Thanks, sis," Emily said as she shoved the medical bag back in the truck, making sure there was no trash left on the side of the road. The less people knew about her and her injury, the better. She hung up with Angelica and walked back to the driver's side door, getting in. As soon as she slid up into the seat, Emily realized it would be nearly impossible to drive with her numb leg. She shifted in her seat and moved her left foot over to the pedals.

As the engine turned over, Emily realized that going back to the hotel probably wasn't a smart idea. If she decided to take any of the pain pills, she could be so drowsy that anyone entering her room would be able to have a second go at her. She did a U-turn with the truck, heading around the edges of town, back to Vicki's house.

The drive took a couple minutes longer than Emily would have liked, but it was difficult getting used to operating the truck with her opposite foot. As she pulled into Vicki's house, she noticed another car in the driveway. It was Liz's.

Emily slid down the side of the truck, landing with her left foot, not wanting to put any sudden strain on her leg. Last thing she needed to do was split a stitch and have her whole leg start bleeding again. She limped into the garage and up the steps, not bothering to knock when she opened the door. As she walked into the kitchen, Vicki was sitting in her spot at the table. A new pot of coffee was bubbling in the corner of the kitchen. Emily wondered for a moment how much coffee Vicki drank every single day. It had to be a lot.

"Emily?" Vicki stood up from the table. She moved faster than Emily had seen her move over the last couple days. "Are you okay?"

Emily looked down and saw the red stain on her jeans, the white gauze stained with blood peeking through the torn leg of her jeans. "Apparently, someone is a little offended that I have come to town asking questions about Sarah." Spots started to form in front of her eyes. She felt her body start to go weak. The last thing she heard was Vicki calling to Liz.

How long passed before she woke up, Emily wasn't sure. She blinked a couple times and realized she was on the floor of Vicki's kitchen, a pillow underneath her head, her legs raised up with more pillows. Vicki and Liz were leaning over her. She felt a cool washcloth on her forehead. She pulled it off as she struggled to sit up. "Take it easy, Emily," Vicki said, her warm fingers wrapped around Emily's forearm. "You passed out. I'm guessing it's from the wound on your leg. What happened?"

Emily grunted, "As I said, clearly someone doesn't want me looking into Sarah's case." She looked around the kitchen, "Let me just sit over there for a couple minutes," she said standing up.

Vicki stayed by her side, her hand lifting underneath Emily's elbow as she limped over to the table. "Liz, get her some juice."

Emily slumped down into one of the kitchen chairs. Vicki pulled another chair closer to her and propped up her injured leg with some pillows underneath it. Liz brought over a short glass of what looked to be orange juice. Emily sipped it. It was sweet and sour at the same time, but it did seem to do the trick. Within a minute or two, she felt like her head had cleared.

Vicki pulled one of the other chairs close to her, frowning, "What happened, Emily?"

"I was at the crime scene in the park. I walked back out to my truck, and the tire was flat. While I was trying to change it, some guy charged me and stabbed me in the thigh. Didn't get a good look at him."

"How did you manage to get the tire changed?"

"I don't know. An older guy wearing some camo came up and gave me a hand getting it finished. I told him I had surgery and popped a stitch."

Vicki stood up and pulled open the tear in Emily's jeans. "Looks like you have this wrapped up pretty well."

"Yeah, I called my sister. She's a doctor."

"You should still be seen by somebody in person."

"Thanks, Mom. I've been a bit busy trying to sort out what happened to Sarah." As soon as the words came out of Emily's mouth, she felt bad. All Vicki was trying to do was to help her. Emily shifted in the chair, pointing to her backpack. "The bag of records you gave me, it's in my backpack." Liz walked over and unzipped the bag, pulling out the paperwork.

"Did you find anything?"

Emily shook her head, briefly remembering the slip of paper with the numbers on it she couldn't decipher. "No, nothing. What they gave you was just junk."

She was just about to tell them about the real records — the ones that Mike had been able to dig up, but then she decided not to. Just then, her phone chirped. "Can you talk?" It was Mike.

"In private?" she typed back.

"Yep."

"Give me two minutes." If Mike was asking to speak to her, then he had some sort of news or had found something. She didn't want to have that discussion in front of Vicki and Liz. "I have to go make a call. I'll be right back."

Vicki pointed out the back door. "There are chairs out on the patio. We'll keep an eye on you from here."

Emily nodded and struggled to her feet, realizing that Vicki had shifted into full mom mode. It had probably been a long time since she had anyone to care for, with no husband and both daughters gone. As Emily limped out and closed the patio door behind her, she could imagine how Vicki had been years earlier with her family around her. It was another layer of loss that made the case that much more difficult. No matter what Emily found out, or the justice she was able to get for the family, nothing would replace the loss of her husband and girls.

The afternoon sun had warmed up Vicki's backyard. Emily slumped down into a stained plastic chair that sat in a corner of the patio just behind the house. The numbness in her leg was starting to wear off. Maybe she didn't use quite enough lidocaine. She grunted. She'd need to take some painkillers soon if she hoped to be able to continue on the case. Emily pulled her phone out of her back pocket and dialed Mike. "What's going on?"

"You don't sound good."

Mike was one of those people who could tell how someone was doing by the most minor changes in their tone. Emily didn't have the energy to explain what happened. The last thing that she needed was to have Mike a thousand miles away worried about her. She knew he wouldn't be effective if that was the case. "I'm okay, just tired."

"I've got two pieces of news. One bad, one worse. Which one first?"

Emily closed her eyes for a second. The last thing she needed right now was more bad news. "I don't care. Just tell me."

"There was a call on your home phone when I got back from running errands. Some old guy. He had a gravelly voice."

Emily frowned. There were very few people that had her home number. She only kept it in case the power went out or she couldn't find her cell phone. "Who was it?"

"Some guy named Anthony, I think. He said the person you had in common died. An overdose. He wanted you to know."

Emily sucked in a breath. The only person that could be would be Anthony Tizzano, her father-in-law. Former father-in-law, to be exact. Her mind raced ahead. Luca died? The shock from the stabbing and now the news that her ex-husband had passed made her feel a little woozy again. She had to focus. "An overdose?"

"That's what he said."

"Do a quick search for me on my ex-husband."

"You think it was Luca he was talking about?"

Emily heard the keyboard tapping in the background. "Just check, okay?"

Mike sometimes didn't know when it was appropriate to ask a question and when it wasn't. This wasn't one of those times she wanted to talk about Luca's issues. It was bad enough that he ran around with other women on her, but right before her arrest, he had started doing cocaine. His father was old school. By the time it had become a problem, Luca had already left her. She couldn't imagine that Anthony would've been okay with his son being a drug addict.

"Okay, yeah, I'm sorry to tell you this, but Luca died last night." There was more tapping on the keyboard. "There's no cause of death in the newspaper. Hold on," Mike paused. "Here it is. It's in the medical record. I guess he was rushed to the hospital. Looks like an overdose of cocaine." There was another pause, "Emily, I'm so sorry."

"Don't be. He's been out of my life for a long time." The last thing Emily wanted to do was spend time thinking about Luca. A mixture of sadness and anger moved through her. Should she go back? Leave the case and attend his funeral? Her sadness wasn't really for herself, she was sad for his family. They had always been decent to her, but she was disgusted at the way that Luca had lived his life. He was one of those people that had a lot of promise, but never lived up to it. Memories flashed in front of her eyes, the feeling she had on their wedding day, the soft white dress being pulled over her head, the day they had bought their house, the day Luca left. It was bittersweet. More bitter than sweet, unfortunately. Emily glanced at the back of Vicki's house, feeling torn between helping them and her obligation to Luca's family. "What's the other news?"

Mike sighed. "You know those numbers you sent me yesterday? The ones from the bag of evidence they gave Sarah's mom?"

"Yeah. Did you figure out what they are?"

"No. I haven't quite figured it out yet. Still working on it."

Emily could never tell if Mike was more mad or disappointed when he couldn't figure out a puzzle as quickly as he would like. "Keep working on it. If you find something, let me know. In the meantime, I gotta go."

As she hung up the phone, Emily stood up, using her left leg as much as possible. Moving would be next to impossible if she didn't take something for the pain. Her mind started to reach for answers. Who had stabbed her? Why? There was no doubt in her mind that whoever it was had a vested interest in keeping Sarah's story quiet. That they would go as far as attacking her took the case to an entirely new level.

Inside the kitchen, Vicki and Liz had resumed their positions at the kitchen table, that was until Emily hobbled in. "Here, let me give you a hand," Vicki said, helping Emily ease back down in the chair and elevating her leg again.

"You're pretty good at this," Emily said, leaning back in the chair. "Can you hand me my bag?"

"I was a nurse before I had kids," Vicki said, handing Emily her backpack.

Emily nodded, the expression on Vicki's face making more sense now that Emily knew she had been a nurse. She hated the fact that she had to ask for help. That wasn't how she operated. A wave of uneasiness covered her. Could she continue the case with her leg banged up? While it was important to Vicki and Liz that she helped them figure out what happened to Sarah, it wouldn't do anyone any good if Emily got killed in the process. As she looked at the two women, she knew she was at a crossroads. Liz finally looked at her, "Are you going to continue with the case? Are you going back to Chicago?"

"I don't know."

The words hung in the air between the three women. Emily knew that Vicki and Liz viewed her as their last and best hope to figure out what happened to Sarah. Clearly, she was onto something, but she wasn't sure it was worth it. She decided to avoid the topic until she had a chance to think, the pain dulling her thinking.

They sat in silence for a little while, Emily calculating what to do. She could go back to the hotel and stay there, but if she took any of the stronger painkillers, she would be completely vulnerable. It had to be better than staying at the Schmidt house, though. "I think I'm going to head back to the hotel. You guys have those records back."

"Absolutely not," Vicki said. "I'm sorry, but from the looks of the way you are walking, that's a pretty significant stab wound. It's bad enough that you came the whole way here to try to help us and got stabbed. The least you can do is allow me to help you."

"I'd stay, if I could, but the kids…" Liz said.

"We'll be fine," Vicki said. "Keep your phone handy. I'll call if there're any issues."

Liz nodded, picking up her purse. "I'll swing by in the morning."

Emily watched Liz walk out the door. Her mind felt divided. She would have preferred to go back to the hotel, to be on her own, the way that she was used to being, but she knew that to some extent, Vicki was right. The injury to her leg was significant enough that even having one person as backup was probably a smarter tactical plan than her being by herself in the hotel. "I'll just go rest on the couch, if you don't mind." Vicki offered to help her, but Emily waved her off. "I'm all right."

When Emily got to the couch, she gently pulled off her

boots and swung her legs up onto it, propping her back up with a pillow. The sun had become low in the sky, the rays pushing through the windows in the back of the house, glinting off of the frames where the pictures of Sarah were. Emily closed her eyes for a moment, feeling the need to rest. She hadn't felt that way in a long time, probably not since she'd had knee surgery in high school.

By the time Emily woke up, it was dark out. She glanced at her cell phone. It was four o'clock in the morning. There was no one nearby. The house was dark, the only noise the nocturnal animals outside scurrying around to find the last bits of food before the sun came up. Emily swung her legs down off the couch, the pain from the stab wound searing through her body. She needed to take some pain medicine. Getting up, she limped to the kitchen, finding a glass that had been washed, draining on the side of the sink. She filled it with water and swallowed pills from her bag and then rested her hands against the sink for a minute looking out the window. A new wave of fatigue washed over her. She limped back to the couch, putting her feet back up, the pain dulling just a bit when she took the pressure off of it. As she lay on the couch listening to the animals outside, her mind floated first to Luca and then to Sarah. She wanted to say she was surprised about Luca, but she wasn't. She turned her head to the side, almost feeling like she was able to feel his touch on her face, but then the memory of the way that he had turned against her when Emily had been accused of bribery ran through her. Emily shifted the other way, trying to get comfortable, hoping the pain pills would kick in quickly. In the dark of the house, she could see the outline of the bookcases, the shelves where the memories of Sarah's life were held. Emily wanted to have the strength to get up and keep working on the case, but she was tired, so very tired.

18

Cameron Nolan hadn't been sleeping well, not since the visitor had come to the police station a few days before. It was still dark out when he woke up for what felt like the tenth time that night. He rolled over and looked at his cell phone. Four o'clock in the morning. He was due in the station by six AM to start his shift. He rolled over, wishing he had a girlfriend or wife to share his bed. Another warm body might have helped him sleep better. Dating in a town like Stockton was nearly impossible. As he sat up, he wondered if he should just get up and give up on sleep for the night. He wasn't sure he had a choice.

Pushing the curtain aside, Cameron looked outside. There was no movement on the road in front of his house, not that he expected any. The only thing that was moving quickly in his life were his thoughts. He couldn't let go of the memory of the woman that had showed up at the police department asking about Sarah Schmidt. He hadn't been part of the department when Sarah went missing, but it was one of the first cases his training officer had briefed him on. "Worst thing that ever happened to this town," his training officer said on their first day together in the cruiser. "One of those things I'm never sure Stockton will ever get over."

As the drapery slipped back into place, Cameron remembered he'd asked the officer a couple follow up questions about Sarah. "Not much to tell. One day she went for a hike and she never came back." Cameron remembered the man had popped a piece of gum in his mouth as he answered. Any more questions had fallen on deaf ears.

Now there was a new person asking questions, and she was an outsider. Just the thought of it made him uneasy. Why, he wasn't sure. Cameron went into the bathroom and took a shower. He knew he wasn't going to sleep, at least not more that night. He quickly got dressed, making sure he had everything he needed before zipping his duty bag closed. There was no point in laying in a bed that wouldn't give him sleep. Might as well get into the office a little early.

Cameron went out and started his truck, running the windshield wipers to get rid of the dew that had accumulated on his windshield overnight. There was a faint glow on the horizon, not enough to be called daybreak, but enough to give anybody watching hope that it would actually arrive at some point. As Cameron turned out of the driveway of his house, he took the back roads to the station, his headlights grazing over the empty pavement. Very few people were moving in Stockton at this hour, save some farmers who had dairy herds to deal with. On the back of his property, Cameron had a small herd of cows of his own. He knew the neighbor would come over and take care of them within an hour or so. It was a small herd at the time, one that Cameron was hoping to develop. He wasn't sure that being a police officer was going to be a career for him. There was something about it he just didn't like, whether it was working in Stockton or the Sheriff Mollohan, he wasn't sure. He had looked into positions in other cities, but the idea of a big city department didn't suit him either, constantly running after drug dealers and rapists and murderers. Cameron knew himself. He was the kind of guy who wanted to help, not chase bad guys around.

When he got to the station, there were two cruisers parked in the lot and three personal cars. He left his truck in the back lot, hitting the key fob and hearing it chirp before he walked into the station.

"You're in here early." Jason Randall was sitting behind one of the desks, clearly trying to keep his eyes open.

"Yeah, I couldn't sleep. If you want to head out, I'll cover for you."

Jason raised his eyebrows, "Are you sure?"

Cameron nodded, setting his duty bag down at the workstation he used when he was in the office. "Yeah. Just do me a favor and clear it with the boss before you leave, okay?"

Jason keyed up his radio and called the sergeant on duty and explained the situation. Cameron heard the radio chirped back a second later. The once drowsy Jason sprung to life, knowing he could get out of the station and home into his bed. "Thanks, man. I owe you one," he said, stuffing some papers into his duty bag and zipping it up.

Cameron nodded but didn't answer. He just went about unloading his equipment for the day. On the workstation, he set a clean thermal mug, hung his jacket on the back of the chair and made sure his duty belt was attached properly. The last thing that he needed was Sheriff Mollohan coming in later on that morning and barking at him for not being uniformed properly. He sat down at the computer in front of him and logged in, quickly getting up and starting some fresh coffee. The guys coming in from the road would appreciate a fresh pot, and so would he. He walked back to the desk, waiting for it to perk and checked his email. There was nothing of importance — just a couple of schedule changes and a report on a couple of horses that had gotten loose at a farm on the outskirts of town. One of them had gotten hit by a car. The local vet had to go out and put the mare down. Though it was sad, it wasn't uncommon in a city like Stockton. Fences failed almost as much as people did, he thought to himself.

Cameron looked at the coffee pot. It was almost full. He got out of his chair and walked over, taking his thermal cup with him. As he unscrewed the top, he started thinking about the woman that had come in requesting information on Sarah a few days before. If he remembered right, her name had been Emily. She was pretty in an intense sort of way, he thought. But he couldn't imagine someone like her putting on a pretty dress and pink lipstick. She'd be more the type of woman who'd help you plant acres of corn or rebuild an engine. He smiled a little, thinking that she might be the type of girl that he could see himself with someday.

As he fastened the top on his coffee and turned, he stopped for a moment. As much as the woman who'd shown up at the office was interesting to him, what was keeping him up at night was the fact that she'd come a long distance to ask questions about Sarah Schmidt. The fact that no one in town talked about the case bothered him. Why was there not an ongoing investigation?

Without really thinking about it, Cameron dropped off his coffee at his desk after taking a single sip, the hot liquid nearly scalding the roof of his mouth. He walked to the file room, glancing over his shoulder as he approached the door. There was no one else in the building at the time. The department had interior surveillance, but no one ever watched it. He pulled a set of keys from his pocket and unlocked the door to the file room. Why the department didn't move over to a digital keypad, he didn't know. Seemed like everything in Stockton was about a decade behind where normal departments were in terms of technology.

As he opened the door, the smell of old paper hit him. He

knew from his training days that the original records from every case were in this room. There was a main set of file cabinets that ran across the wall on his left and then a smaller set of files on the right. The ones on the left were active cases or at least cases that had happened within the last five years or so. The files that had been moved to the cabinets on the right were cold cases from their jurisdiction. Cameron squatted down and pulled open the file drawer that had the letters R through Z, thumbing through the tabs until he found Sarah Schmidt's file. He'd never really looked at it before, but something struck him as funny when Emily had come in earlier that week. It seemed awfully thin for a missing person's case. In fact, he noticed it was one of the thinnest files in the entire drawer.

He pinched the top of the file, pulling it out of the drawer and standing up, opening it on top of the file cabinet. The light in the file room was dim, a couple of the fluorescent bulbs black. Apparently, the maintenance person hadn't figured out those needed to be changed. The bulbs that were working buzzed above him in a way that made his skin crawl. As he flipped open the file, he looked at the pages, his brows furrowing together. Why wasn't there more information? He flipped forward through the papers, seeing basic information about Sarah and a couple of pictures of the crime scene, but that was it. No wonder Emily seemed frustrated. A memory flashed through his mind. The year before, he had been in the Sheriff's office and saw Jerome looking at a couple of files on his desk. Cameron had walked in to deliver some paperwork that needed to be signed. The Sheriff, someone that most people considered a good old boy and only in his office for political reasons, was leaning back in his chair looking at an open file suspended on his lap. The Sheriff barely grunted at him before scratching his name on the paper. Cameron wasn't even sure if he knew what the forms were for. That wasn't Cameron's problem, though. As Cameron closed the file that Sheriff Mollohan signed, he glanced down, past the cowboy boots that the Sheriff always wore, unlike his other officers who were required to wear proper duty boots. There was a large file drawer at the bottom of his desk that was open, a stack of manila files in it. From the file at the top of the pile, Cameron could tell that they were case files.

The memory of that day came flooding back as Cameron looked at the thin paperwork in Sarah Schmidt's file. He pulled his cell phone out of his back pocket and turned on the camera, quickly taking pictures of each page in the file. As soon as he finished, he closed the file, shoved it back in the drawer and stuck his phone back in his pocket. If anyone found out that he had taken pictures of the investigation file, he could be fired, but for some reason it didn't matter. As he walked out of the file room, one of the guys on the road was coming in. Cameron nearly ran into him. "Whoa," the officer said, squinting. "Whatcha doing in there?"

Cameron's heart started to beat a little faster. Typically, the only people that went into the room were the detectives — there were two with the Sheriff's office — and the clerk. Officers did go in there once in a while, but it always seemed to raise an eyebrow. "Filing. One of the guys left a couple files out on his desk. Thought I'd get those put away before they ran off."

The officer nodded, "Good idea. Glad you've got our backs."

"Thanks." Cameron tried to check the time on his cell phone without looking obvious. "Coffee shop just opened. I may run over and grab a dozen for the guys coming in. You want anything?" Cameron needed an excuse to get out of the station so he could get a better look at the images he had taken on his phone.

"A maple cruller, if they've got one." The man smiled at Cameron, "You going for officer of the year or something?"

Cameron attempted a smile. "Something like that," he said, walking away.

Outside, the light had just crested over the ridge, the peak of the promise of morning sunshine pushing its way through the dense trees that were on the edge of town and just beyond the station. Cameron got into one of the two cruisers that were in the parking lot, turning the key in the ignition. The officers always left the keys in them in case they needed to go someplace fast, not that there were many calls in Stockton that required that type of urgency. It wasn't like anyone would steal any of the cars. Stockton wasn't that kind of town, although Cameron was starting to wonder what kind of town it was.

It was a quick drive to the coffee shop around the corner. Cameron left the cruiser running in the parking lot as he went inside, the smell of freshly fried doughnuts and sugar filling his nostrils. He went up to the counter. A young girl named Katie was working. "I'll take a dozen, mixed." Cameron pulled his cell phone out of his back pocket wanting to get a look at the pictures he'd taken. He stopped for a moment and looked back at the girl who had picked up a box and said, "Can you add a maple cruller in there?"

"Sure," she said.

Normally Cameron would've at least tried to talk to her, but he was too preoccupied with the pictures on his phone. As he stood off to the side waiting for her to fill his order, he quickly flipped through the pictures he'd taken. Something about the way the case had been documented simply didn't make sense. He remembered that he had looked in their database to see if the files had been digitized, but they hadn't. He hadn't thought about it much a few days before, when Emily was asking, but now, he had some questions of his own. It would have made sense if the file had all the documentation he expected, but it didn't.

"Here you go," the girl behind the counter said.

Cameron quickly paid her and said, "Thanks, Katie. Have a good day."

"Thanks, you too."

Cameron shoved his phone back in his pocket and carried the box of doughnuts back out to the cruiser. As he got in, he set the doughnuts on the passenger seat and pulled his phone out again, looking at the interior of the file. There was literally so little information in the file he wasn't sure how anyone could begin to solve the case. It seemed suspicious. The whole thing, from the arrival of Emily to her questions about the file, seemed suspicious. And yet, his mind kept drifting back to the drawer in Sheriff Mollohan's office.

19

Emily woke up a couple hours later to the sound of coffee perking. Vicki was up. The morning sunshine pushed through the windows at the back of the house. Emily didn't move for a moment, trying to figure out how her leg was feeling before she decided to sit up. Before she had a chance to try, Vicki walked over, "Did you sleep okay?"

"Pretty good. I got up at about four and took some painkillers."

"Mind if I have a look at your leg?"

Emily remembered that Angelica told her she needed to have her leg looked at shortly. At least Vicki had been a nurse. "Yeah. Let me go use the bathroom and change into some shorts." The last thing Emily wanted to do was sit stripped down to her panties in front of Vicki. She stood up, hobbling for a second, and then made her way into the bathroom, pulling off her jeans and pulling up a pair of running shorts. She'd brought them for the drive home, but they would come in handy now.

Emily limped out of the bathroom and sat back down on the couch, feeling hot and dizzy. She could barely get her eyes to focus. Vicki walked over, bringing her a bottle of water and a cup of coffee. She pulled the tape off the bandage that was wrapped around Emily's thigh and gently peeled the squares of gauze off of the wound. As soon as she did, Emily looked away. From the brief glance at her leg, the wound was red and inflamed, the hole in her leg shades of yellow and green. Vicki stood up without saying anything, gently laying her hand on Emily's forehead. "You have a fever. I think your leg is infected."

"I took some antibiotics yesterday."

"Well, they don't appear to be working. We need to get you some proper medical attention."

Fury ran through Emily. Who was this woman to tell her what she needed to do? She stood up, realizing she was wobbly from the pain and probably from the fever. "No doctors. I am not going to the hospital. There is nothing wrong with me. That's not what I'm here for. I'm going to go get changed. I'll be out here in five minutes." As soon as the words came out of Emily's mouth, she crumpled back to the couch, a wave of dizziness too strong for her to fight.

Vicki looked at her without saying anything for a moment just standing nearby. "I know you're here to try to help us figure out what happened to Sarah. I appreciate that. But I can't have two lives on my hands. I have an idea, though. Give me a couple minutes."

Emily rested her head back on the couch. She knew Vicki was right. Angelica had warned her that if there was any debris left in the wound, it would likely get infected. Apparently, her roadside cleaning job hadn't done the trick. Her mind raced forward to Sarah. She was here for one reason and one reason alone. Whoever had taken Sarah was intent on slowing down her progress. They had won this battle, but not the war. Not yet.

Vicki came back a couple minutes later after the low murmuring of voices in the kitchen had subsided. "I've got somebody who can stop by to give us a hand. Think you can wait here for a couple hours?"

Suspicion filled Emily. After what happened to her, trust wasn't something that she came by easily. She needed to make a decision. Either she was getting in her truck, leaving the Schmidt family and their skeletons behind, and heading into a larger city where she could get medical help, or she was going to stay the course, take the help that Vicki offered and hopefully get answers for Sarah's family. Emily looked away, staring at the pictures in the bookcase, the morning light glinting off of them. "Okay. But who is this person?"

"Friend of the family you could say," Vicki said, quickly sending a text. "Dr. Zuckerman. He's the vet that works in the area, but what a lot of people don't know about him is that he's former military. Was a combat medic. If anyone can get you patched up, it'll be him, no matter whether you decide to stay, or you just want to head back to Chicago." Vicki walked away.

Vicki was worried Emily would abandon the case. Vicki had told Emily when she arrived in Stockton that if Emily couldn't figure out what happened to Sarah, Vicki would give up. By Vicki's comments, Emily knew that she was concerned that Dr. Zuckerman would come and patch her up, give her some drugs and Emily would jump in the truck and head out of town, their only hope leaving them in the dust again.

The memories of the night she had been arrested flooded back to her, another surge of anger rising up. She remembered the looks on the faces of the other officers as she was paraded into the district headquarters in handcuffs, stuffed into an interrogation room like some common criminal. People she had been friends with — other officers that she'd celebrated weddings, births, baptisms, and funerals with — acted like they had never seen her before. There were people that literally turned away from her when she walked into the station, strong hands on each one of her elbows. She had remembered the fight within herself to not look down, to not stare at the floor, to not act like she was guilty when she wasn't.

When she had been found innocent of the bribery charges, some of those same people still never spoke to her. Even her former partner, Lou Gonzales, who had basically adopted Emily and Luca into their family, had slipped away. Emily sucked in a breath, trying not to stare at the blood-tinged gauze on her thigh. She hadn't heard from him in a couple of years. If anyone knew how it was to feel abandoned, Emily did.

Emily looked down at her leg and picked up the roll of gauze that had been set off to the side when Vicki checked the wound. She re-wrapped the gauze around her leg, fastening the tape as best as possible. It wasn't quite as sticky as it was the day before, so she ended up pulling the ends apart and tucking them under another row of gauze tying a knot on the top to keep everything in place. She stood up, "What time does the doctor arrive? I have work to do."

20

After Cameron dropped off the doughnuts back at the station, he hung around for a couple hours going through new emails that had come in and updating reports that needed to be finished. The images he had on his phone felt like they were burning a hole in his pocket. The idea that someone might have skimmed information off the Schmidt case and kept it from the family pushed a wave of nausea over him. That's not what he had sworn to do on the day that he accepted a position with the Stockton County Sheriff's office. He had sworn to serve and protect. Hiding information certainly wasn't part of that description.

He picked up his duty bag and headed out the back door. It was time for him to get out on the road. Besides the fact, sitting in the office, knowing that Sarah Schmidt's files had been compromised was making him sick to his stomach. No one said a word as he left the station. He got into the closest cruiser, radioed the dispatchers to let them know he was out of the station and pulled out into the center of Stockton, passing the gas station and Sandy's Restaurant.

For about an hour or so, he drove the streets, choosing the ones that were farther outside of the city. The fields were filled with corn that was ready for harvest. He knew that within a couple weeks all the local kids would be heading over to the county fair, taking the pigs and horses and goats and rabbits they had been tending to for months to show off to the local judges. That part of Stockton he liked, the idea that a simple life was one worth living. He wouldn't be taking any of his cattle to the fair this year. His herd was new, and he was hoping for a couple of calves in the spring.

There were only a few cars out on the road, with most people who were driving headed off to a late start at work. He waved to a couple of passing cars and trucks, recognizing who was driving them.

Once he'd traveled all the back roads on the west side of town, he decided to cross over the main drag and check the east side of town. He knew where he was going, even if he didn't want to admit it yet. Cameron made a couple of right turns and then a left, which put him on the same road where the Schmidt family lived. He felt like he had met them a long time before, or maybe he just felt that way because of the information he had burning in his pocket. He drove by the house once, seeing Dr. Zuckerman's truck in the driveway. It seemed strange as he hadn't seen the Schmidt's at any of the cattle or livestock sales that happened in the area. He knew most of the people who were in the business. As far as he knew, they weren't.

He passed their house and then drove another couple miles, turning around. When he pulled into the Schmidt's driveway, Dr. Zuckerman's truck was still there. Parked off to the side was a blue truck with Illinois plates. Cameron's heart started to beat faster. He left the cruiser running in the driveway, careful not to block the veterinarian in case he needed to get to another call. Maybe Dr. Zuckerman and the Schmidt's were friends and he was just stopping in for a cup of coffee. That happened a lot in Stockton.

Cameron walked into the garage and knocked on the back door. "I saw the vet's truck here and wanted to see if you needed any help," he said to the woman who answered the door. She was heavyset and blond, the lines of worry etched around her eyes. He knew that was Vicki Schmidt, even if he hadn't met her in person in the few years he'd been with the Sheriff's Office.

"No, Officer. We're fine here."

From just above her shoulder, Cameron could see Dr. Zuckerman. He was kneeling in front of Emily. They were sitting in the kitchen, Emily's leg propped up on a chair. Dr. Zuckerman was reaching for something in his bag when he turned. "Cameron? You need something? Cows okay?"

The fact that Dr. Zuckerman had spoken to him gave Cameron all the push he needed to walk right in the house, brushing past Vicki, even though she hadn't technically given him permission to enter. It didn't matter to him. All that mattered was the fact that the person who had asked for information on Sarah Schmidt was now being tended to by the local veterinarian. "What happened here, Doc?"

Dr. Zuckerman glanced at Emily and glanced back at Cameron. "Not much. Nothing really."

Cameron had known Dr. Zuckerman for long enough to know that he wasn't telling the truth. There was a blue surgical towel covering a section of Emily's thigh. She narrowed her eyes at him, "Wait, you're the officer that gave me the bogus file about Sarah Schmidt."

Cameron felt his face flush. He was hoping that no one in the room could see it, his skin tanned from being outside every minute he wasn't on duty. "I'm not sure what you mean," he said, trying to sound convincing. "I gave you the information you asked for. You weren't exactly even entitled to it."

He watched her for a second as Emily struggled to sit up, Dr. Zuckerman putting his hand on her shoulder. "Emily, don't get up. I haven't finished doing what I need to do."

"What happened to your leg?" Cameron said, taking a step forward.

Vicki stepped in front of him. "Now, I've been polite up until this time. We didn't invite you in. I think it's best if you leave."

The tension in the air was thick. Cameron knew there was something definitely wrong with Emily and that Vicki and Dr. Zuckerman were trying to protect her. Vicki was right, he hadn't gotten her permission to enter the house. Entry without permission with no probable cause could get him in hot water with the department, but he didn't care. After what had been missing from the file about Vicki's daughter, he wasn't sure he could stay silent anymore. He looked at Emily, "You're the one that's snooping around about Sarah Schmidt."

As soon as the words came out of his mouth, Cameron realized that he probably shouldn't have used the word snooping. Emily's eyes blazed at him, "How dare you!" She struggled to her feet, exposing a gash in her leg that was at least four inches long. "I came to this godforsaken town to try to get some justice for Sarah Schmidt because you people are not doing your job!" She slumped back down in the chair, crossing her arms over her chest.

Cameron said nothing for a moment, waiting for things to settle. "What happened to your leg?" he said slowly, each word coming out of his mouth apart from each other.

Dr. Zuckerman stood up, "She was stabbed. Stabbed after walking out to see the site where Sarah Schmidt was taken."

As Dr. Zuckerman continued working on Emily's leg, Cameron leaned over to try to get a better look at what had happened to her. It was definitely a stab wound, probably from a hunting knife. He'd seen jagged cuts like that left on the meat of a deer carcass after hunting. Emily had been lucky that someone hadn't hit her femoral artery. If that had been the case, they probably would have found her body in the park a day or two later. "You think this is connected to the case?"

"Don't you?" Emily said looking away.

21

Sheriff Mollohan had just finished his weekly breakfast with some of his constituents at Sandy's Restaurant when he decided to take a little drive around town. He was headed about ten miles down the road, going to visit Bucky Walters, the local lumber mill owner who'd had some issues with kids vandalizing his property, when he passed Vicki Schmidt's house. There were several cars in the driveway, including the blue pickup truck he knew belonged to Emily Tizzano. He frowned when he realized that one of his own department cruisers was sitting in the driveway as well as Dr. Zuckerman's vet truck.

He picked up his phone and called dispatch. A friendly female voice answered. It was Anna, a dispatcher that had been with them for a few years. "Sweetheart, could you tell me who is on the road right now?"

"Sure, boss. Sanders and Nolan are both out there. Do you need me to send them somewhere?"

"No, that's not necessary. Thank you." He hung up the phone before getting an answer from her. There was no way that Sanders was sitting over at Schmidt's house. He'd been with the department for a long time, long enough that he knew that unless the Schmidt's called, they didn't go there. Nolan, on the other hand, was new enough that he hadn't quite learned the rules of the road yet.

Jerome turned the truck around and headed back to the station, his heart beating a little faster than it probably should. This Emily woman was starting to give him trouble. He didn't need that. Although Stockton looked like a sleepy Midwestern town, there was a lot that ran under the surface, a lot of people that needed tending and situations to manage. New officers like Nolan didn't understand that.

As soon as he got back to the station, he pulled the truck around the back of the building, trying not to get intercepted by anyone who needed something as soon as he walked in. Using the key card to buzz himself in the back door, he walked down the short hallway, unlocking the door to his office and closing it behind him, pulling the blinds. He was hoping no one would notice the truck in the parking lot for at least the next few minutes.

He sat down in the chair, it creaking as he rested his weight on it. He logged into his computer and then accessed the surveillance cameras from the inside of the department. He'd had them installed five years previous, telling the county trustees that if there was ever an incident inside of the station, that kind of information could be critical in protecting the needs of Stockton County. They had bought it hook, line and sinker, but that wasn't really what it was for. Jerome had issues with officers from time to time. Seeing what they were up to when they weren't out on the road could be helpful in cases where he needed to get rid of someone.

A couple of clicks of his mouse opened the surveillance footage. He rolled it back twenty-four hours and then ran it forward at double speed. Within about a minute, he had found what he was looking for. Nolan had come in extra early. By the time stamp, it looked like he had arrived in the office just before five AM. Curious, Jerome thought, given that their first shifts didn't start till six and most of the guys rolled in about two minutes before things started, just enough to be considered on time.

He slowed the recording down, watching Nolan's first few minutes in the office. He set his duty bag down, made some coffee, and appeared to log into his email account. He got up, about two minutes later according to the recording, and walked over to the coffee station, filling his mug. At that point, Jerome saw Nolan look towards the back of the station, towards Jerome's office and the file room.

Jerome eased the recording forward, watching Nolan put his fresh coffee back down on the workstation and turn towards the back of the building. Nolan walked through the main area of the station, at which point another camera picked him up in front of Jerome's office. He didn't stop. At least that was one good thing. Jerome squinted at the screen, watching for another few seconds as Nolan unlocked the records room. The door opened and closed, Nolan going inside.

Frustration filled Jerome. The trustees hadn't given him enough money to install a camera inside the records room, so he had no idea if Nolan went into the room to smoke a cigarette or to look at files. There'd be no way to prove what he was up to.

A few minutes passed before Nolan emerged again. Jerome watched the recording frame by frame, trying to determine whether he had carried anything out of the records room with him. Other than the normal bulges on his body from his required equipment and tactical vest, the only other thing that Jerome could see was a bulge in the back pocket of his pants. That was likely his cell phone. Jerome squinted at the screen, wishing there was something more concrete than just the raging suspicions inside of him. With a couple clicks of his mouse, Jerome ran the recording forward and back a couple times, making sure he didn't miss anything. He let it continue to run as he watched Nolan go back out to his workstation, sit down at his desk and resume working on the computer. He didn't look like someone who was feeling guilty about anything. Jerome would have expected more shifting body language if that was the case.

Jerome leaned back in his chair, the back of it giving another groan. It was possible that Nolan had just stopped at the Schmidt's house because he saw Dr. Zuckerman's truck there. Jerome had stopped at Nolan's house one time about a year before. Nolan had walked Jerome out to the back pasture where he had just bought his first cattle. He'd heard him talking to one of the other officers about how he'd added to his herd and was hoping for calves in the spring. Perhaps he just had questions for Dr. Zuckerman and decided to stop and see what was going on. If that was the case, there was nothing to worry about, but the nagging feeling that of all the places he could've stopped was at the Schmidt's exactly at the same time when a stranger from Chicago was in town looking into the Schmidt case made Jerome's skin crawl.

Jerome closed the surveillance software, logged out of his computer so that no prying eyes could see what he'd been up to, and grabbed his hat off the desk. It was time to make that trip to the lumber mill. Bucky Walters was waiting.

22

After letting Miner out to go to the bathroom while it was still dark, Mike curled back up on the couch to go back to sleep for a few more hours. He'd been up late, scrounging around for leads on the Sarah Schmidt case. He never slept well when Emily was out of town. Whether it was because he was staying at her house and not in his own bed or whether it was because he knew she was in danger, he was never sure. Taking care of Miner wasn't hard, but the dog tended to get him up at all hours of the day and night to run outside to use the bathroom or chase a chipmunk. Just since Emily had been gone, he had managed to dig three new holes in the backyard. He lived up to his name, Mike thought, rolling over, adjusting the pillow under his head. All the dog needed was a hardhat and a headlamp.

By the time Miner got him up again, the sun was well over the horizon. Mike stretched, used the bathroom and then let Emily's dog out into the backyard. As he started a fresh pot of coffee, he realized he hadn't grabbed the mail from the day before. While he waited for it to perk, he walked to the front door, thinking there were probably some magazines or sales flyers that he could bring in.

It was still a little cool, but he could tell by how it felt that the rising humidity meant it would be an almost summerlike day. A couple of cars buzzed down the street as he opened the door and glanced left and right. Was he more paranoid now that he'd started working with Emily or less? Mike wasn't sure. Emily had certainly given him the opportunity to refine his technical skills, that was for sure. As he stepped down off the threshold of the door, he nearly tripped over a bag. He frowned for a second and then reached into the mailbox, retrieving a couple of letters. He bent down, looking at the bag. There was no name on the outside of it. It was just a brown paper bag, the kind that the grocery stores used to pack all the groceries in before they started using the blue plastic bags that seem to end up everywhere.

Mike picked up the bag with the mail and went back in the house, locking the door. Miner was scratching at the back door, ready to come in. Mike let the dog in, who immediately ran over to his water bowl, lapped up some water, grabbed a mouthful of food and promptly curled up in the corner on his dog bed. Mike was hoping to be able to get a little work done before it was time to take Emily's dog for a walk.

For a moment, Mike didn't know what to do about the brown bag. It didn't have anyone's name on it. He wondered if maybe one of his buddies, who knew he was house-sitting, dropped something off without telling him. He checked his phone, but there were no texts saying anything about it. Mike chewed his lip for a second, wondering if he should open it. If it was something private, Emily might get upset, but at the same time, maybe it was for him. There weren't many people that would drop off something for him, but he was curious anyway.

The top of the bag was neatly folded over with three staples spaced evenly across the top. It almost looked like a food delivery, Mike thought, hoping to find doughnuts inside. As he popped the staples off, he unfolded the top of the bag, peering down. There was another bag inside. Mike reached in and pulled out a plastic bag, one of the biggest he had ever seen, much bigger than the typical gallon size that someone might keep in their drawer in their kitchen.

Seeing what was inside the bag, Mike dropped it and slumped down in a chair. He needed to call Emily. He needed to call her now.

23

The cleaning and re-stitching of Emily's leg took about another thirty minutes. Dr. Zuckerman had taken out the stitches Emily put in the day before, quickly snipping them with a pair of surgical scissors and pulling them out with forceps. "For someone with no medical knowledge, you did a pretty good job," he said, setting the scissors off to the side.

Emily sat quietly, just trying to hold still long enough for the veterinarian to finish what he needed to do. He put a headlamp on and pointed it directly into the wound. Emily wondered about it for a second, but then she realized that as a mobile vet, he probably spent a lot of time in dark, musty barns and working on animals at all hours of the day and night. The headlamp probably came in handy.

As the latex from his gloves touched her skin, Emily winced a little, not so much because it hurt, but because she was afraid it would. Dr. Zuckerman had done a good job of numbing up her leg again, though. She leaned back in the chair, staring up at the ceiling, fighting the urge to watch what he was doing. If it had been anyone else who was hurt, she would have been happy to assist, but watching him work on her own leg was more than she thought she could handle.

Even with the amount of anesthesia Dr. Zuckerman had given her, Emily could feel a faint tugging and pulling on her skin. The smell of antiseptic and latex gloves wafted up from her thigh. Vicki moved closer to her side. "You okay?"

"Yeah. Just want this to be over."

Vicki nodded, but said nothing. Dr. Zuckerman worked for the next couple minutes in silence. Emily could feel him moving the flesh around. "Just another minute here, Emily," he said. "I'm going to put some antibiotic ointment down into the wound before I close it again. That should help with the infection." He glanced up at her, "Little trick I learned in the Army."

"Whatever gets the job done, Doc," Emily said, staring at the ceiling.

Another minute passed. Emily could hear Dr. Zuckerman rooting around in his medical bag. "Vicki, can you get the suture kit open for me?"

"Sure thing."

Emily heard paper tearing open and the sound of metal tapping against metal with a clink. She still couldn't look. It was bad enough when she had to watch herself stitch her own leg together. For some reason she didn't feel like she could watch Dr. Zuckerman do it again. As he was getting the first stitch set in her leg, the pulling and tugging on her numb skin letting her know that something else was happening, she heard her phone ring. She had left it in the family room, on the coffee table next to the couch where she had fallen asleep the night before. Without asking, Vicki brought it to her. She saw the call was from Mike. A frown must have crawled across her face because Vicki looked at her, "Everything okay?"

"Not sure." Emily set the phone down on the table, figuring

she would call Mike when Dr. Zuckerman finished. A second later, her phone chirped. She picked it up and saw a text from Mike, "911."

The timing wasn't ideal. She was in the middle of getting her leg stitched back together. Was whatever Mike was worried about enough to make her take the call at that minute? Emily didn't know what to do. She ignored it. A second later, a second text came through, "Emily?"

Mike wasn't giving her much of a choice. Clearly, he had news that couldn't wait. A knot formed in her stomach. What could be so urgent that he was chasing her around like this?

She tapped the call button on the screen of her phone and Mike picked up a second later. "Where have you been?"

"You just called less than a minute ago. What's going on?"

"I just sent you a picture. We had a delivery this morning. You're not going to like it."

Emily pulled the phone away from her ear long enough to see what the picture was. Mike had sent several images in the stack. One was a brown bag, the next one was of a plastic bag holding something. Emily squinted at the image on her phone and then enlarged it with two fingers. It was a pink shoe. She put her phone back up to her ear, her heart pounding in her chest. "Are you kidding me? Is this some kind of joke?"

"I wish. I just went outside to go get the mail. I forgot to get it yesterday. When I did, I found the brown bag on the front stoop."

Emily swallowed, whether from having her leg re-stitched together or the shock of the pink shoe ending up on her doorstep in Chicago, she wasn't sure. "Did you open it? Was there anything else inside?" Mike sounded like he was panting on the other end of the line. Emily needed him to stay calm so he could answer her questions. "Mike, focus. Did you open the plastic bag?"

There was a pause, "No. No, I wouldn't do that. I know better than that. What do I do now?"

Emily knew Mike was comfortable with technology, but she knew the case invading his space in Chicago would throw him for a loop. It certainly was doing the same to her. Her mind raced ahead, realizing that whoever had taken Sarah not only had kept the pink shoe as a trophy of what happened to her, but also knew that Emily was in town and where she was from, down to the exact location. The threat was real. "Okay, we have to think clearly about this. Let me call you back in a couple minutes. I'm with somebody right now." Dr. Zuckerman tugging and pulling on her leg made thinking almost impossible. Emily needed a minute to think.

"Okay. Call me back as soon as you can," Mike said.

By the time Emily got off the phone, Dr. Zuckerman was just about done stitching up her leg. He pulled out more gauze pads and rolled gauze, placing them carefully across the wound and wrapping it around her thigh, neatly tying the ends by wrapping them under one of the wrapped sections. "Animals eat tape," he said. He rummaged around in his bag for a minute after stripping his latex gloves off, pulling out of a large bottle of pills. "It looks like a tiny bit of the wound wasn't quite clean at the base. That's why it became infected. I need you to take these antibiotics three times a day for the next ten days." He handed her a bottle of pills that were marked veterinary use only.

"Are these for cattle?"

"Well, we use them for a lot of different animals. Believe it or not, this drug was developed first for humans. It was adapted for veterinary use, but the formula is exactly the same. Lucky for you, I had the right size pills. If I had given you the ones we use on cows, you would've had a hard time swallowing them," he smiled. Emily noticed he was attractive, but her mind was so focused on Mike's call and the work Dr. Zuckerman had just on her leg, that she couldn't do anything other than notice.

"You should be able to manage the pain with just some over-the-counter Ibuprofen. I numbed it up pretty good so I could clean it, so be careful when you stand up." He stood up, zipping his bag. "Oh, and drink plenty of water. You don't need to get dehydrated with a fever and an infection. That'll end you up in the hospital pretty quick." He looked at her, narrowing his eyes, "You don't look like the kind of person who likes to end up in the hospital."

Emily let the comments slide. "I have some money in my bag. How much?"

Dr. Zuckerman waved her off, "Consider it part of your welcome to Stockton package. Happy to help out." He gave a brief nod to Vicki and Cameron and walked out. A second later, Emily heard the sound of his truck starting up, the tires grinding on the gravel, the same way that the tires of her own truck did.

Vicki slumped down in the chair next to her. "Something happened, didn't it? While Dr. Zuckerman was stitching your leg. That call you got."

Whether it was a mother's intuition or just the change in Emily's body language, she didn't know. Somehow, Vicki had picked up that there had been a development in the case. Emily glanced at Cameron. He was still standing in Vicki's kitchen, off to the side, watching. "Why are you here?" Emily knew it was risky to speak to a local law enforcement officer that way, but she didn't care.

"To get some answers. You?"

Cameron had met Emily's challenge with one of his own. "Why did you feed me that bogus file?"

Emily watched him for a second as he shifted in place. His body language told her he knew what she said was the truth. He looked like the type of guy that liked to be on the right side of things. Emily implied that he wasn't, and it had made him uncomfortable. Good, she thought. About time to move things in the right direction. "I didn't do that intentionally," he said quietly. "I haven't slept much in the last couple nights since you got into town."

Emily raised her eyebrows. If that was his weak admission that his sense of justice had been stirred, she would take it. "So, let's say I agree to the fact you didn't mislead me on purpose, which I'm not saying I believe, but if I did, why would you do that?"

"That's the file we have. I went into the records room this morning to check." He pulled up a chair at the kitchen table. Vicki hadn't offered him coffee yet. It was a slight that was subtle, but Emily didn't miss it. Clearly, Vicki wasn't sure if she should welcome Cameron into her home or not. Emily figured the next minute or two would decide that. She'd either be leaving the house in another set of handcuffs or maybe Cameron would tell her something she needed to know.

Emily uncapped her bottle of water and took a sip, trying to swallow the bile that had risen in her throat, the image of being arrested again floating through her mind. "What are you saying?"

"What I'm saying," Cameron sighed, "is that for some reason, the file I handed you is the one we have in our cold case records. Why there are only five pages in it I have no idea." Cameron grabbed a hold of his duty belt and pushed it down, adjusting it lower on his hips while he sat. "Every other cold case file we have, looks to have at least fifty to one hundred pages in it."

Emily shifted in her seat, the image of the pink tennis shoe rising in her mind. She felt conflicted, not knowing if she should tell Vicki about the shoe. It was a clear threat. Discretion was the better part of wisdom, she thought to herself. "So, you're saying you got a guilty conscience and decided to stop over here?"

"Not exactly." Cameron looked up at the ceiling for a second. "It seems like there's a bigger issue here. I don't like it. Whatever is going on, that's not why I got into law enforcement."

Emily squinted at him. Suspicion rose in her mind. There was no real way to know if he was being honest, or if the county sheriff had put him up to it. She decided not to share the information about the shoe. "There is that," she said. "If you're serious, what are you going to do about it?" She decided that challenging him would be likely the only way to figure out if he was being honest or not.

"Well, I know that Nate Gillibrand was a suspect at the time. I figure I might want to head over there and have a talk with him. Maybe he knows more than he's saying. You up to riding with me?"

Emily could feel Vicki's eyes boring into her. She was sure that maternal instinct in Vicki had risen again. But Emily wasn't her child. She wouldn't be controlled by her. Not by anybody ever again. That was a promise she had made to herself after she'd been arrested. She wasn't about to break it now. "Sure. I already talked to him, but if you want to try again, let's see what you've got."

Without saying anything more, Emily pushed herself up and to a standing position, testing the weight on her leg. The painkillers had started to kick in, and the anesthesia Dr. Zuckerman had used was still working. "Give me a minute to go put some pants on."

Emily picked up her cell phone off the table as she walked towards the bathroom, only limping a little. As she closed the door behind her, she shut the lid to the toilet and sat down, dialing Mike. "Is the bag the shoe in sealed?" Emily didn't bother saying hello. This had to be a quick call. She didn't want to raise any suspicion with Cameron.

"Yes. It's plastic."

"Think one of your friends could get some DNA off of it?" DNA identification had come a long way in the twelve years since Sarah Schmidt's disappearance. The database where DNA results were mostly kept was called CODIS. It was the identification system that police departments across the nation had access to. Whenever someone was arrested all their identification went into that database so they could be linked to other open cases throughout the country. Before getting Vicki's letter, Emily had been doing some research on the improvements in DNA testing. Even the smallest shattered cell could now be used to at least send detectives in the right direction. Not that Emily was a detective anymore, but maybe Mike's conspiracy theory friends might have a way of running the science without her having to use other means.

There was a pause on Mike's end. "I don't know. I have somebody who might be able to help." There was another pause before he answered again, "Let me reach out to her and see if she'd be willing to do us a favor."

"Do that. We need to get this wrapped up."

As soon as she hung up, Emily pulled a clean pair of jeans out of her bag. Vicki had been nice enough to stow it in the bathroom for her. She slid the denim up over her leg, being careful not to disturb the bandages and new stitches on her thigh. She pulled on a pair of socks, which was challenging given the fact she didn't want to bend her knee at any severe angle. As she stood up, she pulled her pistol out of her bag and clipped the holster to the back of her pants, pulling her shirt down over top of it. She wasn't going to take any more chances. She grabbed the bag and slung it over her shoulder, stuffing her cell phone in her back pocket.

A minute later, she was ready to go. As she walked towards

the back door, she saw a look of concern on Vicki's face. "Are you coming back?"

"I don't know. I'm going to take my stuff with me. If we find anything, I'll let you know."

In some respects, Emily felt bad. Vicki had been generous enough to let her stay at her house the night before, but two things weighed on Emily's mind: she didn't want to draw danger to Vicki's house, and secondly, she needed to be able to go where she wanted to go when she wanted to go, even if that meant leaving. She didn't need Vicki holding onto her like a smitten schoolgirl every time she wanted to walk out the door. It wasn't fair to Vicki, and it certainly wasn't fair to Emily. She had Liz to keep her company, Emily thought as she walked out to the police cruiser.

Cameron started up the car without saying anything, the gravel grinding under the tires of the cruiser. He pulled out, checking the traffic right and left before saying anything more. "Want to tell me anything more about your leg?"

A wave of frustration crashed over Emily. "I already told you what happened." The fact that Cameron was that suspicious of her made her start to wonder about his intentions. Maybe getting in a car with him hadn't been a good idea after all. She adjusted in her seat, tilting her body toward him. If he made any kind of move, she'd be able to more easily reach for the pistol on her back.

"You get a look at the guy? Were you able to hit him or anything? I'm just wondering if someone in town had a bruise on them, we could connect it to your case."

His line of questioning put Emily's mind at ease, at least for the moment. "No. I don't have anything else to give you, and even if I did, I wouldn't. I've got no interest in pressing charges. I'm just passing through."

"Once you figure out what happened to Sarah…"

Emily didn't say anything, she just stared out the window,

watching the cornfields pass by. A minute later, Cameron turned the cruiser onto the narrow gravel driveway that belonged to Nate Gillibrand. Cameron seemed to find it with no problems. Emily wondered how many trips Cameron had made to Nate's trailer in the past. Nate had told her he'd been in scrapes with the law over the years — he'd made no secret of it. The ease with which Cameron found the driveway made her believe that visiting Nate's property was a regular occurrence.

Before they could even get out of the cruiser, the trailer door opened, slamming shut with a loud rattle, Nate coming towards them. "Officer Nolan. I see you've brought some company with you today. To what do I owe the pleasure?"

Emily pushed herself up out of the car and followed Cameron over toward Nate. Nate must have noticed the limp, even though it was slight. "What happened to you?"

"I fell off a bull."

Nate raised his eyebrows and then looked back at Cameron. "So, what can I do for you? Here to accuse me of something else?"

Cameron didn't take the bait. For that, Emily gave him credit. He looked at Nate, hooking his thumbs over his duty belt, the way that so many police officers did when they were outside of their cruisers. "You're not at work today?"

Nate shook his head. "Nope. We finished a job yesterday and don't start another one until tomorrow. We're driving up to Minerva. Industrial roof."

Cameron nodded. "Fair enough. Listen, I want to ask you about Sarah Schmidt."

Nate glanced at Emily. "You put him up to this?"

Emily shook her head no, "All his idea."

Cameron sucked in a breath. "This case has been open for too long. What do you know about Sarah Schmidt?"

Nate narrowed his eyes at Emily. "I'm not sure what you're asking me. She came asking the same stuff yesterday."

Cameron wasn't going to take no for an answer. "Tell me again."

Nate sat down on the step by the front door of the trailer. Emily hadn't really looked closely at him before, but she could tell by the wrinkles on his face and the broken blood vessels on his cheeks he'd made choices that had made life hard on him. He was wearing an old T-shirt, a tear near the collar exposing some hair on his chest, and a pair of baggy sweatpants. Emily guessed that he'd slept in the same clothes he was wearing.

"There's not a lot to tell. I was interested in dating Sarah. She disappeared. Nothing happened."

"You didn't go out on one date?" Cameron said, shifting his weight onto his right leg.

"Not really. Just ice cream a couple of times. She wasn't interested. I knew she was leaving to go to college, thought I'd make a play for her, she blew me off, and that was the end of it."

Emily raised her eyebrows. If she hadn't already talked to Nate, she would've taken what he said a little differently than she was sure Cameron had interpreted it. Sure enough, Cameron fired back, "She blew you off? How did you feel about that?"

Nate shrugged, not getting up from the step. "She told me she was going to college. Didn't want to have anybody holding her back. I understood it. Actually, I didn't blame her."

"Any idea what might've happened to her?"

"Isn't that your job?" Nate said, staring at Cameron.

Emily gave him credit. He wasn't going to be manipulated by Cameron, that was clear. "Anything else you want to tell us?"

"No."

As Nate got up to go back in the trailer, Emily could tell that there was a lot more he would like to tell Cameron, but the kinds of words he'd use would likely end him up in jail. Apparently, he learned his lesson at some point, opting to go back in his trailer rather than getting agitated at Cameron.

As Emily walked back to the cruiser, she thought about Nate's reaction to what she said about the injury on her leg. He hadn't flinched and he hadn't looked away. That told her he wasn't involved in the attack on her. In her gut, she believed Nate had been one of those people who'd been caught up in circumstances beyond his control. He looked like a viable suspect, but was he? Probably not.

24

Kathy Barnes was at the end of a long shift. There were more people than usual at Sandy's Restaurant. A busload of people on their way back from an antique buying trip in West Virginia had stopped at the restaurant for lunch. It had been two-and-a-half hours of non-stop movement before she could get outside to take a break. She stopped at her purse on the way out, pushing her tip money down into her wallet and pulling out a cigarette and a lighter, stuffing her phone in her back pocket. She had a whopping fifteen minutes to herself before she had to get back into the restaurant and help clean things up.

As she touched the edge of the flame to the dried tobacco, the pull of smoke into her lungs instantly made her feel calmer. She wished that wasn't the case. Her dad told her repeatedly she should stop smoking before she developed Emphysema, lung cancer, COPD or something worse. It wasn't that she didn't believe him, it was just that she had no reason to quit. More than once she had tried to hatch a plan to get out of Stockton, but every time she'd fallen on her face. In some respects, she wondered if she was a lifer in the little town. She knew her family was, but at least her dad was a doctor. He had made the choice to come back to Stockton, to serve the community. She hadn't made that choice. She had no options, other than the menial work that she did at the restaurant. It wasn't that her family hadn't given her the chance to go away to school. She'd even tried taking some online classes and thought about becoming a real estate agent, but then quit halfway through, each time realizing it just wasn't for her.

Before the next drag on her cigarette, her phone vibrated. Sandy and her husband, the owners of the restaurant, didn't care if she kept her cell phone in her pocket, but they did care if it rang while she was serving customers. On her first day of work, Sandy looked at her over crinkled lips and said "Now, I am more than happy to give you a job, but I've got rules.

If you break them, I will fire you right away. You have to be on time for work every day. No excuses. If something happens, that's okay, but you need to let me know right away, not come carousing in here five, ten, fifteen minutes late for your shift. And I hate those cell phones. If you want to have it with you, that's okay, but it needs to be on vibrate." Sandy used the phrase "That's okay," like she had trademarked it. The reality was not much was okay with Sandy. She expected her staff to work hard for the money they earned.

Kathy looked down at her phone. She recognized the number, although she didn't have it listed in her contacts. "Hello?"

"You at work?" the male voice asked.

She had known Benny Walters for years. They had grown up together and had even dated for a couple of months when he came back from college, toting a fancy business degree that he was supposed to use at his father's lumber mill. Bucky

Walters, his father, was one of the most respected members of Stockton. Whoever was coming through the city, whether it was a Congressman, Senator or CEO, they always stopped at the Walters Lumbermill to have a cup of coffee with Bucky.

After they dated for a few months, he and Kathy broke up over something stupid. She couldn't even really remember at this point what their last fight had been about. What she did remember was finding out two days later that he'd started seeing another girl, Melinda Barrett. A year later they were married. They now had two kids, five and three. Melinda had let herself go. About six months before, Benny had started to call Kathy again.

THEIR RELATIONSHIP HAD STARTED INNOCENTLY ENOUGH. He'd come by the restaurant, sitting at her tables or picking up takeout for his family. Then, he asked her to start delivering the takeout to his car out in the parking lot. He told her, in confidence, things were not going well with Melinda. Would she be able to have a cup of coffee with him to help him sort it out? Not thinking anything of it except for trying to be a good friend, she agreed. Two days later, she found herself in the backseat of his car agreeing to something she probably never would have if she had any kind of life of her own.

It wasn't that she thought the relationship was going to go anywhere. At first, she thought it might. For the first couple months, Benny said he was thinking about getting divorced from Melinda, had even contacted an attorney. Then the talk started to wear off. Benny knew he could get what he wanted from Kathy and still go home to his wife and kids at night. Kathy knew she could be mad at him, but she also knew she could say no, which she never did.

"Yeah. What's going on with you?"

"Not much. Avoiding my dad. I've got end of the month reports due and the sheriff was just here."

There was never much love lost between Sheriff Mollohan and Benny. Kathy knew Benny was busted a couple times as a teenager. Sheriff Mollohan had let him off the hook because of his relationship with Bucky. Even though he'd been given the opportunity to get off scot free and head out of town to college, Benny still didn't like him. He told Kathy one night he felt like Sheriff Mollohan was only interested in his dad because he was a business leader in Stockton. Kathy had raised her eyebrows and looked at him, "And you expected something else?"

Benny shook his head, pushing the hair out of his eyes, straightening his clothes. "I guess I shouldn't. He's more of a politician than a Sheriff."

KATHY PULLED the cell phone away from her ear, checking the time. "What was the Sheriff there about?" She only had a couple minutes left before she had to get back inside the restaurant.

"I don't know. It was a strange meeting, though. Usually, they sit outside and smoke a couple cigars. This time they were in Dad's office with the door closed. I walked by, and Dad looked pretty pale. Probably bad news of some sort."

"Not like the Sheriff to deliver bad news."

Everyone in town knew Sheriff Mollohan was always trying to stay in the good graces of people like Bucky Walters.

"Listen, I gotta get back inside."

"Okay. Can we meet up later?"

Every time Benny asked, Kathy tried to find the willpower to say no. She had told him no before, but he just kept calling. She wondered if that's what had made Benny's dad so successful. Refusing to say no was a lesson she might need to learn in her own life. "I don't know. I've got some stuff to do tonight.

Why don't you call me later?" It wasn't a firm no, but it was all she had at the moment.

"All right. I'll do that."

As Kathy walked back into the restaurant, she saw a vision of herself, not as a waitress, but with a career and a life. She pushed the thought out of her head, not sure it was possible.

25

As soon as Mike hung up the phone with Emily, he sent a quick text. He fed Miner and gave him fresh water. The dog was picky. Mike couldn't figure out what the difference was, but it didn't matter. He had to do what he had to do in order to keep the pup happy until Emily got home.

If she made it home...

Most of the time when Emily was out on cases, Mike didn't really worry about her. But the fact that someone figured out who she was and where she lived and bothered to drop off a piece of evidence a thousand miles away from the crime scene seemed like a new level of intrusion. It was like the case had been dosed with heavy-duty caffeine, everything happening too fast. It was a helpless feeling, one that Mike tried to shake off. He felt like all the nerves in his body had been fried at the same time.

He checked his phone, but no response yet. It might take a few minutes. His contact wasn't always that careful about staying in communication. Mike went into the bathroom, realizing he probably needed a shower. It'd been a couple days. He scowled. He'd been working so hard that he couldn't remember the last time he stopped for a meal or to get cleaned up.

He started the water in the shower, using a bathroom off the hallway upstairs in Emily's house. He paused in the mirror, rubbing his chin, the growth of stubble sticking out like porcupine needles. He looked pale and drawn, black circles under his eyes. Normally, these cases invigorated him. Not so with this one.

After getting cleaned up, he threw on a cleaner pair of jeans than the ones he had been wearing before, tossing his dirty clothes in Emily's washing machine along with another set or two of his clothes. He had no idea how much longer he'd be at her house. The case wasn't moving. That was a fact. And now, someone had decided to leave a little present for them. As if the situation wasn't dangerous enough...

He checked his phone again after putting the load of laundry in, hearing the washing machine click on and the gush of water filling the tub. "You can bring it over. Meet me in the parking lot."

Mike checked the time. It would take him about a half hour from Emily's house to get over to the University, especially in late afternoon traffic. Chicago was notorious for traffic snarls, sometimes even worse than places like Los Angeles. The thing most people didn't realize about Chicago was there was really no rush hour. The freeways were jammed at all hours of the day and night. He needed to be lucky to make it over to see his friend in thirty minutes. "Leaving now. Will text you when I get there." His friend sent back a thumbs up.

Mike picked up his car keys off of the kitchen table, checking on Miner one last time. The dog had curled up in Emily's office in the front of the house. Mike knew he'd be fine if he was gone for a while. Jamming his laptop in a black backpack he always carried, Mike grabbed the paper bag with the shoe in it. His backpack was nondescript, like most everything that Mike owned. He wanted to blend in, to be the gray man, as it was called, someone that was not interesting enough to take a second look at.

He double checked the back door of the house, making sure that the alarm was armed and that the deadbolts on the door were fastened. They were. Once he got into his blue sedan, he pulled on a baseball hat. It was plain, with nothing on the front of it that anyone could remember if he was seen somewhere, plus a pair of sunglasses. He backed out of the driveway carefully, doing everything he could to avoid attention. He drove just slightly over the speed limit, merging onto the freeway.

A couple of miles down the road, Mike realized he was gripping the steering wheel much harder than he needed to, his mind focused on the bag dropped off at her house. They needed to get this case solved, and soon. Clearly, there was something about the Sarah Schmidt case that had stirred up a hive of bees. Mike chewed his lip for a moment, realizing they were fighting an enemy that was different from their other cases. He was on the research side, doing technical work in real time, not running away from trouble. He sighed, putting on the blinker to get off the freeway. He realized that he'd have to up his skills in the future. That was something to talk to Emily about once she got home. Otherwise, he'd have to tell her he'd only deal with the technical side of things in the future. As soon as he had the thought, he realized that just wasn't possible. He'd been doing that on this case, but somehow trouble managed to find him. It was trouble he wanted to avoid at all costs.

The building where his friend Alice worked was a white behemoth that rose up out of a parking lot on the edge of campus. It was the medical research building for the University of Chicago. There were signs all over the side of it showing off their partnership with the Chicago Medical Center and a couple of other hospitals. As Mike pulled in, he chose a parking spot away from the clusters of cars, pulling in where he could see the front entrance, though he wasn't sure Alice would come out that way. He threw the small sedan in park, but left the engine running, picking up his cell phone and sending her a text. Before he could send it, he heard a rap on the window. He nearly jumped out of his skin, his heart pounding in his chest. It was Alice. As he unlocked the doors, she slid inside, tucking her white lab coat underneath her. "I saw you come in. What's with all the cloak and dagger?"

He and Alice had met online in a group that was interested in the forensics of the most famous murder cases in history. After circling each other in the group for a while, they finally started a private chat and met up a couple times to do some gaming. Alice was tiny, with jet black hair and almond eyes. She was half Chinese and half Korean. When she told Mike that, she acted like he should be shocked, but he didn't know better. "Don't you know that it's a big deal for a Chinese man to marry a Korean woman?" she asked one night, late, after they had eaten an entire bag of cheese puffs and played to the fourth level of a new game. Mike had no idea.

At the moment, Alice was sporting hair that looked like it had been cut with a weed whacker, the layers some short, and some long, some sticking out and some close to her face. About a quarter of her hair was fluorescent green. She had on a pair of glasses and wore a pair of jeans and a T-shirt under her lab coat. "Wait, you don't look so good? Are you okay?"

Mike shook his head, "I need some help with the case I'm on." He paused for a moment, "Actually, it's a case that Emily is on."

"You mean the mob boss's ex-wife? The one you dog sit for?"

"Actually, she was married to the mob boss's son, if you want to be precise about it. And yes. It's a complicated case. A piece of evidence was delivered to the house. I need whatever forensic evidence you can pull off of it, especially DNA." Mike reached into the back seat and pulled the paper bag forward, handing it to Alice. She pulled a set of blue latex gloves out of her pocket, putting them on before she touched it.

"Are you the only one that touched this?"

Mike nodded. "This is how it was left at the front door. I found it this morning."

"What's inside?"

"Other than a shoe? I'm not sure. That's up to you to find out. Think you can work your magic?"

Alice pushed her glasses up on her nose and grinned. "Is that actually a question?"

From the amount of time that Mike had spent with her, he knew that she was very good at what she did, even if at times she seemed to be quite a bit overconfident. "The most important question I have for you is: Can you keep this quiet? I need the results right away, but I need them off the books."

Mike had told Alice a little about the work he did for Emily, but not much. She knew he did some consulting work for a former police officer who tried to settle cold cases now and again. In the community of people that Mike chose to run with, secrecy was the norm. The friends he had, they connected over basic things like technology or gaming, but very rarely got into anything too personal. It was just the way they were. Paranoid, maybe. Mike preferred to think of it as smart.

Technology had evolved to such a level that he didn't believe there was much real privacy anymore. Mike stayed in an apartment in town. It was sparsely decorated with just a couch, a big screen and a mattress thrown on the floor. What no one knew is that with the money he had earned doing off the books jobs for people, he'd bought a little campsite a couple hours outside of Chicago. There was a tiny, off the grid cabin on it, and access to a stream. He went out there every week or so, taking supplies with him. If anything crazy ever happened, he knew how to disappear and disappear quick. He swallowed, suddenly wondering if this case would be the one that would send him off the grid.

Alice's voice interrupted his thoughts. "I'll run this up to the lab now and get it started. You sure you're the only one that touched it?"

"Yep."

As she popped the door open, she leaned back inside the car, "I should have some results in a couple of hours. Things are slow in the lab right now. I have some stuff that's processing that won't be ready until tomorrow, so you caught me at a good time."

"Don't you need a set of my fingerprints or something?"

Alice smiled, "I already have those as well as a sample of your DNA. Don't worry, I won't implicate you."

"How did you...?"

Alice giggled, "All those times I took out the trash? Not too hard to snag your fingerprints and DNA off of those red plastic cups you like so much." She tilted her head to the side, "Sorry, I needed a new sample to play with. Guess it's a good thing I did, huh?"

The car door slammed shut and Mike watched Alice march right back towards the building, her green hair bouncing above her slight frame, the swish of her white lab coat rubbing against the back of her jeans. He started up the sedan and pulled out of the parking lot. To anyone who'd been watching, it looked like he'd dropped off a late lunch to Alice, nothing more. They'd be surprised if they knew the truth... He just hoped her results would come back in time to get Emily the answers she needed.

26

As soon as Cameron dropped Emily off at her truck, she left. He hadn't bothered to ask her what she was going to do next. Emily was glad, she thought, pulling the seatbelt across her chest. It really wasn't any of his business, anyway. He said he'd try to help, but the only help he'd offered was in re-interviewing Nate Gillibrand — someone that Emily already knew was innocent.

By the time they got back to Vicki's house and Emily pulled the truck out of her driveway, the sun had started to slump down in the sky. The anesthesia that Dr. Zuckerman used on her leg had worn off. Emily rustled around in the bag she had on the front seat, pulling out a bottle of water. Her phone rang. It was Angelica. "How are you, sis? How's the leg?"

"It's okay."

There was a pause on the phone for a second. "What are you not telling me, Emily? I know that tone in your voice."

It always amazed Emily that even from thousands of miles away, Angelica could sense when there was something wrong. She had an eerie way of calling or texting when Emily needed to talk to someone. There were very few people in Emily's life that knew much more about her than what they saw. Angelica was one of them. "My leg got infected."

Angelica's voice immediately turned clinical, "Tell me what happened."

"Nothing to worry about," Emily said, turning the wheel. Without thinking about it, she drove back to the cemetery. She needed time to think. "I woke up with a fever this morning. The local vet took a peek at my leg."

"I want details."

Angelica's protective side had come out. Emily knew better than trying to blow her off, so she spent the next couple minutes describing all of her symptoms and all the steps Dr. Zuckerman had taken. "He was a combat medic for the Army and then decided he liked animals better, at least that's what he told me while he was busy restitching my leg," Emily said, turning the truck off in the driveway for the cemetery.

Hearing about Dr. Zuckerman's qualifications seemed to calm Angelica down. Once she heard what type of medication Emily was on, she quickly shifted gears, "How's the case going?"

"It's taken a turn."

"A good one?"

"I'm not sure." Emily told Angelica about the shoe delivered to her house in Chicago.

"Are you kidding me? How did they get your address?"

The fact that Emily still didn't know who the "they" was, stung. It was her job to figure this stuff out, even if she wasn't getting paid for it. "That's what I don't know. What it tells me is whoever is behind this has means. They have access to information, and they have the desire to protect themselves."

"Maybe you should go home…"

The very thought of turning tail and running back to Chicago sent a flood of emotion over Emily. "Are you kidding? Some idiot has the nerve to stab me in the leg and scare me off with some random pink tennis shoe delivered to my house in

Chicago? That's small town. Just a bunch of games. I'm not going to fall for it. This family deserves justice."

"You still think you can get justice for yourself by helping other people?"

Angelica's comment hit a nerve. Emily knew it was meant to do exactly that. Angelica had inherited their mother's ability to cut to the bone when she felt like it. Emily bit her lip for a second, trying not to let her anger get the best of her. She knew that it came from a place of protectiveness and love from Angelica. She just wished that Angelica had a better delivery. Emily couldn't fault her, though. Emily had the same issue in her own life. She'd lost a lot of friends because of what she had said in the past, relationships that probably would have been good for her, she thought. "Yes. I'm going to get justice for this family."

It was the first time she'd said it out loud. Though she had committed to the case, she'd done so because she thought she should, not necessarily because she thought she wanted to. There were plenty of things Emily would rather be doing, but after the perpetrator decided to invade her private life in Chicago, things had changed. They'd be sorry they came after her.

A surge of new energy filled Emily. Any weariness she felt from the stab wound or the situation seemed to float off somewhere in the air. She got out of the truck and walked away from it, holding the phone up to her ear, limping towards Sarah's empty plot.

Angelica hadn't said anything for a minute. Emily wondered if she knew that her comments hurt. Not that Emily cared that much. She was beyond that. They'd had similar conversations for years, Angelica sure that if Emily would just pack up and come to Europe that her life would be better. Emily didn't want to, at least not yet. There were still cases to solve and people to help. Every time she ended a case, she felt an inch closer to having her life back. It might not be something Angelica understood, but it didn't matter. Emily needed to do what she needed to do.

Emily heard Angelica sigh on the phone, "All right, I know how stubborn you are. Just be careful, okay?"

Emily nodded, even though she knew Angelica couldn't see her. "I will. I've got to get this wrapped up, and soon, before something else happens."

27

After dropping Emily off at her truck, Cameron left her without a word. There was nothing he could do about Emily. He had no grounds to arrest or detain her or even question her. Not that he would. In his mind, she was just trying to do a solid for the Schmidt family.

For a minute, Cameron's mind reached back to his own family. He had three sisters, all younger than him. He wondered what it would be like if one of them disappeared without a trace. He swallowed, a surge of bile coming up the back of his throat. He wondered if his own mom would look like Vicki Schmidt, worn and weathered with unresolved grief.

Cameron circled Stockton, his mind racing. There was no doubt in his mind the file on Sarah Schmidt wasn't all the information from the case. It couldn't be. There were only two possibilities left: the Rangers had the full copy in their offices, or something had been done to the file in his own department.

Cameron swung the cruiser around, a spray of dirt and gravel flying off the back bumper. He revved the engine and headed for Wayne National Forest. It was time to get this resolved.

Ten minutes later, he stepped out of his cruiser, adjusting his belt. The Wayne National Park Rangers had a main office on the Stockton side of the park and a couple of satellite offices on the other side, which were closer to the West Virginia border. The offices, like much of the park, seemed a little dated. The park rangers, although they were given all the same police powers as any other department, didn't look nearly as police-like as he did in his uniform, or at least that's what Cameron thought.

He pulled open a dark brown door that led inside to their offices. Inside, there was a counter facing him. To his left, a map of the park system had been hung on the wall and the emblem of the State of Ohio was hanging on the other side. The linoleum tile on the floor had years of ground in dirt in its crevices. Musty smells hung in the air, the odor of old upholstery and damp wood. "Hi there," Cameron said. "I wanted to talk to somebody about an old case file."

A park ranger behind the counter stood up, his olive-green jacket shifting over his tan uniform shirt and black pants. "You can talk to me. You from Stockton?"

Cameron nodded. "Yep, just doing some follow-up on some old files we have in the office. You guys were in on a case with us a little more than a decade ago. Just want to see if you had anything different in your files than we do." He tried to make it sound casual, not wanting to create any suspicion. If the park rangers had access to Sarah's file, the last thing he wanted to do was tick them off before he got a look at it.

"Sure thing." The park ranger, a guy about his age with the last name Miller pinned to his shirt, sat down at a computer terminal just past where Cameron was standing. "Victim name or case number?"

"Sarah Schmidt. Happened a little more than a decade ago."

The park ranger smiled, "Yeah, I know that case. Let's see

what we've got." He tapped on the keys. "I think I had just started here when she disappeared. Was she a college kid?"

Cameron found himself gripping the edge of the counter. When he looked down and saw how white his knuckles were, he decided to stuff his hands in his pockets. "Close. High school kid who was getting ready to go off to college."

The park ranger looked back at the screen. "That's weird," he muttered.

"Did you find something?" Cameron said, his heart beating a little faster.

"Well, it's not what I found, it's what I didn't find." He swung the monitor toward Cameron so he could see the results on the page. It was a little too far for Cameron to get a good look. "Why don't you come on back here so you can see this a little better? Door is unlocked."

Cameron pulled it open, the odor of the office getting stronger now that he was behind the door. He walked over to where the Park Ranger was working and extended his hand. "Cameron Nolan."

"Greg Miller. Nice to meet you." Greg pointed at the screen in front of him. To Cameron it looked very similar to the cloud-based record storage that his department had gone to a few years before. "If you look here," Greg pointed at the screen with his finger, "we should see a link to all the documents that belong to the case. It doesn't look like anything is here." He swung the monitor back towards him and started typing again. "Let me check the activity logs for that day and see if maybe the link is in there."

Cameron inched towards Greg, wanting to look over his shoulder while he searched for the records. Greg pasted the record date into a screen that did a search for an activity log. A couple of seconds later, Greg nodded, staring at the screen and pointing. "See here?" he glanced at Cameron who had put the palms of his hands on the edge of the desk so he could get a closer look. "It looks like we had people working the case for a couple days at least, but there's no linked documents." Greg frowned for a second and then clicked on another link. "Oh, here it is. Looks like we turned all of our records over to you guys since you were running point on the case." Greg looked up at Cameron, "Sorry, man. Our chief usually has us hold onto case records from incidents we aren't in charge of for about five years and then we ship off what we have to the department in charge. Just makes record-keeping a little easier on our end," he said, shrugging. He stood up from the workstation. "Anything else I can do for you?"

Cameron shook his head, feeling a combination of frustration and anger, "No. I appreciate you trying. I'll go back and dig through our records some more." As Cameron walked away, he looked back at Greg, "Hey, would you mind keeping this to yourself? If somebody misplaced those files, their career could be on the line."

Greg sat back down in the chair, it giving a little squeak as it compressed underneath him. "For sure. I get that." He turned back to his computer, "Have a good day. Stay safe out there."

Cameron didn't say anything else. He walked out the brown painted metal door of the park ranger office and got back in his cruiser, starting it up. His mind was racing. After talking to Greg, it was clear the park rangers had been involved in the search for Sarah Schmidt. It would've been more surprising if they'd had no record of it at all. If what Greg said was true, then the fact that they sent all their records over to the Stockton Sheriff's Office after five years made sense as well. Cameron knew most departments considered cases cold after a shorter time than that.

He chewed on his lip as he drove back into town, stopping at the only coffee shop around and getting himself a plain black coffee. They had coffee at the department, but the coffee shop's brew was better. He took a sip of the scalding hot liquid and licked his lips, putting the cup in the cup holder. He frowned, pulling back out on the main road. Where were those files? Someone must have a reason to want to keep those records quiet. What that was, he didn't know. Cameron pulled into the parking lot of the local school district. The kids were just starting to get out for the afternoon. An idea began to form in his head. After watching the first busload of kids pull away, he pulled back out on the road, feeling the tension in his jaw. He tried to take a deep breath. He didn't want to seem agitated when he got back to the department.

Cameron left the cruiser in one of the front two parking spots reserved for the on-duty cars. He went in the side entrance, using his key card to get in the door. He stopped just inside, scanning the area. There was no one in at the moment, except for one officer sitting way up at the front of the building in case someone stopped in. He gave a brief wave, trying to look friendly. The other officer didn't even acknowledge him. He looked like he was busy working on something at the front desk terminal. Cameron wondered if it could be scheduling for the next month?

He hadn't brought in his bag from the cruiser. There were still three hours left on his shift, so there was no reason to have it in the office yet. He sat down at his workstation, pulling up his email, every now and again looking up to see what the other officer was doing. He realized as he was typing that his hands had turned cold and clammy. He had an idea, but if it blew up in his face, there would be repercussions, serious repercussions.

Cameron stared at the computer screen for another minute and then pulled open a desk drawer, pretending to look for something. When he looked up, he picked up a thick case file and notebook from his desk and walked towards the back of the building, where the records office and Sheriff Mollohan's office was located. He stopped for a second, kneeling down, pretending to tie his boot, checking to see if the officer at the front of the building had noticed him get up and move. He hadn't. All Cameron could see of him was the top of his head. The rest of him was buried behind the monitor. The officer would actually have to stand up in order to see where Cameron had gone.

As Cameron stood up, he moved quickly to the records office. He pulled his ring of keys from his pocket and unlocked the door, moving toward the cold case file storage where he had found Sarah's file before. He pulled open the drawer and slid the file between the notepad and the other working file that he already had in his hand. Less than a minute later, he was outside of the records room, walking towards the Sheriff's office. Cameron swallowed, stopping just outside of the Sheriff's office. He gave a brief knock, waiting to hear a voice inside. The Sheriff's truck wasn't in the parking lot, but it seemed like a good idea to at least knock. He tried the door handle. It was unlocked, unusual for the sheriff. Sheriff Mollohan usually left his door locked when he wasn't in the office. Why, Cameron was never sure, but he didn't have the time to think about that right now. As Cameron pushed the door open another officer walked by, someone just coming in from on-duty. "Hey," the other officer said, moving past him without even looking at what Cameron was doing. Cameron gave a lift of the head, acknowledging the other man.

Cameron stopped dead in his tracks, just inside the doorway of the Sheriff's office. If he did what he was contemplating doing, it could be the end of his career. He sucked in a breath and clenched his teeth. He'd come this far. He couldn't let this cover-up continue, whatever it was. For a moment, it occurred to him that he could just turn around and walk out of the office, closing the door behind him, like nothing had ever happened. It wasn't really his business after all, was it? Let Emily figure out what happened to Sarah Schmidt. He hadn't been on the department at that time. It wasn't his responsibility.

Or was it? Cameron found himself standing behind the Sheriff's desk, leaning over and pulling on the file drawer before he had a chance to finish any of the thoughts rattling in his head. It was locked. That was it, then. He stood up for a second, staring at the thin file of Sarah's information in his hand. Could he really live with himself if he didn't do something to help?

From out of his pocket, he pulled out his penknife, quickly shimmying the lock on the file drawer. It slid open with a quiet rattle. Inside the drawer, there were a stack of files, clearly ones that Sheriff Mollohan didn't want out in public where any of the other officers could see them. That was against the policies of the department, not to mention against the law. Cameron thumbed through the top five files and found Sarah's real file, buried under the first two. He pulled it out, slipping the cold case file in its place. If Sheriff Mollohan didn't look too carefully, he would see her file in his drawer, not realizing it was the phony one.

Cameron used the penknife to relock the drawer, carefully pushing Sheriff Mollohan's chair back where it had been. He looked up, just in time to see the officer that had been at the front desk right in front of him, "You need something?"

His heart began to beat in his chest, loud enough that he was sure that the person standing in front of him could hear it. He cleared his throat, "Sorry, I guess I need some water. I was just dropping off a case file for the Sheriff to take a look at. He asked me for it this morning." Before the other officer could respond, Cameron slipped past him and went back to his workstation. He stood there for a second, wondering how he was going to get Sarah's real files out of the building without arousing suspicion.

He sat down at his desk for a second, trying to appear

natural, slipping the Sarah Schmidt file under a stack of other paperwork. He looked around, hoping no one noticed how nervous he felt. He figured they wouldn't. The other officer in the building had disappeared again, probably in the bathroom. A second later, he saw the officer come out, adjusting his duty belt. Without thinking, Cameron stood up, carrying the files with him to the bathroom, hoping no one saw him. He went in and closed the door. There was a window at the back of the room. Most of the time it was cracked open to let some fresh air in. Today was no different. Cameron reached up and slid the file under the edge of the window, closing the window enough that no one would see there was a file sticking out if they happened to drive past from the outside. He walked over to one of the stalls, ducking in and flushing the toilet, then walking over to the sink and running the water in case anyone happened to walk by. He walked back out of the bathroom, closing the door behind him and over to his workstation, where his coffee was sitting. Picking it up, he gave a wave to the officer at the front desk. The guy waved back, but hardly looked at Cameron. Taking his coffee, he walked out the side door of the building, casually reaching up and pulling the file off the ledge as he made his way back to the cruiser.

As Cameron got back in the car, he was out of breath from the adrenaline pumping in his system. It wasn't as though walking around the office had been all that strenuous. He knew it was the stress of breaking into the Sheriff's office, his fear of getting caught getting the best of him. He turned the key in the ignition, hearing the engine roared to life. There was nothing he wanted to do more than get away from the office.

As he pulled out, the Sheriff's truck passed him, pulling in. Cameron gave a friendly wave and continued on his way, his eye catching one of the surveillance cameras in his view as he pulled out. If anyone looked at the surveillance camera, they'd come looking for him, and fast. His heart started to pound in his chest. A sense of fear and relief flooded over him at the same time. Fear because he'd just violated pretty much every regulation in law enforcement and relief because he realized he wasn't really meant to be in law enforcement anyway.

As he drove, Cameron lodged the file folder under his duty bag on the passenger side of the car. He glanced at it every couple seconds, anxious to look inside. He made a lap around Stockton, careful to make sure that he wasn't ignoring the job he was paid to do, finally ending up at the little church just off of the main road through Stockton.

The Old Mill Church was his parent's congregation. He went there as well as a child, he and his three sisters packed into red fabric covered pews every Sunday for an hour as they listened to the pastor talk, trying to share hopeful thoughts for the week ahead. He had stopped going to church years before, sometime when he was in high school, when it was too inconvenient with sports and homework. After the police academy, his schedule hadn't allowed him to go regularly, so he just didn't go at all. The reality was he found the services boring. Not to say he wasn't a man of faith, he just had lost his faith in the Old Mill Church.

He pulled into the back parking lot, knowing the few cars that went down the road wouldn't be all that interested in why he was sitting there. He pulled the file out from underneath his bag, feeling the weight of it. It was definitely thicker than the five pages they had in the cold case room.

It didn't take long for Cameron to discover that there had been a ton more evidence in the case than was reflected in the slim folder he had shown Emily a couple days before. There were more crime scene pictures, images of Sarah's shoe, more investigator notes, and even a whole slew of information about people involved in the search in the national park. In fact, just as Greg Miller said, the back half of the file was from the park rangers. Strangely, it appeared to be a digitized version. So, there had been a digital version made at some point, he realized. Where it was stored, he couldn't even begin to imagine. He hadn't been able to find it on the Stockton County Sheriff's office computers, and Greg Miller hadn't been able to find it on the National Park Service computers. He shook his head, flipping the page, realizing that was a bigger question for another day.

As the thin paper slid into place on the opposite side of the folder, an image caused him to suck in his breath. It was a picture he'd heard whispers about but had never seen. A young woman, bound and gagged, sitting in what looked to be the back of the van, with a pink shoe nearby, her feet only covered in socks. It was as if whoever had taken the picture wanted to make it known that he had her remaining shoe. They had found the other shoe at the scene, but that had been returned to her family after many years of no new leads and no new opportunities to solve the case. Cameron stopped for a second, blinking, wondering where that shoe was now. Had the person who'd taken Sarah Schmidt disposed of it, casually tossing it in a trashcan or dumpster where no one would think a second thing of it? After all these years, could it be buried under tons of trash in a remote landfill in a state far away? At this point, the odds of anyone being able to find it or find Sarah were infinitesimal at best.

He flipped through the rest of the pages in the file, frustration growing inside of him. He put his career on the line to go into the Sheriff's office and steal the file. Now what? He closed it, feeling angry at himself, quickly stuffing it under his bag on the passenger seat again. He shook his head. If he hurried up, he could get back to the office and maybe even replace the file the next time the Sheriff left the office. The gravity of what he had done sunk in, regret washing over him like a wave. He started the cruiser, inching forward out of the church parking lot. As he checked left and right getting ready to pull out onto the side street, he saw a blue truck parked off to the side, near the cemetery. He furrowed his brows for a second and then squinted. Was that Emily's truck? What was she doing at the cemetery? He'd only left her a little more than an hour ago. The whole scene seemed strange. The reality that he was hiding in the rear parking lot of a church feeling guilty wasn't lost on him. To top it off, the fact that the investigator who was supposed to be finding out who did it was now at a cemetery seemed to take the case from sad to futile.

As he pulled out of the church parking lot, his intention was to drive down the side street and head back to the station, but he found himself pulling up behind Emily's truck and getting out. He closed the cruiser door and locked it, walking up the driveway towards the interior of the cemetery. He'd only been there a couple of times – for his grandmother's funeral and for the funeral of one of the other officer's mom who had passed away a couple years before. He wasn't a cemetery kind of guy. He knew there were people who would go there on a regular basis to visit their loved ones, but somewhere, deep inside, Cameron believed they were in a better place, at least that's what he thought he'd been taught in church. It had been so long, it was hard to remember.

He saw Emily before she saw him. Emily sat with her back to him on a small white stone bench in the middle of a circular cut out in the cemetery. She wasn't on her phone or with anyone. Emily was alone, just staring off into the distance. Her left leg was at a right angle, but she had extended her right one out in front of her, probably because of the stab wound, he realized. Her jacket hung loosely over her shoulders, a long black ponytail grazing over the fabric. Cameron looked around, the trees gently swaying, the breeze having picked up. Seemed like storms were coming, but so often in Stockton it started to blow like something would happen, and then nothing did.

As Cameron got closer, he didn't want to startle her, so he

called out, "Emily? You okay?" Even with the warning, she seemed jumpy. He saw her quickly twist his direction, her shoulders rising as if she was ready to leap up off of the bench. When she realized it was him, her shoulders dropped, and she seemed to relax, at least a little.

"You following me?"

"No. I was parked behind the church over there looking at some paperwork. I saw your truck when I pulled out."

She turned away, staring off into space. "You can leave. I'm fine."

Cameron stuffed his hands in his pockets. Why Emily was so sharp tongued, he wasn't sure. She acted like a wild animal that had been injured, quick to react and even faster to bite. There was no doubt in his mind that something had happened to her. He felt a wave of sadness for a second and then shook it off. "What are you doing out here?"

She pursed her lips together and then pointed. He couldn't tell by her body language if she was just telling him to go away for what, but she did answer him. "You know what's over there, don't you?"

Cameron shook his head. "Other than a bunch of dead bodies? No, can't say I frequent the local cemetery."

"Come with me," she said, standing up.

By the way she was moving, he could tell her leg was bothering her, but she wasn't the kind that would ask for help. He followed her as she limped forward about fifty feet and then pointed to the ground. He dropped his gaze, seeing a headstone that read Sarah Schmidt. "What's this? I thought they never found the body?"

Emily nodded, a loose wisp of hair escaping from her ponytail holder. She pushed it behind her ear. "It's empty. I found Vicki here when I got into town a few days ago. I guess she comes here regularly. It's the only way she can feel close to her daughter."

Cameron didn't say anything, the image of the grieving mother sitting on a bench staring at an empty grave forming a lump in his throat. "You have any idea who's responsible or what happened to her? That's why you're here, isn't it?"

Emily looked at him. It felt like her eyes were boring into him as if she was trying to figure out if he could be trusted or not. "Yes, that's why I'm here. I'm waiting on some information that might help me."

Cameron swallowed, realizing the file he had in his cruiser parked less than a two-minute walk away was probably the very thing she needed in order to get justice for the Schmidt family. He was torn. Giving her the file would seal his fate. He no longer would be in law enforcement, that is unless he was able to replace the file without the Sheriff knowing. That was unlikely. Without thinking anymore about it, he said, "I've got something in my cruiser you might want to see."

Emily didn't say anything. She just followed him, only showing a slight limp. Cameron hadn't gotten a good look at her leg when they had been at the Schmidt's house, but the fact that Dr. Zuckerman was stitching it meant that was a pretty deep wound. She was walking pretty well for someone in that much trouble.

When they got back to the cruiser, He unlocked the passenger side door, bent over and pulled the file out from under the bag. Without saying anything, he handed it to Emily. She stared at it for a moment, her eyebrows furrowing together and then looked up at him. "Where did you get this?"

It was one thing to offer her the file, it was something completely different to admit how he got it. Cameron had never been much for deception though, "I found it in the Sheriff's office. He had it in a locked drawer. It's not the same file I showed you a couple days ago."

Emily turned and leaned against his cruiser, taking some weight off her leg as she flipped through the pages. "Wait. This entire file was in a random drawer in the Sheriff's office? Is that what you're telling me?"

He could tell by the way that she said it that she was angry. "Yeah." Cameron couldn't keep the story a secret anymore. "The Sheriff keeps a locked drawer with files in it in his office. I thought there was something wrong with the first file I showed you. It was way too thin for this big of a case. Stockton doesn't get these kinda cases but once every ten or twenty years. I went over to the park service to ask them about their file, but they said they had turned everything over to us. The more I thought about it, the more it didn't make any sense. Then, I remembered that one time when I had stopped in the Sheriff's office to ask him a question, I'd seen the drawer open with files in it. On a hunch, I went in and did a little investigating."

"You decided to break into the Sheriff's office and bust open a locked drawer?"

Cameron could feel his face redden, his eyes dipping to the ground, "It sounds a lot worse when you say it like that."

A smile stretched across Emily's face and she started to laugh. "It is bad." She stared down at the file, flipping through the pages. "This might be worth it, though. Have you taken a look at it?"

Although the smile faded from her face in the matter of seconds, Cameron noticed how beautiful she was when she did smile. For a second, he imagined an Emily that was carefree, not one that had been hurt. He brought himself back to reality. "I flipped through it but didn't take a good look at it."

"I need to sit down and go through this carefully." Emily tilted her head to the side, her eyes narrowing. "You wanna help?"

A lump formed in his throat. The fact that he'd just given a civilian a piece of confidential evidence settled over Cameron. There was no way he could walk away now. He looked at his watch, a gift that his parents had given him when he graduated from the police academy. It was a tactical model with a thick black strap. There was only an hour left to go on his shift. "Okay," he nodded. "I have to get back to the station and clock out after my shift. Why don't you come over to my place at six thirty?"

There was a pause for a moment. Cameron could feel Emily sizing him up. She had no reason to not be suspicious. "Okay."

Cameron had a funny feeling she'd agreed with reservations. He meant her no harm, but Emily didn't know that. He could understand how she felt. Since she had arrived in Stockton, she experienced some of the less friendly side of a small town. "Good. Give me your phone. I'll give you my address and cell phone number. I'll pick up some pizza on the way back."

Emily handed over her phone and Cameron quickly put the information in it for her, saving it as a new contact. He was relatively sure she'd delete it as soon as she hit the county limits on her way back to Chicago, but it didn't matter. He felt like he was doing something that would actually help someone, a feeling he hadn't had in a long time.

28

Alice liked Mike Wilson. How much she liked him, she was still trying to figure out. She walked back into building, carrying the brown paper bag, still wearing her blue latex gloves. In any other setting, someone would probably wonder why she had gloves on when it looked like all she was carrying was her lunch, but not in the research lab.

From the time she was little, Alice Chang had been interested in science and math. Luckily, Alice was gifted at both and didn't need to spend all the hours that her younger brother did trying to learn them. He had just graduated from a literature program at Vanderbilt University. Her parents weren't thrilled about his major, but they had come to realize he wasn't gifted in science like Alice.

When she got to the floor where her lab was, she used her key card to enter the negative pressure room, the door popping open with a slight whoosh. The first time she'd been in a pressurized room she thought it sounded much like something you'd hear on some old sci-fi movie, like Star Trek. What she didn't realize at the time was the air getting sucked out of the room and replaced with fresh air was a good plan. You never knew what airborne particles or biologics might be floating around.

Alice set the bag down on a stainless-steel worktable, one she had just cleaned before running down to meet Mike. They had been what she would call friends for a couple years, although she felt like she still didn't know a lot about him. What she did know, she liked. He was technically savvy, as gifted with computers as she was with biology.

Before she opened the bag, Alice sat down at her workstation, logging into her computer. She was about a year away from finishing her PhD in molecular genetics, a relatively new field that dove deep into the role of DNA in a person's health. There were all sorts of applications, everything from preventing disease before a baby was ever born to solving cold case crimes. From her backpack, she pulled a second laptop out. One night, when she was waiting for an experiment to process, she decided to set up a clone account on her own laptop, one that would allow her to access all the lab equipment and evaluate the results, but without anyone knowing. Mike had actually given her the idea a few weeks before when they were eating pizza and playing video games. Their characters had become cloaked. No one could see them. Mike had suddenly gotten serious, "You know, with all this technology, it's hard to get anything done without prying eyes, if you know what I mean."

That's all he needed to say about it. Though she wasn't as technically proficient as Mike, she had been able to dupe the system by creating a dummy account. If anyone had looked closely, they would realize that the person they thought the results were linked to didn't exist. Alice figured if she ever needed to use the account, it would have to be for an important reason. That reason had arrived today in the brown paper bag Mike handed her. Though she didn't know the circumstances, she did know Mike. If he asked her to do something connected to a case, then it was important.

While the lab machines she needed were warming up, their hum adding to the pulsing of the overhead lights, she got up from her workstation and walked over to the brown bag, stripping off the pair of blue gloves she had been wearing and putting on a fresh set. She opened the bag, drawing the two sides apart and pulled out the plastic bag. The only thing she saw was a pink tennis shoe, one that didn't look current at all. She flipped the bag over, noticing there was mud in the treads, as though someone had been hiking. She looked around the lab, grateful that her research partner was on vacation this week. He wouldn't bother showing up until early next week, so she had the lab to herself.

From underneath the stainless-steel table, she pulled out a tray, some glass slides, slide covers, swabs and the plastic containers that housed them. All the reagents she needed were already lined up near the equipment. She could hear it humming and whirring in the background. Often, one of the most frustrating things about science was waiting for the machines to do their job. She had learned early on to get everything set up so it could be working while she was getting things organized. Less frustrating.

Over the next hour, Alice meticulously swabbed nearly every surface of the shoe, the plastic bag and the paper bag, making notes about where each sample had been taken from. She used a small stainless-steel pick to pull the grit out from the tread of the shoe. As a last step, she donned a headlamp fitted with a black light. She shut off the fluorescent overhead lights in the lab and waited for her eyes to adjust, taking another look at the shoe. Laid out on the table were the laces, which he had put on the separate tray, and the shoe itself. Using the black light, she scanned it, pulling the tongue away from the shoe and staring inside.

Bent over the table, Alice squinted. Then her eye caught something — a short fiber or a hair, that had been pushed through one of the holes used for the laces. Not sure which, she grabbed a pair of forceps and gently pulled it out, laying it on a slide and covering it with a thin glass cover, so the fiber didn't get lost. She marked it down and took one last look. The black light picked up something, some sort of cellular residue. Alice grabbed two swabs, popping the tops off of them. The kind the lab used were sterile and had been soaked in a reagent that would help to identify the sources. She rubbed the damp swabs over the area, quickly snapping the tops back on to avoid contamination.

She stood up, feeling satisfied with her work. Alice reached overhead stretching the kinks out of her shoulders and back. One side effect of being a scientist she hadn't expected was the physical toll it took on her. Mike had mentioned a couple times that the woman he worked for, Emily, had taken up boxing. He had offered to take Alice with him. He had told her that Emily wanted him to go to the gym, but he hadn't. Maybe it was time to take him up on his offer.

Alice sat on a metal stool next to the lab table. The feet made a scraping noise as she pulled it in close, staring at the evidence she had in front of her. She took a look at the list of her notes, updating the information on her laptop so the two logbooks matched. You could never be too careful, she thought, pleased that she had remembered to keep a paper copy as well. She'd give it to Mike with the results. He'd have some way of scanning it and encrypting it. How, she wasn't sure. What she was sure of is that he would have a way of protecting the information if it needed to be protected.

A quiet beep toward the back of the lab told her that the equipment she needed was ready. She put a couple of the samples in the mass spectrometer and then came back to her lab table, picking up a small tray that held the slides she found.

Grabbing the edge of the tray, she picked up the swabs, and took them over to the hooded worktable. In order to get any usable information from the samples, she knew she would need to use a four-step process: extraction, quantification, amplification and capillary electrophoresis. She checked the time on her cell phone. It was going to be a long night.

29

The ache in her leg was worse again. Emily reached into her bag and pulled out a couple more pain pills and an antibiotic. She popped them in her mouth and swallowed them whole. The GPS in her truck was talking to her, showing her the way to Cameron's house.

On the face of it, Stockton was a beautiful city, one that looked like something that came right out of a postcard sold on the side of a road at a little stand offering fresh grown corn and tomatoes. As Emily passed a vast field of soybeans swaying in the wind, she remembered the adage "still waters run deep." That was certainly the case in Stockton. She gripped the wheel a little tighter, sliding her right leg back underneath her and using her left to drive. It was a little awkward, but she was managing it just fine as long as she didn't get into a high-speed chase. That wasn't likely in Stockton. The only thing she was likely to have to speed up to pass would be an Amish buggy on their way into town for their weekly groceries. Rural life was a little different than the hustle and bustle of Chicago.

Cameron's house was further out of town, on the south side, toward the West Virginia border. In the few days she had been in Stockton, Emily hadn't traveled that way yet. It didn't look any different from the rest of Stockton, save for the fact that the houses were a bit more spaced out, with more virgin land and fields than she had seen closer to town. It occurred to her that people who lived in a city like Chicago their whole life never understood how much land was actually available just beyond the city borders, how much space there was to be had if someone wanted it. It was an amazing sight to see, she thought, glancing out the window as she passed what looked to be six or eight draft horses in a pasture. She wondered if they'd finished their day's work and had been put out for the night.

The voice of the GPS caught her attention. She pressed on the brake of the truck and made a left-hand turn on the far side of a white mailbox that leaned precariously over the edge of the road, so close that she wondered if winter plow trucks ever took it out. People didn't get much physical mail anymore, she thought, except for someone like her who got cash in their mailbox every month. She grimaced, her mind focused back on Chicago for just a split second, the smells and sounds of her neighborhood, the feel of Miner curled up next to her in her office, the groan of the old boxing gloves she wore hitting the bag when she was at the gym. Traveling through Stockton had awoken something inside of her, the desire for more space and more peace, but she knew she'd be going back to Chicago, or at least that's how it seemed at the moment.

The jarring of the truck hitting a pothole in Cameron's driveway brought her back to the fact that she was in Stockton. His driveway appeared to lead to nowhere. It seemed that there were a lot of those in Stockton, Nate's being another one. If you wanted to get lost, Stockton was a good place to do it.

A stand of trees moved out of the way enough for her to see a small white house on the right and an old red barn across the driveway on the other side, probably about five hundred feet from the driveway. Neither one looked to be new. In fact, they looked like they might be as old as Stockton itself. Emily shut the truck off and slid down out of the cab, checking her phone. There was no news from Mike. She shook her head, feeling frustrated. At least we have the real file to look at, she thought. She checked to make sure the pistol was still in place on her back. After what happened in the park, she didn't want to be unprepared, especially with her leg wounded. Mobility was definitely an issue if she got herself into a fight.

Emily walked towards the red barn. The barn door was open just enough for her to pass through, the metal rails gliding smoothly. She gave it a little push to make it wide enough to get through. Inside, she could smell the combination of animals and feed. The barn was dark, so she went back outside and walked around it. On the other side of the barn, there was a fence. Off in the distance, she could see a small herd of cows, grazing all in a cluster. There were acres of land in the pasture for the cows to eat from, but they all stayed together. Emily leaned on the fence, hoping it wasn't electrified. Did the little herd stay together out of instinct? One of the cows picked up her head and looked back at Emily from the distance. She moved slowly as though she had all the time in the world, the dark brown color of her coat slightly reddened from the late daylight in the sky. Without a noise, the heifer turned back to her grass and her companions.

The peace on Cameron's farm was palpable. Everything seemed to move in slow motion. Emily took a deep breath and exhaled, feeling the tension leave her, if just for a second. She pulled her phone out of her back pocket, checking the time. It would still take a little time before Cameron got back to the house. She turned from the cows and walked back around the front of the barn and over to the house, stopping at her truck for a moment. Going to the side door, she twisted the knob to see if it would open. It was locked. From out of her pocket, she pulled a small lock picking kit and inserted two tools into the handle, popping the lock in just a few seconds. That wasn't something she had learned in the police academy, but something she had picked up along the way. She'd actually learned how to pick locks from her boxing coach. They had got into a conversation after one workout about their past. Like many men in Chicago, Clarence had gotten in trouble with the law from time to time. "I can pick a lock faster than anybody else in this neighborhood," he said to her at the end of one particularly grueling workout.

"Oh really?" she said, wiping the sweat from her forehead with a towel.

"Want me to show you?"

The two of them walked out the back door of the boxing ring, Clarence locking it behind him. In a moment, he had popped the lock on the back door open again faster than Emily could even get a grip on what he was doing. After that, each one of her lessons included free training on breaking and entering. Standing at Cameron's door now, she was grateful for what Clarence had taught her.

Inside Cameron's house, it smelled like stale coffee. She closed the door behind her, her eyes adjusting to the light. There wasn't a lot to see. It was a small bungalow plopped down on some land near an old barn and some cows. It looked like Cameron had done what every single man did — he bought a giant couch and an even bigger television. The television seemed to take up the majority of the living space in the house. The kitchen was small, but neat. No dishes in the sink. The only evidence that anyone lived in the house or had been there recently was the half pot of cold coffee sitting in the brewer.

After taking a quick cruise through Cameron's house and discovering nothing out of the ordinary, she went back out to her truck to retrieve the file, leaving the door unlocked. Knowing she had the file was like having a burr inside her shoe. She was excited to take a look at it, hoping it would offer the answers she needed. She carried it back toward the house, but instead of going inside, she decided to sit on the small porch that faced the pasture. In the distance, she could see the small group of cows. They had moved out from behind the barn. She imagined they were trying to get to fresh grass. Two of the small group were laying down, resting in the evening sun.

Emily pulled her phone out of her pocket, setting it on a table next to a chair on the porch. She eased herself down, glad to rest her leg and sent a text to Mike, "Any news?"

"No," came the reply.

A wave of frustration pushed at Emily. How was it possible that all these hours had gone by and he didn't know anything yet? The only good news was that she was sure he would let her know as soon as he did. He had a little extra time left in his day, given the fact that Chicago was part of Central time not Eastern time, like Ohio. Hopefully that extra hour would give him time to get some sort of information.

At least she had the file. Emily opened it on her lap, paging through the entirety of it once, trying to get a feel for how it was organized. She knew she'd need to go back through with a fine-toothed comb, probably with Cameron's help, to find something, anything, that would give them an idea what happened to Sarah. The memory of Vicki sitting at the cemetery, staring at her daughter's empty grave was lodged in her mind. How many hours had Vicki spent sitting there, wanting to know that Sarah was either home or resting comfortably in the family plot?

The file was organized almost identically to the copy that Mike had sent her. The typical summary sheets and background information were in the front, followed by pictures and investigator notes. As she flipped towards the back, what she discovered was there was one significant difference — this copy of the file included the state park notes, as well as the Stockton Sheriff's Office notes. The copy Mike had gotten for her didn't have those, or at least not as many as were in the file she now held in her hands.

About the time she got done looking through the file for the first time, she heard the crunch of tires on gravel. A truck pulled up the driveway. Emily looked toward the windshield, her heart skipping a beat, instantly on alert for another attacker. It was Cameron. As he got out of the truck, he called to her, "You found it okay?"

"Yeah, I'm getting used to all these gravel driveways. It's a miracle you can find anything out here."

As Cameron came around, he opened the passenger side door, pulling out a pizza box and a twelve pack of beer. "I got dinner. Hope you like sausage."

"I do," Emily sighed, raising her eyebrows. "That's a lot of beer for two people. You planning on getting me drunk?"

"How did you figure that out?" Cameron smiled. "Actually, I have a couple buddies coming over tomorrow."

As Cameron stepped up on the porch, he glanced at the back door. "I didn't leave that open…"

"I broke in," Emily said, stretching her right leg out in front of her, waiting for him to react. The painkillers had done their job. The heat and ache that were in her leg on her way over to Cameron's house had subsided enough that she felt like she could concentrate.

"You broke in? Is that a Chicago thing?" Cameron smiled, setting the pizza down on a small plastic table between the two of them.

"Kinda."

Cameron disappeared back in the house for a minute, returning with a roll of paper towels and a stack of paper plates. He offered her one of each as he settled into the chair on the porch near her, the hiss of the cap on the bottle breaking through the quiet of the farm. "Did you find anything yet?"

"Not yet. Just getting started." She nodded toward the pasture behind the barn. "I spent a little time over there visiting with your cows."

"You did? I wouldn't have thought a city girl like you would have been interested in farm animals," he said, picking up a piece of pizza and biting the tip off.

Emily closed the file for a moment and set it off to the side, letting the peacefulness of Cameron's farm soak into her. The cicadas and peepers started to make their nightly noises, along with a chorus of leaves rustling quietly in the breeze. She took a bite of the pizza, the tang of the tomato sauce and a light flavor of anise from the sausage filling her mouth. "This is actually good," she said wiping her mouth with a paper towel. She cracked the top of the beer that Cameron had handed her. She decided one would be okay. Any more than that might be too much with the painkillers that Dr. Zuckerman had given her.

"You're surprised about the pizza? Don't tell me you're one of those Chicago pizza snobs," Cameron said, putting his second piece of pizza down and taking a sip of beer.

Emily nodded, wiping the grease off her fingers. "We are a little precious about our pizza in Chicago, that's for sure. I don't really like deep dish, to be honest," she said, setting her own piece back down on the flimsy paper plate and setting the whole thing off to the side, "Too much sauce. Gives me heartburn." She stared out at the barn in the pasture for a minute, "Tell me, what's the plan with the cows? Is that just a hobby?"

Cameron finished chewing the bite of pizza in his mouth and shook his head, "After stealing that file out of the Sheriff's office?" He glanced at the file sitting underneath Emily's pizza, "I have a feeling I might be finding a new career in livestock pretty soon."

Emily furrowed her brows. "So, why help me? You're risking

your job. I lost mine over less than that." She watched him for a minute. He stared out at the pasture. Emily imagined that if she lived on the farm she'd spend a lot of time sitting outside staring at the cows, watching their slow movements as they ate their way from end to end of the pasture. She knew there was more to it than just watching them, the milking and feeding and cleaning up after them probably took a significant amount of time, not to mention the veterinary care. That would explain the relationship Cameron had with Dr. Zuckerman. She could imagine a time when Cameron got his first cow and Dr. Zuckerman came out to give him instructions on how to care for it.

He hadn't answered her question. He just stared off in the distance. A minute went by before he spoke, "I became a police officer because I wanted to help. I'm not sure that the Sheriff is on the same page I am."

Emily figured he was on the right track. From what she had seen of Sheriff Mollohan at Sandy's Restaurant, it certainly seemed like he was more of a career politician than a civil servant, the key word being servant. From his giant hat to his shiny boots, he appeared to be almost a caricature, someone who was more interested in kissing babies and trying the winning slice of apple pie at the yearly fair than he was actually making the community a better place. "I can see that, but you're risking a lot. Why?" She needed to know what she was dealing with — she needed to know if Cameron was helping her for the right reasons, as best she could figure.

Cameron set down a half-eaten piece of pizza, the flimsy white paper plate curling underneath his fingers. He took a sip of beer and leaned back in the plastic chair he was sitting on. "I don't know exactly," he started, staring off in the distance. As Emily's eyes followed where he was looking, she saw that one of the cows in the pasture was starting to lead the group to another section, close to where the fencing made a right angle. "They seem to like to sleep in that spot," Cameron said. He looked back at her, as if he remembered her original question. "I guess the simplest answer is that I've got three sisters. Seeing Vicki Schmidt made me think about my own mom and what might happen to her if she lost one of her kids." He shook his head, "I can't imagine what that woman has been through."

Emily bit the inside of her lip, "You've lived here your whole life, right?" Cameron nodded. "You heard about the case before I arrived in town?" Suspicion flooded Emily, but she waited. Her next move would depend on how he answered the question.

"Yeah, I've lived in Stockton my whole life. I heard about the case, but I didn't really know the case, if that makes sense." He picked up his piece of pizza again and took a bite. "Listen, I'm a simple guy. I enjoy being outside, I like helping people — that's why I took a job in law enforcement. Could never see myself sitting in a cubicle somewhere, not that there's that many of those kinda jobs around here. I just take things as they come. So, to answer your question, no, I hadn't really thought about the ramifications of the case before today."

"And you're willing to risk your job because of that?" Emily looked at the manila file that was sticking out from underneath the pizza box. If Cameron was being honest with her, then a fresh set of eyes would be helpful for the case.

Cameron turned and stared directly at her, "I feel like you're questioning my motives." He suddenly sounded angry.

"I am." Emily wasn't going to back down from asking the hard questions. That was how she got the information she needed.

"I've told you the truth. The Sheriff is a scumbag. I'm not sure I can work for him for the next twenty years. Now either you want my help or you don't. Which one is it?"

Emily nodded, the suspicion that had risen in her seeming to subside. In her years of working cases, she had discovered that sometimes the simplest explanation was the right one. If what Cameron was saying was true, then his love for his family would motivate him to do the right thing by the Schmidt's. In detective work, the experts were always talking about means, motive and opportunity. In her experience, motive was most of the time the critical factor. Means and opportunity would appear if someone was motivated enough. Emily took another bite of pizza, not saying anything for a moment, staring back at the cows. Of the small little herd of seven of them, three of them had already laid down, their thick lips chewing. It was interesting to her they chose the closest corner to the barn and the house they could find as the place they wanted to rest. She realized they must have felt safe there. Someday, she hoped to find a place she felt the same. After wiping her hands on a paper towel, she pulled the file from underneath the pizza box, laying it on her lap. "Okay, let's get started."

Over the next couple of hours, Emily walked Cameron through the information they had. She had at least seen part of it with the help of Mike's contact, whoever that had been. "How did your friend get a copy of the file already if it's never been digitized?" Cameron asked, at one point when Emily handed him another five pages to read.

"I've learned not to ask."

As the sun began to set, it became harder to read the print in the file. Cameron looked at her, "I can't really read this very well anymore. How about if we go inside and spread this out on the kitchen table?"

Emily nodded, carrying the papers into the house, following behind Cameron who had picked up the pizza box, paper towels and the rest of the plates.

As they went inside, Cameron flipped on lights, bathing the small house in a yellow tinged glow. Seeing the house at night made Emily realize it was homey. It wasn't the same worn brick as her bungalow, which had been built in the 1920s, but Cameron's house was friendly, in a way that Vicki's hadn't been.

It was as if the ghost of Sarah's loss, Vicki's destroyed marriage, and her estrangement from her other daughter had taken over the house just a few minutes from where they were now.

Without saying anything, Cameron pointed to the kitchen table, picking up some magazines. Emily glanced at the titles as he stacked them, putting them on the kitchen counter. "Rural Livestock Management," "Natural Breeding for Livestock," "Agricultural Business Today." "That's some serious reading you have going there," she said, handing him a copy of "The Farmer's Almanac."

Cameron sighed. "My family thinks I'm weird," he said, laying the almanac on the top of the pile he had assembled on the kitchen counter. "I don't know why, but I have a passion for livestock and being outdoors. I don't know," he frowned, looking towards Emily, "for some reason, it seems real to me. So much of life doesn't seem real anymore."

Emily had finally heard what she needed to hear from Cameron. He was identical to Mike Wilson, just in another way. She liked people who thought outside of the box, who questioned why things were the way they were. She had gone through the darkness of questioning her life when she had lost her job. In some respects, she knew it was one of the best things that could have happened to her. It caused her to question all the things that people so quickly adopted — social media, technology, social constraints. What she discovered was she was most interested in people who were true and honest. Unfortunately, she had learned very few people had that quality. She looked up at Cameron, as if seeing him for the first time. "If that's what you've been called to do, then by all means. Maybe you've been waiting for a reason to walk away from Sheriff Mollohan." She held up the file, "Maybe this was just your way of doing it."

Regardless of the revelation she had about Cameron, they needed to get to work. Cameron didn't say any more, going into the kitchen and starting a pot of coffee. The smell of the hot water dripping over the grounds filled the small kitchen with an aroma that seemed to link much of life together, her own morning routine, the pots of coffee Vicki Schmidt drank endlessly, and now the work that she and Cameron had in front of them. "Have you found anything out of the ordinary yet?" she asked as Cameron set a mug in front of her.

"Nope, I'm just getting the gist of the case." He sat down, frowning, "What I don't understand is why the state park notes aren't better integrated with the case? I mean, they all work together on an incident like this, right? It almost looks like the state park had their own records."

Emily tilted her head to the side, shuffling through a couple more pages, "I wouldn't say that it's completely out of the ordinary. Often, when more than one agency is working a case, they have their own protocols." She handed him another pile of papers. "Let's get to work on these and then see what we need to do next."

The next several hours passed quickly, Emily only taking one break to go outside to her truck to retrieve more painkillers and antibiotics. The night had descended in a thick blanket over Stockton with hardly any stars in the sky. Though Emily had been there for a few nights, it was the first time she'd been away from the center of town. It was a stranger expierence than she anticipated, the vastness of the sky stretching over top of her. She took a couple of deep breaths, enjoying the cool air filling her lungs.

As she limped back to the house, she realized her leg was starting to feel better. Whatever Dr. Zuckerman had done to it earlier that day must have been working. Earlier that day felt like a million years ago, she thought, wrapping her fingers around the handle to the door back into Cameron's house. When she walked in, she saw him frowning, staring at a page in the file. "Have any idea what these numbers are?" he said, sliding a piece of paper towards her.

It looked to be a photocopy of the slip of paper she had found underneath the edge of the frame of the bed in the hotel. She shook her head, "I have someone working on that. Did you find anything else?"

Cameron shook his head. "There are a lot of pages in this file, but very little information." He stood up, carrying his mug back to the kitchen, "More coffee?"

Emily nodded.

As he brought the pot of coffee over and filled her cup, he said, "What I don't understand is why all the secrecy about this file if there's really nothing in it? There has to be something here we are missing."

Emily knew he was right. It made no logical sense to have a sanitized version of the file accessible to the public and the full file hidden away in a locked drawer in the Sheriff's office if there was no value to it. It just didn't make any sense. Emily leaned back in her chair for a second, tilting her head left and right, trying to work the kinks out of her neck. She hadn't felt this stonewalled in years. Most of the time when she worked a case, the person who did it was pretty obvious. This situation reminded her more of the cold cases she used to work when she was part of the Chicago PD. No leads, little information. The whole environment around the case seemed foggy. The only thing that was crystal clear was that Sarah Schmidt was missing and Vicki Schmidt was paralyzed by grief. All of a sudden, she had an idea. "Let's try looking at this a different way." Emily stood up, making piles of the papers in the file. "Let's put all the pages that are reports and notes over here," she pointed to the back part of the table. "Let's try actually looking at the case."

The technique was something that her supervisor, Detective Aldo, had taught her years before. Sometimes the visual clues for a case were stronger than the written reports. As they laid out the images on the table, there were too many of them. Without saying anything Cameron went and got a roll of masking tape. He started taping them to the wall, one after the other, lining them up. Emily sat back down in her chair as he did, not wanting to be on her feet too much. Her eyes scanned each picture. The pink shoe found at the side of the trail, the footprints on the trail, the picture of someone that Vicki saw was Sarah months later in the back of what looked to be a van — there had to be two dozen or more images by the time Cameron put them up.

When he was done, he sat down next to Emily. The way they were sitting reminded her of being at a sporting event. They were staring at the same thing, both caught up in their thoughts. Cameron was the first to speak. He stood up, pointing at the picture of Sarah that was found at the gas station eight months after her disappearance, "Is that really her? I mean, if that is her, then the fact that a picture emerged eight months later means she could still be alive, right?"

Emily shook her head, "Not necessarily. We have no way of knowing when that picture was actually taken. The only information we actually have about that image is that it was found eight months later. The picture could have been taken that same afternoon." Emily stared at the picture again, the face of Sarah staring back at her. That they had gotten no traction on this case in several days was eating at her. "What I do know is that is Sarah."

Cameron looked back at her, his eyes narrowing, "Are you sure? How do you know?"

"I just know. I have proof. It's her."

Having the issue of whether that was Sarah or not settled, Cameron sat back down in the chair next to Emily. They sat in silence for a few more minutes. Revelations about this case seem to be few and far between. Emily stood up, feeling the frustration nipping at her. She kept coming back to the one mysterious fact in the case, the reality that Sheriff Mollohan had hidden this file in his office. Why? Even with the dull ache of the wound in her leg, Emily started to pace, watching the pictures as she moved past them. Her eyes kept settling on the picture of Sarah, bound in what looked to be the back of a truck. For a second, she thought her eye caught something, but then she wasn't sure. Emily picked up her phone and walked over to the image, opening the camera function. Holding it in front of the picture of Sarah, she zoomed in, scanning the corners of the picture. She wasn't sure what she had seen, but there had to be something there. There just had to be...

30

"I was just about to call you," Alice said when she picked up the phone.

It wasn't the first time Mike had texted to see the progress on the bag of evidence he passed off to her earlier that afternoon. He seemed to be calling every couple of hours, anxiously awaiting news of what was in the bag, at least what the eye couldn't see.

"You were? Do you have news?" The words came out quick and snipped.

Alice carried her phone through the lab. Mike had set her up to use a VOIP line, one that couldn't be tracked, so she felt like she could speak freely. Somehow, he managed to bounce the signal all over the world. Anyone who wasn't standing right in front of her would have no idea who she was talking to or what they were talking about. Mike's quirkiness was sweet in a kind of paranoid way, she thought, walking back to the stainless-steel lab table, grabbing a few papers she had just pulled off of one of the machines. As she sat down, the stool at the lab table giving out a quiet squeak, she said, "I do."

"Did you find anything?"

As much as Mike was an expert on technology, Alice was an expert in science. She could barely contain her excitement. She loved it when information emerged from even simple testing. But what she thought as simple testing was highly complex to most people, so she spoke slowly, "So, you know that inside of the brown paper bag was a plastic bag that contained a pink shoe."

"Yes," Mike conceded. "Did you find anything else?"

Alice nodded, "As I told you a couple of hours ago, I retrieved a few samples from the shoe. This included a couple of hairs, some residue, some dirt or other organic matter that was in the tread of the shoe and a couple other miscellaneous samples that I wasn't sure what to do about. I spent the last few hours running identification tests and DNA sequencing." What Mike didn't know about Alice's work is that she was part of the team that was testing a brand-new DNA sequencer, one that could get results when needed, and just under three hours. The current technology took twenty-four to forty-eight hours, which in many cases, could lead to delays in medical treatments and even in the arrest of suspects who had DNA evidence as part of their case. The application for the new technology was wide. It was one of the things that excited Alice most about the work that she was doing.

"Did you tell me a while ago that DNA sequencing could take a couple of days?"

"Yep, but what I didn't tell you is that my lab has some newfangled equipment that can make things happen a lot faster than that."

"What kind of equipment?"

Alice could almost see the scowl on Mike's face. He was known to do that when he was skeptical. "I could tell you, but then I'd have to kill you. Suffice it to say, I have confidence in the results." She took a sip of water from the bottle she had brought into the lab earlier, her throat drive from the environmental controls in the lab. She cleared her throat, "Okay, the samples resulted in some normal things, some things you might expect. Like the dirt in the bottom of the shoe, for instance."

"What about it?"

"Well, if you'd let me finish, I was about to tell you that the organic material that was stuck in the bottom of the shoe was dirt that's common to the Midwest. Based on the composition of clay, cinders and the spores of a few oak trees that I found, I would guess that it came from somewhere in southern Ohio, West Virginia or maybe even southern Indiana. I'd need a larger sample in order to get you more information than that." Alice stopped for a second, wondering who the shoe belonged to, but it really wasn't her business to ask. Her relationship with Mike had moments of feeling tenuous, only because of his level of privacy and suspicion.

"Did you find anything more specific? What about the DNA?"

Alice cleared her throat, taking another sip of water, "So, that's where things start to get very interesting. There were a few samples of organic material, other than what you would normally find outdoors on the shoe."

"Did you find any fingerprints anywhere?"

"If you just let me get through one topic at a time, I'll give you all the information you could ever want in about two minutes. Think you can be patient that long?"

"Sorry. Just feeling a little under the gun on this one."

Alice scowled. Now she had a better idea of how he felt when he was trying to explain a technology to her she didn't understand. "One thing at a time. No, there were no fingerprints I could find on any of the bags. I checked them inside and out. There were a couple partial fingerprints, but not enough information to run them." She stood up from the stool she was sitting on and started to pace. "So then, I turned to the other methods I have of finding biologic information. I spent a couple hours just going over the shoe, pulling samples off of it. That's where things got interesting." She stopped in front of the lab table for a moment, taking a look at her notes. "I found a hair wrapped around one of the laces and pushed through one of the holes in the shoe. I also found some sort of other fluid that I tested."

"What kind of fluid?"

"Semen." Alice waited for a moment, letting the idea that the shoe had been part of some sort of a sex crime set in. "There were also a couple smudges of blood."

"How did you see those? I didn't see any of that when I looked at the shoe."

"Ultraviolet light. I think the color of the shoe obscured some of that from the natural eye, but once I lit it up, it was easy to see." Alice sat on the lab stool again, flipping the pages in her notes. "So, what I have figured out is that the hair and one of the blood samples belongs to a white female. I ran it against the CODIS database but got no hits. I tried a couple of private databases as well, but nothing there. Whoever it is isn't someone who has any DNA records on file." Alice hoped Mike wasn't disappointed with that part of the report, but she felt a surge of excitement as she got to the last part of the information she had to tell him, drumming her fingers on the stainless steel surface of the table. "The fluid came back with something more specific. I ran the DNA sequencing and then sent it over to CODIS. We got a hit, but don't get too excited yet."

"What do you mean?"

"Well, when I ran the DNA, it came back with a hit, but not a direct one. The databases are becoming more sophisticated, so I can tell based on the results if it's a direct hit with an individual or someone in their family."

"I've never heard of that before."

"Probably because it's a relatively new field, one that's in its infancy, called genetic genealogy." Alice stood up and started to pace, as if she was in front of a lecture hall of wide-eyed freshman, "Here's the way it works: Each one of us carries a certain amount of DNA from the generations previous to us. It's only a portion, but it can at least send us in the right direction and help us narrow down what family someone's DNA has come from. Now, whether they are a brother, sister or cousin, that remains to be seen."

"What's the deal with the sample? Who is it?"

"That's what I'm trying to tell you — I don't know. What the database came back with is a partial hit on a relative. The sample I got back is related to someone named Sam Walters. His DNA was in the database because he was picked up for armed robbery." Alice leaned over her computer and pulled up the records she had saved to tell Mike about. "I'll send you a copy. The important thing to know is the fluid on the shoe is related to someone who is related to Sam Walters. It's someone in his genetic line. I don't know who, you'd have to consult with a genetic detective to figure that part out. But whoever the fluid belongs to is part of Sam Walters's family."

31

Initially, Mike wasn't all that overly excited about the information Alice had given him. It all sounded way too vague. After they hung up, he waited for a minute or two, the information that she had collected arriving to him over a secure email link. He wanted to take the time to go over the information and have it all packaged and ready for Emily, but he knew she would want the information sooner rather than later, even if it was one o'clock in the morning.

He picked up his phone and called her after doing a few minutes of research. He bit his lip, wishing he had more concrete information for her. "You awake?" he said, standing up in her kitchen and walking back and forth beside the table where his laptop and papers were spread out.

"Yeah. I'm up. We're looking at the original file from the case."

"We're?"

"Yeah, me and one of the local sheriffs. He managed to get it for me."

Mike felt a whisper of disappointment. He was the one that

was in charge of getting information for Emily. Who this other guy was, he wasn't sure, but he didn't like it. He hadn't run a background check on him or had any information about him. He could be a plant. "Emily, I'm worried…"

She cut him off, "Don't start with me. I'm not in the mood. What's going on?"

They'd known each other long enough that Emily knew what his objections would be before he ever said them. "I have the results back on the shoe. Do you want them now or should I wait until the morning?"

"Now. I'm gonna put you on speaker so Cameron can hear what you're saying."

"Okay." Mike could hear Emily in the background telling whoever Cameron was that Mike was her technical consultant, and he had information for them.

A low voice came on the line, "Nice to meet you, Mike. Sorry it's not in person."

The voice sounded pleasant enough, but even Jeffrey Dahmer had a nice voice, Mike thought. It was Emily's hide, not his. "Yeah, nice to meet you, too," he said awkwardly. "So, I had a friend of mine run some tests on the information that we got earlier." He wanted to be as vague as possible, still not trusting that whoever the person was with Emily had good intentions."

"What did they find?"

"Well, she found some organic material that looks like it belongs to the side of the road or somewhere outdoors near where you are. It was a combination of dirt, cinders, and some tree spores — I think oak."

"Where did she find that?" Emily asked.

"In the tread." He didn't want to say shoe. At least if he said tread, it could be a tire.

"Anything else?"

Mike paced in the kitchen, turning every few steps to go back the other direction. "My friend ran some DNA sequencing on a few other samples she found on the shoe," he said the word, even though he didn't want to, "and she found some organic material."

"What kind of organic material?"

He could hear the questions in Emily's voice. "She found a hair, some blood and some man juice."

"Man juice?"

"You know what I mean. Anyway, when she ran the test, the first one came back to a white female, but there's nothing in the DNA databases that my friend has access to that gave her a match."

Emily didn't let him finish, "Did she run it through CODIS?"

"Yeah, and a couple other databases, but nothing."

"What kind of hair was it?"

"I don't know, brown?"

"Sarah Schmidt had brown hair. If we got you a sample of Vicki's DNA — the mom — do you think your friend could run it to see if there is a connection?"

Mike thought for a second. He didn't want to burn Alice out, but running one more sample didn't seem like a big deal, at least not for this big of a case. Maybe if he told her what she was working on, she might want to do it, "I can ask. I think she'd help."

"What about the other sample?"

"Well, that's where things get a little interesting. My friend was able to run the DNA and got a hit, though not a direct one."

"What do you mean?"

"I guess that some sort of relative popped up in the database, but it's not a direct match to the person that left their sample on the shoe, if you know what I mean."

"So, what you're saying is that it's a relative, but we don't know who the actual person is?"

Mike nodded. "Exactly. She sent a name to me along with the guy's criminal record. She said we need a genetic detective to figure out how they were related, but she said it's definitely somebody in that family."

"Why was the guy in the database?" It was the first time Cameron had said anything during his conversation with Emily. Mike wasn't sure how he felt about that. Clearly, the guy was still listening. Maybe he was the strong, silent type. Mike didn't know.

"Armed robbery."

"That makes sense," Emily said. "Most departments now grab a DNA sample when they book someone along with fingerprints. It's just another layer of information that can be used to either convict or acquit someone." There was a pause for a second, "Who's the guy?"

"Sam Walters."

Silence hung in the air for a second. Mike wasn't sure what to make of it. He could hear some murmuring in the background at Emily's end of the conversation but couldn't quite make out what they were saying. He couldn't wait any longer, "Do you know him?"

Cameron spoke first, "I just told Emily that Sam Walters is the son of one of the most prominent community members here, Bucky Walters. It's his oldest son. Hasn't been around in a long time, though. From what I heard, he left about ten years ago. Moved somewhere north in a big city. Can't remember which one, though."

Emily jumped into the conversation, "But, Mike, you said it's a relative of Sam's, correct? It's not Sam we're looking for?"

"From my understanding of what my friend said, yes, that's the case. She couldn't tell me if it was an uncle or cousin or who it was, just that it was a relative."

"If it's a relative, that doesn't leave us with too many options. We'll get back to you," Emily said.

As Mike put the phone down, he slumped down in the chair, wishing there was more he could do. Opening up his laptop, Mike mumbled, "There's gotta be something here that I'm missing…"

32

As Emily ended the call with Mike, she turned to Cameron. "This all centers around the Walters family. What do you know about them?"

Cameron sat back down at the kitchen table, resting his forearms across the wooden surface, "Well, I know the Sheriff spends a lot of time out there with Bucky. He's one of the Sheriff's main donors. I think the family has three boys. Sam is one of them. The middle child, David, he moved out of town, I think. He's more my age."

"You said there's three?" Emily wanted him to finish his thought.

"Yeah, Benny." Cameron rubbed his forehead, "He's younger, probably about Sarah Schmidt's age. I think he's married with a couple of kids of his own now. Works for his dad at the lumber mill. I see him around town from time to time. He hangs out at Sandy's Restaurant."

Emily popped up out of the chair she'd been sitting in and started to pace, being careful not to put too much weight on her bad leg. The information was coming in fast and furious and she wanted to make sure that she was drawing the right conclusions. "So, what we're saying is that whoever took Sarah Schmidt is related to the Walters family?"

"Hold on for a sec, how is it that your tech guy in Chicago has the shoe?" Cameron stared at Emily.

"Oh, that," she sighed. "I got a call from Mike this morning, while Dr. Zuckerman was working on me. Mike's taking care of my dog while I'm here." Talking about her private life caused a stretch of discomfort across Emily's chest. "He called me, all frantic, because he went out to grab the mail and someone had left a brown paper bag by the front door. It had a shoe in it that matched the one in the picture, the same one that Vicki has at her house." Emily pointed at the image that was still taped on Cameron's wall from the police file. "Apparently, someone wanted to get a message to me that they know where I'm from. Probably trying to get me off the case."

"I guess it didn't work, huh?"

"No. You were talking about Bucky Walters's youngest son, Benny?"

"Yeah," Cameron furrowed his brow. "As I said, he's about the same age as Sarah, although I'm not exactly sure. He got into a bit of trouble when he was younger, then his dad sent him off to college, from what I heard. He's been back here ever since, the only one that was interested in running the lumber mill. Not sure he had much of a choice."

It was Emily's turn to furrow her brow, "What do you mean by that?"

"Well, from what I heard, Bucky has been insistent that one of the kids take over the lumber mill. He's getting up there in age and doesn't want to work forever. My guess is he's more interested in making sure that what he's built gets passed on to someone in the family so the company doesn't have to be sold to some stranger. From what I heard from the other guys at work, Sam was always troubled and David was never interested — more bookish if you know what I mean.

Benny was really the only choice Bucky had for running the business."

Emily needed to know more about Benny, particularly his age. She sent a quick text to Mike who responded right away that he would get back to her in a few minutes.

"What was that about?" Cameron said, nodding at her phone.

"Just asking Mike to do a background search on the Walters family for us." Emily started to pace again, the next steps unfolding in front of her like dominoes dropping in a line after the slightest touch. "If we think that someone in the Walters family is the perpetrator, then some of the things we've heard make sense. Like, the fact there's been a rumor going around that everyone in town knows who did it. Prominent families tend to have big mouths." Emily thought back to the time when her father-in-law, Anthony, had to silence someone in his organization who had developed the habit of getting drunk and talking loudly at the local bars. She remembered him saying over dinner one night, "It's not good for business." She remembered how awkward she felt at the time given the fact she was a sworn law enforcement officer, but the simple fact was Anthony hadn't admitted to anything at all. He knew where the murky depths of obscurity were, what he could say and what he couldn't.

"If their ages were about the same, that might make sense, too," Cameron said, walking into the kitchen and filling a glass with water. "Want one?"

Emily shook her head no. "From the pictures I've seen of Sarah, she was a beautiful girl. Maybe he had his eye on her in addition to Nate and that was why he went after her."

"It's all conjecture unless we can prove something." Cameron came back to the table and sat down.

"I know. What else do you know about Benny?" For some reason, Emily's mind had locked on Benny as the target. It seemed natural, given the fact that he was approximately the same age as Sarah. She could imagine his frustration at being thrust into the role of having to save the family business, especially if that wasn't his dream. Her ex-husband, Luca, had suffered with some of the same issues. Although his dad had happily paid for him to go to architecture school, there were ways he was responsible for the family business that he never talked to Emily about. He couldn't. It wasn't just because she was in law enforcement, but because she wasn't family, at least not blood. Emily wondered if Benny was suffering under some of the same family weight and expectation that Luca had been. Ultimately, it had driven Luca to drink and chase skirts. She wondered if it had driven Benny to do something worse.

Before she could say any of that out loud to Cameron, her phone chirped. It was Mike. "Here's some basic information on the Walters family. They've been in Stockton for generations. Started at the lumber mill more than a hundred years ago. Three boys in the family — Sam, David and Benny. Only Benny is near your location. Currently married with two kids. Ran his finances. There are a lot of charges to a local motel. Wondering if he has a girl on the side?"

It felt like the sun shining after a long week of rain. Emily leaned back in her chair, thinking through the information. "Looks like you might've been right about Benny," she said to Cameron.

"Was that your tech guy?"

Emily nodded, "Yeah, he said that of the boys in the Walters family, it looks like Benny would be the only one who was a likely suspect." Emily's mind raced ahead. What if Benny was the one who'd taken Sarah? Was it possible he had her stashed somewhere still? Emily had read about a case solved in northern Ohio where three women were kept by a kidnapper for more than ten years, each of them shackled to a wall and having to succumb to his whims whenever he felt like it. Two of the three, on the day they were rescued, left the house with children in tow. Was it possible that Sarah was suffering the same fate? Emily's stomach turned. In some ways, she hoped Sarah was dead. Suffering through that kind of torment might be more than someone's spirit could ever recover from. With the lumber yard and the mill attached, it was possible that Benny had Sarah in one of their remote outbuildings that no one ever bothered to check on. He could have even moved her from place to place, if he was the person that had taken her. They needed proof. They needed to get it quickly before anything else happened.

The ache in her leg reminded her it was probably time to take more painkillers. Having the knowledge there was actually someone she could look at as a suspect gave her hope. Her mind wanted to keep going, but her body was demanding rest. They needed a plan. "If it is Benny, we need proof."

Cameron nodded, "We do. How are we going to tie him to the DNA results your friend got?"

Emily knew that for her own sake, she needed to know for sure if Benny's DNA matched what Mike's friend had isolated on the shoe. In all reality, she could take care of the problem, but she knew that wouldn't allow her to sleep at night. That was one of the promises she had made herself when she decided to work on off-the-books cold cases. She'd only take action if she was sure, really sure. If she ended up getting caught, she wanted to know what she'd done had merit. "We need to get a DNA sample from Benny." Emily looked at the time on her phone. It was just after two o'clock in the morning. Their best shot would be to take action after daybreak. "Do you know where he lives?"

Cameron nodded, stretching his arms up over his head. "Yeah, I do. What are you thinking?"

Emily stood up, reaching into her bag and taking out the painkillers and antibiotics again. Washing them down with a swig of water, she said, "I think we should spend a little time tailing him in the morning. I gotta get back to the hotel. I need some sleep."

Cameron squinted at her, "After you just slugged down painkillers and after the day you had? Nah, you can sleep in my bed. I'll sleep on the couch tonight. That way we can get an early start."

Emily chewed the inside of her lip. She wasn't sure what to say. Someone had broken into her hotel room, that was a fact. She didn't want to go back and stay at Vicki's house. It was too late. The idea of waking the woman up in the middle of the night to crash on her couch again, even though she was sure it would be fine with Vicki, didn't sound like a good plan. "All right, but I'd prefer to sleep on the couch."

Cameron shrugged, "Have it your way." A minute later, he came out carrying an extra pillow and blanket. "Here you go. I'll see you in the morning. We should probably get a pretty early start."

Emily nodded, "Will do." She set her alarm for five, not sure she would need it. They were so close to the end of the case, she wasn't sure sleep would come.

33

Somehow, Emily had drifted off to sleep, only the creak of the door opening and closing rousting her. Cameron had gone outside. In the fog of painkillers that were wearing off, she realized he would need to go out and tend his livestock before they took off for the day. She swung her legs down onto the floor, testing the pain in her leg. It had subsided, but she wasn't eager to un-bandage the work that Dr. Zuckerman had done. She blinked a couple of times before hearing the door to the house slam. "Emily, are you up?"

She could tell by the tone in Cameron's voice that something was wrong, very wrong. He was standing silhouetted in the door, the morning light just breaking over the horizon, framing him from behind. "Yeah, I just woke up. What's wrong?"

"Someone got to my herd."

By the tone of his voice, Emily could tell he was angry, but she wasn't sure what he was saying, "What?"

"Three of my cows are dead."

The word settled over Emily like fog rolling in off the coast. The progress they'd made on the case all of a sudden seem to be both dampened and accelerated at the same time. "What are you saying?"

"I'm telling you, someone got to my cows. Three of them don't die just for nothing." The door slammed behind him.

Emily got up, slipping her boots on and pulling her jacket off of the back of the chair where she had left it in his kitchen. As she followed him outside, the sun sending rays of light streaming over the field and the barn, she saw that Cameron was already halfway back to the herd. The cows that were remaining stood staring in Cameron's direction as if they were looking for answers. It took Emily another minute to reach Cameron, who had hopped the fence and was kneeling down by one of the chestnut colored cows, stroking its coat. Emily stopped at the fence and looked for a second. Three of the cows we are laying on their sides, their tongues hanging out of their mouths. "They've been poisoned," Cameron said, standing up. "I'd bet my life on it. Someone is trying to send us a message."

A wash of anger ran over Emily. The secrets of Stockton County were being threatened, and someone didn't like it, someone who knew she was with Cameron and also knew what was important to him. But she knew she needed to be careful not to let her emotions get out of control, "You're sure that someone poisoned them. It couldn't be anything else?"

Before Emily could get the full sentence out, Cameron already had his phone in his hand, "Doc? Hey, listen, sorry to bother you so early. I came out to check on the cows and I've got three that are down." There was a pause in the conversation, "No, I think they're gone. Any chance you can come out here and tell me why?" There was another pause, "Thanks. I'll be here." He looked at Emily, "Doc will be here in ten minutes. He was just headed to another call, but he's going to come here first."

Emily didn't know what to say. She knew Cameron was attached to his cows. It wasn't something she understood, save for her attachment to Miner, but she did understand the pain of losing something that was important to you. In the few minutes that it took for Dr. Zuckerman to drive over to the farm, rage inside of Emily started to build. Who were these people that thought they could protect their secrets by destroying the lives of others?

Neither she nor Cameron said anything, only the grind of gravel on truck tires breaking the silence as Dr. Zuckerman's truck pulled up, the cab silver, the back of it equipped with the white compartments that held all of his supplies. He got out of the truck and nodded to both of them, hopping the fence with a surprising amount of agility. He knelt down by one of the cows and then walked over to the other two. "I don't need to do a blood test here, Cameron. No reason to put you through that. I can already tell you they've ingested something toxic. What? Not exactly sure, but I can tell by the color of their tongues and the broken blood vessels in their eyes that whatever it was, was pretty powerful. My guess," he said, brushing off his coveralls, "is that somebody gave them a big dose of Rompun." Dr. Zuckerman looked toward Emily, "That's a heavy-duty tranquilizer used on large animals. Doesn't take much to calm them down, and just a little more will kill them." The vet looked back at Cameron, "You want me to run a blood test to be sure?"

Cameron shook his head no, his face ashen. "That won't be necessary. Nothing I can do about it now."

Dr. Zuckerman walked back towards the fence and climbed back over, "One of the farmers just outside the city has some calves he's ready to sell. They're really nice. Shoot me a text if you want the information. I'm sorry, Cameron."

Emily had expected Dr. Zuckerman to be enraged or at least slightly perturbed that someone had killed three of Cameron's cows, but she guessed that in his line of business he had to be like Switzerland — as neutral as possible. In reality, there was nothing he could do for the cows now. They were long gone. As his truck pulled out of the driveway, Emily looked at Cameron, who was texting someone on his phone. He looked back at her, "The truck will be here to get them in a little while."

"Are you okay?" Emily said, surprised at the words coming out of her mouth. She didn't really know Cameron and wasn't really fond of cows, but she could imagine how she would feel if something happened to her dog, especially if it was of the unnatural sort.

"No, I'm going to get whoever did this," he said, his cheeks reddening. "You don't come onto someone's land and kill their livestock because you're trying to hide something."

"Seems like there is a lot of hiding in Stockton," Emily said, turning on her heel and walking back towards the house.

"Where're you going?" Cameron called, stepping up and over the fence.

"To tail Benny. You coming?" They needed to get back to work if Emily had any hopes of returning to Chicago and resolving this case anytime soon. She was gritting her teeth, which sent a sharp pain up the side of her head. Someone knew they were working the case. They knew she had spent the night at Cameron's house. They probably also knew Cameron had the file. They just weren't bold enough to come through the front door. Emily had no respect for people who did business like that, people who would hurt innocent animals or take innocent lives but never deal with their own problems head on. She could feel the heat building in her system, the same anger she felt when she'd been accused of taking money as a bribe to pass over a case. She realized that Cameron was probably feeling the same way that she did — violated, furious. He had every right to if someone had poisoned his cows.

As Emily got into the truck, Cameron slid in next to her. "Where're am I going?" she said, throwing the truck into drive, a spray of gravel being thrown off of the rear wheels. Cameron didn't say anything, just pointed.

As they drove, Emily glanced at Cameron once or twice, trying to judge his mindset. His face was set, hard as stone, filled with anger. She hadn't realized he would be that kind of guy, the kind that had a temper. From every interaction she'd had with him he was easy-going, almost to the point of what she thought was being passive. In that moment, she realized that he was more like her than maybe she wanted to admit. He was someone who had worked within the system until the system turned on him. She knew how he felt. When the system turned on her, they snapped cold metal cuffs around her wrists. His reckoning had just happened this morning. She knew he would never be the same.

As they passed through town, Cameron pointed out a street, "Benny lives up there. If we park over here, behind the store, we should be able to see him come down the street."

Emily turned the truck in behind a store that looked to be abandoned. There was no sign on the front and no evidence of anything inside the windows. She backed the truck into a spot, threw it into park and then cut the engine, straightening out her injured leg. Emily had forgotten to take her painkillers before they left, the shock of dealing with Cameron's cows making her forget. Frowning, she realized she was a little surprised that Dr. Zuckerman hadn't asked her how she was feeling, but he was probably all too eager to leave the farm, given the look on Cameron's face. People like Dr. Zuckerman needed to stay out of the fray. There was no telling what a powerful family like the Walters could do to his practice if they got wind of the fact he was interfering. That was, if it was the Walters family.

Emily glanced at Cameron, who had leaned back in the passenger seat. He was looking at something on his phone and glancing up at the road. "Who do you think did that to your cows?" She knew the question could open a firestorm, but she didn't care. She needed to know his thoughts.

"There's really only two options. It was either the Sheriff or it was the Walters family, if that's who took Sarah. If it wasn't the Walters family, then I have no idea who would have a big enough beef with me that they'd want to kill three of my cows." He rubbed his forehead with his hand, suddenly looking really tired to Emily, "I mean, who does that? Why would you kill some innocent animals because you're upset about an investigation?"

Emily looked at him, her eyebrows raised. "Apparently, someone who would like to encourage you to not hang around with me anymore."

Cameron scowled and shook his head, "That's not gonna happen. You're right, there are too many secrets in Stockton. Somebody needs to open the door to the closet and let the bones fall out. At this point, it might as well be me."

Emily knew that in reality, it wasn't going to be Cameron who got justice for Sarah's family. That was her job, but if he felt like he needed to think that way to make himself feel better about the loss of his livestock, then so be it. Emily didn't care. She picked up her phone and sent a quick text to Mike, "Trying to get another DNA sample. What's the fastest way to process it? Things are heating up here."

Even though it was early, Mike responded right away. Emily was never sure if he actually slept or didn't. "Is there somewhere nearby that has a lab? That tech can probably send the results to my friend."

Emily frowned. She was surprised Mike would suggest getting someone else involved, someone he didn't know. "Not an option. Gotta keep this quiet, but I'm going to need them right away. Can you get your friend to come down here?"

There was silence on the other end of their text conversation for a couple of minutes. "No can do. She's on a big project.

If you get something overnighted to me. I'll get it to her. That's the best I can do."

Emily knew that DNA testing could take time. Mike was right, although Emily wasn't happy about it. It would be faster if they got a sample overnighted to him and then had his friend run the results. She sighed. She didn't want to spend one more minute in Stockton, let alone another day or two. But at least she could see the light at the end of the tunnel, that was if Benny was who they were looking for. If it wasn't, then Emily was afraid she would be getting back in her truck and heading home without solving the case. That seemed like an impossible decision to make at the moment as the memory of the poor dead cows crossed her mind. The idea that someone had hopped the fence and injected three innocent animals with enough drugs to kill them just to make a point caused bile to surge in Emily's throat. Who were these people? Emily knew about the darker side of justice from her father-in-law, but even the Mafia had rules about innocent women, children and animals. You didn't touch them. You just didn't do it.

Before she had a chance to think any more about what had happened, Cameron spoke up. "There," he pointed, "that's him leaving."

An enormous black SUV passed them on the street. Emily only got a brief look at the driver, a man wearing a baseball cap and holding a cell phone up to his ear. She started the truck and pulled out slowly, not wanting to attract attention. Up ahead, he was stopped at the light, his blinker on, making a right turn.

Emily saw Cameron crane his neck, his gaze following the black SUV. He said, "Okay, so fill me in on the strategy here. I'm not sure I understand exactly what we're doing." He waved his hand across his brow, "Sorry, I'm still a little flustered from this morning."

Emily couldn't blame him. Knowing the amount of time

and energy he had put into his little livestock herd, she couldn't imagine how he felt. Yes, they were cows, but they were his cows. And someone had come onto his property and violated something he felt was near and dear to his heart. Emily understood that, better than she probably wanted to. Emily turned the truck into the local First National bank branch as the black SUV pulled into the drive-through coffee shop next door. She put the truck into park before answering. "Based on the information we got overnight, we know that DNA evidence links someone in the Walters family to Sarah. The thing is, we don't know exactly who. It's not Sam, otherwise the DNA would have been a match with what is in the law enforcement databases. So, that leaves us with David and Benny."

"Unless it's some other relative we just don't know about," Cameron said.

The idea that it was someone other than David or Benny was frustrating. Emily rubbed her fingers together, the pads of her fingertips turning in little circles while she waited. "Yes, it could be someone other than David or Benny, but they are the most likely suspects. If we can get a DNA sample, we will have an opportunity to test it and then rule them out, or rule them in." Based on what Mike had told her, the whole field of genetic-based investigations was new. It was a field in its infancy, but sounded reliable, like good science. Emily just wondered for a moment how far the leads would take them. Trying to get a sample from Benny, other than tackling him and forcing a swab in his mouth, would be a long shot. He'd have to throw something away or leave something where they could pick it up. The idea they would have to resort to force to get his DNA wasn't something she was all that interested in, although it was an option.

A minute later, Emily saw the black SUV pull out of the coffee shop line and turn back down the road. She started the truck, backing it out of the spot at the bank slowly and then tailed the SUV, hanging a couple cars back. Her heart beat a little faster in her chest. "Keep an eye out for him throwing anything out of the car, okay? We need something like a cigarette butt or a coffee cup. Something his mouth has touched." Emily knew that even if they could get something, time wasn't on their side in terms of resolving the case quickly. It was going to take time to get the sample back to Mike, time for him to get it to his contact, and time for him to have his friend process it. Her chest tightened along with her grip on the wheel. She didn't want to spend one more minute in Stockton, but she knew she wanted to see the case through. It was like her desire to get home and her desire to solve the case were having a tug-of-war inside of her. Easy, Emily, she told herself. Just one step at a time.

Without saying anything, they followed the SUV out of town. A few miles down the road, Cameron cleared his throat, "He's getting close to the lumber mill entrance. I don't think we should drive on the property. Especially since we don't have a warrant."

Emily realized Cameron was still thinking like a law enforcement officer. She was past that. Though he did have a point — they didn't want to alert the Walters family that she and Cameron knew what was going on. As Benny drove past the sign for the plant, the entrance flanked by six foot high cyclone fencing, Emily slowed down, pulling the truck off the side of the road. "What are we going to do now?" Cameron said.

Emily did a U-turn in the road and headed back the way they came, pointing as she saw the sign in front of her for Treetops Park. "We're going to wait here. Ever been on a stakeout before?"

34

Benny showed up at work just like he did Monday through Friday, arriving late and leaving early, as was his habit. He passed one of the administrative assistants that worked at the lumber mill as he walked in, giving Janice a nod. She'd been with the lumber mill for about ten years. Benny remembered when she started. She had been cute at that point, always wore her hair in a braid. But, years of working in a male dominated industry made her sloppy. She had on the pair of leggings and a sweatshirt, her hair pulled up in a ponytail. "Morning," he muttered, walking past her. Janice didn't reply.

The door to his office creaked as he pushed it open. When he started with the business, his father had given him the second largest office in the building, other than his. "One day, you'll sit in my office," his father had said, handing him the keys to the door. "Until then, make this your home." Over the years he'd worked for his father, he had migrated a few things from his life into the space. Benny's wife, Melinda, had brought in a few fake plants and pictures of the family as decoration, ones that were now covered in dust. Janice was supposed to clean his office as part of her duties, but it didn't seem to get done.

Benny set the cup of coffee he bought at the coffee shop down on his desk and woke up his computer, scanning his email. There wasn't anything interesting in it, just a couple requests for quotes on larger orders, two emails from people who were begging for more time to pay their bills, and a short message from his dad asking him about monthly reports. His dad hadn't come to using technology naturally, so it was kind of a miracle that he managed email at all. Benny was grateful for that. It was better than having his dad hanging in the doorway of his office all day long.

Out of his pocket he pulled his phone, scrolling through a couple sites he liked to visit while he was at work, checking the football scores and the schedule of upcoming games. He glanced back up at his computer and his mind began to wander. He'd left the house without talking to his wife that morning. Not that he cared, that was pretty typical for their daily routine. Melinda was focused on the kids, he was focused on everything else. As long as there was something to eat at home at night, he didn't care too much. But he had needs, that was a fact. And his wife wasn't interested enough to satisfy those.

He pulled up a string of text messages from Kathy Barnes. Why he hadn't married her, he wasn't sure, though a part of him wondered if she would have turned out exactly the same way as Melinda — plain, boring and sullen. Maybe all wives became that way. The thought passed in his mind, but he didn't spend much time on it, quickly typing a message to her. "Noon?"

"I have to work today."

Kathy liked to play it coy, he knew that. She'd been a tease as long as he knew her. But the one thing he knew about her was that if he was persistent, he'd get what he wanted, all of it. "What time do you go to work?"

"Noon."

It figured that exactly the time Benny wanted to meet her she had to be at work. It was too bad he couldn't get her a job at the lumber mill, but he thought that would probably raise a few eyebrows, especially if anyone caught them sneaking off to take advantage of one of the outbuildings. He and Kathy had met there one night, but then he decided it was better to choose a more neutral site for their rendezvous. He looked at the time on his phone. It was just after nine o'clock in the morning. "How about if I meet you in an hour?"

He drummed his fingers on the table, waiting for her reply. Sometimes she got back to him and sometimes she didn't. It was part of the game they played. He set his phone down and then picked it up again. A minute passed, then two. He sent a short reply to one of the emails he'd gotten. Four minutes after he sent the text, she replied. "Okay."

Benny's nerves tingled, the same way they used to when he was in high school and he scored a touchdown on the Stockton High School football team. He hadn't scored yet, but it was coming. "Our regular place."

35

She'd done it again. Kathy stared at her phone in disbelief. It was like her fingers had a mind of their own. Somehow, she'd agreed to meet Benny before work. She knew how the visit would go. He would get to the motel room before her, take a shower before she arrived and meet her at the door. They would fall into bed, spending fifteen or twenty minutes getting their needs met and then lay together, talking for another fifteen or twenty minutes, at which point, Benny would get up, go take another shower and tell her he had to go. It was the same every single time. She shook her head. Who was using who, she wasn't exactly sure.

There was one glimmer of hope, though. Lately, Benny had been talking more about leaving Melinda. He was tired of her bitterness and her silence, he said. He was ready for a fresh start — a fresh start that didn't include the lumber yard or his father or Stockton, for that matter. He said he had enough money stashed away that the two of them could leave. They could go wherever they wanted, he said, and get a fresh start. Kathy wasn't sure she could believe him. There were too many stories on television of men who had said the same thing to their mistresses and then never made it happen. Unfortunately, Benny was the only hope she had at the moment.

When Benny texted that morning, Kathy had just gotten out of the shower in her little basement apartment. She could hear footfalls above her, her mother probably cleaning up the kitchen after her dad left for work. She pulled the hair dryer out of the drawer and plugged it in, hearing the whirl of the motor and feeling the warm air on her shoulders as she dried her hair.

Kathy put on a clean set of work clothes and stuffed a few things in her bag while she waited for her curling iron to heat up. Benny liked it when her hair was curled. She paused for a moment walking into her bedroom, wondering what she was doing. She shook off the thought, realizing she'd prefer to just move forward. Too much thinking led her into a dark place. She didn't want to be in that dark place today. Stockton was dark enough on its own.

From the nightstand next to her bed, Kathy grabbed a fresh box of condoms. It was her responsibility to get them. After all, she was the one who could get pregnant, Benny said, after the first time they hooked up. An unexpected pregnancy was the last thing she needed. Kathy stuffed the box down in her bag and set it just outside the bathroom door, going back to use the curling iron to put a few waves in her hair. Not that they would last. Between the fumbling around she knew was coming with Benny, and the fact she had to go to work, she knew that within an hour or so, her hair would be back in its typical braid for work. "This has to be the last time," she whispered, promising change to herself again, for what had to be the hundredth time. There had to be something better than the meager life she'd built for herself in Stockton. A pit formed in her stomach. There had to be a way out of Stockton, she thought. There had to be.

36

Cameron had just gotten back in the truck after relieving himself behind a tree when Emily spotted the black SUV passing their hidden spot at the entrance to a local park. "He's moving. Come on," she said, starting the truck engine. She pulled out, following him, watching the driver's side window for any movement, any movement at all. She needed him to throw something out — a piece of gum, a cup, a cigarette butt — anything that would have his DNA on it.

Emily glanced over at Cameron, who was leaning forward in the seat. His color had improved in the few hours they had been away from his farm. He seemed to be more focused on figuring out if Benny was the person that had taken Sarah than he was the fact that someone had gone after his personal property. Emily wasn't sure she would ever be able to get the image of the three dead cows out of her head, but she'd seen worse. "Where do you think he's going?"

Cameron shrugged, "I have no idea. He just got to the office. Maybe he has to meet a client?"

Emily shook her head, using her right hand to cover the

wound on her leg. The warmth seemed to make it feel better. She wished she had remembered to grab a couple more painkillers on the way out the door, but she hadn't. In some respects, it was probably better. Painkillers made her dull and sleepy. It's not what she needed at the moment.

The SUV made a couple more turns and then seemed to make almost a complete loop around Stockton. "Does it feel like he's driving in circles?" Emily said.

"I think he's trying to avoid construction on the west side of the city," Cameron said. There's a bridge out. People are driving crazy routes to get back and forth. There aren't that many roads in Stockton. I'm sure you don't see that problem in Chicago."

"We might have more roads in Chicago, but we definitely have our fair share of construction. Seems like as soon as the snow melts the orange barrels go up," Emily shook her head. That was one side benefit to not having to go into the police station every day. She could at least wait for the morning traffic to settle down, although it was never easy driving in Chicago, that was for sure.

They followed Benny for a few more minutes. He seemed unaware that they were following him at all. Emily was being careful, though. She hung back, keeping two to three cars in between his SUV and her truck at all times. The reality was there were a lot of blue pickup trucks in the area. Unless Benny was looking very carefully or he'd been trained in counter surveillance, it was unlikely he'd see them. He probably had other things on his mind.

The SUV turned off onto a side road and then pulled back into a parking lot of a motel. It wasn't the kind of hotel Emily was used to seeing in Chicago, except in the seedier parts of the city. It was a single story, with rooms she imagined hadn't been updated in decades. "What's he doing here?" Cameron said out loud.

"Mike said there were quite a few charges to a motel." Emily scanned the parking lot as they drove past. She didn't want to follow him in. That would be too obvious. She drove past the motel and then pulled into the parking lot of a feed store, circling back. She wanted to give him a minute to get inside of the room. It wouldn't be too hard to figure out what room he was in since there was only a single story. People were creatures of habit, Emily knew. They liked convenience and comfort. If that held true for Benny, he would park right in front of the room he was occupying.

"I'm gonna circle back here and then park in the back of the lot, so we can see what happens," Emily said. She took the blue truck in the back route, changing her mind about the circling back. There was a dumpster in the rear of the lot, with a full view of all the doors to the rooms. She pulled in, facing the truck away from the motel, not wanting to make a big show of backing it in. It was better if no one noticed they were there.

As soon as Emily got the truck stopped, she unclipped her seatbelt and twisted in her seat, trying not to bang her leg. Cameron did the same. She sent Mike a quick text, "What was the name of the motel you found on Benny's financials?"

The text came back right away, "Red Door Inn."

"What's the name of this motel?" she asked Cameron. She'd been so busy tailing the SUV that she hadn't paid much attention to the actual name on the sign.

"Red Door something, I think," Cameron said. "I don't come down this way very often."

Emily nodded and focused her gaze back on the black SUV. "We need to keep an eye out. He has to be meeting someone here. Hopefully, that will get us the information we need."

"It'd better."

37

Whatever sense Kathy had left in her head, she turned it off on the way to the motel. As she got out of her car, she noticed there were only a few vehicles in the lot. That was pretty typical for the time of day. The Red Door Inn seemed to be busier on the weekends and in the evenings. With how few people lived in Stockton, she wasn't sure how they stayed in business. There was a nicer hotel on the other side of town, a chain that offered a free breakfast. Not that she and Benny would spend the night. He had to get home to his family. Just thinking about it formed a knot in her stomach. Would he ever leave his family for her?

Kathy saw his SUV in the parking lot right away. It was hard to miss it. Long and boxy, she wasn't sure how he could park it anywhere. It seemed to be the size of an aircraft carrier to her. She pulled in the parking spot next to him, checking her lipstick in the mirror before getting out. The smell of her perfume filled the car. It was one that Benny had bought for her, one that he liked. Why she went to such great lengths for him, she didn't know. As she slammed the car door, she realized that it wasn't that she didn't know, it was that she didn't want to face the fact. She was in love with Benny. Thinking about it while walking to the motel room door felt like getting punched in the stomach. He had texted her the room number so she could go directly there. So many times, he said he was ready to leave Melinda, but it never seemed to happen. Maybe this time would be different, she thought, knocking on the door.

Benny opened the door, wearing only a towel around his waist, his hair wet from the shower. Kathy pushed the door closed behind her as she went in, noticing the smile on his face.

When they were done, Kathy rolled over and laid her head on his chest, pulling her blonde hair away from her face. She liked pretty much everything about Benny, the way he looked, the way he smelled, the way he talked, and even the way he looked at her. Resting there for a second, Kathy turned back on her side looking at him, "How are things going at home?" She knew it was a sensitive subject but admitting to herself that she loved him pushed her to speak.

Benny's eyes were closed. He opened them, looking at her and then turned away, closing them again, one arm around her, the other arm up under his head, "Do we have to talk about this?"

Kathy looked down, wondering if she had made a mistake bringing it up. "It's no big deal, I was just curious. You know, I worry about you." The truth was she wanted to know where she stood with him.

"Things are the same. Melinda is just... Melinda."

"A while ago, you said you talked to an attorney. You said you were thinking about leaving her. Is that still the case?" Kathy knew she was treading on thin ice, but she didn't care. She needed to know where they were going with the relationship, if you could even call it an actual relationship.

Benny rolled away from her, sitting up on the edge of the bed. "Yeah, I did say that," he said, without looking at her. "But things have changed. I have kids." He looked over his shoulder, "We're just having some fun, right?"

"It's just," Kathy said, sitting up, covering herself with the sheet, "I thought maybe we'd have a future together. Like you said before, you might leave Melinda and we could go start someplace new." Kathy was furious at herself for sounding so desperate, so needy. But she had to know. She had to know where their relationship was going.

Benny stood up and faced her, the grin she loved so much all over his face. "Now, you didn't really think that I was gonna leave Stockton with you, did you? I mean, not that I have any objection to it, but you're just a waitress. You don't have any education. I guess your family is nice, but I can't leave my two kids. That's not ever going to happen." Benny didn't say anything more. He went into the bathroom. Kathy could hear the water running. She knew what would happen next. He would come out in about two minutes, say goodbye, give her a kiss on the cheek and then leave. He'd go back to his life at the lumber mill with his wife and kids, and she would go back to hers at the restaurant, scraping dirty dishes and serving the old men that liked to look at her as she walked by.

Kathy rolled over on her side, trying not to cry. Knowing she loved Benny made it worse. She felt like she'd been stabbed in the gut. How could he do this to her? How could he string her along and lie to her? She used the corner of the sheet to dab at her eyes. It wasn't as if they hadn't had fights before. They had. But there was something in the way that Benny spoke to her — it seemed so cutting — that she knew he was speaking the truth. It was a truth that she didn't like.

A couple minutes later, Kathy heard the bathroom door open. She could smell the scent of the soap being carried out into the room on a cloud of steam. Normally, she would have sat up, so Benny could see her body one more time before he left. She stayed where she was. He walked by her without saying anything. When he got to the door, he turned back and looked at her, giving her a wink and nothing more. The door clicked closed behind him.

In a fit of anger, Kathy stood up and flung a pillow at the door. Tears rolled down her face. She was stuck in the same cycle that she'd been in for years. Go to work, mess around with Benny, and then go hide in her parent's basement. What kind of life was that? Kathy sat on the edge of the bed for another minute, wrapped up in the sheet. He was just using her. She knew the reality all along, but she didn't want to face the fact because she had fallen for him and his lies. The tears stopped, replaced by a surge of white-hot anger that ran up the back of her neck. She went into the bathroom and got cleaned up, quickly putting her hair in a long braid and wiping the smears of mascara out from under her eyes. He wouldn't have her again. She was done.

38

Emily and Cameron slumped down in the truck seats as they saw Benny Walters leave the hotel room. "That was fast," Emily said. He hadn't been in the room for more than forty-five minutes.

"Probably has to get back to work."

"Any chance you know the girl that followed him in?" They had both seen a blonde woman pull into the parking lot and stop, but she had parked on the other side of Benny's SUV, completely blocking their view. The only hint of identity they had about her was that her hair was blonde. They had seen a glimpse of it as she passed through the door. Emily knew it would've been better to get closer, but she didn't want to risk being spotted by Benny.

"Nope. I didn't get a good look at her."

Emily stared out the window, watching as the black SUV left the parking lot out the front entrance. She opened her door, "Let's go."

"Where are we going?" Cameron said, opening the passenger door and getting out before she had a chance to answer.

"We're going to go see who that was."

Cameron trotted to catch up to Emily. "Are you crazy? We don't know what happened in there!"

Emily didn't bother to look back. "That's the point. If you don't want to come, stay in the truck." She knew that her comment sounded sharp, but her gut was telling her that this was an opportunity she shouldn't miss. Her gut was rarely wrong.

As soon as she got to the door, she rapped on it. The door creaked open, a blonde woman standing inside, her hair in a braid and a bag over her shoulder. "What are you doing here?" she said, her eyes narrowing.

Emily didn't say anything, pushing her way past her into the room. "You remember me, don't you, Kathy?"

Kathy reached into her bag and pulled out her phone. "I'm gonna call the police. You shouldn't be here."

Cameron came through the doorway. "Hey, Kathy," he said with a casual tone, "No need to do that. I'm already here." He shut the door behind him.

Emily could tell by the look on her face, Kathy knew she'd been caught red-handed. Red handed with what was the question. Cameron stayed by the door, blocking her exit. Flustered, Kathy plopped down on the edge of the bed, keeping her bag on her shoulder, as if she'd have an opportunity to escape. Emily felt bad for a second about cornering her, but they needed answers about Benny. There was no other way.

Kathy looked at Emily, her eyes wide, "I don't know what you want, but we weren't doing anything illegal in here. We don't have any drugs or anything. You can check my bag if you want."

Emily narrowed her eyes and squared herself off, a technique that she had found to be particularly effective with other women. "I don't care what you were doing. I do want to know if Benny Walters was in here. Was he?"

"Well, if you were following me, then you know he was in here. What do you want with him?"

Emily looked carefully at Kathy and realized that her eyes were red, not the redness that came from doing drugs, it was the kind of redness that came from crying. She decided to soften her stance and sat down on a chair that was across from the edge of the bed. "We weren't following you," she said, leaning forward and folding her hands in her lap.

It took a second and then Kathy looked at Emily and then glanced back at Cameron, "You were following Benny? Why?"

Emily glanced at Cameron, hoping that he would jump into the conversation. He did. "Kathy, listen, I know you've been around Stockton your whole life. I have, too. But there's some shady stuff going on that Emily and I are trying to solve."

Emily watched Kathy for a second. It was as if a light bulb went on in her head and she was quickly putting the pieces together.

"You asked me about Sarah Schmidt when you first got here."

Emily nodded, watching Kathy try to piece things together. "I'm a private investigator. I'm here to see if I can get some closure for the Schmidt family."

Cameron cleared his throat, "Kathy, Emily used to be a detective with the Chicago Police Department. She's trying to do something good for Stockton. What's going on between you and Benny Walters?"

Emily was grateful that Cameron had cut to the chase. Someone with a personality like Kathy's could take hours to sway. They didn't have hours. She needed a DNA sample she could get back to Chicago and she needed it right away. If Benny Walters still had Sarah Schmidt tucked away somewhere, every minute that went by was another minute of torture for the poor girl.

Kathy sighed and her expression changed. She cocked her

jaw off to the side and looked at each of them, "He's been cheating on his wife with me. It's been going on for years." The words came out clipped and short, as if it was the first time she'd admitted out loud that she was having an affair with a married man. She licked her lips, "I know I shouldn't have done this. He's married. I know that. But, until just now, I thought he was leaving his wife." Kathy stared down at the floor, as if she was ashamed she had gotten caught up in the lies. "He's been leading me on for years." She glanced at Emily and Cameron, "Is that what you wanted to know?"

Emily leaned back in the chair, sizing up Kathy. It was impossible to know how far she could push before Kathy shut down. Emily decided to do a little probing before she got to the heart of the question. "So, he told you he was going to leave his wife?"

Kathy stood up, her arms folding across her chest. "Yes. He has said that for years. He even told me he found an attorney. He's a liar!" Her voice boomed off the walls of the small hotel room. Emily could tell there wass fury building inside of Kathy. That was a good sign.

"He's been taking advantage of you this whole time?" Emily glanced at Cameron as if saying to him to stay quiet. She had Kathy moving forward. She didn't want anything to stop that progress now.

Kathy kept pacing the room, "Yes!" She unfolded her arms across her chest and started waving her hands in the air, her voice getting louder and louder with each syllable, "He told me he had enough money for us to go anywhere and start all over. He told me he didn't love his wife anymore. He told me he'd help pay for my education. He even told me he hates the lumber mill." She wheeled around and stared at Emily, "What was I supposed to think?"

Emily fought back the urge to look at Kathy and tell her she was a fool. An "I told you so" wouldn't get Emily what she wanted. "Kathy, this happens to lots of women. You are not alone. It's normal for you to feel betrayed and angry." Emily knew she needed to stoke the fire of fury in Kathy. It seemed to be working.

"What am I supposed to do? How am I ever going to get out of Stockton?" Kathy flung herself down on the edge of the bed, tears starting to flow again. Emily moved over and sat next to her, giving a little nod to Cameron, who stayed quiet at his position by the door.

"I'll tell you what. If you help me, I'll help you." Emily stared at Kathy, waiting for her response.

Kathy turned and looked at Emily, the black mascara she had been wearing running down her cheeks, "What do you mean?"

"Well, I need information, and you need to get out of Stockton. Right?"

Kathy nodded. Emily could tell she was starting to calm down, the more logical part of her brain taking over. Emily would have this one window to get what she needed before Kathy shut down again. "I have three questions I need to ask you. If you answer them truthfully, then I will give you five thousand dollars so you can get out of Stockton." In reality, Emily could've made it much harder on Kathy. She could have given the money to a university towards classes for Kathy, but Emily didn't care that much. However Kathy chose to spend it, that was up to her. Emily knew it was likely that even if Kathy answered her honestly and she gave her the five thousand that a year from now, two years from now, ten years from now, Kathy would still be working at Sandy's Restaurant.

Kathy's eyes bulged out of her head, "Are you serious?" She looked at Cameron, who nodded.

"She's serious," he said, still staying by the door.

"What are the questions?"

Emily paused for a minute, trying to judge whether she

thought Kathy was actually ready to give her the information she wanted or not. She sucked in a breath, deciding the time was now. "Did you and Benny have sex this morning?"

Kathy nodded, her attitude suddenly very serious, "Yes."

"Did you use a condom?"

Kathy blinked, but answered, "Yes."

"Where is it?"

Kathy pointed at a small wastebasket next to the bed. Emily got up, her heart beating in her chest. She stared down into it, the interior lined with a clear plastic trash bag. Inside, she could see the wrapper from the condom on the top. She bent over and pulled up the corners of the bag, lifting it out. At the bottom, there was a used condom. "Thank you." She tied a knot in the top of the bag and handed it to Cameron, "Take this out to the truck." She handed him the truck keys, "There's a lockbox under the front seat. Open it and get Kathy her money. One envelope."

Cameron nodded, not saying anything. Emily pulled her phone out of her back pocket and quickly sent a text to Mike, "Have sample. What now?" She said a silent prayer that Mike had a better plan then sending the DNA sample through regular mail. If that was the best he had, they would have to do it that way, but there had to be a better option. Once she'd sent the text, she looked at Kathy. "I'm going to give you the money I promised." She stared at Kathy, "It's not ultimately my business how you spend the money, but if you continue to let opportunity pass you by, you will never leave Stockton. Never."

Before Kathy could answer, Cameron came back, a white envelope in his hand. "This it?"

Emily nodded. She checked the inside of the envelope. There were fifty hundred-dollar bills in it. She always grabbed a couple envelopes on her way out the door to a case in the event there were expenses she needed to handle. She could see Kathy eyeing the envelope as she checked the inside. As Emily extended it to Kathy, she practically grabbed it out of her hands, stuffing it down low in her bag. She stood up, putting the bag on her shoulder. "Before you leave," Emily said, "give your cell phone number to Cameron in case we have any follow-up questions. Those you can answer as a courtesy." Emily didn't want Kathy to think that just because they had paid her for information once that they would do it again. Five thousand dollars was a pretty hefty fee for handing over a used condom, but if it got the job done…

Kathy nodded and gave her number to Cameron as she walked out the door. It clicked behind her. A moment later, Emily heard the engine of her sedan start and saw the shadow of it pull back in front of the shaded windows. Cameron looked at her, a half-smile on his face. "Can't say I've ever been so happy to find someone's leftovers," he said. "Now what?"

Emily chewed her lip. A couple minutes had gone by and she hadn't heard from Mike. "Let's take a look around the room and make sure we didn't miss anything before we leave." She shoved her cell phone in her back pocket and went into the bathroom. She could still smell the scent of the cheap motel soap, seeing a couple wet towel strewn on the floor. Though Kathy hadn't said anything, her hair wasn't wet. Bucky must've taken a shower after they had sex. Emily cocked her head to the side. He was smart. No reason to go home smelling like another woman, she thought.

"There's nothing in the bathroom that's worth anything to us," she said to Cameron. Cameron closed the drawer next to the bed. "They weren't really here long enough to leave anything behind, but I checked all the drawers and under the bed as well. Nothing there."

"Let's head out to the truck," Emily said. Waiting for Mike to get back to her gnawed at her stomach. She opened the truck door, glancing in the back. The bag with the used condom and the wrapper sat on the floor. Emily opened one of the storage areas and pulled out a small plastic shopping bag, picking up the evidence and dropping it in. She didn't want to look at it. She started the truck and stared forward for a moment and then turned to Cameron, "I'm waiting to hear from Mike. Do you want me to take you back to your farm?"

"Honestly, I could really use a cup of coffee after that."

Emily smiled. They could probably both use something a little stronger than coffee but given the fact it was about eleven o'clock in the morning, it was probably a little too soon for anything stronger. Besides the fact that she needed to keep her wits about her. "Sure enough."

Emily backed the truck out of the spot next to the dumpster and used the back entrance of the motel to get out onto a side street. She pulled out onto the main road and then right back into the coffee shop, the same one they had seen Bucky go to on the way to work that morning. They ordered using the coffee shop's drive through, a young man with wavy brown hair, wearing a baseball hat with the name of the coffee shop on the front of it handing them two paper cups with sleeves. "Man, that tastes good," Cameron said.

Emily put her cup in the drink holder in the truck, waiting for it to cool for a moment. She took a deep breath, realizing her gut told her they were getting close to a resolution. Tension creeped up the back of her neck. Where was Mike? They couldn't close the loop on this case without his help. She checked the time on her cell phone just before pulling out onto the main road. It had been almost a half hour since she texted him. It wasn't like him to not respond. "I'm gonna run you back to your farm so you can check on things there. I need to pick up my bag anyway."

Cameron nodded. He stared down at his phone. "That's fine. I just got a text from the guy that was coming to get the cows. He got them. They're gone."

As Emily glanced over at him, she saw a streak of sadness

pass over his face. He was right about one thing — she didn't think he'd have the stomach for law enforcement over the long term. She had seen it happen over and over again. Rookies came out of the Academy, their jaws set and their eyes steeled as soon as they were given their gun and their duty belt, only to come back later, quivering when a call went bad. Some of them were able to go through that and brush it off, others were not. Not that she didn't think Cameron could handle the trauma of being out on the street, she just wasn't sure he had the stomach for knowing how truly evil people could be. She had seen so many cases where people had lost their lives or their loved ones or their business or their reputation or even their freedom, just because someone was greedy or dishonest. It didn't need to be that way.

Driving back to Cameron's farm, they were both quiet. Emily's mind circled around details in the case. Every time she glanced at Cameron, he was staring out the window. She guessed he was replaying the morning's events. "Will you get more cows?" she said, trying to make conversation.

"I think so." There was a pause before Cameron answered.

"You sound unsure. Why?"

Cameron sighed, "To say things have changed rapidly in the last twenty-four hours would be an understatement. I think I'm just trying to catch up. You know, I thought I always wanted to be a police officer."

"And you don't?" Emily asked, but she already knew the answer.

"I don't think so. Not after what I've seen. Kinda changes my opinion."

Emily nodded, "Well, for what it's worth I think you're a good officer. There are lots of good officers out there. Unfortunately, a few bad apples can sour the whole barrel."

The truck bumped up and onto the gravel driveway for Cameron's farm. As soon as the truck stopped, Cameron got out and walked over to the fence. His remaining herd was huddled together as if they were talking about the friends they'd lost overnight. Emily watched Cameron as he hopped the fence and walked over to each of them, running his hand along their hide, talking softly. She couldn't hear what he was saying, but she imagined he was telling them how sorry he was.

While he was out in the field, Emily walked back to the house, wanting to retrieve her bag. They had left in such a hurry that the house was unlocked. For a moment, Emily scanned the room, afraid that someone came in and trashed it while they were gone. Nothing was out of place, though. Her bag was still sitting by the table where she'd left it. She reached in and grabbed antibiotics and some Ibuprofen, finding a glass in the kitchen for some water. Just as she swallowed the pills, her phone buzzed. She pulled it out of her backpack and looked. Her heart started to beat a little faster.

As fast as she could, she ran out the door, limping, and yelled for Cameron, "Hey! Do you know where the Grove City Airport is?"

Cameron had just jumped down from the fence when she yelled at him. He nodded, "Yeah, it's a little tiny airport about twenty minutes from here. Why?"

"We gotta go." Before Cameron could ask any more questions, she got in the truck and started it up, pulling as close to him as possible so he didn't have to walk the whole distance back to the house. She goosed the engine leaving the driveway, the tires grinding on the gravel.

Cameron reached for one of the passenger handles and held on as Emily spun the truck out onto the road. "Whoa, Nellie. Let's try not get pulled over before we get there."

"We don't have a lot of time." Emily focused her eyes on the road, "Mike said it's north of Stockton. Where do I go from here?"

"Just stay on this road. I'll tell you when to turn, as long as you don't decide to go warp speed on me."

The truck whipped by cornfields and pastures filled with cows and goats and horses. Emily didn't notice much of it at all, everything seeming to be a blur of the yellowish green that comes in the late summer and early fall in the Midwest. Mike had come through, but there was a ticking clock. If they missed their window, there was no telling how they would be able to get the sample back to Chicago. "How much further?" she said, her knuckles white on the steering wheel.

Cameron craned his neck forward, "We're about two minutes out, I think. Take the next left. That'll take you right into the airport."

Emily glanced down at her cell phone, checking the time. If Cameron was right, they would be fine, but just barely. If he was wrong, they wouldn't.

The tires of the truck squealed as Emily made the last turn, gunning the engine again as they drove through the entrance to the little airport. It wasn't much more than an oversized barn and a long strip of concrete runway. There was no tower, there were no guards and no gates. Definitely way different than O'Hare. Off in the distance, Emily could see a white plane with the side door open. It was small, probably nothing more than a two-seater. She pressed the accelerator on the truck again, seeing the side door close, the plane inching away. Hopefully, they weren't too late. Emily laid on the horn, trying to get the pilot's attention, the plane rolling ahead without stopping. Emily leaned forward in the driver's seat, still pounding on the horn.

The plane made a jerk to the left and then stopped abruptly, the fuselage rocking back and forth on the wheels, just as the truck got close. Emily reached around back and grabbed the grocery bag that had the sample and it, launching herself out of the truck as quickly as she could, half running and half walking over to the plane, the pain in her leg sending jolts through her body.

The side door on the plane popped open, the pilot looking over his left shoulder at her. He pulled the earphones off of his head. "You Emily?"

She nodded, "Thought we might miss you."

"You just about did." He glanced at the bag in her hand, "Just set that down on the floor." Glancing at his watch, he said, "I'll get this to your friend in about a couple hours, give or take a bit for the winds."

Emily dropped the bag right behind the pilot's seat and stepped away from the plane. She had barely gotten ten feet away when the door slammed shut and the propellers started to rev again, the little plane giving a shutter as it started to roll forward. She walked back to the truck and watched, the plane traveling down the runway, quickly picking up speed. By the time she got back in the truck and closed the door, she could see the top of the plane, the nose angling up into the air, the propellers moving so quickly they weren't even visible. She leaned back in her seat and sighed, letting out a deep breath.

"What was that?"

"Apparently, our courier. Somehow, Mike found a guy who was flying up to Chicago today. Mike will meet him at the airport and get the sample to our scientist." She picked up her phone and sent a quick text to him, "Package is on the way."

"I'll let you know as soon as I have anything..." came the reply.

39

After dropping off the sample at the airport, Emily took a more relaxed approach driving back to Cameron's farm. There was nothing more she could do except wait. Knowing that Benny Walters was out, living his day like any other, having his needs satisfied by his mistress that morning, made Emily furious. If he was the one who had taken Sarah Schmidt, Emily couldn't figure out how it was possible that he could do even the basics in life — walking, breathing, eating. People like that shouldn't be allowed to exist. Emily knew from her time in law enforcement that even in jail, the criminals who went after kids were maligned, often killed within a week or two of them being incarcerated. Even criminals even had their code of conduct. Kidnapping and abusing a teenager was certainly not part of it.

"Do you mind if we make a stop on the way back?" Cameron said, as they pulled back on the main road leading out of Stockton.

Emily hadn't really absorbed the names of the streets yet. The area was set up on a square grid of north, south, east and west. She just tried to keep the general sense of where she was going, the GPS in her truck spinning every single time she made a turn, the map changing direction. "Sure. I don't think we're going to hear anything until closer to dinnertime. You aren't on duty today?"

"It's my day off. Lucky, I guess," Cameron said, sarcasm in his voice.

Over the next few minutes, Cameron directed Emily down a couple side roads, finally ending up at a muddy farm that seemed to be off the beaten trail. "You can stay here. I just want to check on those calves Dr. Zuckerman said old man Miller has for sale."

Emily furrowed her brows. "So soon?" It hadn't been more than a few hours since Cameron had found the three cows dead in his pasture.

"It will be better for the herd if they have some new members. Doc said old man Miller felt bad when he heard the story. He knows how things are here in Stockton. I just want to go check them out and see how much he wants."

Emily nodded. She stayed in the truck, watching Cameron as he shook hands with a grizzled farmer with a white beard. He looked exactly like someone Emily would guess had lived in Stockton his whole life. Worn jeans, worn boots, flannel shirt pulled on over a T-shirt to fight off the fall chill. The men stood and talked for a moment and then Cameron followed him, disappearing into one of the barns. She glanced down at her phone and decided to call Mike.

"You got to the plane in time?" he said without saying hello.

"Just barely. Thanks for that. Not sure how you pulled that one off."

"Friend of a friend of a friend. You know how that works. He was headed up to Chicago anyway."

"How long will it be before he lands?" A couple of butterflies fluttered in Emily's stomach. She wanted to know the results. She was tired of waiting. It was time to resolve Sarah's case or head home. Emily didn't know what she would do if it wasn't Benny. She wasn't sure she would say anything to Vicki. Maybe she would, maybe she wouldn't. She didn't like to leave cases unfinished, but he was their only — and best — lead. If it wasn't him, they'd have to start the investigation all over again. Emily wasn't sure she was up for that.

"My friend just texted and said the pilot will be on the ground in two hours and twelve minutes. I'll meet him at the airport and run the sample right over to the lab. With any luck, we'll know something later on tonight."

Emily nodded, "Thanks. How's everything going at home?"

For the next few minutes, Mike regaled her with stories about Miner and his escapades — the new hole he dug in the yard and how he had chewed one of the toys Mike had bought for him practically down to nothing. "I think he misses you."

"I miss him, too." There were very few things that Emily was willing to be sentimental about. Her dog was one of them. She sucked in a breath, "Okay, send me a text when the pilot gets there. Let me know as soon as you know something. I'm ready to get out of here."

"Will do."

Cameron walked back to the truck just as Emily put her phone down. He hopped in, "They were nice looking calves."

Whatever had happened between Cameron and old man Miller seemed to brighten Cameron's spirit, Emily thought. "You going to get them?"

"Yeah, I think he's going to bring them by this afternoon and let them loose in the pasture for me. He gave me a good deal."

It was interesting to Emily to see how quickly Cameron bounced back. She wondered if people in the livestock business were that way. It wasn't like their cows and goats and pigs were actually pets. They were commodities, like gold and corn and wheat. If they got attached, it would be nearly impossible to send them to the meat market. "Good. I'm glad to see you moving forward."

Cameron shot a glare toward Emily, one that she knew wasn't meant for her, but meant for whoever had attacked his herd. "They'll get theirs."

Emily stared out the window, wondering if she could say the same about whoever took Sarah.

40

When they got back to the farm, Cameron insisted that Emily stay for lunch. "Where are you going to go? I can't imagine you'd want to go back to Vicki's house. It's way too sad over there."

He was right. The specter of Sarah's ghost seemed to hang over Vicki's house and her life. Going back there and waiting for news from Mike might suck the life out of Emily, the way it had out of Vicki and Liz. "All right."

Cameron reached into the refrigerator, pulling out bread, cheese and some packages of cold cuts. "Lucky for you, I actually went to the grocery store a couple days ago." He opened a cabinet door and pulled out a bag of chips. "Selfishly, I would like to know how this case ends up, anyway, especially since I may have lost my job over it."

Emily frowned for a second, realizing that Cameron hadn't heard from Sheriff Mollohan. Strange, she thought. "Have you heard from the Sheriff about the file?"

Sitting down at the kitchen table, where Emily was already resting her leg, he said, "No. Funny thing, that. Maybe he doesn't look at those files all that often. Maybe he just wants to keep them out of public view. I don't know."

Whether Emily would ever be able to figure out why Sheriff Mollohan had files hidden in his drawer, she wasn't sure. Only Cameron had seen the files that were in there. "Did you get a look at any of the other files that were in the drawer?"

He shook his head, "Not really. I was focused on getting Sarah's file and getting out of there. Why?"

"Don't you find it strange that he has files hidden in his office and not with the rest of the records?"

"Of course. What am I supposed to do about it, though?"

"I don't know. Just food for thought." Emily didn't have the time or the energy to deal with the political ramifications of what was going on in Stockton. From a legal perspective, if Cameron did want to do something, he'd have to get a district attorney or judge involved — someone who had more power and authority than the sheriff did. In a small town like Stockton, those people were few and far between.

Getting some food in her stomach made Emily tired. Neither of them had slept much the night before. "Is it okay with you if I put my leg up on the couch for a bit?" she said to Cameron.

He nodded. "Your friend probably won't know anything for a while, huh?"

"Yeah. He said closer to dinnertime, or maybe after. Just depends on how quick we can get the results back."

Emily got up from the table and walked over to the couch, laying down as gently as she could. All the moving around had definitely irritated something inside of her leg. She was glad she had taken the Ibuprofen when she did. She positioned a large pillow under her leg to elevate it, just like Dr. Zuckerman had told her to. Turning her head to the side, she closed her eyes, her cell phone in the front pocket of her jacket, in case Mike needed anything.

. . .

By the time Emily woke up, the sun was low in the sky. She blinked a couple of times, her heart starting to pound in her chest, afraid she had missed a call or text from Mike. By the position of the sun, she'd slept a lot longer than she'd planned. A blanket covered her legs. Cameron must've done that, she thought. She swung her leg down, realizing how stiff it had become, but at least the pain had receded with some rest. Emily pulled the phone out of her pocket, checking. There was nothing. Standing up, she looked out the window. She could see a truck and trailer sitting outside, Cameron standing at the back, holding the lead to one of the calves in his hands. He had a smile on his face. After the day they had, she was glad to see it. She walked outside, sitting down on the porch, wrapping the blanket around her shoulders. Cool night air had started to push into Stockton. Shivering a little, she watched Cameron as he walked over to the gate with what must've been the third calf, the other two already standing next to the others in the herd. He slipped the halter off and the calf trotted toward the group. Their numbers were whole again. The end gate of the trailer clanked closed, the old truck pulling out. It left the driveway before Cameron noticed she was sitting there. He called to her as he walked towards the house, "How are you feeling?"

"Better now that I had some rest." It was probably the most relaxed Emily had been since she arrived in Stockton.

"Any news from your friend?"

Emily shook her head, "I was just about to text him." She nodded towards the pasture, "The calves came."

"Yeah. I'm glad. Better to get these kinds of things resolved quickly rather than letting them fester. If I had to look at a small herd day after day that wouldn't be good. Better to just move on."

Emily wondered about that, "You aren't angry that somebody killed three of your cows?"

"I am, but that will be handled as well. Just not right now."

Cameron surprised her. She didn't expect that he would be the kind of man who would wait to get justice. It seemed like the slow pace of the Midwest impacted even the pace of retribution. Emily looked down at her phone and sent a message to Mike. "Any news?"

"Thought I'd hear from you hours ago," Mike responded right away.

"Catching up on some sleep while I was waiting. Any news?" It was irritating that Emily had to ask the question twice, but she knew Mike was prone to forgetting things.

"I was just going to text you. I should have news in thirty minutes. My contact at the lab is just finishing up the tests now."

Knowing an end to everything was coming, and quickly, made Emily's heart beat a little faster in her chest. "Okay, I'll keep my phone with me," she texted back. She looked up at Cameron, "Thirty minutes. We should know something in a half hour."

With the clock ticking, new life was breathed into Emily. She shook off any sleepiness that remained from her nap and went back inside, checking her bag. She hadn't left anything at the hotel or at Vicki's, so however things got resolved, she was ready to go, immediately.

After cataloguing all the things in her bag, Emily took it out to the truck. Cameron called after her, "You leaving so soon?"

"In a few minutes. This part I need to handle on my own."

41

Exactly thirty-two minutes later, Emily got a text from Mike. "Results are in. The DNA you sent me is a match to what we found on the shoe. Good luck."

Emily's chest tightened. She'd been leaning on the side of the truck, waiting for news from Mike. Instinctively, she reached around her back, checking to make sure her gun was holstered. Her phone chirped again, "One thing I forgot to tell you. Remember the numbers you sent me?"

The image of the strange sequence of numbers that Emily found on the back of a piece of paper in the hotel room had slipped her mind. "What about them?"

"It's a location. Some sort of strange, convoluted GPS coordinates. Took me a while to decipher them. I'll send you the address."

A second later, a location ping came through on Emily's phone. She tapped at the icon in the message and it pulled up a map, a map that led to somewhere in Stockton. "Hey, Cameron," she called to him. "Can you come look at this?"

Cameron walked up from the pasture, glancing back to

check the calves even though they had only been out of his watchful eye for a few seconds, "What's going on?"

"You know this location?" she said, showing him the information Mike sent.

"Yeah," he said, staring at her for a moment. "That's the address for the lumber mill."

It was all coming together, Emily thought. Not only did the DNA match Benny Walters, but now someone who knew the case well enough had written down the location of something at the sawmill. Could it be that Sarah was still alive? Maybe there was a building there? A trickle of hope rose up through Emily. "Can you do me one favor before I go?" she said to Cameron.

"Sure."

"Text Kathy Barnes and find out where Benny is."

Cameron sent the text and they waited. Emily knew it was likely that Kathy would have to reach out to either Benny or someone they knew in common to find out where he was. A couple of minutes later, Cameron's phone chirped, "Kathy called the office and asked the assistant. She said Benny has an eight o'clock appointment out at the lumber mill with a big client."

Emily nodded, wondering why Benny was having such a late meeting. She checked her phone. That was just a little more than an hour away. "Thanks for your help. I don't think I'll be seeing you again but take good care of those new calves." Emily put her hand on the door of the truck, pulling it open.

"You want me to come with you?" Cameron said. "I mean, are you sure you want to do this alone? Whatever it is you are about to do?"

Emily looked at him and blinked. He knew that she would go and confront Benny. He could pretend he didn't understand the ramifications of that, but she knew he did. "No. It's best I do this part on my own. Thanks for your hospitality and your help."

Without saying anything else, Emily got in the truck and started it, heading out towards the lumber mill, for what she hoped would be the last time. The more she thought about Benny and the self-serving, smug way he'd treated Kathy Burns, the more she wondered how many other women — including Sarah Schmidt — had fallen prey to him over the years. That would end. Tonight. One way or the other, things would get resolved.

As she drove, she found herself gritting her teeth. She hoped the information Kathy Barnes had shared with them was reliable. There was no reason for it not to be. After all, Emily had spent five thousand dollars to gain her loyalty.

The sun was setting quickly, darkness rolling over Stockton almost faster than Emily's eyes could adjust. In her gut, she knew this was a one-way trip. She wouldn't rest until she found Benny and got the answers she needed. There was no traffic on the road out to the lumber mill. It was as if people had hunkered down in their homes for the night. It seemed strange to her. Chicago was alive and vibrant every hour of the day. Stockton had shorter business hours, people rising early, getting their work done and then heading back to their homes.

As Emily got close to the lumber yard, she checked the time on her cell phone. There was about forty-five minutes before the meeting that Kathy Barnes had told them about. Emily decided to pull the truck off to the side, using the same park entrance she and Cameron used earlier that morning, to camouflage the truck. The last thing she wanted to do was roll into the lumber yard and have Benny find her rather than her find Benny. The element of surprise was important, especially in this case. The hope that Sarah was still alive twitched in the back of her mind. Was it even possible? Twelve long years had passed. She shook the thought away. There was no point in thinking that part through until she actually had answers. Conjecture could get you killed. She knew that.

Waiting for Benny's black SUV to drive past her seemed to take forever. At exactly seven fifty, ten minutes before his appointment, Emily saw the SUV pass, shrouded in darkness. She decided to wait for two minutes, watching the vehicle go through the gates of the lumber yard before she started up her truck. She set a timer using her phone. It was the only way she could keep her mind occupied while she waited and wondered. Emily drummed her fingers on the steering wheel, wishing for that two minutes to pass, but knowing that she wanted to give him time to do whatever it was he needed to do. Just as she was ready to start the engine, the timer ready to start beeping, another vehicle passed her, a white sedan, a luxury model. It must be the client, Emily thought. She decided to wait another two minutes to give Benny and his client a chance to connect.

Emily continued to drum her fingers on the steering wheel. As soon as the timer on her phone went off, she started the truck and drove slowly into the lumber yard, not using her headlights. She didn't want to give Benny any forewarning that she was on his property. With the size of his ego, she was sure he'd never suspect that someone would be coming to confront him.

As she pulled into the parking area, she could see the black SUV and the white sedan parked next to each other in front of the office entrance. Emily pulled her truck back around the side of the building, where it couldn't be seen from the front. She slipped out of the car and walked quickly to the front of the building, as fast as she could manage, pain streaking through her leg from sitting in the car for too long. She knew that in a minute or two it would loosen up but getting there sent jabs of pain up and down her leg.

Staring through the office window, she saw the two men had stood up. They were coming her way, out of the office entrance that faced the mill. She slipped around the corner of the building, where neither of them could see her. The next time she glanced around the corner, they had their backs to her, Benny laughing loudly and pointing, "Let's go up to the mill, so I can show you more about our operations."

Emily trailed the two men in the shadows. Benny was talking so much and laughing so loudly, that a nuclear bomb could go off over his head and he probably wouldn't notice. At least that made Emily's job a little easier.

The actual lumber mill was an enormous structure, something that looked like it had been pulled out of a magazine on old farm buildings from a hundred years ago. The smell of sawdust filled the air. Emily peered around the corner as the two men disappeared inside. The lights were on inside the building, large can lights suspended from the ceiling. The echoes of their conversation could be heard bouncing off the walls, but Emily was too far away to hear exactly what they were saying. They had stopped about forty feet inside of the doors, Benny pointing at various machinery and stacks of wood that were lined up against the walls.

It was time.

Emily stood in the doorway and called to Benny, "Hey. I need to talk to you."

As he turned toward her, she saw that he had on a baseball hat, jacket and a pair of jeans, the cuffs covering boots that were noticeably similar to Sheriff Mollohan's. Must be a trend among the powerful in Stockton, she thought, almost laughing.

"Who are you? We're closed. You'll have to come back in the morning." Benny turned away trying to continue his conversation with the client, a bald man wearing a sport coat. He didn't look like he belonged in a lumber mill, any lumber mill, for that matter.

"No, I need to talk to you now."

As Benny's eyes adjusted to the darkness, Emily saw that he

recognized her. "Oh, you're the little woman who keeps asking questions about Sarah Schmidt, aren't you?"

A surge of fury ran through Emily. Benny's level of disrespect was no surprise, but it was evident, nonetheless. Emily didn't address him, but pulled the pistol out of her holster, leaving it dangling at her side. She looked at the bald man, whose eyes had grown wide. "Sir, if you'll excuse us, Benny and I have some business to do. Head on out."

The man glanced at Benny and glanced at Emily and then at her gun. He didn't say anything and didn't ask any questions. He scurried past Emily, not making a sound. A moment later, Emily heard the engine on his sedan roar to life. She was sure he would call the Sheriff's office on his way out. Time was ticking. "Where is she?"

"Who? And who do you think you are coming into Stockton demanding answers?"

Emily raised her eyebrows, the gun hanging in her grip on her right side. "Well, if you know that I'm here to demand answers, then you know who I'm here to demand answers about. Sarah Schmidt. Where is she?"

"That little tramp? Who knows? She's been gone for twelve years."

"A little fairy told me you would know where she is." Emily moved the gun in front of her, adding her left hand to the grip.

Benny's eyes narrowed. "Who would say something like that? Maybe that Vicki? Her mother? She doesn't know what she's talking about. Or her crazy cousin Liz? She's a drunk."

Emily's patience was running out. "Nope, it wasn't anyone here in the city. You made one mistake. You decided to send evidence to my house. It's been tested and guess what? You're it."

"What does that mean exactly?"

Benny had turned and was facing her, not denying he'd sent the shoe to Emily's house. He'd taken a few steps closer to Emily but was still a good twenty feet away. It was a shot Emily knew she could make quickly and accurately if he decided to charge her. In a way, she kind of hoped he did. "Well, your DNA might not have been on file, but your brother Sam's was. We found DNA on the shoe you dropped off at my house. DNA from sperm." Emily let the information settle over Benny for a second before she continued. "And your friend Kathy was more than happy to donate your used condom from this morning. So, as I said, you're it. Now, where's Sarah?"

Benny pursed his lips together. "You're wrong. There is no way anyone could do DNA testing that fast. There must be something wrong. I'm not responsible."

"Like you're not responsible for messing with Kathy for years? I wonder what your wife might think about that?"

"I'm telling you, I had nothing to do with Sarah's disappearance."

Emily was tired. She was tired of the games. She lifted the gun in front of her, pointing it directly at Benny. "I'm sure your little friend in the snazzy sedan has already called the Sheriff's department, so I don't have a lot of time. Take me where you have her."

"I told you, I don't know anything."

Something snapped inside of Emily. She tipped the gun slightly to the left and pulled the trigger, shattering Benny's shoulder. He screamed in pain. "It's time to tell the truth, Benny. Since you can't be reasoned with, maybe a little pain will help you remember."

Benny fell to the ground with the impact of the shot. He scrambled to his feet, wrapping his left hand over his shattered right shoulder, blood seeping out from between his fingers. "Okay, yes. I found her on that trail that day. I just wanted to have a little fun. She'd been playing hard to get," he moaned. "Things got out of hand."

Emily took two steps forward, the gun still aimed, this time at his chest. "How out of hand?"

Benny's face had gone pale in the dim light of the lumber mill, "She kept saying no, but I didn't believe her. I might've put my hand on her throat, maybe a little too hard."

"What about the picture? The one found at the gas station."

"I took it the day I was with her. Lost it."

In that moment, Emily knew Sarah was dead. "Where is she?" Emily lifted the gun a little higher this time pointing the barrel between Benny's eyes. "If you ever hope to see your family again, or Kathy, for that matter, tell me where she is right now."

Emily could tell by the look in Benny's eyes that he knew that she was serious. He started to stammer, "Out back." He motioned with his head, "I buried her out there. I felt bad about it, but I couldn't tell anyone. You understand, don't you?"

Emily wagged the gun at him, "Show me."

On the way out of the lumber mill, she stopped him for a second. "Pick up that shovel. Don't try anything funny. A bullet is always faster than any other weapon."

The two of them walked for a minute out into the darkness. The faintest glint of moonlight prevented things from being completely black. Benny carried the shovel in his left hand, his right arm dangling at his side. Following him, Emily could see the dark stains of blood running down his jacket. Luckily, she hadn't hit an artery. She would never have gotten the answers she wanted if that had happened.

They walked up an incline, to an area that looked like it had been dug up at one time. Only a few sparse spots of grass grew. Benny stopped and pointed, "Here. She's here."

Emily pulled her phone out of her pocket and matched the coordinates Mike had sent with where they were standing. It was the spot. "Dig. I want to see her bones."

"I can't," Benny moaned. "My shoulder..."

Emily raised the gun again, "Don't make me ask twice."

Benny took the shovel and pushed it into the earth. It was softer than Emily expected it to be. That was probably why he buried Sarah there in the first place. Emily stepped back, closer to the wood line, in case anyone happened to show up while she was still standing there.

It took a few minutes of shoveling, but Emily limped out of the shadows when she heard the clank of the metal blade on something hard. "Here," Benny said, leaning on the shovel. "Is this what you wanted to see? This make you feel better? There's nothing left, just her skeleton."

Emily peered down into the hole, ignoring Benny's sarcastic tone. She used the flashlight on her cell phone to see what was at the bottom. Sarah Schmidt's skull, clavicle and left arm were visible, poking out of the dirt. It was undeniable, Benny was the one who had killed her. Emily looked at him, as if she was seeing him for the first time, narrowing her eyes. "Did you ever for once consider what you did to her family? Did you ever think about the fact that you took Sarah's life before she ever had a chance to live it?"

Benny shook his head, a smirk forming on his face. "In Stockton, you take what you want. That's the way we do things."

At that moment, all the pieces of the puzzle snapped into place in Emily's mind. Benny's desires, the powerful history of his family, the way he'd attacked Emily at the park—the evidence was right in front of her. Benny had gone after what he wanted more than once. There was nothing to say he wouldn't do it again and again.

A taunt from Benny broke through the silence, "What are you gonna do, shoot me?"

"Yes," Emily whispered. Without saying anything more, Emily lifted the gun, lining up the sights. Putting pressure on the trigger, she pulled it, the shot echoing off the woods behind her. With wide eyes, Benny's body dropped and landed on top of Sarah's, a bloody stain soaking the center of his shirt.

Emily took one last look at Benny and Sarah, hearing sirens in the background. Benny wanted to be with Sarah. In a way, he'd gotten what he wanted. Emily holstered the gun and disappeared into the darkness.

EPILOGUE

After an all-night drive back from Stockton, Mike greeted Emily at the door with Miner, who was barking and whining, his tail wagging so fast she couldn't even see it.

By the time Emily unpacked her bag, a few small stories had shown up on online news sources about the son of a wealthy lumber mill owner who had been shot and killed in a small town in Ohio. Authorities were puzzled about the fact that a body had been found underneath him, more specifically, a skeleton. Authorities were waiting for DNA results.

Two days later, Emily got two emails. One was from Vicki Schmidt. It only had two lines. "Thank you. I can never repay you." The other was from Cameron. How he had found her email address, she wasn't sure, but she was glad he did. "The Sheriff is looking for a new job. If you're ever down this way come and see me." Attached to the email was a picture of the three calves, their faces wide-eyed, with white blazes that stretched all the way to their nostrils. Also attached was a link to an article. A newspaper in Columbus had reported that Sheriff Jerome Mollohan had been arrested on dereliction of duty and bribery charges for falsifying records and taking payoffs from people in the community. The State Highway Patrol had taken him away in handcuffs, much to the embarrassment of the department. The reporters in the article stated they weren't sure where the information came from, but an investigation was underway.

Mike leaned over Emily's shoulder, reading the email, a grin spread from ear to ear. "I wonder who could've gotten that kind of information to the state government?" he said, standing up and pouring himself a fresh cup of coffee.

"You didn't…" Emily said, scratching behind Miner's ears.

"I would never…" Mike said with a wink.

Emily leaned back in the chair and let the image of Vicki Schmidt rest in her mind for a second. She pictured Vicki visiting at the cemetery, now sitting guard over her daughter who was finally where she belonged, back with her family.

Get an exclusive prequel from the Emily Tizzano series now!
Click here to have it instantly delivered!

A NOTE FROM THE AUTHOR

Thanks so much for taking the time to read *Twelve Years Gone*!

After reading *Twelve Years Gone*, I hope that you've been able to take a break from your everyday life and join Emily on her adventure to get justice for Sarah. There are more stories to come! Click on this link and enjoy an exclusive prequel for this series.

Enjoy!

KJ

P. S. Would you take a moment to leave a review? Reviews mean so much to indie authors like me!

Printed in the USA
CPSIA information can be obtained
at www.ICGtesting.com
LVHW012301180424
777863LV00032B/880